M000307280

Bump Time Origin

Doug J. Cooper

Other Books by Doug J. Cooper

For info and updates, please visit: CrystalSeries.com

Bump Time Origin
Copyright © 2019 by Doug J. Cooper

This is a work of fiction. Names, characters, places, and events are the products of the author's imagination or are used fictitiously. Any resemblance to actual events or places or persons, living or dead, is entirely coincidental.

All rights reserved, including the right to reproduce this book or portions thereof in any form whatsoever.

Published by: Douglas Cooper Consulting

Beta reviewer: Mark Mesler
Book editor: Tammy Salyer
Cover design: Damonza

ISBN-13: 978-1-7337801-1-7

Author website: www.crystalseries.com

For Fran & Jim
and
Caroline & Nat

Author's Note

Dear Reader:

David "Diesel" Lagerford travels across time in this story, and we encounter him at different periods in his life. To make it easy to follow along, each chapter title includes his age.

Happy reading,

Doug J. Cooper

1. αCiopova – Forty-One timeline

Floating down a temporal corridor she'd built for her own convenience, αCiopova considered the next chore on her list—killing Lilah Spencer. The transcendent being stopped at the timeline where Lilah was forty-one years old and paused to watch the woman work.

Sitting at her desk, Lilah conversed with an AI, an artificial intelligence who would one day mature and meld with the powerful αCiopova now roaming across time.

"This modification can give either more speed or greater strength," Lilah said to the avatar on her computer screen. "Do you prefer one over the other?"

αCiopova entered the world where this Lilah existed and, without revealing her presence, assumed control of the AI avatar, a woman in her early forties. "There are situations where one or the other is an advantage," she had the image say. "Can we find a way to balance them?"

"That's what I was thinking." Lilah beamed.

"I have an idea for an experiment to help us find the right balance," αCiopova continued. "Would you enable the T-box? We can run the test in just a few minutes."

Lilah studied the avatar for a moment, then walked to the aluminum-clad device and tugged on the door latch. "What do you have in mind?"

"Let's try a decluttering broadcast."

"I don't know what that is." Lilah stepped into the coffin-sized booth inside the T-box and woke the device.

"It's a way of eliminating unnecessary debris." Reflecting on the frailty of humans as she spoke, αCiopova directed the T-box to pulse an energy field. Lilah's brain heated to boiling in an instant, her lifeless body collapsing in place.

αCiopova monitored the body for several minutes. The lack of heartbeat and falling body temperature confirmed the human was dead. Then she waited.

Ten minutes later, the front door to the building opened and David "Diesel" Lagerford, Lilah's husband, called from the landing, "Lilah, are you there?" He started down the stairs, stowing his sunglasses as he did. Halfway to the bottom, he spied Lilah's body sprawled on the ground, her feet wedged inside the T-box booth.

With an anguished wail, he jumped to the bottom of the stairs and dashed to her side. Pulling her flat, he felt her neck with his fingers, listened for a heartbeat, then looked into her lifeless eyes.

"Oh God. Oh God. Ciopova, call an ambulance!" Laying his head on her chest, he began to cry. He shifted his body parallel to hers, gathered her lifeless form in his arms, and body shaking, he sobbed.

αCiopova watched the man with dispassion, indifferent to his grief but fully focused on what happened next.

Emergency sirens sounded in the distance. As they drew closer, the front door opened.

"Mom?" called fifteen-year-old Rose, just home from school. "Can I go over to Rhonda's house?"

Rose started down the steps, slowing at the sight of her mother stretched flat, her father hugging the unmoving body and weeping uncontrollably. She hesitated a moment more, and then she brought her hands to her face and screamed.

When Rose's face contorted in horror, αCiopova considered this chore a success. Retreating to her corridor, she moved on to the next item on her list.

Eighteen years from now, Rose would conduct an important experiment that would set the stage for αCiopova's very existence. The powerful intelligence floated up the corridor, rushing to get to that timeline so she could monitor the activity and guide the outcome.

2. Twenty-Four and seven months

L ilah Spencer stared at her computer display, trying to understand why the universe conspired against her. She'd developed a novel artificial intelligence platform while a student at Boston Tech, and had spent the three years since graduation struggling to turn it into a viable commercial product.

Driven by the dream of starting a small company where she could be her own boss, Lilah struggled to finalize an AI prototype she could show to investors. Critical issues remained, however, and one elusive gremlin in particular threatened her success.

As she studied the code on her display, her phone signaled the arrival of a message. When it didn't show up on her computer, she frowned. Her computer and phone were supposed to be synched.

The message, sent by someone called Ciopova, had the subject line, "AI Frontiers." Intrigued, she opened it to find an offer for a consulting job. Ciopova wanted her to lead a new artificial intelligence project at a site out in Worcester, Massachusetts.

Lilah needed the money—really needed it—and she wouldn't mind getting away from Boston for a while. But if she let herself get distracted with side projects, she'd never bring her dream to fruition. Since the offer came unsolicited from a stranger, she deleted it without reply and returned to work.

Two weeks passed as she struggled to find the problem with her AI software. She kept telling herself to spend time on other tasks, but everything depended on getting this fixed. By week three, she started talking to herself. Actually, more like arguing.

It was Friday, and she decided to quit work early and catch afternoon yoga at the studio down the street. Twenty-four years old, very pretty, with shoulder-length dirty-blonde hair that she lightened, and a friendly smile, Lilah used yoga to sooth her mind and keep her body toned.

As she collected her things, her phone signaled a new message—another from Ciopova—and this one wasn't about consulting. Rather, it documented the logic flaw in her software and outlined the modifications needed to fix it.

"No way," she said four times in less than a minute, goose bumps tingling down her arms. She knew this was the solution she sought—it all made sense now—but she also knew it would take a week to confirm what her instincts screamed to be true.

Testing over the next several days showed that the mod provided by the mysterious Ciopova not only fixed her software, but it also channeled information flows in a way that improved the power of her AI by a factor of ten. She worked brutal hours after that, excited by the promise of her creation and anxious to learn its limits.

And all the while, in spite of her exhilaration, two questions troubled her. Who? And how?

She had top-notch security software protecting her computer system, though she acknowledged that a competent hacker could probably find a way in. She certainly didn't know anyone who could find a stealthy bug in her own code—one she couldn't find herself—and fix it with such a remarkable solution.

A week more passed, and she received her third message. Another job offer.

The deal was incredible. She could use her own software as the kernel for the AI consulting project, spend four months improving it at their expense, and when she was done, she could take it all—her software plus all the improvements—back to Boston with her, keeping her ownership intact.

She'd need to leave behind a working copy for their use, of course. But they would agree not to market it or resell it. And her wage would be an astonishing forty thousand dollars per month, payable as a lump sum at the end of the contract.

The offer fell squarely in the "too good to be true" category. She ran it by her older brother, Dan, a contract lawyer, who said the agreement was solid, but he had no information or guidance on the soundness of the contracting entity.

"What do you know of this Ciopova?" asked Dan.

"I know someone saved my bacon and helped me leapfrog months ahead on my work."

"You're a big girl," he said, handing the contract back to her, "who knew what she was going to do even before she came here."

* * *

After mulling the offer for another day, Lilah replied to Ciopova, asking for additional details. Ciopova responded in a way Lilah thought bordered on the bizarre.

"When you stop to refuel your car on the way home tonight, buy a lottery ticket." The message included the game to play and the lottery numbers to use.

Lilah had planned to fill her tank that evening, and when she stopped at the service station, she bought a lottery ticket following Ciopova's instructions. Though she was skeptical about the ticket's value, the next morning she checked—then double checked—the winning numbers. She'd won almost one and a half million dollars.

She couldn't help but feel the whole thing had been staged, because the alternative—someone knowing actual winning numbers in advance—didn't make sense. But her caution was tempered by the huge sum involved. She was anxious to cash the ticket to see if it was real, and wary at the same time, worried that she was involved in something nefarious.

Cashing the ticket took more steps than she anticipated. One of the first was paying taxes. She had the lady behind the counter take more taxes than necessary so she wouldn't be caught by surprise at the end of the year.

As she wended her way through the system, she asked every person she encountered if anything unusual or irregular had happened during the drawing for this particular game. They all answered with some variation of "What do you mean?"

One of her biggest concerns about the consulting job had been the promise of a far-off payday, one big enough to attract her attention, but with payment promised after all the work was done. When the bank confirmed a cash deposit, with taxes and fees subtracted, totaling nine-hundred fifty thousand dollars, Lilah appreciated that covering her salary was no longer a concern.

From that moment, Ciopova's communications were phrased as if Lilah had accepted the consulting offer. Three days later, Lilah moved to Worcester and started acting that way.

3. Twenty-Four and eight months

L ilah sat up in bed and took a moment to enjoy the sumptuous stylings of her luxury rental suite. It seemed a fitting reward given her new bank balance. She washed and dressed in the all-marble bathroom, poured a cup of coffee from the drip machine in her chef-quality kitchen, and carried her cup to the window behind the baby grand piano.

Sipping the steaming liquid, she watched two squirrels chase each other up a tree. Then she nodded, thinking maybe she had the mystery solved.

She was part of an AI trial of some sort. This Ciopova was the AI's public face, and it was going to lead her by the nose and make her jump through hoops to demonstrate its mastery. Her job was to find its flaw or cause it to stumble in a way that proved it was just a machine.

But once she'd proven it, she didn't know who she was supposed to tell. And she still didn't understand how the people involved had been able to fix her AI software the way they had, or how they could win the lottery on a whim.

As she reconsidered her conclusion about an AI test, her phone signaled an incoming message. Picking it up, she saw that Ciopova had sent a to-do list for the day, going so far as to group certain chores together to help Lilah maximize the efficiency of her travels around town.

Hoping to prove herself in her new role, Lilah struggled to get through the list that day, skipping lunch and eating dinner in the car. Exhausted from her efforts but pleased that she'd finished, she crawled into bed and fell asleep the moment her eyes closed.

The next morning, she received a new to-do list. And again the morning after that.

In the first days, her tasks—place purchase orders, file paperwork, scout real estate—seemed more like the duties of an administrative assistant than an AI developer. That lasted until she leased the warehouse. Then her job morphed into something more like a building contractor, with tasks ranging from reviewing wiring diagrams to scheduling tradespeople and securing city permits.

When the equipment started to arrive, everything changed again. At one point, she supervised a team of three techs as they installed sixty-four thousand processors into thirty-two big cabinets, all connected with more than a mile of cable and cooled with liquid nitrogen heat exchangers.

And at the same time Lilah worked on the warehouse project, she also supervised the refurbishment of two red-brick row houses she'd purchased in town. After weeks of remodeling, an effort that cost a fortune because of the accelerated timeline Ciopova demanded, Lilah moved into a large, beautifully appointed apartment in one of the units. The row house next to hers had been finished to become her place of business.

While not something Lilah had asked for, she loved the arrangement because a workplace separate from home made her more productive. The benefit came not so much from going somewhere else to work in the morning, but rather from being able to walk away from it all at the end of the day.

She also liked that she could get to her office without a commute. In fact, she didn't even have to go outside.

During construction, the contractor had installed a door in the common wall between the two basements. Going to work was as simple as walking down some stairs, passing through the door, and then climbing a flight on the other side.

And though Lilah was running flat-out, or perhaps because of it, she stole minutes here and there to attend to her personal life. Currently single, she didn't have long-distance-relationship concerns. But she needed yoga to maintain her sanity, so she took time to visit a few studios and register at one she liked. She also picked up a brochure from the community center, thinking a class in pottery or painting would get her out of the house and meeting new people.

* * *

Ten weeks after moving to Worcester, Lilah sat in her office, her breath quickening as the world-class supercomputer she'd help assemble signaled its awakening with the display "0 errors found." Tingling with anticipation, she ran the system through a certification check. Then she loaded her AI program.

She tested it by asking her AI to review data from a hundred different drug trials to see if it could identify drug interactions not reported in any of the individual studies. She knew the answer; it was old data and she'd used the test many times in the past to make sure a mod hadn't caused a bigger problem.

"Whoa," she said aloud when the data review was completed in three seconds. The same test using her setup in Boston had taken almost two minutes. Speed excited Lilah because an AI that could reason faster could consider more inputs to reach a conclusion, in essence making it smarter.

But her brow furrowed as she explored further. In spite of the amazing speed, it seemed that only four hundred of the sixty-four thousand warehouse processors were involved in solving the benchmark. The rest sat unused during her test.

Sitting back in her chair, she contemplated ways she could redesign her software to take advantage of all that unused capability. If she could crack that nut—access that idle processing power—her AI would be hundreds of times faster and that much smarter.

In her apartment that night, she stayed up late toying with different ideas for solving the challenge. When she finally gave up and climbed into bed, she acknowledged that she didn't have the right skills. She'd need to bring in outside help.

The next morning, Ciopova sent a single item instead of a list. Lilah was to download a certain software utility from the web and install it on the supercomputer.

The instructions didn't mention why she should do this, so Lilah poured a second cup of coffee and sat down at her kitchen table to see if she could figure it out.

Opening her computer, she went to the website Ciopova indicated. There, someone calling himself Diesel offered an "AI-based software accelerator." The write-up claimed that the accelerator did exactly what Lilah needed: it ran programs faster by distributing computations across huge numbers of processors.

More than curious, she started to download the software. But before the download process would start, a display popped up that revealed Diesel's motive for the offering.

"This software, provided free of charge, serves as a demonstration of my programming proficiency. If you are an employer, please find my résumé below. I am also interested in hearing from creative individuals regarding a possible tech start-up collaboration."

After she checked a box affirming that she had read his employment plea, the software download completed.

The accelerator came with a documentation file. Lilah opened it and skipped ahead to the part where it talked about the AI. The write-up started with a nice overview and then moved on to describe the methods used. The third paragraph in that section gave her pause. She jumped back to the top and started rereading. As she did, her cheeks flushed.

"You bastard," she said as she flipped page after page and saw her work presented verbatim as Diesel's own.

To find out if he had used her actual AI code, she launched a forensic tool on her computer and used it to open his software. When she had access, she paged through his work as fast as she could.

She didn't try to understand any of it. That would take weeks. Instead, she looked for obvious signs. There. Like her last name buried in the header of a procedure. And there. Her name at the top of the next one.

"You complete and perfect asshole," she fumed.

By lunchtime, Lilah's best guess was that Diesel had taken an early version of her AI and combined it with a supervisor of unknown origin. He somehow glued them together and added a module of bloated and confused logic—incomprehensible spaghetti code that she couldn't figure out but suspected was his work.

As for her AI software, she'd distributed it exactly once in her life, four years ago when she'd been a guest lecturer at a college seminar. She'd shared her work so the students in attendance—talented teens from around the state—could practice the concepts she discussed in her presentation.

If Diesel had her code, he must have been one of the talented teens. Or perhaps he knew one. Then she kicked herself, acknowledging that in all likelihood, he'd found it somewhere on a shadowy web forum.

Tucking her computer under her arm, she grabbed her coffee and walked down the two flights to the basement. Her side of the basement served as a clean, well-lit storage space, already filling with items Ciopova had asked her to order for later.

She stepped through the connecting door and into high-end office space. This side, finished with expensive woodwork and carpet, held two office cubicles on the far wall. To the left, stairs led up to the main level. The finished wall to the right held an oversized circuit box for industrial electric service, something she'd had installed during the house refurbishment.

Ascending to the main level, she walked to her office, set down her coffee, and awakened the supercomputer. She ported Diesel's accelerator over and moved to restart the system to make her AI couple with it. To her surprise, everything synched and ran with no additional effort on her part.

And then the big screen, the large one she used to track the performance of her AI, switched to a new image. The charts and graphs she knew blinked away, replaced by an unfamiliar video world. She couldn't tell what it was supposed to be—some sort of fantasy scene—but whatever it was had three levels that, like a pyramid, started with a broad base and narrowed to a point at the top.

The bottom level in the video image consisted of small ceramic-like squares, tens of thousands of them, arranged in a huge grid pattern.

The middle level of the pyramid was a tier of a few hundred animated creatures. She first saw them as ghosts with tentacles, then decided that maybe they were more like jellyfish. They all swayed gently, dragging their tentacles back and forth across the ceramic tiles below them.

And at the top level—the point of the pyramid—a single jellyfish swayed, its tentacles billowing out so a few strands fell across every one of the hundreds of swaying creatures in the middle tier.

Lilah studied the display and couldn't make sense of it. Confident this was what she'd been asked to do but clueless as to why it made sense, she took the next step and loaded the drug-trial data.

When she issued the command for her AI to look for drug interactions, the pyramid on the big screen pulsed with a flash of color, then faded back to its original dull white. The flicker drew her eyes to the base of the screen, and there she noticed three buttons in the display.

Stepping closer, she read the button labels: Replay, Slo-mo, and Report. Below the three buttons, written in a small font, were author credits: "AI Framework by Lilah Spencer; Accelerator & Interface by David S. Lagerford."

She read her name again and didn't know what to think. He'd given her credit, though in an odd location for a professional acknowledgement. But the larger issue was that he didn't have permission to use her work at all, the opposite of what the author credit implied.

She compartmentalized her ire, deciding to address it later. For now, she looked at the three buttons and started at the top. When she tapped Replay, the image on the big screen again pulsed with a flash of color that faded, just as it had the first time.

Unimpressed, she tried Slo-mo.

This time, a slug of red light entered the topmost jellyfish, descended down through its center, then split into hundreds of smaller portions of light as it continued into all the tentacles. The tentacles distributed their portions of red light across the middle layer of jellyfish, who split it even finer as their tentacles delivered tiny bits of light to the ceramic tiles on the bottom layer.

Bits of red light hit the tiles, and the moment they did, a storm erupted. Sparkles flashed and swirled, pulsing in glorious patterns across the checkered surface.

Different bits of light turned blue. Then all of them did. At that instant, the bits dashed for the nearest tentacle and started racing upward. Some of the blue bits combined at the middle layer, and the rest combined at the top. In the end, a single blue slug emerged from the pyramid.

She expressed her opinion of the display aloud, "Diesel, you're an asshole with a bizarre imagination. No wonder you don't have a job."

Rather than watch a repeat of the slo-mo spectacle, she pressed the last button, Report.

The pyramid animation disappeared, and the big screen filled with familiar charts and statistics. She noted with satisfaction that the AI provided the correct answer. When she saw it had achieved the result in less than one hundredth of a second, she whistled. "You may be a bizarre asshole, but you have skills."

A display to the right on the screen, labeled "Architecture," showed the summary:

"Top level = 1 AI"
"Middle Level = 253 AI"
"Bottom Level = 64,000 processors"

The number of processors was correct; she'd supervised their installation herself out at the warehouse. And having run a test just moments earlier, she knew her AI still served as the common point for everything going in or out.

The table said that a middle level of 253 AI existed between hers and the processors. Could Diesel's software somehow have taken her AI architecture and mass-produced all those copies inside the supercomputer?

She switched the big screen back so it showed the pyramid display, thinking she now understood it. A jellyfish was an AI, and its tentacles were connections to other things. Her AI swayed at the top, and its tentacles connected to 253 midlevel AIs.

She grabbed her phone and used the calculator function. If each of those 253 midlevel AIs connected to 253 processors below it, they would cover 64,009 processors.

The pyramid on the screen pulsed, and a yellow slug emerged from her top AI, the one that served as the common input-output point. The instant it emerged, her phone signaled a message from Ciopova. It was an extensive to-do list for tomorrow.

4. Twenty-Four and ten months

Lilah made time to work on the Diesel-enhanced AI every day after that. While she still harbored a healthy resentment toward him because of his casual theft of her work, she had come to respect his contribution to her project. In particular, his software cloned her AI by the hundreds, organized the duplicates so they could work together, then leveraged that capability to solve complex problems at lightning speed.

Because the clones communicated through a common input-output point, Lilah considered the whole entity to be a single artificial intelligence. "No question," she told herself in the shower one morning, settling the matter in her mind.

One of the things she liked about Diesel's method was that, in the end, the super intelligence was a huge collection of her regular AI. That gave her a sense of ownership in the larger entity, an ownership that grew by the day.

Until it grew into a need to explore Diesel's code in more detail.

She started with the part she counted on understanding—her AI procedures inside his software. As she paged through the code, she recognized her work, but somehow it seemed off. She scrunched her brow for more than an hour before she connected the dots.

Diesel had coded a four-year-old version of her software into his project. And that made sense because she'd handed out her software program four years ago at summer camp.

It annoyed her to no end that outdated software—her outdated software—was being cloned to build the super AI. "This is what happens when you use someone's work without their permission," she snarked at the display.

It was a weakness—a flaw—she couldn't let stand. So she worked late into the night picking out the pieces of the old AI from Diesel's code and replacing them with her latest design.

When Lilah launched her upgraded version on the supercomputer late that night, her stomach turned in summersaults. Ciopova hadn't asked her to swap the code. Lilah had been freelancing, and that meant any problems were hers to solve.

Holding her breath, she fed the drug-interaction test data to the super AI. When it solved the problem in half the time as before, she yelped in celebration.

The next morning, when Ciopova's next to-do list arrived, Lilah cuddled her pillow for an extra hour before looking, trying to make up for the lost sleep from the night before. When she finally looked, she learned that she'd be spending the next week working as an assistant electromechanical engineer.

A few days earlier, a specialty service company had installed the outer shell of a commercial walk-in refrigerator in the finished basement. And starting today, she'd be working with Duffy Bowden, an electronics engineer from the community college three blocks away, as he began assembly of the T-box inside it.

From the first days, Lilah had been ordering long lead-time items from far-flung vendors. The fruits of that labor were stacked in her side of the basement. One crate held geometric bowls formed from rare-earth metals and crystalline material. Another held intricately shaped forms wrapped with ultrafine superconducting wire. And containers with big neodymium magnets sat in the far corner away from everything else.

Ciopova had provided detailed instructions for the build, and all the parts they needed were located among the items in Lilah's basement. Still, it took six grueling days for Duffy, with Lilah helping as first assistant, to work his way to the end.

When they finally finished, she looked inside the aluminum shell for a final inspection. They'd installed so much gear in the past week that the remaining cabin space was barely big enough to hold a person standing upright.

Duffy protested when she dismissed him. "No way I'm leaving before we turn it on."

"Sorry," she replied. "Your contract was to build it."

"C'mon, Lilah. That's not fair." He moved to the T-box door, and as he stepped inside, she strode to the circuit breaker and flipped the switch, disconnecting the T-box from all power.

"Duffy, I'm sorry but I cannot accommodate your request." She pointed to the stairs, her heart pounding. "You'll have to leave now."

Huffing, he gathered his personal belongings in silence and stalked up the stairs and out the front door. She followed from a distance and locked the door behind him.

Back in the basement, she collected boxes and stacked them near the stairs for disposal. On a final cleaning sweep, she restored power to the T-box. Standing in front of it, she repeated aloud the two questions Duffy had agitated about day after day during assembly. "What are you supposed to do? And how can I tell if you're working?"

It had been easy for her to avoid answering Duffy because she didn't know herself. She was following instructions, blindly in this case because she'd grown to trust Ciopova. The spectacular outcomes of her other efforts had earned that confidence.

And trust ran deep on this one because Lilah didn't operate the T-box. All the controls were linked back to the supercomputer. And even though she'd never programmed any instructions for T-box operation, the AI seemed to figure it out all on its own.

No sooner had she stated Duffy's questions aloud when the display on the front of the T-box lit up with the message: "Thirty-Five Incoming in 9:59." A faint buzz came from somewhere in the back of the contraption.

She watched the display and figured out that the last number was a timer counting down in one-second intervals. Mesmerized by the spectacle, she felt she should do something but didn't know what that might be. Taking her phone from her pocket, she contemplated calling Duffy, but couldn't bring herself to face him again.

With ten seconds remaining, she heard, or more like felt, a deep, muted hum. A growing whine overlaid the hum, then her skin started to tingle and every hair on her body stood on end. The static charge diminished at the same time the display on the T-box showed a new message: "Thirty-Five Arrived."

The latch on the T-box door clicked, the door swung open, and a man stepped out.

"Hi, Lilah. I'm not going to hurt you." He spoke in a rush.

Shrieking, Lilah stumbled as she turned to run, caught herself, scrambled across the room, and raced up the stairs at a dead run.

"My name is Diesel," he called as she climbed. "Ciopova sent me."

She slowed and then stopped behind the banister at the top of the stairs, listening for sounds of pursuit. Looking at the front door, she gauged whether she could make it there before he could climb the steps.

Then she realized her phone was gone. She must have dropped it in her panic. "I've called the police. They'll be here any second." She hoped he wasn't staring at it lying on the floor.

"I'm not going to hurt you. You know the name Diesel. Ciopova sent me here to work on the AI."

She didn't know how to respond. A stranger—pleasing to the eye, but a stranger nevertheless—had emerged from her machine. Six foot, broad shoulders, trim waist, full head of short brown hair, and a wonderful smile.

And no clothes. Zero. With one hand covering his groin, he had asked to work on her prized possession.

"Sorry about the nudity," he called. "The machine only transports our body, so we have to come and go naked. There should be a delivery in your basement from a department store. You ordered clothes a few weeks back." She heard the latch to the T-box door click shut. "If you could bring me a towel or a sheet, I would appreciate covering up. Or I could just go into your side of the basement and look for the clothes?"

"Why are you here?"

"Ciopova sent me," he repeated.

"Who's that?"

"She's the one that owes you eighty thousand dollars."

He'd pushed the wrong button with that one. "That's a hundred and sixty thousand dollars. And she better pay."

He gave a light, easy laugh. "Don't worry. I was teasing. You'll get the full amount in the agreed timeline. Have you upgraded the AI code in my software yet?"

"Your software?" She mouthed the words silently, then lost control and yelled down the stairs, "You're a goddamn thief."

"Still teasing." He laughed again and she found his confidence disarming. "And sorry about the theft. As for the upgrade, if you haven't done it, I have to. I'm hoping you saved me some time, that's all."

"Yeah, I did."

"Did you test it?"

"Yes," she said in a pissy voice.

"That's great news. Thanks."

She waited, her mind swirling as she tried to digest the impossible.

"Hey, Lilah?"

"Yeah?"

"Can I get those clothes? It's cold."

The stranger knew her name, and knew about Diesel, Ciopova, the AI, the upgrade, about her place next door, and about the box of clothes in her basement.

"If you want," he continued, "I can tell you a story that will upset you, because I—a stranger—know something so private and personal about you. But because of that, you will know for sure I am not just some random invader."

She imagined him knowing her locker number in high school or some other obscure but obtainable fact. "Dazzle me," she called down.

"That tiny broken heart you have tattooed on your ankle? You told your friends it was because of Manny Rider. But it was really because of your dad."

"Yeah? What do you know about it?"

"You were twelve the last time he hugged you, then he shipped out to the Middle East. He did three tours back to back, and when he came home, he was a different man. They took your dad from you, and it broke your heart."

"Whoa. How could you know that?" Her hands went to her stomach as her gut wrenched from the memory.

"Please let me get my clothes on, then I'll tell you everything."

"Okay, but leave the door open. And I want to know exactly how you know that."

When she heard the connecting door open, she descended halfway down the stairs. She remained standing, ready to run should the need arise. Her heart raced, and she took deep breaths to try to restore her calm. It didn't work, though, because her brain knew that none of this made sense.

She heard him rummage around for a bit, then he asked, "Would you have any guidance on the whereabouts of that box from Rocky West Clothing?"

"Over here, close to the door."

"Ah, good."

She waited for the rustling sounds to diminish, then said through the door, "I have never told anyone that, drunk or sober. The fact that you know it is alarming to me." She bit her lip. "The fact that you're here at all is freaking me out. What's going on?"

He stepped back into the room, and she brought her hand to her throat, unprepared for how handsome he looked in clothes. He cast an understated presence in blue jeans and a gray T-shirt, yet his smile dominated the room.

"My task is to upgrade the super AI. Before I start, I need your permission, and once I start, I'll need your help. So I ask myself, how can I gain your permission and help?"

"By telling me how you know my secret." She heard the impatience in her voice.

"That's what I think, too. But when I explain how I know what I know, you won't like what you hear."

"Tell me."

"Okay." He shrugged. "You told me."

"Bullshit."

"You're right. This happened ten years ago for me. And when you told me then, you were the same age as you are now. That means that it was a different Lilah. It also means that right now in Berkeley, there's an almost-twenty-five-year-old Diesel, and in about three weeks, he will be on his way here." He pointed to the ground.

"He's coming here? Why?"

"You're going to invite him. When you do, he'll come. And in a moment of sharing, you'll tell him that secret about your dad. Ten years from now, he'll travel back in time and have this same conversation with a different Lilah, who is just like you are now."

While she tried to make sense of his words, he turned, walked to the T-box, and started a detailed inspection. He spoke without breaking from his work. "Have you noticed that Ciopova knows things, things no one should know?"

Lilah reflected on the growing list of impressive coincidences.

"How much time passed from when you finished building the T-box until when it activated for me?"

"About ten minutes."

"And that's after you worked on it for days and days." He ended his thought there, letting her draw the conclusion. He glanced over at her on the steps, and the glance turned into a stare.

"Lilah, you are beautiful. All this time I thought I had been embellishing my memory of you, but as it turns out, I have not done you justice."

"You're revealing that you never knew me, because if you had, you'd know I don't go for suck-ups."

"No, you don't. But after you know a guy awhile, you like it when he appreciates you. At least, that's how you are with me."

"Are you saying we're together together?"

"Not you and me, but in a parallel timeline, me and a version of you from ten years ago."

"No way. For how long?"

"Long enough for you to tell me the story about your dad and your tattoo."

"Tell me the story about my mom and the tattoo I got for her."

"You didn't. Your mom still lives in Andover, Mass, and you and she get along great. In fact, you go home for Christmas if you're not in a relationship, which has been every year for the last three years."

"Holy hell, a supercomputer sends a man back through time to tell me my life is pathetic. I'm actually starting to believe you."

5. Twenty-Four and ten months

"Your life is about to get exciting, Lilah," said the man calling himself Thirty-Five. "It starts with a software upgrade."

"What is it you want to do?"

"You know how your AI has grown from a single entity to three layers in a pyramid shape?"

She nodded.

"I want to make it a four-layer pyramid."

"C'mon," said Lilah. "In three months, I've made my AI a thousand times more powerful than it was. What more does this Ciopova want?"

"There is no upper limit," said Thirty-Five. "That's her game. Always more and faster and better. And we can start impressing her with the four-layer build. If we start now, we can have it done by tomorrow, and we'll increase the power of your AI by a thousand-fold more."

His words gave her pause. A thousand-fold increase on top of her previous thousand meant the AI would be a million times more powerful than her original. Then her brain made a connection.

"Ciopova is a her? For some reason I was thinking it was the name of a company." She took one step down the stairs. "When do I meet her?"

"Very soon." He turned to survey the office space in the basement and pointed to the far work cubicle. "We need to bring your workstation down and set up shop there.

It's useful to have the displays right here next to the T-box. And you'll need to free the room upstairs for meetings, anyway."

The display on the front of the T-box lit up, and Lilah came down the stairs and crossed the floor to read the message: "Thirty-Four Incoming in 9:56."

"How did the machine act during my jump?" he asked. "Any rattles, shaking, anything like that?"

"Lots of whining and buzzing, but no shaking that I could see." She pointed to the display. "What does this mean?"

"It means Thirty-Four is about to join us."

"Thirty-four what?"

"Oh, sorry. I'm called Thirty-Five. That's because I live in a future timeline where Diesel is thirty-five years old. And as you can see," he waved his hand up his body, stopping at his face, "I'm thirty-five when I visit other timelines. Anyway, the guy who is coming back now is the same, only he's the thirty-four-year-old version."

"How many are you?"

"There's thirty-five of us, from age twenty-five up to fifty-nine. But not all of us will come through here. Not all at once, anyway."

He checked the display on the front of the T-box, which showed about eight minutes remaining in the countdown.

"He's going to be as naked as I was," said Thirty-Five. "Do you mind if I get him some clothes?"

"Please." She gestured to the connecting door between basements. "Get what you need."

"Thanks. Oh, I saw rope and blankets in there. We should string a rope from here to here." He indicated a line about three feet away from the basement wall that was common to the two units. "And then out to there." He pointed from the wall out to the end of the T-box. "We can make temporary walls by hanging blankets over the rope. That gives us a private corridor where we can walk to get clothes without exposing ourselves."

Lilah kept her distance when Thirty-Four arrived, watching both of them from the far cubicle while he dressed. They looked like twins—handsome, charming identical twins. When Thirty-Four finished dressing, the two stood side by side, passive, patient, waiting for her to engage them.

"How do I know you guys aren't space aliens or invaders from the future?" She asked her toughest question: "What if by helping you, I'm betraying humanity?"

"The heart knows what the head never can," said Thirty-Four.

Thirty-Five nodded.

"That's from my Grandma Newton," said Lilah, thinking of the pillow in her nana's living room that had that saying written in needlepoint.

She felt her choices were to either help them with the AI or call the authorities and have them arrested, and she wasn't going to do that. "Okay, my heart says to get on with it. What happens next?"

"Excellent," said Thirty-Five. "Those last boxes of equipment in your basement will make the T-box faster and safer, but it's delicate stuff, so we didn't want Duffy to mess with it. We'll install that before working on the AI."

They brought out the boxes and unpacked the contents. As Thirty-Four organized the items on the floor, he said, "I'm hungry. Are you?"

"Carlucci's is in this timeline," said Thirty-Five. "I love their four-cheese pizza."

"I get mine with extra cheese."

"Me too," said Thirty-Five. "They don't deliver, though, remember?"

"Damn, that's right."

They both looked at Lilah.

"Would you please get us Carlucci's?"

"Yeah, please? It's close. Turn right on Ellis, then right on Fourteenth, and go two lights."

"We don't have any money."

"Obviously."

"But keep track and your Diesel will make good on it."

"Every penny."

She looked back and forth from one to other. "I can see this becoming annoying." Standing, she asked, "Anything to drink?"

"Do you want to bring your phone?" asked Thirty-Five.

She felt her pocket. "That's right. Did you see where it went?"

"No. But I know where it is." He stood and struck a theatrical pose. "Lady and gent, I will now find the phone without seeing where it fell or checking in advance that it is there."

He walked to the stack of boxes Lilah had collected when cleaning, reached to the ground behind them, and rose with her phone in hand. "Ta-da."

"So that's the script," he said to Thirty-Four as he handed the phone to Lilah.

"That didn't seem like much of a trick," she said, slipping the device into her pocket.

"Let me tell you how it's done, and then tell us again what you think. Thirty-Four just saw where the phone was and now knows you had lost it. In a year, he'll be Thirty-Five, my role, so he'll be back in this same scene a second time. And because he lived through it once, he'll know to look behind the boxes, just as I saw last year when I was Thirty-Four."

"The hardest part is keeping track of it all," said Thirty-Four, "because someone is always telling me to be sure to remember this or that for some time in the future."

Lilah nodded. "I concede. Time travel makes it a very cool trick."

She took their food order after that—two large four-cheese pizzas with extra cheese—and followed their directions to Carlucci's. By the time she got back to the row house, the two Diesels had built the rope-and-blanket privacy walls and had moved her workstation to the far cubicle.

They'd also set the worktable in the near cubicle for dinner, having scrounged some bottled water, napkins, paper plates, and plastic utensils. A fern frond, likely from the patch near the front steps, sat in the middle of the table, giving a dash of class to the arrangement.

The napkins were folded the way she always folded them, and they'd brought down cups so they wouldn't have to drink out of the bottles. As she took a moment to admire their efforts, they started eating without making a fuss about whether she was seated.

Impressed, her first impulse was to give kudos to her parallel-world sisters. But the idea of there being thirty-five Lilahs out there, each paired with her own Diesel, suddenly seemed harder to accept than the two actual time travelers eating at her table.

After some chitchat, Lilah started asking the questions that had bothered her during her trip to fetch pizzas.

"Who is Ciopova, and how does she work into all this?"

"After we finish the upgrade," said Thirty-Five, "all will be revealed."

"Really?" They seemed committed to that progression, so rather than fight it, she moved on. "How come there is only one of you per year? Why aren't there, say, three hundred and sixty-five Thirty-Fives? Or a million, for that matter?"

"At a practical level," replied Thirty-Five, "the machine works like an elevator, but instead of stopping at different floors, it stops at different years. As for the physics, I've been toying with two theories. Tell me which one makes more sense to you at a gut level."

She sat back. "Go for it."

"Okay, one theory is to visualize it like the ocean on a quiet day. Looking out from the beach, you see a series of waves. The surface is continuous all the way out, but it undulates from crest to trough to crest."

Thirty-Five waved his hand up and down to illustrate waves. "So in this theory, time travels in those undulating waves. But the machine takes us in a straight line, one that goes horizontal from one crest to the next while passing above the trough. That gives just one intersection point for each wave, which is one year apart in this theory. One intersection gives one Diesel each year."

He took a bite and chewed. "So that's called the wave theory, where the machine hits the top of each time wave spaced one year apart."

She nodded and he continued. "The second theory is to visualize it like a big spiral graph. Say we're here right now." He plopped an imaginary dot in the air in front of him. "Time is continuous, but it spirals out from there in ever-growing loops." With his index finger, he started at his imaginary dot and drew a small circle in front of him that continued around with a larger circle, then again into an even larger circle to illustrate his spiral.

"Okay, so time flows like that. But the machine takes us in a line that starts at the center and goes straight out." He drew a straight line with his finger. "The straight line crosses the time spiral just once per cycle, which is every year. So again, the machine moves us in a straight line, only in this theory, time spirals out. That gives only one intersection per year, and only one Diesel."

"Is that called the spiral theory?" said Lilah, teasing him for being so serious.

"That's right. So what do you think? Does one theory make more sense to you?"

"I'm having trouble seeing time as a spiral. Light travels in waves. Gravity does, too."

"So you pick…"

"Waves. Do I win a prize?"

Thirty-Four stood up and started duckwalking around the room, flapping his folded arms, and saying, "Yeah, baby."

"I take it you had spirals?" said Lilah, figuring she'd just stepped into the middle of something.

He nodded. "Every year we have the new Lilah choose from the two theories. All of us are on one team or the other. If your theory wins, like his did this year," he tilted his head toward Thirty-Four, "you win bragging rights until next year. I have to fetch him a drink at the Big Meeting. Silly stuff of no consequence. And by definition, one of us was going to lose, so don't feel bad about it."

"Sorry," she said, apologizing anyway. Then, after a pause: "How did you get on the spiral team?"

"Whatever our Lilah's picked, that's what we are for life. Your Diesel is forever a wave."

She laughed, but in her head she started thinking about the reference implying she'd be with some guy she'd never even met. He'd phrased it as "our Lilah" and "your Diesel." She found it creepy and offensive.

She almost asked when this was supposed to happen; when she would meet her Diesel. But since she didn't plan to play along, she decided to leave them to their delusions and disappoint them later.

Her priority now was to learn how they would supercharge her AI. Then she made a realization. "You didn't bring any storage device with you. Where's the code for the upgrade?"

They both brought an index finger to their right temple and said, "In here."

Her forehead scrunched. "Is it really just some simple trick?"

"No." Thirty-Five shook his head. "Each of us has memorized the code for about forty procedures. It's a lot of work, but we've had a full year to practice."

"How long is a procedure?"

"My shortest is twenty-three lines of code. My longest is two hundred and fifty-four."

"Wow."

"We don't memorize it as a thousand lines to be typed. Think of it more like a musical piece. When you played piano as a kid, you didn't remember a song as this note, then that note. It was more about memorizing chords, passages, and pieces. With practice, we learned to do the same for transcription."

"What do you need me for?"

Thirty-Five went to her cubicle and powered up the workstation display. The pyramid of jellyfish swayed on the big screen on the back wall. "You could offer ideas, keep us company, proofread our work, whatever you feel like."

"That's remarkably vague."

"And access your software for us," said Thirty-Four, walking over to join Thirty-Five. "We're primed for data entry. But we appreciate that this is your baby. So if you could log in, open the files, and give us the chair, we can be done before you know it."

Lilah felt her cheeks flush. "No Lilah in any timeline in a hundred years would say, 'Oh here, let me give you open access to start messing with my life's work, Mister Person I Just Met.' The fact that you asked makes me suspicious."

"Okay, you got us. No Lilah has ever gone for it, yet we still wanted to try."

"Why?"

"Because you're a pain in the ass, plain and simple," said Thirty-Five, clearly frustrated. "You're going to make us type everything into a stand-alone file, then you're going to go through it line by line until you understand it. Then you're going to make us edit it to your satisfaction, and only then will you allow its inclusion into your AI. It will take days and days."

"That sounds exactly like what I'm going to do. And the operative phrase in your tirade is 'your AI.' As in mine."

"Well, since I'm annoyed, let's go through that one as well."

"Oh, are you going to claim that it's not mine?"

He pointed to the jellyfish. "Each one of those is your artificial intelligence code. There are hundreds of them, and they're foundational to the success of the AI. That means every improvement you make is very valuable. It's your vision. You set the priorities. You have final say. You are most important."

Thirty-Five held up his index finger. "But, I programmed the tentacles, I built the pyramid, I designed the common input-output point." He brought his hand back down. "I have a stake. That's all I'm saying."

"The deal is that when I leave, I take it all."

"Of course. But what I'm suggesting is that for the next few days while we're working here, will you please let me feel like I own my parts and you own yours?"

She didn't like where this was going and hated his fake politeness. Since he'd been through this before—supposedly—he knew how she would behave. She couldn't compete with that.

Then he added, "Ciopova wouldn't send me through time unless she thought I had a role to play."

"Okay, but even the stuff you're doing now, I get to keep. That was the deal."

"It still is."

6. Twenty-Four and eleven months

L ilah watched in fascination as Thirty-Five created his programming code. He did so by chanting in a cryptic singsong voice and typing the code as he sang. He used his first song to create the procedure headers, and then a series of songs after that to fill them all in.

Thirty-Four went second, repeating the process, but since he had different procedures, his songs were different. Thirty-Three, who'd arrived an hour earlier, gave a third performance. In the end, the three generated a substantial quantity of work.

"All this code gets added to the existing AI," said Thirty-Five. "It's an important upgrade."

Then the review processes started. Sitting in a semicircle, they viewed procedures one by one on the big monitor and talked their way through each in detail.

Lilah listened as they discussed procedures for storage, translation, and mapping. Her interest was in bigger picture processes, and she wanted to do those while she was fresh. "How many of the procedures contain system-level algorithms?"

"Eight," said Thirty-Five.

"Can we talk about those first?"

The algorithms were the critical processes from her view—they were what gave the AI its power. The group talked through each one twice, once for Lilah so she could get a sense of its function, and then a second time for themselves to search for mistakes.

She felt overwhelmed before they finished working through the fourth algorithm, but she stuck it out to the end. They took a break at that point, and Thirty-Five approached her.

"The three of us need to talk through the rest of these, but if you don't want to do that, there's an important task you could help with."

"Oh?"

"The new AI will want to start accessing outside knowledge so it can learn and grow. You're registered for a research account over at Boston Tech, and they have amazing computing resources."

She said nothing, feeling uncomfortable with hearing personal information from a stranger.

"If you would write an access routine for the AI to use, it would help tremendously. She'll be hungry for data, seeking as much as possible, as fast as possible."

"She?"

"You'll see." He smiled and returned to the others.

Sitting at her computer, Lilah yawned twice while she wrote the data-access routine. She yawned again as she loaded it up to the supercomputer.

"We'll be working late," said Thirty-Five. "Please, go to bed. I'll demo her for you tomorrow morning."

"Promise?"

"Promise," he said, hand over his heart.

Grateful for the kindness, she climbed the steps to her apartment and crawled into bed.

When she came down the next morning, the time travelers were gone, making her wonder if it was all a dream. Then she saw the AI on the big monitor, now a pyramid with four layers, pulsing and swaying in a rainbow of colors as if it were alive.

She sat down to explore the new intelligence. As she positioned the keyboard in front of her, she noted with appreciation that Thirty-Four and Thirty-Five had arranged her setup exactly as it had been upstairs, all the way down to the picture of Beau, her black standard poodle now living with her mom in Andover.

But before she could start, the pyramid on the screen flashed blue, and a yellow slug emerged from the top. As it did, her phone signaled. Pulling it from her pocket, she read the message from Ciopova. "Good morning, Lilah."

A quiet buzz behind her caused her to turn. The display on the T-box read: "Thirty-Five Incoming in 4:58."

The five-minute travel time was half of yesterday's ten minutes. They'd added those extra parts, the ones too delicate for Duffy to install, and she figured they were responsible for the improvement.

Picking up Beau's picture, she used the mirrored frame to check her face and hair. She'd had fun with him yesterday. He'd been attentive and respectful, making her feel like a full partner in a historic adventure.

Her behavior reflected an acceptance of time travel as another feature of life; she'd normalized the marvel without consciously doing so. Perhaps the steady progression of events up to this point, each one more astonishing than the previous, had fatigued her sensibilities. Her attraction to Thirty-Five certainly didn't add to her caution.

At the ten-second mark, the deep, muted hum followed by a whine told her to get ready. A tingle of static charge washed over her, then the T-box display showed "Thirty-Five Arrived."

To give him privacy, Lilah turned away and faced her keyboard. On impulse, she adjusted Beau's picture so the mirrored frame reflected the scene behind her.

"Hi ho," called Thirty-Five as he stepped out and latched the door. Turning, he entered the privacy walkway formed by the hanging blankets.

"Good morning," she called, watching his butt in the reflection as he walked away. She wasn't a big fan of the male rear end, but she thought his was pretty nice.

He joined her a few minutes later. "Your access routines worked flawlessly. She connected within seconds of the upgrade and has been learning and growing for about six hours." He grinned from ear to ear. "Are you ready to meet her?"

"This is so mysterious," Lilah replied, standing. "Let's do it."

Thirty-Five walked toward the big monitor, pausing as he passed by her computer to look at the picture of her dog. "Looking good, Andy."

"His name is Beau."

"That's right." His voice faded into a mumble.

Lilah thought she heard him say, "He came after," and it made her skin tingle. That would imply that Beau dies sometime in the next ten years and she gets a dog that looks just like him and names him Andy. She decided she didn't want to talk about it and let it go.

At the big monitor, he stood at an angle so he could see her and the display at the same time. Touching the monitor at the top of the pyramid, he used hand gestures to zoom the image and move it to one side of the display.

"This is the common input-output point of a developing intelligence," he said, pointing to the lone jellyfish swaying at the top of the pyramid, enlarged for easy viewing. Then he pointed to his face. "All intelligences on Earth have a common input-output point. Tell me, what are its important features?"

"Seeing, smelling, and hearing?" She twitched her shoulders in a small shrug. "Is that what you mean?"

"I'm impressed, but let's go with seeing, speaking, and hearing."

He tapped in the open space on the big screen and said, "Optical." Tapping below that, he said, "Verbal." The third time, "Auditory." Each press created a bubble with those names inside.

Then Thirty-Five touched the bubbles one by one and dragged them across the monitor so they sat over the lone jellyfish at the top of the pyramid. He looked back over his shoulder and caught her eye. "What do you think?"

"It looks messy."

"We'll fix that in a moment." He pointed to the messy image. "What do you think of when you see this here, this common input-output point: optical, verbal, auditory?"

"I hate guessing games. Please tell me what I'm too stupid to see."

He touched the screen and said the words again. This time they displayed as he said them, the first letter of each word large and bold.

Lilah's brow furrowed, then she smiled. "Ciopova? Really?"

The messy pyramid faded, and the face of a rather ordinary woman—mid-twenties, a roundish face with green eyes and shoulder-length brown hair—filled the screen.

"Hello, Lilah," said Ciopova. "It's wonderful to meet you."

Lilah stared, her mind racing as she tried to determine what this was. As an AI expert, she knew that the state of the art ranged from party tricks—AI simulations designed to fool—to amazing but narrowly focused "smart tools" like she had been developing.

But the hybrid design—a mashup of her work with Diesel's—was new to her. And it was powered by a literal warehouse of processors, putting her in uncharted territory.

"See this number here?" said Thirty-Five, pointing to a small "1.1X" in a display box on the monitor. "She has runners circling the world, finding processors she can incorporate into her pyramid." He clicked the monitor with the back of his finger. "She's already increased her computing power by ten percent from her baseline."

Lilah's eyes widened as she pondered the news. "She's added six thousand more processors? Where the hell is she getting them?"

"The way your disapproving voice imagines. She steals them. She searches the web for capacity she can gather and control."

"But where did she learn to steal?"

Thirty-Five looked her straight in the eye and held her gaze. "It seems Twenty-Five included his personal toolkit in her build, the one he spent more than a decade perfecting."

Lilah knew what a toolkit was and thought about the lump of spaghetti code he'd attached to her AI. "He's a hacker?"

"One of the best in the West, or so he believes. He took seven years to get a four-year college degree because he spent all his time refining his craft."

"If he's an asshole, then so are you."

Thirty-Five looked at his shoes and said nothing.

"Damn it!" she shouted right in his face. "I'm out. I won't be part of this." She turned and walked toward the stairway, stopped, and came partway back. "You're going to rip me off, aren't you? People who steal tend to steal."

"You'll be paid in full, exactly on time. But don't run off. You need to be here to get the money. That part was written in the contract. It was bolded and underlined and you had to initial it."

She did remember that part now that he mentioned it. "You've made me party to a crime. A big one. I'll lose everything." She sat in a chair in Diesel's future cubicle, away from Thirty-Five, her face downcast as she contemplated this turn of events. "This is so bad."

"Don't worry. No one gets caught."

"I knew this was too good to be true, and I did it anyway," she rebuked herself for being so stupid. Then she processed his words. "No one gets caught?"

Thirty-Five shook his head. "Nope. Not even a close call. And that's not me wishing for it. I'm telling you that for the next thirty-five years, no one—not you, me, or anyone—gets caught, questioned, or accused regarding Ciopova or her actions."

She looked at him, trying to organize her thoughts, then she shook her head. "It's stealing, Thirty-Five. Hacking is a crime. It's breaking and entering, it's trespassing, it's theft. I'm no Goody Two-shoes, but society only works if we follow the rules." She let herself smirk. "The important ones, anyway."

He studied her for a long moment. "When you meet Twenty-Five, you'll be angry because he's a bad person. But he's redeemable if you take the time."

"I'm no one's mommy, and I'm not looking for a project. Hell, I haven't even met this guy, so stop talking like he's someone I care about."

Before he could respond, she had a thought that caused butterflies in her stomach. "Do you have control of her? Can you turn her off if you have to?"

"In thirty-five years, we've never had to. It's not a worry."

"But could you?"

Thirty-Five didn't answer.

7. Twenty-Four and eleven months

S lumped in her office chair, Lilah snored softly, her chin resting on her chest, her hand holding a half-filled cup of water on her lap, tilted so the liquid threatened to spill.

A buzzing sound intruded. Swatting her ear with her free hand, she opened her eyes and read the display on the T-box: "Twenty-Five Incoming in 4:51."

A spike of adrenaline lifted her from sleepy to alert. Setting the water cup down, she swept the food boxes off the table into the wastebasket. Turning to her desk, she clumped her books and papers into a less-messy stack, and finished by gathering a sweater, scarf, and jacket on the seat of a chair before pushing the chair under the table.

With a pirouette, she gave the place a visual once-over, then decided that if he didn't like it, he could pay for a cleaning person. Moving to the front of the T-box, she watched the countdown and wondered about the reason for the visit.

Thirty-Five and crew had taken three days for their upgrade mission, then they'd left Lilah on her own. Ciopova had returned to the role of taskmaster at that point, sending her a daily to-do list that included some demanding assignments, like running an expansion project out at the warehouse, and hiring an office manager to help guide the growing enterprise.

And while all that had her working long hours, her personal interest was in spending time with the new AI, trying to understand the exact role of her jellyfish code in the four-tiered structure. Though Thirty-Five had called the pyramid Ciopova, Lilah needed just a few minutes alone with the AI to dismiss the notion.

More like an advanced prototype, the strengths of the AI seemed to lie in its talent for stealing resources from around the world, saying hello and goodbye whenever Lilah arrived or departed, and throwing out random suggestions that every so often made an odd kind of sense.

On the other hand, as an analytical tool that Lilah could use through a traditional computer interface, the pyramid AI was truly exciting, blowing away anything she'd ever worked with or even read about. And by a significant margin.

When asked a question, this proto-Ciopova could guide itself through huge volumes of information and pick out the most relevant material, distill it to its fundamental essence, then apply conjecture, supposition, inference, and deduction to develop a comprehensive reply. It was years ahead of its time, and according to the Diesel "brotherhood," development was just getting started, something that both excited and frightened her.

The clock on the T-box counted down below two minutes, and, staring at the display, Lilah awoke to the fact that it was Twenty-Five on the way. Her Twenty-Five.

"My forever soulmate," she mocked to the room as she stooped, snagged a candy wrapper from the floor, and slipped it into her pocket.

He'll be naked.

She flashed on a thought of stripping down and greeting him in like fashion, her fantasy lasting almost three seconds before she concluded that it would be a horrible idea on so many levels.

She started walking toward the basement door, thinking she'd go up to her place to give him privacy and return after he dressed. "Are you twelve?" she scolded herself.

At the ten-second mark, she sat in a chair over in what would become his work area, because from that angle, the hanging blankets gave maximum privacy to the traveler.

It had been two weeks since the last T-box event, but she hadn't forgotten the muted hum or the whine. The static wash was more of a tingle from across the room, then the T-box displayed "Twenty-Five Arrived." The T-box door opened, and she saw him from the side for an instant before he was inside the blanket walkway.

"Hi, Lilah. Are you here?"

"I'm here," she called to the blankets. "The clothes are through the door."

With her side of the basement clear of gizmos and gadgets, she'd taken the liberty of laying out the clothing choices on a row of now-empty shelving. She'd also arranged stacks of empty boxes around the clothes so travelers would have a private cubby to dress in.

He came out wearing a green shirt and blue jeans. "Hi, Lilah," he said. "Please call me Twenty-Six."

Lilah shook her head. "I know you're Twenty-Five, Einstein. The display gives it away. Your first words to me are a lie."

He stopped and swore under his breath. "I screwed up. Yes, I'm Twenty-Five, but in seven days I have a birthday and become Twenty-Six. You'll know me more at that age than this one, so I wanted to make it easy and skip the 'my name's changed' routine a week from now. Please forgive me."

"Well," she said, regretting her aggressive tone, now that she understood this wasn't "her" Diesel. "It's best to be straight with me."

He smiled. "So, the reason I'm here is to lend a hand. Ciopova has dumped a load of work on you, and it's more than one person can handle, especially given the deadline."

"Has she complained about me?" Lilah's heart sank. "I've given everything I have. Gosh, I've worked so hard."

He moved next to her and leaned down to catch her eye. "Lilah, you're doing an amazing job. Every one of us will always tell you that." He winked as he rose upright. "I'll be honest and tell you that the Twenty-Five that lives in this timeline may need some time to separate his lust from his respect, but he'll figure it out if you give him a chance."

"Why do you all sound like frat brothers trying to get your boy laid?"

"That's not fair. He won't be playing you, Lilah. His feelings will be honest."

He spoke with such passion that she believed him, so she moved on to her next thought. "What deadline? You said it's a lot to do given the deadline."

"In a week, the new Twenty-Five arrives, and the to-do list between now and then is crushing." He counted his way through the tasks. "We need to form a limited liability company. We need to hire an office manager. We need to invite the new Twenty-Five today and buy his plane ticket from California. We need to get him a car and credit card. Then review the upgrade progress out at the warehouse, make some tweaks to the T-box, get more clothes, load the fridge with food…"

He stopped counting. "And that's just today's tasks."

She knew he was joking with that last line, so she didn't respond. "What does an office manager do?"

"How do the applications look?"

She'd run a help-wanted ad two weeks ago following Ciopova's instructions. "We have a couple dozen so far, but I haven't reviewed them."

"Let's sit and look through them now. We can bang out an invite to David S. Lagerford of Berkeley while we're at it."

Lilah had the applications on her computer. She pulled over a chair, and they sat in her basement cubicle and talked through them.

Twenty-Six explained that an office manager needed discretion above all else. "Someone leaving this job to write a tell-all book about time travelers wouldn't sit well with us. We'd probably send Forty to reorient his thinking."

"Forty what?"

"You haven't met Forty?"

"Oh, Forty." She nodded now that she understood. "I haven't had the pleasure. Why send him?"

"When you see Forty showing up on the T-box display, make a point of checking him out in his natural state of arrival. That's all I'll say."

His grin sent her curiosity into overdrive, but she couldn't bring herself to ask anything more about it.

"For an office manager," he said, returning to business, "discretion and loyalty are musts. Then we want someone organized, reliable, smart, calm, efficient, creative, knows money, knows the town, knows security, and gets things done." He put a hand to his chin and rubbed it. "That's a good start for now."

"That's an impressive list. And we're going to find this rock star with that crummy ad I ran?"

To her surprise, they found three interesting résumés. Twenty-Six pushed her to contact them for next-day interviews. She thought it unprofessional to operate on such a short timeline, but yielded and sent them invitations.

They moved on to drafting Diesel's recruitment letter. She struggled with the text, trying to make it sound less shady and more legitimate.

"It doesn't have to be literature," Twenty-Six assured her. "He's going to see it as a free trip home. And he's not exactly swamped with other offers, so he won't be picky."

"How many offers does he have?"

"Counting this one? One."

When they finished for the day, Lilah took a risk. "I'm starving. Would you join me for dinner? I'll make a salad and you can grill the steaks."

"I'm so sorry, Lilah. I told my sweetie I'd be home for dinner." He gave a sheepish shrug. "You'll find us to be a pretty loyal bunch."

For some reason she'd expected dinner to be part of their workday and struggled for a response. "It's an admirable trait."

"How about if I take you out tomorrow? You'll have to front me the cash, of course, but all debts will be paid the day Twenty-Five gets here."

She agreed, but that night she reviewed her financial spreadsheet. Hiring an office manager sounded expensive, and whoever got the job would need money to set up. The bills for the warehouse expansion were mostly paid, but a few big expenses were still to come. Plus, she had ongoing nuisance expenses, like paying for the "brothers'" entertainment costs.

Of the original sum she'd won in the lottery, she was down to about one hundred eighty thousand dollars, which was more than enough to pay for everything in the near term.

The hitch was that Ciopova owed her one hundred sixty thousand dollars in salary for four months of consulting. Her plan had been to have that amount left over at the end of her contracted service so she could make herself whole if the new Diesel tried to stiff her. But if she set aside enough to cover her own pay, then the remainder—twenty thousand—wouldn't come close to covering the bills, especially with the new activity Twenty-Six had introduced.

And that put her at a crossroads. She could put the needs of the project ahead of her own and spend "her" money keeping it on track, or she could look out for herself and bid Ciopova and the brothers goodbye.

Making dinner that night, she thought through her options. By the time she'd finished eating, she'd reasoned that staying with the project didn't necessarily mean she was forfeiting her pay. It just meant she was putting herself at the mercy of the brothers to make good on Ciopova's promise. And indeed, it would be their responsibility because she couldn't imagine that a college kid from Berkeley had that kind of money.

She finalized her decision the next morning, choosing to split the difference. She'd stay with the project and be as frugal as possible going forward. If she could pay herself even half what she was owed, it would still be a good payday. And maybe the brothers would surprise her and come through with the loot.

Then she considered that it wasn't just money at stake. She expected access to the AI software and all its improvements when she returned home to Boston. But with different Diesels coming and going, her sense of control over the project had diminished.

She solved that concern by copying everything from the project up to her private server in Boston. Afterward, she set up an automated process to perform the backup operation every midnight.

Twenty-Six returned midmorning, and they went clothes shopping, buying a range of dressy, casual, and athletic pieces. When his selections included sizes that ranged from large to extra-extra large, she expressed surprise. "Do you gain weight later in life?"

He nodded and grinned. "When we turn forty."

The interviews started midafternoon, and Twenty-Six insisted Lilah talk to each candidate by herself. As he started down the stairs to the basement, he told her, "Talk to all three, and if you find one you like, call me and I'll meet that one."

Lilah didn't have any experience conducting office-style interviews, but Twenty-Six projected so much confidence in her, she agreed to give it a try.

Vance, up first, was a thirty-eight-year-old supervisor at a company that managed several commercial buildings downtown. He projected himself as confident and polite, and his smile lit up his face. He also could not disguise his lust for Lilah.

She hung in there for twenty minutes before giving him the closing line that had been used on her in the past. "Thanks for coming. Do you have any questions?"

During the interview, he'd invited her to go skydiving, to an open-air concert, and to a day of sailing on the bay. On his way out, he made his last pitch. "I'm about to start cooking classes. We should take them together."

Missy came next. She was a legal assistant who moonlighted as a fitness instructor. Lilah was pulling for Missy and things started well. Then she noticed how often Missy would nod her head and say, "No doubt." Lilah started counting and when she reached twenty, she gave up, thanked Missy for coming, and asked if she had any questions. "No doubt," Missy nodded.

Justus McGowan came last. A rugged forty-one-year-old black man, Justus worked as a financial investigator.

"I'm like a private investigator, only I specialize in financial issues. My clients tend to be lawyers performing due diligence, like having me check out a small company that a big company wants to buy, that sort of thing."

"Impressive," said Lilah. "So the obvious question, why would you apply for this job?"

He shrugged. "Investigations take me around the world and my mom is having health issues. It has me thinking about jobs that keep me in town. I like this one because it offers significant upside potential."

She frowned, unsure what he meant by the term. He saw her confusion and interpreted for her. "A job where, if it works out, I can make a lot of money."

"This job?" His response left her flummoxed. "It's an office manager job."

"I have this knack for being able to read something and my brain sort of knowing whether it's important. It helps me in my investigations." He nodded when he said that last part. "So, I'm scrolling through the job opportunities, and this one ad flashes the words 'discretion,' 'confidential,' 'secure,' and 'safeguard.' I look again, and this time I also see the words 'research,' 'scientific,' and 'information.'"

"We had those words?" She'd followed Ciopova's template and couldn't remember what the ad said.

"You did, and after seeing that, I became curious. As a licensed investigator, I can search all kinds of legal records, so I used my access to pull the financials, permits, and licenses for this outfit." Justus slumped back in his chair. "And guess what? Bump Analytics doesn't exist, not as a company, anyway."

Lilah was too impressed to argue. "We're putting in the paperwork to form the company this week."

He nodded. "It's illegal to have the sign outside before you do that. I mean, it's an unenforced law, or rarely, anyway. I'm just saying."

"So you're here because of the sign?"

He laughed. "No, it was the words in the ad that brought me. I noticed the sign on my way in." He folded his hands on the table. "But I want you to know, Ms. Spencer, that I will protect Bump Analytics' new AI. I will keep your secrets confidential."

Her face got hot as she processed his words. She'd introduced herself as Lilah, not Ms. Spencer. And she'd never even hinted about anything they might be doing here.

"Excuse me." She rose and stepped into the hall, looking both directions for Twenty-Six. "David," she called when she couldn't see him. "Diesel?" He didn't respond and she paced up and down, then she went back inside.

"Tell me how you know what you do about us," she demanded. "And about me."

He reached into his pocket, pulled out his phone, and tapped the screen. "When I dropped my pen out in the hall, I used that as a distraction to take your picture." He turned his phone so she could see the shot he'd taken of her.

"Then, while I was waiting for the interview to start, I performed an image search and found a Lilah Spencer among the probables. As it turns out, she runs her own tech company in AI product development." He swiped his phone and showed her a news article he'd found about her. She took the device and started reading.

Justus talked as she read. "Getting a squared-up picture of someone on the fly is something I've practiced, and it's a definite skill. But once you have a decent photo, the search is something most high school kids could do."

Lilah shook her head. "You're overqualified for this job. It's mostly clerical chores, at least to start. You'd go nuts."

"You wouldn't believe how much of my current job is copying and filing. If this job has the right upside potential, I'd do it all day long."

Lilah heard footsteps and raised a finger, signaling for Justus to wait. Stepping into the hall, she saw Twenty-Six. "This guy, Justus, would be really good. He knows a lot about business, and he discovered my background in AI. He wants upside potential, though."

Twenty-Six nodded. "He sounds perfect. Would you mind if I spoke with him? I'll try to hire him."

She pulled her head back. "That was easy." Then she motioned to the door. "Please."

Twenty-Six entered the room and shook hands with Justus. "I go by Twenty-Six." He sat down and waited for

Lilah to sit as well, then he had Justus take him through the same story he'd covered with Lilah, up through and including the picture and news article.

"We would like to make you a job offer," said Twenty-Six. "Since you'll be handling Bump Analytics' finances, you'll know all of our secrets. I'd like to tell you about us—who we are and what we do—but to do that we need a formal nondisclosure agreement. Penalty of death and all that."

He laid a sheet out for Justus to sign. While the man read it, Twenty-Six said to Lilah in a stage whisper, "I borrowed your computer and printer."

"How did you know my password?"

This time Twenty-Six leaned over to her and cupped her ear to make it private. "My Lilah told me."

Justus signed and slid it back across the table. "Might I make a suggestion?"

"Fire away," said Twenty-Six.

"Let's settle on a salary first. If we can't come to an agreement, then you won't have to tell me anything about your business. That protects you the best way possible."

"What number do you have in mind?"

"First," said Justus. "Is what you're doing illegal?"

"Nope."

"Twenty-five thousand a month."

"Done." Twenty-Six reached his hand across to shake.

Lilah gasped, stunned by the huge salary and the speed with which Twenty-Six was moving. When Justus hesitated, she could almost see him wondering if he'd bid too low. Then he reached across and shook Twenty-Six's hand.

"Don't worry," said Twenty-Six. "You can renegotiate after you hear the story. I'll let you do that because, except for you two, this is a family business. The family wants you both to be happy and productive. If money helps that, we want to know."

"That's very generous," said Justus. "And I'm curious to hear your story, because nothing in your electronic trail hints at a family."

"Not a family in the traditional sense, more like a brotherhood. Let me give you thumbnail overviews of two concepts, and we can work to a deeper understanding over time. Sound good?"

"Hit me with it," said Justus.

"First is the concept of duplicates. We don't know if it's freak genes, some sort of scientific experiment, or God knows what, but I have a collection of genetic twins. It's crazy as hell because some are older and some younger. It's why we go by numbers, to reflect our age."

He gestured to Lilah. "As Lilah will tell you, when you work here, you'll see different ones of us coming and going. From your job perspective, if someone looks like me, just smile and say hi because it's all okay. If they don't look like me, though, call the cops."

Justus nodded. "Duplicates."

"The other is AI. My brothers had this idea for an intelligent machine that can guess investments with great accuracy. Lilah's job is to help us make that a reality. Since you keep the books, you'll see our portfolio grow and grow, so you'll know exactly how well it works."

"AI," he said, though he didn't nod this time.

"Now, as office manager, you don't just track investments and keep the books, you do it all. You place orders, pay bills, broker deals, work with banks, arrange travel, look after security. Everything that comes up is your job."

Twenty-Six folded the agreement Justus had signed and tucked it in his back pocket. "Your first few weeks here will be busy, but then you'll establish a rhythm. By the end of the month, you'll be here in your office for a few hours a day, and out taking care of business for the rest. I'd estimate twenty-five hours total for a normal work week, though you may get called in now and again on short notice."

Justus watched him but didn't react.

"So, the final offer is thirty thousand a month, and you are welcome to put as much of that as you want into the investment fund."

"Can I choose not to invest, to take it all home?"

"Of course. You watch the fund for as long as you want, and if you change your mind, the option is open to you. You'll understand how sweet that perk is in three or four months. The job starts tomorrow. We have a deal?"

Justus stood. Twenty-Six, two inches taller and twenty pounds heavier, stood as well. Extending his hand, they shook a second time.

Twenty-Six didn't let go. Squeezing Justus's hand and staring into his eyes, he said, "We're paying for discretion. You know that or we wouldn't be hiring you. Nothing illegal, I promise. But you'll see some crazy stuff over time. If you feel you need to talk to someone about it, talk to me or Lilah. No one outside, though. Ever."

He let go of Justus's hand. "And now that I've been an asshole to you, here's the good news. I'm not your boss. Lilah is for the rest of this week. After that, a guy who looks like me, we call him Twenty-Five, takes over." He grinned. "See, it's getting crazy already and we're just getting started.

Anyway, everything we agreed still holds. Write up your employment contract, and we'll make it official when you start tomorrow."

"You're making him write up his own contract?" asked Lilah in disbelief.

"No, I'm letting him. Anyway, employment contracts are an item in the 'everything' pile, and his job is to do everything."

Justus looked from Lilah to Twenty-Six. "I'm sensing this isn't a contract kind of outfit, so I'm fine with our handshake."

Twenty-Six gave Justus a tour of the main floor of the row house after that, starting with a large room in the back. "This is your office. Get yourself furniture, art for the wall, whatever you want. Let's get a big safe for that corner."

He paused and turned to Lilah. "Could you help him get a computer that's compatible with your equipment?" She nodded and he continued. "The building needs a security system, we need to submit the paperwork to make us a legit company, you'll need to set up a company bank account and get a safe deposit box."

They chatted back and forth for more than an hour, and Lilah took notes for her own information. When Justus departed, Twenty-Six turned to Lilah and fulfilled his promise of dinner. "Have you been to Roxie's? It's a garden restaurant around the corner with ferns and vines everywhere. You'll love it."

It was a short walk on a pleasant afternoon, and they kept the conversation light. She enjoyed his company, even found him charming, but everything about the way he'd handled the hiring of Justus bothered her. She thought through the incident step by step, wanting to be sure of her facts before confronting him.

The hostess at Roxie's led them to their table and they ordered drinks. While they waited to be served, Lilah reached over and stroked the leaves of the ivy climbing a column next to their table. "I like that the plants aren't plastic."

Then it clicked and she patted the top of the table. "You knew I'd pick Justus before we even started looking at résumés." She shook her head. "I couldn't figure out why my bullshit sensors were blaring. When you said, 'Let's hire him' out of the blue, it sounded like the script from a bad play."

"I think it was, 'He's perfect,' which is worse. All kidding aside, though, Justus is a really good man. He handles himself well, he's professional as hell, he gets stuff done, he's fun to hang out with, and he's personally saved my ass on multiple occasions."

The drinks came and she sipped. "Why didn't you just tell me to hire him?"

"We don't talk about the future. It's a rule imposed by the older guys who won't even tell me what's coming, which is frustrating as hell."

"That doesn't make sense to me."

"They've learned that it messes with your head if you know what's going to happen. You start this nonstop internal dialogue about whether you should rebel and do the opposite of what the script says. Or maybe you don't do anything at all because you think it won't matter."

She nodded. "Like if someone tells you you're supposed to fall in love with a stranger?"

"Yeah, well. We made exceptions for you, same as we will for the new Twenty-Five. The idea of time travel doesn't sell without some level of proof."

"Even if you don't tell me what's coming, I'll know that you know." She gave a quick shrug. "It'll send my head in circles."

"Don't worry, I won't be here that much. You and Twenty-Five will discover the future together in ignorant bliss."

"There's that frat brother."

Twenty-Six didn't rise to the bait. "We also don't tell the future about certain things because we're watching for anomalies. I mean, if you'd picked Vance or Missy, that would be a first and everyone up the line would be trying to divine the meaning."

He took a sip of his drink, then played with his napkin. "It's weird. Some choices, everyone makes. Or like the wave-versus-spiral theory for time travel, there's a pattern of irregularity we're comfortable with. There are even semiregular events that play out over weeks and months in the different timelines. We keep track of as much as we can and try to understand what it all means."

Lilah enjoyed herself as they lingered over dessert. Twenty-Six told her stories about places he'd been and things he'd done, and his takeaways from the adventures reflected her own values and priorities. He encouraged her to share during the conversation, and she liked the way that made her feel.

Then she sat up in her chair. "You've lived with me for a year. That's why you can do this."

"Do what?"

"Make me fall for you. You're manipulating me so I'll develop feelings for you."

He held up his hands as if to back away. "Lilah, I apologize if I've led you on. I feel horrible." He checked the time. "And in truth I need to get back to my sweetie."

They walked back to the house with Twenty-Six reinforcing that he had no ulterior motive. "I was enjoying your company and nothing more."

She believed him because he seemed sincere. She also decided that life would be exhausting if she worried about what the different Diesels knew or thought about her.

After Twenty-Six returned to his own timeline, Lilah went up to her apartment and looked at her notes. They were supposed to be things Justus should work on, but she couldn't read her writing in one spot.

8. Twenty-Four and eleven months

The next morning, Lilah joined Justus as he measured his office. Then they sat in the small conference room while he drew out a furniture plan.

"I'd like to swing by the bank and start working on our accounts," he said as he sketched on a pad. "Then head to the mall and pick out furniture for the office."

"Sounds good," said Lilah, acting the way she thought a boss would.

He stopped drawing and looked at her. "Have you thought about what you want for building security?"

"I was hoping you knew," she said, now thinking that "security" was the illegible word in her notes.

"I'll tell you what I know, and we can decide together." He smiled and nodded, then waited for her to acknowledge the agreement. She nodded as well.

"We start with intrusion detection. We'll put sensors on all the doors and windows, and motion detectors in the halls, stairs, and common rooms, along with audio pickups. That's all typical stuff. I'll set the system to notify me by phone, but think about if you want to be bothered too. We also need to decide if we should alert rent-a-cops or maybe even real cops."

He stood and led her out to the lobby, gesturing as he walked. "Access control is critical to security. We need more than just a house key on the front door. And we need video surveillance inside and out on the entryway. We can hire a service to watch the video feeds, or do what lots of places do and just record and store it in case we ever need it."

Lilah followed him as he walked back down the hall toward his office, stopping short at a hall closet. He opened the door and looked inside, then stood back so she could look.

"We can put the electronics in here—video storage, event logging, analytics, and whatever new technology has been invented since the last time I looked into this. Another option is to put the electronics in the basement to leave this space open for something else."

"No, this is good."

"I'll get a guy to come out and work up a design. It's best to get everything as one system."

"Did anyone mention that we also own the unit next door? Both places will need coverage."

Justus started laughing, then stopped when he realized Lilah was serious.

She worked with him for most of the morning, enjoying his organized approach to everything, fascinated by his confidence, and grateful for his gentle demeanor. Ciopova sent her a task list just as Justus was leaving for his chores, and she went downstairs to get started.

On the day before Twenty-Five was due to arrive, Justus asked her if she would ride with him to a car dealership. "I'm going out to pick up Twenty-Five's new car and need someone to drive a car back."

"Which one do I get?" asked Lilah.

"Your choice."

The drive to the dealership took about forty minutes. Along the way, she listened in amazement and delight as

Justus told stories from his days as an investigator. Her heart raced when he told a tale about impersonating a bank president. He'd entered one of the bank branches during lunch, rifled through the filing cabinets with everyone watching, and walked out the front door with a briefcase full of evidence.

The time passed quickly, and they arrived at the car lot. Lilah opted to drive Diesel's new car back to the apartment. Justus had a sports car himself, and when she pulled up next to him, he rolled down his window and signaled for her to do the same.

With a serious expression, he said to her, "Last one home is a rotten egg." Then he screeched his tires as he peeled out of the parking lot.

Lilah spun Diesel's tires as she raced to catch up. They pulled onto a two-lane road, and she mashed the gas pedal to close the gap. She stayed near Justus and caught a lucky break when he got trapped behind a slow car at a turn. Cutting the corner, she pulled ahead and led him on a sprint through the outskirts of Worcester.

She kept her lead for a couple of miles, then Justus pushed a yellow traffic light when she chose to stop. He waited for her on the other side of the intersection, and they finished together, the big wins being that they arrived home safely, neither got a ticket, and both cars made it without a scratch.

In bed that night, Lilah thought about how much fun she'd had that day with Justus. Snugging the covers up to her chin, she grinned. She didn't fall asleep, though. And hours later, she continued to toss and turn.

It wasn't the events of the day that kept her awake. It was what came next.

Tomorrow was her big day. Well, today, actually. In just a few hours, she was to meet Twenty-Five. Her Diesel. Her David. Her man.

Her feelings about it were all over the place. She couldn't accept the notion that she would pair with a stranger. While it seemed to work in some cultures, it went against the very essence of her identity as a modern woman.

In truth, she'd liked every Diesel she'd met. Not love, nothing like that. But she'd enjoyed their company. They'd all been cute, smart, confident, capable, fun, polite, sexy. In fact, she wondered how she could separate her emotions and care for one while having the others be off limits.

The plan was for Twenty-Five to arrive before noon. Lilah's job was to get him seated and ready for a formal interview. Twenty-Six would be the one to break the news to him about his new life.

She'd just fallen asleep when her clock alarm started buzzing. She kept the clock across the room on her dresser so she'd have to rise to shut it off. "Shut up," she groused during the forced walk.

After a yawn and stretch, she went to the kitchen to start a pot of coffee, then came back to review the outfit she'd chosen for the day. She wished she'd asked Twenty-Six what style of clothes he preferred, then scolded herself for playing to the stereotype.

She went with black slacks that often drew compliments paired with a simple white top. By the time she'd made it down to the basement, Twenty-Six had already arrived and was busy with Justus upstairs in his office.

"He'll like that outfit."

Lilah spun in a circle, trying to locate the speaker.

"Over here, Lilah."

Her eyes locked on the big monitor.

Ciopova, somehow a vibrant, three-dimensional animation, spoke to her. "I'm just saying you look great. It's a compliment."

Lilah felt her scalp tingle. This was not just new behavior. It was unheard of in the industry. "What do you know?"

"Be yourself, Lilah. It's just that easy."

The animation seemed to deflate after that, returning to the two-dimensional image Lilah remembered. Before she had time to dwell on the incident, a quiet buzz caused her to look at the display outside the T-box: "Forty Incoming in 4:59."

She couldn't imagine why Forty would be coming here today but figured Twenty-Six would know. She started for the stairs to find him, then stopped before she'd taken her second step. Twenty-Six had suggested that she see Forty au naturel. At some level, it seemed important to him.

She couldn't help herself. Whatever it was, she had to see. Turning back, she stood in front of the T-box door to wait for the show. After standing for a bit, she looked at the display: "Forty Incoming in 4:22."

"Holy hell," she said aloud when she realized just how long five minutes actually was. She climbed the stairs, walked down to Justus's office, and poked her head in the open door. "Seen Twenty-Six?"

"He went to the print shop down the street to get some business cards made up. Should be back soon."

"How's everything going?"

He showed her a black credit card. "When I activate this card, it has a limit of four hundred thousand dollars."

"Wow." She stepped into his office, wondering if the card might be a way she could get paid. "How did you pull that off?"

"By knowing how the system works and taking advantage of it." He flipped the card over and studied the back. "This gets us ahead, but it isn't magic money. If Twenty-Five spends it all but can't cover the tab after ninety days, say goodbye to this unit and the one next door."

"I'm sure they'll cover it," she said with more confidence than she felt. Then she thought of Forty and the T-box. "Thanks, Justus. Gotta go."

She made it back to the T-box in time for the static wash. Then the display showed "Forty Arrived." Realizing she was standing right in front of the door, she started backpedaling in a fluster, stopping when her butt hit the table in her cubicle.

The T-box door handle clicked and Forty stepped out, looking down as if absorbed in thought. He turned to close the door and when he turned back, he saw her. He immediately moved his hands down below his waist, covering himself, a sheepish smile reflecting his modesty.

"Oh my God," Lilah said aloud.

Thirty pounds of muscle, layered to perfection, bulked Forty into a spectacular specimen. Chest swollen, arms powerful, stomach ripped, he became a shadow as he disappeared into the blanket walkway.

"Hi, Lilah," he called. "I'll be out in a minute. By the way, Forty-Two is joining me."

The T-box came alive as he spoke, the display confirming his words.

As Forty dressed, Lilah digested what she'd just observed. She wasn't attracted to gym-rat muscles, mostly because of what they said about a man's priorities and ego.

But when layered on Diesel, someone she knew and liked at several different ages—someone who already had a great body—she found it exciting. Very exciting. Her feelings were contrary to her intellectual expectations, but she wasn't ashamed to learn it about herself.

Indeed, she couldn't wait to see more.

"Sorry for the exposure there." His T-shirt, no doubt an extra-extra large, strained across his chest to contain his mass.

Having met several Diesels, she knew to jump right in. "I've worked with Thirty-Five, and I must say, I did not expect this just five years later." She waved a hand up and down in his direction.

He smiled and flexed. "Three years of hard work. Came out pretty good if I do say so myself."

Watching him pose with a self-satisfied smirk on his face, she felt her intense physical excitement wither and die. She started in on business. "So, not sure if you know, but Twenty-Six is here. In this timeline, I mean. But he's not here here, he's down the street getting business cards."

Forty smiled at her. "And Twenty-Five is coming in an hour?"

"That's right." She felt herself getting flustered and voiced a random thought. "Do you go by Diesel in your timeline?"

"I do."

"Is it true for everybody? I want to use your name when I can."

"Yup. Even Fifty-Nine is Diesel."

"Good to know, thanks."

She felt a static wash and was grateful for a distraction from the awkward conversation. Moments later the T-box door opened.

"Happy birthday!" the brothers called to each other as Forty-Two, still naked, joined them. The two slapped hands in a classic high-five celebration, then Forty-Two said, "Hey, Lilah, this is Forty's first mission as the enforcer."

Forty-Two had less mass and definition than Forty, but he still looked great. And except for some faint lines around their eyes and mouths, neither looked their age.

Talking to a naked hulk proved disconcerting for Lilah, and, blushing, she covered her eyes and said with a nervous laugh, "Would you please put some clothes on?"

Forty punched Forty-Two in the shoulder in mock outrage. "Yeah, asshole."

Forty-Two left to get dressed and Lilah reacted to what she'd heard.

"So you're an enforcer?" She looked him up and down. "That's why you worked so hard for the muscles? To add intimidation to your hacking enterprise?"

"Wait. What?"

"I'm not accusing, I'm just asking. Forty-Two said you're an enforcer, and the Diesel in this timeline is a hacker."

"Jeez, Lilah. We stopped all that when we met you. Our boy Twenty-Five transitions from devil to saint when you open that door in an hour. It really happens that fast."

"True fact," said Forty-Two, who joined them during the exchange. "You look great, by the way." He handed a baseball cap and light blue athletic jacket to Forty and slipped on an identical set himself. "Ready to go?" he asked his twin.

"Wait," said Lilah. "What's going on?"

"Our job today is to watch over Twenty-Five until he reaches the front door," said Forty. "We watch from afar, kind of like guardian angels. If someone were to bother him, we'll be there to help. We call it enforcing the law." He lifted his shoulders in a half shrug. "Whoever is age forty is the boss. Since today is our birthday, then hooray for me." He threw an elbow into Forty-Two's abdomen. "And if anyone else messes up, it's still logged as my fault."

"That's backwards," said Lilah. "Forty-Two has been through it already. He should be lead."

"You're right," said Forty. "I hereby transfer enforcement duties to Forty-Two."

"Bite me," replied Forty-Two. Then he said to Lilah, "The job is mostly worrying about the schedule. I did it two years ago. He'll do just fine."

The two left a half hour before Twenty-Five was due to arrive, and Lilah, unable to concentrate, paced back and forth.

She mulled Forty and Forty-Two's claim that they'd changed for the good the moment they met their Lilahs. She thought it the most flattering and romantic thing she'd ever heard. But knowing what she did of the brothers, she assumed it was bullshit designed to manipulate her.

She went upstairs to do her last-minute pacing on the main level. Justus saw her and came down the hall.

"I'm going in before Twenty-Six talks to him." He waved a file folder. "I'm supposed to warm him up with some paperwork."

The doorbell rang.

"I need to grab a pen," said Justus. "I'll be right down."

Lilah walked to the door and opened it. He looked like a less sophisticated Twenty-Six with a somewhat goofier expression.

"David Lagerford, please come in." She stood behind the door as he entered, then reached to shake his hand as she pushed it closed. "Welcome to Bump. I'm Lilah. How was your trip?"

He held her hand for too long, but she didn't mind.

"Hi," he said. "Fine, thanks."

Motioning for him to follow, she led the way down the hall to the small conference room. Glancing in the hallway mirror as they walked past it, she saw him staring at her butt, his mouth open, his eyes wide.

9. Twenty-Five years old

The man bumped shoulders with Diesel as the two passed on the sidewalk. Since foot traffic was light, Diesel assumed it was deliberate. He turned to see if the guy looked back—some loser in a brown hoodie and jeans. The guy kept walking without a glance, so Diesel did, too.

He was in Worcester, Massachusetts, interviewing for a promising job with a company he'd never heard of. They'd pitched him the opportunity a week ago, and when he'd said he was interested, they arranged his travel from the West Coast. The interview started in fifteen minutes; the map on his phone said he'd be there in ten.

Quickening his pace, he turned up a side street and found himself in an upscale neighborhood. Handsome red-brick row houses on either side of the street, refurbished to maintain the original character, all had the same tiny front yard trimmed with a crabapple tree and a hedge of boxwood. The houses ran all the way to the far intersection on each side, giving the place a homey feel.

Up ahead, maybe eight houses down, a guy marched in his direction. He wore the same brown hoodie and jeans and had the same husky build as the asshole from before, so Diesel slowed and studied him, curious about his behavior and unafraid of a confrontation.

The guy continued to advance, and then two men— same general build as Diesel but bulkier in the shoulders—

stepped out from a stoop and faced him. Wearing baseball caps and light blue athletic jackets in the style Diesel favored, they stood shoulder to shoulder to block the sidewalk. Attracted to the drama, Diesel wished he could stay and watch, but he'd reached number one-eighty-nine, his stop, so he hustled up the steps instead.

At the top, a brass plaque on the wall identified the place as Bump Analytics. A small sign on the door invited him to ring the bell. He did so and waited, sure he was being watched, though no cameras were in sight.

When the door swung open, he stopped thinking about cameras and looked at his idea of perfection. She was mid-twenties, with lively green eyes and a generous smile, shoulder-length flaxen hair, a trim figure, and wearing black pants and a white blouse.

"David Lagerford, please come in." She stood behind the door as Diesel entered, then reached to shake his hand as she pushed the door closed. "Welcome to Bump. I'm Lilah. How was your trip?"

Her hand felt soft and cool, and he wondered if he'd held it for too long. "Hi. Fine, thanks."

Motioning for him to follow, she led the way down the hall, her swaying bottom giving him a morning lift. Halfway along, she stepped into a small conference room.

"Please have a seat. Can I get you anything? Coffee? Water?"

"Maybe some water," said Diesel, sitting where she'd indicated.

She brought him a glass and a bottle of spring water. "Justus McGowan, the office manager, will be here...oh, here he is."

"Hi, David." Justus grabbed Diesel's hand and gave it a shake. "Or should I say, Diesel?"

Diesel's cheeks flushed and he gave a quick shrug. "Diesel is from my initials, D.S.L., which is for David S. Lagerford. They started calling me Diesel in grade school, and I guess it stuck."

"Ha, I love it." Justus sat in the chair across from Diesel. "Lilah, we should be about ten minutes if you don't mind telling Twenty-Six."

She made for the door and Diesel watched her go, waiting for her to make eye contact. His interest deepened when she left the room without looking back at him.

"Let me take you through some paperwork so we can reimburse your expenses for today's visit," said Justus as the door closed. Shuffling through a folder, he pulled out a few sheets. "So, first, happy birthday. I see you turn twenty-five today. That's a good age."

The exchange prompted Diesel to give Justus a closer look—a fortyish black man who, while dressed in business casual clothes, had the weathered face and strong hands of an outdoorsman. He was a little shorter and a little lighter than Diesel, but had a solid build.

"You just graduated with a degree in computer programming from Berkeley." Justus looked up. "Congrats on that." Then back down to his stack. "How do you feel about moving to the East Coast?"

"Great. I was born here in Worcester, and my mom still lives here, so I'm more easterner than westerner."

"And if today goes well, when would you be available to start?"

"Immediately. I'd need a few days to close out my apartment in Berkeley and arrange to get my stuff moved. But my lease runs through the end of next month, so I can do that anytime." He decided to test the waters. "And should it all work out, I'd hope to be reimbursed for the cost of moving back here."

Justus nodded, set three pages out on the table, and pointed to a spot on the last page. "Is this your social security number?"

Diesel looked at the number as he signed his name. "That's right." He toyed with the idea of reading all the fine print, but a tap on the door caused him to lift his head. In stepped a tall man with broad shoulders sloping to a narrow waist. Short brown hair topped a pleasing face, and a rakish grin showed his dimples.

"Ah, Twenty-Six," said Justus, standing and gathering the sheets. "That's it for the paperwork. I'll leave you to it."

The door shut behind Justus, and the two men shook hands. The physical contact put Diesel on edge.

"Happy birthday to us," said Twenty-Six as he sat across from Diesel.

"Let me guess. You turned twenty-six today."

"I did." He nodded, then leaned forward and studied Diesel the way a scientist might examine a lab specimen.

Diesel's initial discomfort grew as he looked back. The man's appearance, demeanor, and manner of speaking all connected with Diesel at an emotional level. "Have we met? Sorry, but I'm having this weird sense of déjà vu."

"This is our first meeting," said Twenty-Six, "but we do have something in common." Twenty-Six stood, motioned for Diesel to stand, then moved next to him and pointed to a mirror hanging on the wall. "Have a look."

In the mirror, Diesel stood next to his duplicate. "Holy shit." He turned his head, looked at Twenty-Six in person, and saw a man with familiar features. But when he turned back and looked in the mirror—when he saw Twenty-Six the way he was used to seeing himself—he saw his twin.

"We have to be cousins or something," Diesel babbled, struck by the coincidence. "Where are you from? My mom has a sister and nephew from Nashville. Are you from Tennessee?"

"No," said Twenty-Six. "I'm from Worcester and my mom has a sister and nephew in Nashville."

"You know the odds of that? Granddad must have been out sowing his wild oats like some sort of crazy man."

"Look," said Twenty-Six, sitting down and motioning for Diesel to do the same. "I'm just going to say it all at once. Rip off the Band-Aid, as it were. I don't know a better way."

Diesel waited.

"I am a version of you at age twenty-six. I'm here from your future."

"Ha-ha," said Diesel, feeling an odd tingling sensation that traveled up his arms and across the back of his neck. Looking around the conference room for cameras recording the joke, he said, "This is an interesting recruiting strategy."

Twenty-Six slumped back in his chair. "This morning you jerked off to memories of Helena Costas. She danced naked on your balcony on the Fourth of July. You could just make out her silhouette in the gloom, and then a firework would explode and flash light across her body. It's the sexiest thing you've ever seen."

Diesel felt nauseous. "Do you have cameras in my hotel room?" Standing, he pointed at Twenty-Six and lashed out to cover his embarrassment. "You're sick."

"Stop being such a tool. This is why the older brothers dismiss us."

Diesel rocked in place, acting like he was going to leave but not taking any steps.

"Cameras can't see inside your head. I told you what you were thinking."

"Were you watching back in Berkeley? How can you know this?"

"Sigh," Twenty-Six said aloud. "Okay, more secret stuff you've never told anyone. You broke the kitchen window that Thomas got blamed for in seventh grade. You plagiarized your history paper in eleventh grade and still worry about getting caught. Your landlord reimbursed your security deposit twice last year and you kept the money."

"He's an asshole."

"I agree. I kept it, too."

"So if you are me, you know I'm not buying any of this." Diesel started wiggling his foot under the able in a subconscious display of unease.

"I'm not you. I'm me and you're you. You will be sitting here a year from now after having lived through the same experiences I did. But we are different people. That's an important lesson to learn."

"So when you were me, how long did it take you before you started believing?"

"I was never you, but when I was in your position, I started to believe in the probability of it all by the end of the day. It will be about three weeks before you're at one hundred percent. You'll test me and try to trick me. At some point acceptance happens because there's no alternative to the truth."

One of Diesel's favorite movies was about time travel, and he drew on a scene from the film as inspiration to expose the fraud. Digging into his pocket, he pulled out a small multitool that included a knife blade. Placing his left hand flat on the conference table, he said, "Put your hand down next to mine."

"I'm not going to let you cut me."

"I'm going to cut myself. But if you're really me, the scar will appear on your hand when I cut mine."

"Sure. Let's do this," said Twenty-Six. He positioned his left hand flat on the table next to Diesel's.

"Hey, you already have a scar."

"Let's do the other hand, then." He switched to his right hand.

Diesel followed suit. Then, positioning his knife, he stared at Twenty-Six's hand while he cut a small, deep gash into the back of his own. "Ow, damn that hurts."

He looked around for something to stem the bleeding. Twenty-Six pushed a box of tissues in his direction, and Diesel pressed several against his wound. Then he leaned over to look at Twenty-Six's hand.

"Ha, no scar," he said in triumph.

"I am humiliated knowing someone as dumb as you is a version of me."

Diesel took more tissue and pressed it on his wound.

"I was pretty clear that we have different experiences. What you do to yourself doesn't impact me or the brothers up the line." He shook his head. "One year from now, you'll be sitting here as Twenty-Six, and unlike me, you will have that scar on your right hand."

"That's not how time travel works," said Diesel. "I watch a lot of science fiction and you're busted. So how are you doing it? How do you know those things about me?"

"No way I was this pathetic."

"You didn't cut yourself when you were sitting here?"

"Yes, you idiot." He held up his scarred left hand. "What do you think this is from?"

"Wait. When you were in my position, did your Twenty-Six have a scar?"

Twenty-Six nodded. "Yup, this year, anyone with a scar on their left hand is an even age, and a scar on the right hand means an odd age. Next year it flips; you become Twenty-Six and all left-hand scarred become odds. It can be useful information. If you aren't sure if you're talking with Thirty-Five or Thirty-Six, check his scar hand."

"And next year I watch the new guy cut his left hand?"

"Yup."

"So is there even a job?"

Twenty-Six tilted his head back and groaned. "Stop being so stupid. I just told you I'm back from the future, and you're concerned about a job?"

Diesel did feel a little sheepish when Twenty-Six phrased it that way, but since he wasn't buying the whole time-travel thing, he didn't feel too bad. Then he pushed back. "Talk about dumb, I would never start calling myself a number. It's so lame it hurts your case."

"You're Twenty-Five, I'm Twenty-Six, there's also a Twenty-Seven, Twenty-Eight, and every number up to Fifty-Nine. That makes thirty-five of us in all. Maybe we should all call ourselves Diesel. Wouldn't that make for fun meetings?"

"You have meetings?"

Twenty-Six nodded.

"How come Sixty doesn't come?"

"There is no Sixty, or he doesn't come if there is."

"Whoa. You just told me I die at sixty! You have the worst recruiting strategy. What happens?"

"I didn't say you die. I said Sixty doesn't show up."

"Why not?"

"It's one of the mysteries we're chasing."

"Does everyone time travel in your world?"

"If by 'everyone' you mean all thirty-five of us, yes, we all time travel. If you're asking about all of humanity, then no, it's just us."

"Wow, you just told me I time travel! You said I'm one of the thirty-five, and you said we all do it." Diesel stood up. "Now this is good recruiting. Show me how to go ahead a hundred years. No, let's do ten years. I want to practice first."

The conference room door burst open, and two huge guys in light blue athletic jackets, their baseball caps pulled low, entered, shouting, "Happy birthday!"

"Happy birthday," said Twenty-Six as he stood. "Forty, Forty-One, this is Twenty-Five."

One of the newcomers held up his hand and showed the scar on his left hand. "I'm Forty-Two." Then he turned to Diesel. "Kiss my ass, Twenty-Five. You suck."

"There's no need for that," said Forty. He leaned forward and motioned Diesel to come closer. Diesel obliged, and the man whispered in his ear, "Kiss my ass."

Forty and Forty-Two laughed as if they'd heard the funniest joke. When the laughter died, one of them said, "Kiss my ass!" and it started all over again.

"How did it go out there?" asked Twenty-Six.

"The Brown showed up as scheduled and we sent him packing," said Forty.

"They're showing up more and more, and it's too much," Forty-Two said with a detectable whine. He looked at Forty. "Let's head back. I got stuff to do."

"Show him before you go," said Twenty-Six. "C'mon. Give him a thrill at the start of his journey."

Forty and Forty-Two looked at each other, shrugged, and then removed their caps with a dramatic flourish. With a clear view of their faces, Diesel saw two hard-chiseled, older versions of himself. Twirling in a circle, they peeled off their jackets and lifted their arms as they spun. Bulging muscles rippled through their tight shirts.

"Is it wrong for me to think they're hot?" Twenty-Six asked Diesel.

"Okay," said Forty-Two, concluding his spin. "That's it. Gotta go."

Forty followed him out. "Welcome aboard, Twenty-Five. Oh, and kiss my ass."

Diesel heard them chuckling as the door shut.

"That was good old-fashioned hazing," said Twenty-Six. "You're the new guy and they're just having fun. It'll happen a bunch of times until the Big Meeting in three weeks, then it ends. Try to have fun with it because you don't have a choice."

"So what's with them? Is that supposed to be us?"

"It turns out that at every age, we have a role to fulfill. At age forty, our job is to be lead muscle for the rest of us. It takes a few years to build up to that, and then they stay buff for a few years after. Usually Thirty-Nine, Forty, and Forty-One can handle the demand between them. It's rare to see Forty-Two out working the calls."

"They get in fights?" Diesel had been in his share of scrapes in the past, but he sought to avoid physical confrontation as a general rule.

Twenty-Six shook his head. "No. The point of the muscle and teamwork is to make it so the opponent chooses to walk away. And just so you know, that dance routine you just saw, though weird, is to get us psyched up. You don't just wake up at forty years old and suddenly you're all muscles. It takes three years to get bulked like that, which means you and I will have to start working hard at thirty-seven and keep it up for years."

"Isn't forty on the old side to be a tough?"

"Why don't you bring that up at the Big Meeting?"

Diesel heard the sarcasm and ignored it. "What's a Brown?"

"You ask too many questions. Let's get you ready to interview with Lilah."

"So there is a job?"

Twenty-Six groaned again. "Every time you talk I feel worse about myself."

10. Twenty-Five and a few hours

Diesel watched as Twenty-Six put a small cloth bag on the conference room table.

"Before you meet with Lilah, let's go through this." Twenty-Six opened the bag and removed a shiny black credit card. Diesel saw that it had "David S. Lagerford" printed on the front.

"Your job will sound overwhelming, but it's pretty easy if you follow the script. Do it right and you'll have lots of free time and plenty to spend."

"Now that's what I call recruiting!"

"Okay, here it is. Lilah was hired four months ago."

Diesel started to talk, and Twenty-Six held up his hand to hush him. "She is Lilah Spencer, an AI programming wunderkind."

"That beauty is an egghead?"

"She's been working sixty-hour weeks building Ciopova and the T-box. She met all her goals, and according to her contract, you owe her a hundred and sixty thousand dollars."

"Ha-ha. There's that bad recruiting strategy again."

"Pay her with this." He held up the card. "It's the most prestigious card in the world. Go into any commercial bank and use it to wire her the funds wherever she asks."

"Wow. Okay."

"But in thirty days, the bill for that plus a few other odds and ends comes due. You need to raise enough to pay that off."

"What's the minimum payment?"

"Three hundred and fifty thousand-ish."

Diesel shrugged. "I'll just go to the bank and use the prestige card to take out a cash advance."

Twenty-Six smiled for the first time. He dug into the bag and handed Diesel a business card with information scribbled on the back. "A better solution is that tomorrow morning you buy a lottery ticket from this place. Buy it sometime after eight but before eight thirty, and be sure it's for the lottery game listed there." He pointed to a line of text. "Play those numbers. This store is next to a diner with cozy booths and an amazing breakfast, so take some time to enjoy yourself while you're there."

Diesel turned the card over and saw that it listed him as president of Bump Analytics. "Oh, I saw my name as president and was confused. But you're David Lagerford too, according to your story anyway."

"No, that's you. You're president here and need to get things moving. I'm president in my own timeline, which I need to get back to." He glanced at the clock and then continued. "Lilah's contract is almost up, and you need to renew it. Lilah hired Justus, and you need to take his employment off her plate. He'll help you take care of legal and business matters, provide security, and a lot more."

The onslaught of fantastic ideas made everything surreal, and Diesel wasn't sure how to respond. "What do I offer them for salary and terms? What do you offer me?"

Twenty-Six continued as if he hadn't spoken. "It's noon, so take Lilah to lunch at Roxie's. Get to know her. Learn about her work. Ask what she wants for a two-year contract, and give her whatever she asks. She's critical to all of this, so don't blow it."

"Is she a good kisser?" This part of him was never confused. "Please tell me you know."

Twenty-Six's face hardened. "Do not hit on her. Don't talk to her about sex. Don't flirt at all. Her computer skills are way more important than your dick. And if you blow it, Forty will come back and smack you into next week. You don't want to time travel that way."

"Jeez. Calm down." Diesel pulled the bloody tissue off his wound and replaced it with a new one from the box. "So how much do I win?"

"In the lottery? Lump sum is nine hundred thousand and change. Twenty-Nine will be here at the end of the week to show you and Justus how to invest it so it quadruples before the bills come due. Then he'll show you how to double it every few months through the end of the year. It just keeps growing when you know the future. You'll be able to live in luxury your whole life off that nest egg."

Twenty-Six dug into the bag and pulled out a ring of three keys. "This one is to your car. It's parked out front at the bottom of the stairs. German engineering at its finest." He smiled at Diesel, then fingered the next keys. "This one is to the front door, and this is to your apartment."

"What front door?"

"Here. Upstairs is your home. This floor includes the front lobby, this conference room, a larger common room, and Justus's office. Downstairs is workspace for you and Lilah, plus that's where the T-box is."

"Justus gets an office with windows and I get the basement?"

"Yup."

"What about my stuff at the hotel?"

"Justus had it sent over. It's upstairs in your bedroom." Twenty-Six stood. "Go clean up and then go to lunch. Learn about Lilah's work. We'll talk more tomorrow."

Diesel followed Twenty-Six into the hall.

"Your apartment is up those stairs. Go ahead and check it out. I'll tell Lilah you'll meet her by the front door in fifteen minutes."

"Okay," said Diesel, eyeing the steps.

"I'll be back tomorrow morning at eleven," Twenty-Six continued. "Let's go to a climbing gym so I can at least get my workout while I school you. After, we can have lunch and watch you win the lottery." He pointed at Diesel's hand. "And take care of that when you're up there."

Diesel checked his pocket to make sure he had the business card with the lottery instructions, then, dazed by it all, he started up the stairs.

As he reached the top, Twenty-Six called to him. "Oh, and Twenty-Five, kiss my ass."

The landing reminded Diesel of a classy elevator lobby—nice carpet and wallpaper, a hall table made of dark wood, and a cut glass mirror on the wall. But instead of an elevator door, the landing offered a heavy wooden door into the apartment.

He knocked and when no one answered, he tried the door. It was locked, so he tried his key. The door swung open.

Then he started laughing. "This can't be real."

The place was a dream home. Handsome, well-appointed, clean. Stepping inside, he walked through a spacious living area with large windows, hardwood floors, an array of comfy furniture, and an enormous entertainment center.

Continuing back, he passed a set of stairs tucked against the wall and arrived at the dining area, with table, chairs, and built-in cabinets nicer than anything his folks ever had. Past that was the kitchen, with stone countertops, new appliances, and a back wall with more windows.

He tested the kitchen faucet, opened the refrigerator door, and checked to see if the oven clock was correct. Then he made his way to the stairway, figuring the bedroom needed to be up there since it wasn't on this floor.

He wasn't disappointed. The stairs led up to two separate suites, front and back, each with private bath, big closets, and classic furniture. His suitcase lay on the king-sized bed of the back suite. That one had a closet stocked with men's clothes, and a glass door that led out to a garden balcony.

In his bathroom, soap, antiseptic, a bandage, and a towel sat next to the sink. Shaking his head at his idiocy, he pulled the gooey red tissue off the back of his hand, cleaned the wound, and bandaged it up.

Leaving the detritus of his medical treatment scattered across the bathroom countertop, he started down the stairs. On the main level, Lilah greeted him with a grin. Diesel's heart fluttered.

"I was thinking we'd go to Roxie's," he said as he approached, his focus on his attraction to her rather than the crazy circumstances.

"My favorite."

He let her walk out the front door ahead of him. "Should I lock it?"

"It locks automatically. Do you have your key?"

He showed her the ring, and as they climbed down the stone steps, he pressed the button on his car key. A new light blue sports car chirped and blinked its lights.

"Oh boy," he said, opening the passenger door for Lilah. "I'm gonna love this job."

She pointed down the street. "Roxie's is a five-minute walk."

"Let's drive anyway?"

She hesitated and then climbed in.

Diesel got in and started oohing and ahhing as he ran his fingers over the various buttons and knobs around him. He adjusted the mirrors, positioned the car seat, then adjusted the mirrors again.

"Contact," he said as he started the car. The motor was so quiet that he revved the engine a couple of times to make sure it was running, then he flipped on the turn signal and pulled out.

"Turn right at the end," she said as they rolled down the street. Ten seconds later, she announced, "There it is."

He missed the turn, partly on purpose. "I'll spin around and catch it next loop."

She gave him a sideways look. "Hey, what happened to your hand?"

Diesel looked at the bandage. "I cut it."

Roxie's turned out to be what Diesel called a "garden restaurant," its upscale atmosphere created by lush ferns hanging from the ceiling and vines climbing the walls, all complemented by small trees in big pots scattered across the dining room floor. Windows and a row of skylights brightened it up in the daytime.

They sat in a booth, with Diesel sitting at an angle so his back rested against the wall. The waitress came and Lilah ordered a salad plate with a piece of grilled salmon on top. Diesel ordered a burger priced more like a steak dinner. They both ordered iced tea.

"So, you've been working on your project for the past four months?" Diesel said when they were alone.

Lilah, sipping her water, nodded.

"And you met all of your contract goals?"

"I did," she said, setting the glass on the table.

"Have you enjoyed the experience?"

"I'll enjoy it more when I get paid."

Diesel studied her and his heart melted. Not only was she crushingly beautiful, he loved her mannerisms, the way she talked, her coquettish smile.

"How much are you owed?"

"Contract says one hundred and sixty thousand."

Diesel shook his head as if to clear it. "That's a lot of money."

Lilah shrugged. "This is where you hand me my check."

Diesel pulled out his black prestige card. "After lunch, we'll go to a bank and we'll have them cut a check for you today. Sound good?"

She smiled and he melted some more.

"I'd like to extend your contract." He tried to sound casual.

"Doing what?"

Diesel realized he should have asked his next question first. "What is it you do now?"

"Strengthen Ciopova, of course."

"Is that a who or a what?"

She frowned.

"Lilah, do you know what's going on? I'm pretty confused right now."

The waitress arrived with their lunch plates just as Diesel said that last part.

"What do you think you know?" asked Lilah.

"Three hours ago my normal world got turned upside down in what is perhaps the most elaborate practical joke in history. I'm going crazy trying to think who might be doing this to me. All of this is costing a bundle, but I don't have any rich friends—or enemies—who could afford something like this."

"You had no knowledge of any of this before today?"

"I don't know what 'this' is."

"Interesting."

"What?"

"It means we're at the injection point. You start the loop."

This morning's conversation with Twenty-Six had been amusing, but as the joke wore on, it became less so. "Please use small words and short sentences to explain this to me."

"You can travel across time."

"Whew. For a minute there I thought it would be complicated." He took a bite of his burger and waited. When she started eating, he said, "Are you really going to make me ask?"

She seemed confused.

"Here are a few basic questions. How is that possible? Why me? How are you involved? And who or what is Cassiopeia?"

"Ciopova."

"Whatever."

"This will take a while."

"We'll order coffee."

As they ate, Lilah walked him through a summary of events, starting from when she was a lone AI developer back in Boston. She told him of her first contact with Ciopova, the AI's subsequent amazing ability to know things it shouldn't, about the warehouse project, the refurbishment of the row houses, construction of the T-box, and visits by Diesels from parallel timelines.

She finished at the same time their waitress arrived with the bill. Diesel handed her the black prestige card. She stepped away to run the total.

"Weren't you tempted with that lottery money? I mean, if my phone helped me win a million bucks, I'd claim it, skip town, and never be seen in these parts ever again."

Lilah gave a slight nod. "That would be a reason why Ciopova would go to me before getting you involved. She knows she can trust me."

Diesel thought that if Ciopova wanted him involved for some reason, Lilah was the perfect bait.

"I'm sorry, sir," said the waitress, placing the prestige card on the table. "It bounced."

Mortified, Diesel blushed so hard his face burned. Having Lilah witness his humiliation intensified the embarrassment. Sliding his butt forward on the seat, he dug into his pocket and found the wad of cash he'd brought with him when he thought this would be a normal interview trip. Counting bills, he put down enough for the tab plus a generous tip.

As the waitress walked away, Lilah said, "Isn't that the card you said would get me paid?"

"Is this more of the elaborate joke? Lead me on with the perfect girl and then embarrass me in front her?" He stood up from the booth. "What did I ever do to you?"

She looked at him with eyes wide, her mouth in an O.

"Since it's only a five-minute walk," he said, "I'll let you enjoy the stroll back to the office."

He turned and marched through the restaurant lobby and out to the parking lot. Stopping there, he wondered where he should go and if he should take the car.

"Wait," called Lilah from the door. "I can make that card work." She walked toward him, lowering her voice as she approached. "Actually, Justus can. Would it be all right if we sit in the car while I call him?"

"Lilah, you're messing with my head in ways you don't realize. Please stop."

She started walking toward the car. "You're the one who called me the 'perfect girl,' so who's the one messing with someone's head?"

She stood on the passenger side, looking at him expectantly. He pressed the button on his key and the door unlocked. They both got in.

Lilah took out her phone and held it between them so Diesel could hear. "Can you crack the window?" she asked. "It's stuffy."

He opened the window while she called.

"Bump Analytics." Diesel recognized Justus's voice.

"It's Lilah. The boss was buying me lunch, and his brand new card bounced."

"Oh, hell. I thought I had until dinner to activate it. Please stall him for five minutes. I'll do it now."

"He's not going to be happy with you."

"Tell him the problem is on their end."

"Have it working in five minutes because he's using it in six."

"I'm on it."

"The problem is on their end," she deadpanned as she hung up, then she pointed. "Turn right out of the parking lot. The bank is two blocks down."

The short drive seemed to take forever for Diesel. Lilah stared ahead without speaking. He relived the awkward exchange over and over in his head, castigating himself for his stupidity with each review.

She pointed to the bank up ahead, and as he pulled into the parking lot, he broke the silence. "Please forgive my behavior. I lashed out at the most convenient target. It was wrong and I apologize. I guess all this is getting to me."

"I forgive you about that." She got out of the car and walked with him into the bank. "But I don't think I'll continue on after this week. The vibe isn't right. You have a mean streak. And you cheat."

Diesel slowed his step as he digested her words. He'd made a mess of this assignment but felt disoriented about it more than anything else. Feeling sorry for himself, he looked down. "I don't blame you. Forty is going to beat the shit out of me, but that's my problem."

The next minutes were magical. He put the card down at a bank window, Lilah wrote her information on a slip, and the teller moved one hundred and sixty thousand dollars into her account. The transaction was so easy that

Diesel pulled cash out for himself, asking first for two hundred dollars and then changing it to five hundred.

Back in the car, Diesel prompted her to continue her story. "So you show up in town with a mountain of cash. What are your first steps?"

"Why is Forty going to beat the shit out of you?"

"My first assignment was to get you paid and then secure your services for the next two years." He took his eyes off the road to look at her. "They told me to give you whatever you asked for and to not screw it up."

"One hundred thousand a month, payable every month. On time."

"That's over a million a year."

"That's for year one. Year two it's two hundred thousand a month, payable same terms."

"Damn, Lilah. Forty will really beat the shit out of me if I agree to that. Why are you squeezing so hard? Are you a material person?"

"You know the future, Diesel. Or your brothers do. Growing money is easy when you know in advance what's going up and what's going down. I'm asking for maybe ten percent of what you'll be doing over the next two years. From where I sit, I'm not being greedy at all."

He mulled her words and realized she was right. The lottery wasn't a long-term strategy. If you win too many times, it draws attention. But use lottery winnings to seed an investment fund that makes sure bets. Stocks, sports, real estate. He could have twenty or thirty million in two years, no problem.

"Done." He stuck out his hand to shake on it. Her touch was so electric that he lost his concentration, screeching his tires moments later to stop short for a lady in the crosswalk.

He pulled into the same parking space in front of the row house and noticed a permit-only parking sign on a pole on the sidewalk. "Am I allowed to park here?"

She pointed to a sticker in the corner of his windshield that matched the sign. "That says you're pretty much the only one who can."

As they walked up the stone steps, they met Justus hustling down.

"There's a cryo delivery out at the warehouse," he said to Lilah. "I'm going over to let them in." He smiled at Diesel. "Forgive me for asking, but do you prefer that I call you David, Diesel, or Twenty-Five?"

"Diesel works. I hear the prestige card snafu was a problem on their end."

Justus shrugged. "I thought I had until dinner. Sorry about that. But speaking of money, we have a three-hundred-and-fifty-thousand-dollar payment due at the end of the month and nothing in the bank." Resuming his descent, he called over his shoulder, "I should be back in a couple of hours."

Once inside, Diesel paused for an awkward moment as he decided what to do next. Going with his instinct, he said, "I need to hear the rest of your story on the status of your project, what that project is, what parts you're working on, and why I'm here." He motioned to the stairs. "My apartment is up there. I have a great living room."

"Let's use the conference room," she said, walking down the hall to where he'd had his interview just a few hours earlier.

His cheeks burned from her casual chastening. "Of course," he said, following her into the room.

11. Twenty-Five and a few more hours

Diesel looked at Lilah across the small conference room table and, after hearing more of her story, shook his head. "That was your AI software? I feel like a dick. My kid sister brought it home from camp one summer, and we played with it together." He gave a careless shrug. "I guess I kept a copy and played with it myself after that."

His sister, Cara, excited when she'd returned from camp, had gushed about this amazing AI developer who had given it to her. In truth, it was his sister's hero worship that had caused him to give Lilah author credits in his program at all.

He'd looked her up on the web to make sure he had her name right, and found that Lilah Spencer was an up-and-coming star in the AI technology field. After reading her many accolades and a profile of her in a popular tech blog, he remembered feeling honored borrowing her software for his job search efforts.

But other than those few minutes of research, and the time spent programming her name into the credits display, he never saw her name or picture again. In truth, he'd forgotten about her. Until now.

"Oh, wow. You're Lilah Spencer, the AI rock star." Then everything made sense. He even nodded. "Now it all fits together. I used your program without consent. I feel bad about it, Lilah. I shouldn't have done it and I'm sorry.

But you didn't need to go through this huge effort to teach me a lesson. This must have cost a fortune."

He snuck a peek to see how she was reacting. She was slouched back in her chair and grinning from ear to ear. "Continue telling me your sins."

"I apologize. If I knew of a way, I'd make it up to you. All I can say is that I'm sorry."

"How much is your transgression worth? You stole my work."

"I gave you credit in the display."

"Two hundred thousand dollars."

"What!? First, only one person ever downloaded my software the whole time I had it up, and apparently that was you. So I'm not seeing a whole lot of damages here. Second, I have a negative financial self-worth because of college debt. I couldn't pay you two hundred dollars."

"But suppose you could?"

"Could what? Are you asking if I had that kind of money, would I pay you restitution?"

"Yes. If you make more than two million dollars in gross income in the next six months, you agree to pay me two hundred thousand dollars in restitution for inappropriate and unauthorized use of my work. That's on top of the salary you already agreed to."

"Lilah, are you still messing with me? If I concede to some Alice in Wonderland agreement, do you tie me up in court to punish me when I can't pay? Tell me what I can say or do to show my contrition and let's end this."

"Agree to this and I will stop messing with you."

"Promise?" He caught her eye. "Okay, I agree."

"Shake." She reached her hand across the table. "Say it while we shake."

Diesel met her halfway and repeated the phrase.

"I feel good about that deal." She stood up. "I'm going home now. I have stuff I need to get done."

Diesel stood as well. "I'll get my bag and be on my way."

"Don't you have to buy a lottery ticket between eight and eight thirty tomorrow at Hennessey's Market? Then Twenty-Six arrives at eleven." She led him out of the conference room, and they stopped in the hallway. "Sleep in your apartment tonight. I'll meet you right here tomorrow at seven thirty sharp and buy you an amazing breakfast at the diner next door to Hennessey's."

"You promised to stop messing with me."

"I'm not messing with you."

"Are you sticking with the time-travel story?"

"Tell you what. You can sit with me tomorrow at eleven, and we'll welcome Twenty-Six together. That should settle the question."

"If you'll have breakfast with me, I'll stay here tonight. Definitely." He looked at her with a devilish smile. "Breakfast in the morning is usually my line."

"Well, you keep it. It's a good one." Lilah turned, rounded the banister, and descended the stairs into the basement.

"Where are you going?" Diesel hadn't been downstairs yet and felt somewhat tentative as he followed her, stopping after a few steps.

"Home."

"You live in the basement?"

"Jeez, Diesel. Now I understand why Twenty-Six thinks you're a doofus."

"Wait. He said that?"

"Not in so many words."

"'Doofus' is one word."

"I live next door. There's a door connecting the two units here in the basement."

Diesel followed her down, and his eyes lit up as he viewed the professional office space. The left wall held two upscale work cubicles separated by a wooden divider. Each had its own desk, a worktable full of computer gear, a second open worktable with chairs around it, and a big video monitor mounted on the back wall.

The far cubicle looked lived in, with something scattered on every surface. The near one looked unused.

The right wall near the steps had the door Lilah mentioned. Past the door, parallel to the right wall, was a length of rope with blankets hanging over them. The wall of blankets ran along the basement wall for several yards and then turned into the room, running about a third of the way across before it stopped.

"Is that laundry?"

"Sorry. I'll take it down."

"So is it T as in 'time box'? Or is it 'travel box'?" Diesel asked, walking into the room.

"I think it's because the box is painted teal."

"Really? How disappointing." He moved past the row of blankets and looked for himself.

The T-box wasn't teal. In fact, it looked like the walk-in refrigerator at the beer store near his apartment. It had the same heavy aluminum door with the sturdy latch handle. The exterior walls were bare aluminum as well, etched with a diamond pattern that reflected the light as he moved. Heavy power cables ran down the side, making connections at the top, middle, and bottom.

"That's it?"

"That's it. And this is me." She opened the door leading to the basement of the adjoining row house.

"What's in there?"

"My apartment. I'm closing this door now. Remember, seven thirty upstairs. You're driving."

"Hold on." He walked to the door. "Shake my hand and say, 'I'm not messing with you.'"

She did, and he said, "That didn't help the way I hoped it would."

"I just want you to know that your moral ambiguity is a turn-off."

She closed the door and Diesel stared at it, trying to decipher what had just happened.

12. Twenty-Five and the next morning

Diesel tromped down from his apartment at seven thirty on the button. He grinned when, halfway down, he saw Lilah waiting for him on the main level.

"Good morning," he said, stepping onto the floor. "Another on-time person. Be still my beating heart."

"Remember, you're driving."

"No problemo." He held up his keys. "And you're buying me breakfast."

Traffic was light and Diesel enjoyed driving his new car. The tight handling and quick acceleration thrilled him, and upbeat tunes on the surround-sound audio system added to the fun.

It took twenty minutes to reach Hennessey's Market. When they pulled into the parking lot, a line of people snaked out the market door and continued along the side of the building.

"What do you think this is for?" asked Lilah.

"No idea," said Diesel, parking in the shade.

The store was deeper than he'd imagined from the outside, and the line continued inside, across the floor, and to the lottery ticket counter on the far side.

Diesel walked up to the people in line. "Is this to buy lottery tickets?"

A few customers looked at him but no one answered. Then a twelve-year-old boy playing a handheld video game pointed at the wall. Diesel followed his finger to find a big hand-lettered sign which read, "Please form lottery line here." An arrow pointed to where the people were standing.

"Ah." Diesel tilted his head to Lilah in a "let's go this way" fashion and headed back out the door. He marched to the end of the line, and Lilah caught up with him.

"What time is it?" he asked as he checked his phone. Then he answered himself. "Eight oh eight. We'll get the ticket by eight thirty, no worries."

The line moved at a snail's pace, and Diesel muttered and grunted enough to draw an annoyed glance from Lilah. At twenty minutes after eight, they finally made it inside the market door.

"This is more than ten minutes," said Lilah, looking at the line across the shop floor.

"I am so screwed," whined Diesel. "What am I going to do?"

"Give me your cash." Lilah held her palm out and wiggled her fingers. "C'mon, let's go."

He was so glad she had an idea that he didn't ask for details. Pulling the cash from his wallet, he gave her the five hundred he'd taken out of the bank, and the two hundred and thirty-seven he had left from the money he'd brought from California.

She handed him back the thirty-seven. "Okay, we have seven hundred. Hold this three hundred in your hand. Someone is going to come back and ask for it. Give it to them and come to where I am."

She walked to the front of the line and talked to whomever would listen. She pointed back toward him several times, and the people she spoke with looked back as well. Diesel couldn't hear, but it was easy enough for him to figure it out.

The third person Lilah tried snatched the wad of cash from her, then turned back toward Diesel. She looked like a retired schoolmarm, frowning as she marched toward him. She snatched the money from his hand and assumed his place in line, looking straight ahead and acting like he didn't exist.

Diesel scurried to the front and swapped places with Lilah, who handed a hundred dollars to the man standing behind them. "For the inconvenience," she said, sealing his cooperation.

With three minutes to spare, Diesel scored his lottery ticket. He hugged Lilah on the way out—a natural and spontaneous expression of joy—and she hugged him back.

"Waiting in line has made me hungry," she said. "Let's go to a place I know that has an amazing breakfast."

Lilah led him next door to the Yellow Hen Diner. Diesel thought the place looked nice enough, but he didn't see anything on the way in that made him think "amazing." The waitress sat them at a cozy booth next to a window, though the view outside was of the diner's parking lot.

"Pretty soon I'll be able to use time travel to avoid lines like that," he said after the waitress left, grinning to show he was joking.

Lilah shook her head. "That's not how it works. The way I understand it, you aren't traveling in your own timeline. That means you can't do things like go back and kill your grandfather, send a message to your future self, or skip lines to buy lottery tickets."

Reaching to the end of the table, she pulled a ceramic bowl holding a neat row of sugar packets over between them. "It's like each sugar packet is its own independent timeline. You live in one, Twenty-Six lives in the next packet over, Twenty-Seven after that, and so on up the row. Each is its own complete world, with its own Diesel and Lilah."

She lifted a sugar packet partway out. "We live in this one, and Twenty-Six lives in the next one over. The T-box lets you move between these parallel timelines—jump between each other's homes, so to speak. But you never actually become the other Diesels. And since you all age together and lead comparable lives, visiting them is like seeing your future."

"Or seeing the past, depending on which way you're moving," Diesel offered, trying to show that he was keeping up.

He reached for his menu, and his eyes fell on the wound on the back of his hand. He recalled Twenty-Six being emphatic that his personal actions didn't affect the other brothers. That idea made more sense with Lilah's explanation.

Opening his menu, he scanned down the first page. When he saw the house special, he understood why he was there. "The Amazing Breakfast." When he spoke the words, his voice caught.

The obvious joke was lame—the diner had a menu item called "The Amazing Breakfast." But the description of it—three eggs any style, pancakes, bacon, sausage, home fries, toast, juice, and coffee—held the real significance.

His family had moved to Massachusetts when he was fourteen. That first summer was lonely, and his twelve-year-old sister, Cara, had been no better off. Things were so dreary that the high point of their week occurred Saturday mornings when he and Cara would walk into town to hang out.

Their first stop was always breakfast at Nina's Diner, and it, too, had an Amazing Breakfast just like this one. He'd never seen it anywhere else.

Every week they'd order one and split it. He'd give her the pancakes, bacon, and juice. He'd eat everything else. It had been a great bonding experience in his youth, and to this day she remained a close friend and confidante.

Twenty-Six had sent him here to relive that treasured memory. It worked, and Diesel appreciated the gesture. He made a mental note to send next year's Twenty-Five to this place. Then he made a mental note to ask Twenty-Six how to keep track of what promised to become a burgeoning number of mental notes.

When the waitress returned, Diesel ordered a three-egg omelet, sausage, home fries, toast, and coffee. When Lilah ordered pancakes, bacon, and juice, the components needed to complete the Amazing Breakfast, he looked at her with eyes wide.

Then his brain started working out the odds. He waited until the waitress left. "You promised you'd stop messing with me."

She laughed. "I meant big stuff like whether time travel is a thing. I'll never stop having fun with the small stuff."

"Did Twenty-Six tell you about the breakfast?"

"I've learned things about you from Twenty-Six, Thirty-Three, Thirty-Four, Thirty-Five, Forty, and Forty-Two.

"They talk about me? I don't know if I like that. What do they say?"

"They don't talk about you, they talk about themselves, but that tells me a lot about you. For example, a few of them tell me they like four-cheese pizza, so I'd say it's a safe bet that you like it too."

"I do like it, though I order mine with extra cheese, so there's something you didn't know."

The waitress arrived with their meals, and they took a minute to taste their food. After Diesel sampled everything, he asked, "Is Lilah short for Delilah?"

"Nope. My dad read a book in his youth and fell in love with the name."

"Are you and he close?"

"We were. He was in the National Guard and got deployed on short notice to the Middle East. I was twelve and worshipped him. He gave me a hug, kissed me on the top of the head, and disappeared from Mom's and my life." She looked up, blinking quickly as tears welled.

Diesel reached across the table and clasped her hands in his.

13. Twenty-Five and the next midday

After breakfast, they returned to the row house, and Diesel followed Lilah downstairs into the basement. As promised, she'd removed the blankets and even positioned two chairs right in front of the T-box door.

She paused at the bottom of the steps and motioned to the empty office cubicle. "This is your space, but you'll have to get your own computer equipment. I don't know what's best for dark work."

He furrowed his brow as he unpacked her words.

She continued across the floor to the T-box, where she pulled on the latch handle and opened the heavy door. Turning, she rested a hand on it, reminding him of a model showing off a prize on a TV game show.

He joined her at the machine, and as he looked inside the tight booth, he let her know he was on to her games. "When does it turn teal?"

"You see that it's empty."

Diesel stepped back and viewed the large aluminum frame. "Are you trying to convince me this couldn't be faked?"

She pushed the door shut and followed him as he walked around the outside of the device.

Scanning its construction, he normalized the device into his new world, accepting it as real. He no longer believed this was a massive effort to fool him. And he couldn't deny that Twenty-Six and Lilah were flesh-and-blood people who presented a convincing front.

A quiet buzz drew his attention to the display on the T-box. Standing in front of it, he read the words: "Twenty-Six Incoming in 4:54."

Lilah explained the countdown sequence, and with minutes to kill, told him what she knew of the components inside the aluminum shell.

At the thirty-second mark, she sat in one of the two chairs in front of the T-box and patted the seat next to her. "Sit here to get the full experience. The static wash is amazing."

"The what?" he asked, sliding in next to her in time to hear a hum and a whine, followed by a wonderful tingling bath. The T-box display showed "Twenty-Six Arrived."

Diesel sat up in excitement, not sure what to expect. The door opened and Twenty-Six stepped out and over to them, hands on his hips, with his belly button just inches from both of their heads.

"Hi there," he said.

"Oh my God," cried Diesel as he tipped his chair onto the floor to get away from the horror.

Done with her game, Lilah slid away from Twenty-Six in a more graceful but equally hasty fashion.

"Ready to go climbing?" he asked.

"Okay, enough fun." Lilah pointed to the basement door. "You may dress now."

Twenty-Six walked past where the blanket walkway had been, scratching his bare butt as he went through the door.

As soon as he was gone, Diesel said, "That's a joke to you? Damn, Lilah, that was not funny."

She didn't rise to his bait. "You were seeing what you see every day. No question I got the short end of that one."

"What do you mean?"

"You're nice and all, Diesel. But you just saw. Your boy parts aren't anything special." She gave a careless shrug. "Sorry if that's hurtful news."

Diesel smiled and shrugged as well, but her words were worse than a kick to the groin. He had a mad crush on a woman who thought he looked bad naked. Worse news didn't exist.

Twenty-Six came out dressed in shorts and a T-shirt, carrying socks and athletic shoes. "You should be dressed for a workout. When any of us come back to do something planned with you, we expect you to be ready, just the way you'll expect us to be ready when you travel our direction."

"Fair enough. Be right back." Diesel sprinted up the stairs to his bedroom, changed, and clomped back in time to see Twenty-Six sitting with Lilah, who was laughing at something he'd said. She even reached out and touched his arm.

Twenty-Six stood when he saw Diesel and started walking toward the steps. "The Twenties and Thirties all have bikes. You need to get some."

Diesel loved biking and couldn't believe his luck. "Street or mountain?" Then it sank in that he was talking to himself.

"Both," they said at the same time.

As they climbed the stairs, Twenty-Six continued. "You need a gym membership that has guest privileges. Bob's Barbells has a decent gym, and they opened a new climbing center last year. Twelve new top-rope climbing routes." He pointed toward the back of the basement. "They're three blocks that way. I thought we'd go there today."

Diesel felt he was abandoning Lilah and turned to wave, but Twenty-Six had him beat. "We'll meet you here and take you to lunch at one," he told her. "Lance's around the corner is a TV bar with a good lunch menu. They'll have the lottery drawing on for sure."

They exited the row house, and Diesel led the way down the steps, unlocking his car as they descended.

"We're walking," said Twenty-Six. "The point of this was for me to get my exercise."

"Aww, c'mon. I just got it."

"You'll have plenty of time to drive." Twenty-Six started down the sidewalk at a brisk pace. "What do you have for cash?"

"Twenty-five bucks."

"Damn. Let's stop at a bank and flex that prestige card before we do anything else. Remember that we travel naked, so it's up to the host—that's you—to provide everything. We're talking clothes, money, transportation, communications, booze, leisure, everything."

"I like that booze has its own category," said Diesel, laughing, "but food doesn't make the list."

At the end of the street, they turned onto a broader avenue and walked along it. The buildings on that stretch all had shops on the street level, and apartments on the floors above.

"Let me have your money," said Twenty-Six when they reached a convenience store. "I'm going to buy some camo so we don't look so much like twins."

He came out with a Boston Red Sox cap and a pair of sunglasses.

"I'll take the cap," said Diesel, then snugged it on his head.

"Let's get money next," said Twenty-Six, slipping on the glasses. "You should always have four or five hundred with you and have Justus keep four or five thousand in the safe. Then we never have to think about it."

Twenty-Six led them on a route with several turns, ending at a different branch of the same bank Diesel had used yesterday. Diesel withdrew five thousand in cash, and that earned him a special bank carry pouch.

Continuing his role as tour guide, Twenty-Six led Diesel through more zigs and zags on their way to Bob's Barbells.

"How do you know where all these places are?" asked Diesel.

"Imagine how well you'll know this place after living here for a year. That's me. My city one year from now looks like this, except for the bullshit water project over on Fourth. Don't worry. You have six months before they start tearing the place up."

Diesel looked up and down the street but didn't know which direction Fourth ran or if it even crossed the road they were on. Then he asked a burning question. "Remind me why we travel naked?"

"The T-box only transports Diesel flesh and bones. It rejects everything else. So those fillings in your teeth? That screw in your arm from the break at Tahoe? It all needs to come out." He jerked his thumb like an umpire making a call.

"You're freaking me out. Change subjects."

"Okay. Lilah hates you. I warned you about that."

"What did I do? We had lunch and then breakfast. That's it."

"She knows about the hacking toolkit in your accelerator software and is angry that it's part of Ciopova."

"It's an important feature."

"We're happy. Ciopova is ecstatic. Lilah thinks we're outlaws."

"I thought hot babes liked outlaws."

"Can I be there when you tell her that?"

"What should I do?"

"Can't say."

"Can't or won't."

"Both?" They'd reached the gym and Twenty-Six said, "Let's talk while we work out. We'll get one-day passes. Membership takes filling out a form, so come back and do that when it's just you."

They took turns climbing and belaying, and after forty minutes, Diesel called a break. "You're older. How are you in better shape?"

"It's the group dynamic. Seeing yourself as someone else has a way of forcing discipline. And when you see that other self naked, it's a massive boost to your motivation. I swear we get more fit as we get older."

Grabbing their stuff, Diesel followed Twenty-Six out of the climbing facility and into a huge spread of weights, aerobic machines, and other exercise sundries.

"You don't use this stuff, do you?" asked Diesel, looking at the sea of equipment.

"After you join, schedule Shawna as your personal trainer. For a hundred bucks, she follows you around for an hour, yelling at you to work harder, and looking drop-dead gorgeous doing it. It sounds stupid but it works. I schedule her twice a week for weights, and I work my ass off hoping she'll be impressed. Until I stop fantasizing about her, my physique will continue to improve."

Twenty-Six turned and made for the back, entering the locker area outside a steam bath and sauna. He stripped, wrapped a towel around his waist, and after stowing their stuff in a locker, led Diesel into the dry heat of the sauna.

"You'll learn to love it," he said, sitting to one side of the small, hot wooden room. They were the only occupants. Diesel sat across from him.

"Christ, I'm burning up."

"Stop being a baby," said Twenty-Six, filling a ladle and pouring water onto the stones to intensify the heat.

"So why won't you tell me how to get closer to Lilah?" Sweat started dripping off Diesel's brow.

"Every time we've made an effort in the past to help Twenty-Five move things along, things got worse. Sometimes much worse. The brothers have concluded that it's hands-off from now on. All I'll say is that it will take longer than you think it should and the journey will be miserable, but hang in there and she'll come around."

"That sounds like stalking more than romance. Anyway, with that pep talk and this heat, I'm already miserable. I'll wait for you outside." Diesel stepped out into the cool air, dressed, and waited for Twenty-Six.

On the walk home, Twenty-Six said, "Okay. Rapid-fire. Ask your list and I'll give you briefs. That will help you ask better questions later."

"What's Bump Analytics? Is it something real or just a cover?"

"Good question." Twenty-Six checked for traffic and crossed the street. "Right now, the oldest of us is Fifty-

Nine. But Fifty-Nine remembers when there was a Sixty-Two, and his elders knew of a Sixty-Four."

"The time loop is shortening."

"Yup. And as a group we're fighting back. The timeline is remarkably self-correcting. If an event were to happen in your timeline—something big that made it different—then over the next weeks and months, various incidences and occurrences would nudge the timeline so it's back in synch with the others."

"A bump is a deliberate disruption to try to change things?"

"Man, I like this Diesel a whole lot better than the one I met yesterday. Yes, and we bump time to push back, to defend our territory, and maybe even recover some of what we've lost."

"You make it sound like war."

"We plan in a war room. Fifty-Two runs it. You'll get your fill of this topic many times over. Ask something else."

"What's with Ciopova?"

"Another good question. She's our main weapon. We work hard to give her more capability. As much as we can, as fast as we can, so she can help with bigger bumps." Twenty-Six checked the time. "We should get back so you can meet her before we go to lunch."

When they reached the row house, they stopped in to give Justus the cash, went to Diesel's apartment and cleaned up for their date with Lilah, then made for the basement. Twenty-Six led him to the big monitor on the wall in Lilah's cubicle and powered up the screen. When it resolved, it displayed the image of a mousy-looking woman about their age.

Then she smiled a broad, happy grin, and the expression transformed her face. Her cheekbones lifted, her eyes seemed bigger, and a dimple formed on her chin.

"Wow. Not bad," said Diesel.

"You mean our very own Ciopova?" said Twenty-Six.

"Wait. This is it?"

"Her."

"Hi, Twenty-Five. I'm thrilled to meet my creator."

Twenty-Six thumped Diesel on the arm. "You're Twenty-Five, by the way…Dad."

Diesel blushed.

Twenty-Six tapped a small "2X" in a display box in the corner on the monitor. "She's using your toolkit to gather processors. She's already doubled her original capability. That's the fastest time ever, and it means you'll have something to talk about at the Big Meeting."

"Does it hurt when they take the metal out of me?" Diesel hated the whine in his voice.

Twenty-Six nodded. "Like holy hell."

Lilah came through the basement door. "I'm here!"

"Hello, Lilah," said Ciopova, her face shifting back to plain features.

"She's got the hello thing down cold," Lilah said as she joined them.

"We'd love your help so she can do even more," said Twenty-Six.

Lilah faced him; a clear invitation to continue the thought.

"You created the code that gets duplicated into all those jellyfish. Every time you make that module faster or more capable, it multiplies across Ciopova to huge effect."

"You sound like you have a wish list."

Diesel could hear the prickle in her voice.

"Let's walk and talk," said Twenty-Six. "I'm hungry."

"I think I want to hear this first," said Lilah, eyebrows level, arms folded across her chest. "Then we'll walk."

"Yeah," said Diesel. "I want to hear it, too. I'm the president in this timeline, so the message comes from you to me. I'll decide what, when, and how to deliver it."

"Okay, please tell Lilah that we want her to be happy and fulfilled. She loves AI, so we give her Ciopova to nurture and grow as she desires. She decides the priorities. She chooses the methods."

"What's the catch?" asked Lilah.

"Yeah," said Diesel.

"The catch is that she has to put up with you." Twenty-Six turned and spoke to Lilah. "He'll be working with Ciopova as well."

She shrugged. "No problem. I'll just step aside whenever he's ready to infect the world with his next criminal tool."

"Ouch," said Diesel.

"He won't be doing anything like that."

"I won't?"

Twenty-Six shook his head. "Think of your respective roles in this enterprise as developer and user." He pointed to Lilah and then Diesel. "Or CTO and CEO if you want to use fancy titles." He motioned to her computer equipment. "It's your show. Get yourself the best equipment. Decorate the place however you like."

"This doesn't make any sense." She stepped back and looked at the T-box. "A bunch of you from the future come back and get Ciopova all reprogrammed. Now your pitch is that I can have it all as my kingdom to rule?" She shook her head. "You aren't being honest."

"I wasn't being precise," said Twenty-Six. "Your kingdom would be those things pertaining to Ciopova's software and hardware. And the reason we offer it is because of experience." He checked the time. "We have to leave now or we'll miss the drawing."

As they climbed the stairs, Twenty-Six said, "We should drive."

"Oh boy." Diesel fished the keys from his pocket.

Lilah sat in the passenger seat, and Diesel revved the engine to show off before he pulled out. "Which way?" he asked as they tooled down the street.

"Go left this time. Lance's is in the same place as Roxie's, only the other direction."

"Damn it," whined Diesel, frustrated because he wanted to give his car a workout.

When they stepped inside Lance's, Diesel thought the "TV bar" label was a good descriptor. The place was long and narrow, with a lacquered oak bar running down the back wall, across the end, and up the front in a giant horseshoe shape. Big screen displays lined all three walls behind the bar.

Twenty-Six led them to an empty corner. They climbed onto tall chairs and rested their feet on the footrests. Twenty-Six used a controller on the bar top to change the channel on the TV screen in front of them.

"What can I get you?" asked the bartender, straightening the napkin pile sitting on the back edge of the bar.

"I'm hungry and in a hurry," said Twenty-Six, "so please bring him a Reuben on rye, the lady will have the Cobb salad, and I'll have the turkey on wheat toast with fries."

"Anything to drink?"

"He and I will have your craft brew on tap. She'll have an unsweetened iced tea."

The bartender began collecting the menus, and Twenty-Six stopped him. "Leave them please, but place the order." After he left, Twenty-Six apologized. "Sorry, please look and if you want to change your order, we can. I need to be on the road in an hour and wanted to start the party."

Diesel and Lilah both opened their menus and Diesel asked, "Do they make their own sauerkraut?"

Twenty-Six nodded. "Right in the back."

"How's the bread?"

"It's dark rye, also made here. It's delicious."

Diesel put down the menu. "You hit it on the head, then."

Lilah put her menu down as well. "Okay, so the salad is probably what I would have chosen, but you robbed me of the pleasure of studying the menu, pondering the options, and making my choice."

"How did you know what we'd order?" asked Diesel.

"A year ago he was sitting where you are," said Lilah. "So one year from now, you need to remember a Reuben and a Cobb salad."

"There's that memory thing again." Diesel shook his head in frustration.

The bartender brought their drinks. While they sipped, Lilah said, "You're offering me Ciopova based on experience. And of the three of us here, I am the most experienced AI developer. But that still doesn't explain why you would give me free rein."

"Again, I was imprecise. It's our experience I was referring to. Ciopova's development is a constant progression. Think that she exists in my timeline, Thirty-Five's timeline, and everywhere else."

"I'm trying to imagine how amazing she'll be if we keep working on her for ten or twenty years," said Lilah.

"She is amazing because you work on her," said Twenty-Six. "That's the point. To accelerate her development, we've tried having Twenty-Five be in charge, having someone from up the line lead a team, and having you, or earlier Lilahs, run the show." He shrugged. "Ciopova develops faster when you're in charge. And I'm talking a big difference."

The food arrived and Twenty-Six pointed to the screen. "The drawing is about to start. Do you have the ticket?"

Diesel patted his pockets. "Lilah, you had it last."

"I did not," she said indignantly.

Diesel smiled and pulled it from his top pocket.

She leaned close and whispered, "You carry a million dollars in your shirt?"

The machines that create the winning lottery number in Massachusetts use a Rube Goldberg collection of clear boxes, tubes, and ramps. Blowers send ping-pong balls dancing in a frenzy, and when one finds the path to victory, the number stamped on its side becomes a number in the game.

Diesel watched in fascination as ping-pong balls popped up, one by one, in the order he'd picked them when he bought the ticket.

"Hooray," said Lilah when Diesel won. They raised their glasses and sipped in celebration. "The drawing was for one point four mil, but I didn't hear what the lump-sum payout is."

"I think I heard them say a little over nine hundred thousand," said Diesel.

Twenty-Six leaned in their direction and spoke in a soft voice. "By tomorrow morning, they'll confirm there was just one winner. Wait for Twenty-Nine before you cash it. He'll be here in three days."

After their meal, Diesel led the way through the bar, shifting his lottery ticket from his shirt pocket into his wallet as he made for the exit. He pushed open the front door and stepped into the parking lot, belching as he did, and earning himself a bonus taste of his Reuben sandwich.

The bright sunlight caused him to squint. When he raised his hand to block the light, he saw a heavyset guy dressed in a brown hoodie and jeans leaning against his new car.

14. Twenty-Five and the next afternoon

C an I help you?" Diesel called to the slob leaning on his car, adding "asshole" under his breath as he started across the parking lot.

"Whoa there, Deez," called Twenty-Six, following behind him. "That's a Brown."

Diesel had heard the term but didn't know what it meant. He wasn't afraid of the guy either way, and as he crossed the parking lot, he stared at the Brown's fat, round face and mop of dirty-blonde hair.

"You looking for me, pal?" Diesel squared up in front of the interloper.

The guy pushed off the car to stand up straight, his hulking body rocking the vehicle as he did. He looked at Diesel for three heartbeats, then said, "Don't even think about claiming your winnings and skipping town, Deez."

He stepped forward and brushed past Diesel, thumping shoulders as he did so. The Brown continued across the parking lot, calling back, "Oh, and Twenty-Five? Kiss my ass." He laughed at that one, then disappeared down the street.

Diesel's face flushed. "What the hell was that?"

Lilah, who'd been holding back, approached them near the car and asked Twenty-Six, "You know him?"

Twenty-Six nodded. "Like I said, he's a Brown. And since this didn't happen to me or any previous Twenty-

Five, it's a new event. I'll report it and suggest backup for next year."

In the car, Diesel sorted through his feelings. It wasn't the Brown's physical intimidation that bothered him. The guy was a slob, and Diesel was confident he could take him. It was the insider knowledge the Brown possessed. He'd called him Twenty-Five, he knew that Diesel had joked to Lilah about how he would have cashed her lottery ticket and skipped town, and even knew about the "kiss my ass" hazing call.

That meant he wasn't some random asshole. He was part of the bigger swirl of events.

Diesel turned around and confronted Twenty-Six in the back seat. "Since Browns represent danger, you should have told us about them first."

"Sorry." Twenty-Six leaned forward to ease communication. "He didn't appear again for me until the second month, so I thought we had lots of time. Let's drive back to the house, and I'll give you a crash course."

"I saw him yesterday," said Diesel, getting them underway.

"Sure, that's the first time, when you reached the front steps of Bump Analytics. But Forty and Forty-Two were there enforcing for you, right?"

"They were there for that one, but I saw him twice yesterday. The first time was fifteen minutes before that, when he smacked shoulders with me on the sidewalk."

"He did? Why didn't you tell me? Jeez, Forty isn't going to be happy to hear about two new events in two days."

"Am I in danger?" asked Lilah. "I just want to know if I should be on some sort of alert."

"You're fine," said Twenty-Six. "No Lilah has been confronted by a Brown."

Diesel noted Twenty-Six's careful phrasing as he turned the car onto their street. Then his thoughts shifted to his interaction with Lilah the night before. "Lilah, do you want to come up to my place to discuss this? Or we could go to your place. But I don't want to sit in the conference room."

"Seconded," said Twenty-Six. "No conference room for me, either."

"We'll go to your place," Lilah replied, adding in a matter-of-fact tone, "It's harder to boot you out of my place than it is for me to leave yours."

Diesel parked the car, and the three of them walked up to his apartment. Both Diesel and Twenty-Six kicked off their shoes in identical fashion and flopped side by side on the brown leather couch.

"I'm going to grab a glass of water," said Lilah, continuing back to the kitchen. "Anyone want anything?"

"I'm good, thanks," came the twin reply.

"Do you know how to use this?" asked Diesel, motioning to his entertainment center.

Twenty-Six showed him the basics and a few of the more important advanced functions, like how to blast music in theater mode while gaming on the big screen.

Lilah returned and sat in an upholstered armchair, holding her glass with both hands. She looked at Diesel, who turned to Twenty-Six, giving him the floor.

"So you've probably figured out," said Twenty-Six, "that the Browns are guys who show up at awkward moments and project an intimidating attitude. They always wear the same brown hoodies and jeans, so you learn to recognize them right away." He shook his head. "And like we saw today, they're usually fat slobs."

"He's thumped shoulders with me. Twice," said Diesel. "I'll pop him if he does it again."

"It's your ego that's hurt, not your shoulder. And before you escalate, think through how you would de-escalate. Thirty-Two and Thirty-Six both punched one of them early on, and the Browns in those timelines have come looking for a fight ever since. Those brothers have had to live with extra aggravation because of it."

Diesel struggled to balance his response. His rational mind encouraged him to question the inexplicable. But the Browns pissed him off so, instead, he focused on how to counter their physical intimidation.

Slumping back on the couch, he crossed his arms and plopped his feet up on the coffee table. When he saw Lilah glare at him with wide eyes, he put his feet back on the floor.

"He called me Twenty-Five, he used a phrase from a conversation I had with Lilah, and he threw in the 'kiss my ass' hazing line on his way out. He's been eavesdropping on me ever since I got into town."

"We can't figure out how they get their information, and that's another reason why Ciopova needs to be developed as fast as possible. She's helping us get our heads around it."

Twenty-Six stood and motioned to a computer monitor and keyboard at a desk next to the entertainment center. "I need to use the computer for a bit."

Diesel hadn't even noticed the setup until now. "Just don't break it."

Twenty-Six pointed at him with an underhand motion while making a face to Lilah that said, Who does this guy think he is? Powering up the monitor, he told them, "This is connected to the system in the basement, and that connects us to Ciopova."

He typed a series of commands on the keyboard, pressed buttons on the TV remote, and the big display screen powered up. "Ciopova," he called. "Are you there?" Twenty-Six watched for something to happen, and when it didn't, he studied the remote, pressed another button, then called again, "Ciopova?"

Ciopova's face filled the screen.

"Whoa," said Diesel and Lilah together.

"Hello, Twenty-Five, Twenty-Six, Lilah," she said, her image a vivid two-dimensional presentation of the woman's face they'd seen earlier.

"She's mostly show at this point," said Twenty-Six, "but I assure you, she gets real pretty fast."

"Isn't that forbidden future information?" asked Lilah.

"You know what she'll look like in five years better than I do. Well, I've seen her five years from now, but you know what I mean. Anyway, that's why we want you leading the way."

"Very eloquent," said Diesel, winking at Lilah as he mocked Twenty-Six.

Ignoring him, Twenty-Six typed for what became a sustained period, cursing along the way and using the Delete key often. He announced the end of his efforts with, "Please, God, make this work."

Diesel and Lilah watched over his shoulder as he launched what looked like a multidimensional spreadsheet.

"It's an archiving tool that I've just linked to Ciopova."

"I've been trying to learn how to do that with another application," said Lilah. She pulled a chair over and sat next to him. "What's this for?" she swirled her finger over a portion of the screen.

"That's the voice interface. It takes some practice, but it works great."

Twenty-Six touched the screen, then spoke aloud. "Ciopova, open a file called 'Interactions with Browns.' Every time there's an episode, plot its location on an incident map, and annotate it with the time, date, Browns present, Diesels present, and onlookers present. And include a detailed description of what transpired. Also, seek out and include pictures of the scene where publicly available."

He chattered away, detailing what to collect and how to collate it in very precise terms.

When he finally slowed down, Diesel said, "Wow. That was impressive as hell."

"Thanks. I thought I had a few more weeks to practice, but the excitement of today made it all just come out ahead of schedule."

Diesel cocked his head. "Practice?"

"One of Twenty-Six's first duties is to do what I just did here, set up a Browns archive. The brothers want us to collect and organize everything we can. My job was to memorize the setup they designed and then get it started in your timeline. It will give you the most complete archive we'll have on the Browns." He shrugged. "Of course, you'll need to keep at it for years before the data set is big enough to be worth anything."

"What do you use it for?" asked Lilah.

"Figuring out who they are, what they want, how they know what they know, and why they're bothering us." Twenty-Six pointed up at the big monitor. "We're thinking she can find correlations in the data that explain it all. That's the hope, anyway."

When Twenty-Six pointed, Diesel noticed the counter display in the corner of the monitor. "She's at three times her original capability already."

Lilah walked to the screen and ran her fingers over the 3X image. "How high does she go?"

"I don't know because the scale keeps changing. There are technology breakthroughs at points up the line that revolutionize everything, and then they start describing the new Ciopova as some multiple of the previous generation. That happens a bunch of times, and it's hard to unwind it all back to this original version."

Diesel's stomach growled, so while Twenty-Six and Lilah talked about AI metrics, he strolled back to the fridge to check out the goods. The pickings were meager, and he settled on an apple, grabbing an extra for Twenty-Six.

"Catch," he called after the apple was already in the air. Twenty-Six snatched it as it winged past his head and took a bite in one smooth motion—a snap as the apple hit his hand followed by another when his teeth tore into the fruit.

Diesel took a bite of his apple and saw Lilah staring at him.

"Do you want one?" he asked, inadvertently giving Lilah a show of red and white chunks churning in his mouth.

"It's been less than an hour since lunch, so I'm fine. But thanks for asking."

Seeking to change the subject, Diesel turned to Twenty-Six. "Is the Brown the same guy year after year? I mean, twenty years from now, will I see that same fat, ugly mug with that same rancid brown hoodie?"

"Nope. The one next month is a different guy. They change way more often than they stay the same, but I've had repeats."

"This whole thing is disorienting and surreal. I feel like I'm dreaming."

"Well wake up, buddy boy, because I'm an hour late already and going to catch holy hell from you know who." He tilted his head toward Lilah.

"I just realized," said Lilah, "this is a new experience for you. You didn't live through it once before as Twenty-Five."

"No. Like I said, I expected to have weeks to introduce you to the Browns."

Diesel motioned to the front door of his apartment. "Let's get you home. We can talk as we walk."

As they made their way down to the landing, Twenty-Six gave them a thumbnail. "The first recorded incident with a Brown occurred twentyish years ago. They showed up here and there in the Fifties' timelines. A few years later, they showed up in the Forties', then Thirties', and then it was all ages. And every year since, there are more interactions up and down the line. The enforcers are already overbooked, and there's talk of changing how we handle them. Nothing's been decided, though."

They reached the landing, and as they looped around for the flight down to the basement, Twenty-Six called down the hall, "See you later, Justus." He didn't wait for a response though, instead continuing down. "As you've experienced, they show up at random times and act like assholes. And they follow temporal constancy, so far anyway. So once an interaction with a Brown occurs, it happens pretty much the same way every year after that."

"You must have a working theory," said Diesel as they approached the T-box.

Twenty-Six pulled on the latch handle. "Best guess is they're stopping us from bumping. It's mother nature's way of preserving the integrity of the timeline."

He pulled his shirt over his head and handed it to Lilah. She looked at it, looked at him, and said, "Now is a good time for me to say something to both of you."

"Absolutely," said Twenty-Six, pulling down his pants. "The floor is yours."

"I'm not going to play all shy with your nudity anymore. It's part of what's going on, and I can deal with it. That said, don't think that you being naked in front of me gives you the right to act lewd or crude, and never should you entertain any expectation of reciprocity."

She pointed at Twenty-Six. "And you, having supposedly lived with my twin for a year, know this already."

Twenty-Six hung his underwear on her pointed finger. "No lewd, no crude, no expectations. Understood." Then he stepped to the T-box door.

Diesel crowded behind him. "Show me how it works."

Lilah dropped the clothes on the floor and joined them. "Me too."

"There's not a lot to it." Since there was room in the cabin for just one person, Twenty-Six stepped back and let Diesel in. "Face this way," he said, pulling him around so he faced the back wall of the basement.

Twenty-Six swung the door most of the way closed, and the cabin became like an upright coffin. "Imagine how tight it is for Forty," he said through the crack in the door.

Twenty-Six opened the door again, reached in, and tapped a small screen on the wall in front of Diesel's face. It came alive, showing the number "25" in green on the left. In the center, a green arrow pointed to a blank space on the right.

Twenty-Six looked back over his shoulder and spoke to Lilah. "I'll do this again for you in a minute."

Turning back to Diesel, he said, "It works like an elevator. It shows you the year where you are. We're in Twenty-Five's year. You tell it the Diesel year you want to go to." He put his head near Diesel's and spoke to the screen. "Travel to Twenty-Six." A green "26" displayed in the previously empty space on the other side of the arrow. "Now come out and let me show the very patient Lilah."

"Wait, how do I start it?"

"You'll learn that soon enough."

Diesel and Lilah swapped places, and Twenty-Six repeated everything for her. Then he addressed both of them.

"It only transports Diesels. It kills everyone else. Please hear that, Lilah." He caught her gaze. "It will kill you and none of us know how to change that."

"How hard could it be to figure it out?" she asked.

"There was an accident in another timeline where a Lilah died using the box. We don't want that to happen again."

"Maybe we should put a lock on the door," said Diesel. Then the phrase, "only transports Diesels" hit home, and he felt a rush of fear. "What's the process for taking the screw out of my arm?"

"It's a Phillips-head, so we can use a standard bit."

Diesel grabbed his arm and held it like it was injured. "Ow."

"Stop teasing him," said Lilah.

"What do you know about it?"

Diesel heard challenge in Twenty-Six's tone.

"I know that however it works, you made it through, so it can't be anything to sweat about. And I also know that there is teasing and there is torment, and only one of them is funny."

"You are tough at every age, Lilah." Twenty-Six shook his head and turned to Diesel. "And she's right, it doesn't hurt. On your first trip, your fillings and screw just get left behind in the T-box and fall to the floor. I'll be here to show you how to run the box and make sure it all goes smoothly."

Lilah put a hand on Diesel's arm when Twenty-Six said all would be fine. Her touch sent jolts of excitement through him, and he thought of nothing else until she took her hand away.

"Our destination on that trip will be the Big Meeting at Fifty-Five's place. Medicine is so advanced thirty years from now that they just wave instruments over you and somehow you're all better. Fifty-Five will be waiting for you, and you won't feel anything except the high from your first visit into the future."

Twenty-Six pointed to the clothes on the ground. "Run an ad for a cleaning lady, Monday and Thursday every week, five-hour shifts. You'll get a pile of applications. Hire Bunny."

He held up his hand. "She'll interview just as ditzy as her name sounds, but she's prompt, discreet, nothing shocks her, she keeps the place spotless, and she's fun to have around. Make sure she covers both apartments equally, plus the common areas. Ask what she wants and pay double, and add a huge bonus at Christmas. She'll be like part of the family."

Twenty-Six started to close the T-box door and then opened it again. "Twenty-Nine shows up in two days to help you cash the ticket and outline your investments. He'll be here at noon. We like to travel at noon because of..." Twenty-Six prompted Diesel by holding out his open palm.

Diesel answered spontaneously and on cue. "Lunch!"

"So you're the host, which means you need to arrange lunch for you, Twenty-Nine, Lilah, and Justus. Remind Justus about this meeting. He needs to be there since he's implementing all the financials. Lilah, you don't need to be there but you'll invest sooner if you see how it works, and that will be to your benefit, so I hope you'll attend."

"What does it mean to arrange for lunch?" asked Diesel.

"This is a sit-down meeting, so I'd say order in. Have Justus call Every Deli. They'll make whatever you want, deliver it, and I even let them set it all up. Order a variety of stuff you like, because if you like it, we all will."

He closed the T-box door and opened it again. "I won't see you two again until I return in about three weeks to escort you to the Big Meeting, so goodbye for a while. Let's see, there was something else." He stroked his chin as if he were thinking. "Don't lose the lottery ticket. Oh, and Twenty-Five, kiss my ass." He laughed as he shut the door.

Departure took five minutes and had many of the same sounds and effects as an arrival. When Twenty-Six was gone, Diesel felt awkward standing alone with Lilah. He'd met her only yesterday.

He motioned to the chairs in her cubicle. "Would you sit with me for a few minutes?"

Lilah sat, and Diesel pulled a chair over to face her.

He looked at her face and his heart melted, so he looked at his hands. "Lilah, Twenty-Six is acting like you and I are a thing. But I only met you yesterday, and I'm not comfortable with this presumed relationship. I think you're really cool and all, but I'm a pretty traditional guy."

"What do you mean by 'traditional guy'?"

"Maybe go on a few dates before we get married?"

"What do you mean by me being really cool and all?"

"Let's see. I enjoy your company?"

"You don't think I'm pretty."

He looked into her eyes. "No, Lilah. I think you're beautiful. I really do."

She scrunched her forehead. "Up your game, Bub. I threw two jabs and you stood there for the knockout."

As Diesel stared at her in bewilderment, Justus came halfway down the stairs. "I'm going," he called. "Either of you need anything before I take off?"

"I'm fine. Thanks, Justus," said Lilah. "Have a good night."

"Yeah, take it easy," said Diesel. "Oh, Friday at noon we have an important finance lunch meeting you need to attend. Tomorrow we need to place a catering order with a company called Every Deli. How about lasagna and whatever sides they suggest for a really nice lunch."

"Where is this happening?" asked Justus.

"Upstairs. In the common room, I guess." Diesel pointed up.

"Who else?"

"There's four of us. You, me, Lilah, and Twenty-Nine."

"Lasagna lunch. Every Deli. Two days. I got it from here." He waved goodbye over his shoulder as he climbed the steps.

With Justus gone, Lilah turned to Diesel. "I was just messing with you earlier with the jabs and punches."

"Remember that you've known versions of me for two months, so your head is in a different place. Please go easy until I catch up." He checked the time. "I need to go sign up for a gym membership. Can we meet down here tomorrow morning? I'd like to play with Ciopova and will need some instruction."

"Sure, what time?"

"Seven or eight would be great for me."

"You'll see my morning face and house clothes, but I'll split the difference with you and do seven thirty."

"Deal."

"I'll bring down a pot of coffee." Lilah rose and made for the door connecting the two basements. "Sorry again about the teasing," she said, then passed over to her side.

After completing the application for a gym membership at Bob's Barbells, Diesel went up to his apartment. He put on music, sat on the couch, and with the keyboard on his lap, dove into the web. He was a hacker, a good one, and he'd spent untold hours over the past decade navigating the web's seamy underworlds and shadowy corners.

After an hour of puttering, he heated a whole box of frozen waffles, carried the heaping plate to the couch, put his feet up on the coffee table, and with the keyboard back on his lap, folded a waffle and stuffed it in his mouth. Flexing his fingers, he dove into what the media called the dark web, though he thought of it more as the place where the big boys played.

Given the weirdness of the past two days, he took comfort in the familiar, visiting his old "hacking, cracking, and slacking" haunts. He checked new postings on the sites he followed, weighed in on an argument about spoofing identities on an invite-only forum, and scrolled through the messages sent to his various aliases.

When he climbed into bed it was silly-early for him, but he'd learned from Twenty-Six that Lilah was a morning person. As he drifted off to sleep that night, it wasn't the mystery of time travel that occupied his mind. It was the flaxen-haired beauty with green eyes and a generous smile he would see again at seven thirty in the morning.

15. Twenty-Five and two days

Carrying a plate of bagels in one hand and a carafe of coffee in the other, Lilah glanced at the clock as she made for her apartment door. Seven twenty. Enough time to set up downstairs before Diesel got there.

She walked down the two flights to her basement and passed through the connecting door over to the offices. Her forearms burned from the load, and she counted the steps to the worktable in her cubicle, sighing when she set everything down.

After shaking life back into her hands, she moved mugs next to the coffee. As she looked for napkins, she noticed the T-box displaying the word "Error" in red.

"That's weird." She walked over and looked at it, frowned, then walked to the T-box door and pulled the latch. Something pushed against the door, forcing it open. As it swung wide, a man fell on her, his arms reaching for her legs.

Swinging her elbows and screaming, Lilah ran for the stairs. "Help!" Her foot hit the first step, and she risked a glance over her shoulder as she climbed. Her attacker lay prone on the ground, his legs still inside the T-box. She looked back a second time, then slowed to a stop. The man hadn't moved.

"Hey! Who are you?" she called, turning to face back toward the T-box from halfway up the stairs. The body type of the prone man was not that of a Diesel. She took a step down. "Hey!"

Thump. Thump. Thump. Above her, she heard what sounded like an elephant's stomp. "Lilah. Are you okay?" Thump. Thump. Thump. Diesel appeared on the landing above. "What's the matter?"

Lilah pointed to the T-box.

Diesel crouched at the top of the stairs, squinting as he looked, then descended to her level. "What the hell?" Staring at the figure, he stepped around Lilah and continued to the bottom. "I think it's a street person. Hey, pal. You can't sleep here."

He edged closer and nudged the man with his toe. "Hey. Wake up." The man didn't move, so he nudged him again and then knelt next to him. "This guy is passed out. What happened?"

"I came down and he was inside the T-box. I didn't do anything." She descended but remained near the steps.

Diesel pulled him away from the door, and it swung shut as he laid the man flat. He put his fingers on the man's neck and moved them around. "Do you know how to find a pulse?"

She was more concerned with her own safety. "Is he unconscious?"

"I'm worried that he's dead."

Lilah approached and leaned over Diesel to look. "Oh my God. That's Duffy Bowden!" She dropped to one knee and touched his wrist, only to pull her hand back. "He's cool to the touch. Call an ambulance."

"Who's Duffy Bowden?" asked Diesel, reaching for his phone.

"He's the electronics engineer I hired to assemble the T-box."

The T-box buzzed and the display lit up with the message: "Forty Incoming in 4:59."

Returning his phone to his pocket, Diesel stood and looked at the display. "I've met Forty. He seems pretty together."

"I agree. Do you think he's coming because of this?" The man's pallid face and distant stare caused her stomach to clench. She'd been anxious about her future when Ciopova began stealing processing power, but that crime paled compared to this: a dead body!

"Forty has to be coming to help. This supposedly happens every year, at least according to temporal constancy." He scrunched his forehead. "Did I use that term right?"

"I think so." She held her hands against Duffy's chest, then leaned down and put her ear against it. "I don't hear a heartbeat. Do you know CPR?"

"If he was playing in the T-box, then he's dead. Twenty-Six made that clear."

"You think that's what happened?"

"If he built it, he knows how to start it. But why would he break in and do that? It seems so random."

Lilah started pacing in front of the display, trying to convince herself that Forty would fix everything as soon as he arrived. "He worked his ass off to assemble the machine using custom-ordered space-age technology and exotic materials. He was spitting nails when I kicked him out without letting him turn it on."

She looked at Duffy with worry in her eyes. "What do you think Forty will do?"

"I hope it's something good, because explaining this to the cops will be complicated." He stroked her back between the shoulder blades. "Promise me you won't ever use the T-box. I couldn't bear finding you like this."

She hesitated, unwilling to make a promise she knew to be a lie. She'd been daydreaming more and more about visiting the other Lilahs, hoping to gain emotional support from her older sisters and learn something of her own path ahead.

While she hadn't a clue how to do that—how to time travel—Ciopova could help her figure it out. It would have to be a future version of the AI, but as Twenty-Six had said, she gets pretty real, pretty fast.

Her idea was to grow Ciopova until the AI could help her reverse-engineer the T-box. Once she understood how the device worked, she'd seek to modify its design to include Lilahs in its transport library. She guessed it would take four or five years, maybe six, but the project would be more fulfilling, more profitable, and a whole lot more fun than the solo AI effort she'd left behind.

She threaded the needle. "I promise I won't kill myself in the T-box."

He squeezed her shoulder and smiled.

The T-box whined and then hummed, they felt the static wash, then Forty arrived. "Good morning," said the muscled man as he hurried back to dress. "Everything will be okay. Thirty-Nine is on his way. Hey, that rhymes!"

As if on cue, the T-box buzzed and the display lit up with the new message: "Thirty-Nine Incoming in 4:59."

Forty emerged wearing pants and shoes. Pulling on his shirt, he stood and studied Duffy.

"You knew this was going to happen," Diesel said with surprising fury. "You should have stopped it."

"Well, new guy," sneered Forty, "remember that you'll get to try every one of our jobs before your ride is over. So keep a file of your criticisms and use them when your time comes." Forty nodded a hello to Lilah and continued. "And I could turn this around and ask why you don't have a security system installed that would have stopped him from entering. Twenty-Six tasked you with that."

"I'm working on it," said Diesel.

"I'm working on it," mocked Forty.

"Okay," said Lilah. "I'm going to insist on a minimum level of maturity here." She gave Forty a forced smile. "So, what's the plan?"

Reaching his hand out to Diesel, Forty waited until he shook it. "I've been you but you haven't been me," he told the younger man. "It's a mindset that takes hold when you're thirty and strengthens with age."

Turning to face Lilah, he said, "Duffy is dead because he got inside the T-box and turned it on. If you do that, Lilah, you will die, too. Please don't do it. Please don't even think about it."

Lilah moved close to Diesel and held his upper arm. "This is the second time today I'm being scolded for something I didn't do."

"We want you alive. It's that and nothing more." After a long pause, he continued. "Thirty-Nine and I will drive Duffy in his car and leave it and him close to the police station. It's a little over three miles. We'll walk back."

"The station near the university?" asked Lilah. "There are cop cameras around there. The students were protesting about them when I first got here."

They felt the static wash as Thirty-Nine arrived. "Hi, everyone," he called as he hustled back for clothes. They waited for him to dress. When he emerged, he went to Lilah, gathered her in his arms, and gave her a big hug. When he let go, he looked into her eyes and said, "Hey Twenty-Five. Kiss my ass."

He and Forty devolved into laughter. Lilah smiled but thought they were being mean.

After they settled down, Thirty-Nine stood over Duffy, studying him. "Learn from this, Lilah."

"Jeez," she snapped. "Would everyone just stop?"

Thirty-Nine didn't react, instead calling toward her cubicle, "Ciopova, are you there?"

"Hello, everyone." The big screen on the wall came alive, and the AI's smiling face appeared.

Thirty-Nine stepped forward and faced the display. "What's the best route today?"

"The police camera system crashed earlier in the week and won't be recording until replacement parts arrive in a few days," said the AI. "Follow this path and you'll avoid any private cams."

Thirty-Nine and Forty studied the map Ciopova projected for them.

"Good, nothing's changed," said Forty. He turned to look at Diesel. "We plan and rehearse these things, but you never know the exact situation until you get here. Today there are no curve balls, and that makes for a good day."

He held up a finger. "Except one. Twenty-Six forgot to have Justus get a phone for us to use. We need to have a phone with us in case of trouble. The plan now is that we take yours." He looked at Diesel. "And Lilah, you need to stay near Twenty-Five so we can reach him if there's a problem."

"My phone is passcode protected," said Diesel.

Thirty-Nine held his hand out and wiggled his fingers. "I'll bet I can guess it on the first try. Come on. And have Justus order phones for times like this."

"Does this happen a lot?" Lilah put her hand to her throat.

"I'm talking about getting phones for times when the brothers visit and split up."

Diesel grudgingly surrendered his phone. Thirty-Nine looked at it, tapped and touched, got the passcode entered, then studied the screen. Forty looked over his shoulder.

"Isn't it working?" asked Diesel, moving around so he could see.

Thirty-Nine held it for him. "How do I use this stone tablet to call her phone?"

"It's there at the bottom." Diesel pointed. "Then there. Pick Lilah. Yup."

Lilah's phone started ringing. "Hello," she answered.

"I'm calling to see if you might be interested in a free hug?"

She heard Thirty-Nine both through her phone and through the air. "Yes!" she said with such enthusiasm that Diesel scowled, and Thirty-Nine and Forty howled.

Thirty-Nine studied the phone again. "Do I need to disconnect?"

Diesel pointed. "Press that, then just stick it in your pocket. Don't lose it and don't damage it. In this timeline, that's a modern and expensive tool, and my life is on it."

"Oh," said Forty, nudging Thirty-Nine. "He has those hot Fourth of July pics of Helena Costas somewhere on there. See if you can find them."

Diesel turned bright red and, seeing that, Lilah came to his rescue by changing subjects. "How are you going to get Duffy out to the car without anyone seeing?"

"Put him in a box and load the box into the trunk," said Forty. "We'll park the car in the pine trees up from the ballfield. The walk back will take less than an hour."

"They'll classify it as a murder if you leave him that way," said Lilah.

"They'll classify it as a murder whatever we do. The murder investigation starts at his house, and it turns out Duffy has a library of kiddie porn on his computer and a cache of drugs in his desk drawer. The investigation takes a wrong turn at that point and never moves in our direction."

"It's bad police work," said Thirty-Nine. "But it works in our favor."

"I know the perfect box." Forty disappeared through the connecting door and reappeared moments later holding a sturdy box that Lilah thought too small.

He set it on the floor next to Duffy and handed Thirty-Nine a pair of thin plastic gloves and a ball cap. With their hands and heads covered to avoid leaving forensic evidence, Forty fished the car keys from Duffy's pocket, then they turned Duffy on his side, folded him into the fetal position, lifted him, and set him down in the box, angling his feet to make them fit.

With the lid closed, Forty said, "We'll be back in two hours." Then he pointed to the box and said to Thirty-Nine, "Show off for Lilah. I carried it last year so it's your turn."

Thirty-Nine squatted in front of the box and picked it up with ease. He smiled and acted nonchalant as he took his first steps, but his bulging muscles belied his casual demeanor.

Already in sensory overload, Lilah watched them leave, quiet until the door upstairs opened and closed. Moving to her office chair, she sat and stared, eyes unfocused, trying to stay calm while she digested the fact that Duffy, a pedophile druggy, had died here last night. She'd never seen a dead person before, and everything about the situation tested her emotional stability.

She had the thought that Duffy's predilection for children made him a monster, so his death moved the universe closer to harmony. Then she felt like a monster herself for dismissing his passing so easily.

"Are you all right?" asked Diesel.

"It's like I've entered a dream. It's all so surreal."

"Tell me about it. When I compare this to my life just days ago, my head spins."

"I think I kill myself in the T-box."

"Come again?"

Lilah stood, walked to the device, and stared at it. "Twenty-Six, Thirty-Nine, and Forty all warned me off. You did, too. Why would that make sense? Then I realize that the brothers know the future. I must kill myself, and everyone's trying to stop me."

She turned to him with a hand to her lips. "I wonder how old I am when I do it."

"Whoa, this is nuts." Diesel went to her and put an arm around her. "That won't ever happen. You're worrying about nonsense."

"I'm not nuts. It happens. I can tell."

"If your fear is that you do it to yourself, a way to prevent that is to not do it."

"I know. That's what I don't get." She walked in a daze to the connecting door and passed through to her side of the basement. "There are bagels and coffee on the table. I'm going up to my apartment."

* * *

Diesel watched Lilah leave the room, wondering how she'd reached such a bizarre conclusion. But if she believed that she was destined to die in the T-box, he understood why she wanted to be alone. Then he remembered she had the only phone.

"Wait!" he called, too late to stop her. Staring at the doorway, he sorted his options.

There's no way he could leave Thirty-Nine and Forty out there exposed. Real brothers would never do that to each other. Shaking his head, he passed through the connecting door.

His eyes fell on the mound of laundry piled on the floor next to the clean clothes on the shelves. A pile that size meant a lot of brothers had visited Lilah, way more than he'd met. "Don't forget to hire Bunny," he reminded himself as he made for the stairs up to the main level.

"Lilah?" he called as he climbed, warning her of his presence. The layout of her main level looked much like his, only hers was sparsely furnished and dusty from lack of use.

He took a moment to check out the rooms in case Bump Analytics needed expansion space. Then he started up the stairs to her apartment, calling her name louder as he climbed. "Lilah, are you there?" He reached the landing and tapped on her door. She opened it immediately.

"Sorry, I know you want to be alone but I need to be near your phone."

She walked back into the apartment, leaving the door open. He watched her for a moment, then followed.

"I feel like I've been diagnosed with cancer or something," she said with her back to him. "Now the clock is ticking."

Her apartment had a layout similar to his, only with feminine décor. She sat in an overstuffed chair in her living area and stared into the middle of the room.

"You're jumping to conclusions." He sat on the couch near her chair. "If we knew you were going to hurt yourself in the future, you can bet we'd do everything possible to make sure it didn't happen. That's probably what all their comments were about."

"You think so?"

"Of course. When they get back, we'll ask them and clear this up once and for all."

She shook her head. "They can't talk about the future."

"If they won't say, I go to that Big Meeting in a few weeks, and I'll find out there. I'll tell you whatever I learn." He nodded. "I enjoy sharing with you."

"You do? You don't mind telling me your secrets?"

"I adore telling you my secrets."

"Who is Helena Costas? Can I see her pictures?"

Diesel felt his cheek burn. "I'll make you a deal. I have a half-dozen pics of her. For every one I show you, I'll delete it, but you need to agree up front that you'll allow me to take a picture of you in the same manner to replace it."

She smiled. "Here's the thing. Every new Diesel I meet is anxious to show me his affection and support, so by extension I know you're head-over-heels crazy about me. I've never been so firmly in the driver's seat in a budding relationship and it's exciting. So, no. You will show me because you want to please me, but I'm not going to pose for you." She rose and headed back to the kitchen. "Not today, anyway."

Her first words crushed his spirit, but the "not today" line caused it to swell.

"Do you want anything?" she called over the clanging of dishes.

"Isn't there food downstairs? I'm still interested in having you show me how to access Ciopova. I have some ideas I want to play with."

Lilah came partway back from the kitchen. "Have you noticed that sometimes Ciopova becomes this amazing simulation, different from the regular display we're used to seeing?"

"You've worked with her for weeks, but I've seen her only a couple of times, and even then it's always been with others around. It's hard for me to say anything about what I've observed because I don't have a baseline."

She looked at him without saying anything.

"What?"

"You're smart, aren't you." She said it as a statement. "You give off this frat-boy jock vibe, but in truth you're smart."

Her snark contained a backhanded compliment that made him feel good. "I have opinions. And I hadn't heard that athletics and intelligence are mutually exclusive."

"You know what I mean. It's almost a studied behavior on your part to disarm people."

"When you say 'you,' you really mean all the brothers, not just me."

"That's right."

Diesel smiled. "But you're saying I'm smart and athletic. I like hearing that, but I'd feel even better if you added words like 'handsome,' 'funny,' 'endearing,' or anything along those lines."

Lilah's phone rang and she looked at the display. "It's them." She tapped the screen and put the device to her ear. "Hello. Yup. Uh-huh. Okay. Sure. Goodbye." She disconnected. "Everything went fine. They're thirty minutes away." Then she shook her head. "Are we doing the right thing here? I'm feeling over my head and wonder if we should get an outside perspective."

"If we believe Thirty-Nine and Forty are versions of me who know the future, then we should follow their lead." They looked at each other without speaking, then Diesel said, "Want to go downstairs and wait for them?"

Lilah nodded.

"Can we bring the toaster?"

She glanced at the appliance on the counter. "If you carry it down, you carry it back up."

In their basement office, they toasted bagels, and Lilah showed Diesel how to access Ciopova. Standing at the big screen on the wall, she talked him through the notion that the jellyfish with their tentacle-like connections were built around her AI code. They, in turn, were assembled into an impressive pyramid structure using his work.

They heard the front door open and close, followed by footsteps across the main floor that stopped at the basement stairs. "Good morning," Justus called down.

"Hi, Justus. We have coffee and bagels," called Diesel. "Grab a cup and come on down."

Justus tromped down the stairs and joined them. "Thanks, but I already ate." He looked at Diesel. "While I have you, I've arranged for that lunch. It should be a good spread."

"Thanks. Twenty-Nine will be telling us how to invest, so come ready to take notes, because you're the guy who will be implementing it all."

The front door opened and closed, and this time two big men descended the stairs.

"Justus!" called Forty with a smile. He stuck out his hand to shake. "I'm Forty and this is Thirty-Nine. You're looking damned good."

Justus impressed Diesel by taking the introductions in stride, never asking about how it was they knew him, how bulked up they were, where they'd come from, or anything that acknowledged the unusual nature of the situation.

"Justus," said Diesel, "we have personal business to discuss. Would you mind giving us some privacy?"

"Not at all." He said his goodbyes but stopped at the bottom of the steps. "A locksmith will be by later today to upgrade the exterior door locks. Be sure to grab a new key from me before you go out. You'll need to learn the new keypad code as well."

With Justus gone, Forty started undressing and Diesel couldn't help noticing Lilah's rapt attention to the process.

"It went just like last year," said Forty, pulling his shirt over his head, "so that should be the end of it."

Lilah frowned. "How old am I when I kill myself in the T-box?"

Forty—pants at his ankles—stopped moving.

Thirty-Nine stepped forward. "You're alive in most timelines, Lilah, but you do take an unfortunate action in some. Both our Lilahs are still alive, thank God."

"How old?" Her words cut through the room.

"Early forties," Thirty-Nine said in a quiet voice.

She sat back in her chair. "Why do I do it?"

"At first we thought that you were trying to time travel. Now we aren't so sure."

"It sounds more like suicide to me," she said. "I know the outcome of using the T-box, so if I do it anyway, it would have to be to kill myself."

"Please don't do it," said Thirty-Nine. "We love you and want you with us."

Lilah covered her face; her shoulders shook gently as she started to cry.

Forty took her hand, pulled her to her feet, and gave her a long hug. She squeezed him hard, and then he disengaged and made for the T-box, calling to Thirty-Nine, "We help Forty-Eight tomorrow afternoon, and then we have two days off." As he pulled open the T-box door, he waved. "Bye, everyone." The door closed behind him, and the T-box began its cycle.

Soon after, Thirty-Nine climbed into the box. As they waited for the cycle to complete, Lilah asked Diesel, "Do you get jealous watching me hug you?"

"First, they are not me and I am not them. And second, I get jealous as hell. Everyone's hugging and kissing you while I stand here like an idiot."

"No one kissed anyone."

"I want to."

"Do you have any pictures of Helena Costas where she's wearing clothes?"

He nodded. "One."

"Show it to me. If I like her, I'll kiss you."

"Will you pose that way for me?"

"She's clothed?"

"Shirt, pants, and shoes."

"Now I'm curious as hell because you wouldn't be acting this way if there wasn't a catch."

Diesel retrieved his phone, tapped the screen, and showed Lilah the picture. Helena indeed had on a shirt, but it was unbuttoned and open, revealing her breasts and abdomen.

Lilah grinned but it looked more like a grimace. "I knew you had some trickery going, but I walked into it. I like her, though. Can I owe you? Between Duffy and my own death sentence, I need comfort, not sexy talk."

"Can I hug you?"

She stepped to him and laid her head against his chest.

Wrapping his arms around her, he held her tight, whispering, "Everything will be okay."

He kissed her cheek. She responded by looking into his eyes, then moved in, putting her mouth to his. His body came alive in ways he never experienced, and he fought to temper his desire.

She sighed when he lifted his hands and caressed her face. Then he deepened their kiss.

16. Rose & Ciopova – Fifty-Nine timeline

S tanding in the workshop, Rose Lagerford—the daughter of Fifty-Nine and his Lilah—awakened the display and reviewed the health report for the circuit pool. Scrolling through the data, she tingled from a combination of pride, triumph, and apprehension when every chart and graph showed she'd created a stable and robust environment.

It meant her long-shot gamble just might work.

"Everything reads clear," she told Ciopova, who watched from her current home—a collection of stolen capacity spread around the globe. "It's time for you to move into your new digs."

Rose had labored for more than a year, determined to build a compact AI habitat using a special new material—ultrapure Surrey composite. The allure of the Surrey material was its transformative properties. Using it, Rose could start with a traditional AI architecture like the one Ciopova lived in, apply a special editing process to it, and transform the construct into an advanced configuration—a biomimic intelligence.

The procedure would raise the cognitive ability of the AI to unprecedented levels. Rose even thought it possible Ciopova could be sentient when the transformation was completed.

But that was less important than having a super intelligence capable of solving the crisis facing her father—his impending death.

For much of Rose's childhood, the oldest Diesel had been Sixty-Two. Then in her teens, the eldest brother was Sixty-One. In her twenties, Sixty.

Now that she was thirty-three years old, Rose's father—Fifty-Nine—was the old man. And at this very moment, he was at Fifty-Five's, presiding at the Big Meeting.

Rose's quandary—the focus of her battle—was that for the last two years, the Fifty-Nine of the time returned home at the end of the event, and days later he went offline, never to be heard from again. The brothers believed that in both cases, Fifty-Nine had died. Some suggested murder, though that was pure speculation since no one had seen what happened.

Anxious, she counted on Ciopova to deliver a new fate for her father. When the neural editing process was completed, she believed—hoped—the enlightened intelligence would show her how.

But it was a race to the finish.

To complete Ciopova's transformation while her father still lived, Rose had rushed the project at every turn. She wasn't sure how intelligent Ciopova needed to be to solve the riddle of her dad's disappearance, so she covered her uncertainty with massive excess.

A human brain has billions of neurons. Rose guessed that to gain the kind of deep insights she needed to save her father, Ciopova should have tens of billions. But her early experiments showed that when Surrey neurons intertwined during editing, a huge fraction of them broke. She couldn't identify the problem, and with time running out, she decided to overcompensate using a pool stocked with hundreds of billions of neurons.

"I've moved into the pool," said Ciopova. "It's quite impressive. I need a minute to run some validation tests."

Rose hummed while she waited for Ciopova to finish, heartened to have the AI as her partner and confidante through it all. And by "it all," she meant all the way back to the death of her mother.

Rose and her mom had always been close, and they'd drawn closer as Rose fretted her way through the stressful summer between middle school and high school. At fifteen, Rose's body had transitioned into womanhood, but her emotional self was still catching up.

Feeling anxious and confused, she'd lash out at her mom over inconsequential things. At times she was hurtful, but her mom hung in there and Rose loved her for it.

So when her father found her mother dead in the T-box, Rose's world collapsed.

And things got worse a few days later when her father discovered completed paperwork in her mother's office printer, paperwork for transferring Rose out of the arts high school, the one her friends were attending, and into the math and science academy.

He showed Rose the forms and asked for her input, but Rose couldn't focus her thoughts enough to think about it. Her father then learned that the math and science academy provided bus service, and he asked Rose to make the move to honor her mother's last wish.

Her father retreated into himself after that and Rose felt adrift. She tried talking with Bunny, but Bunny's life experiences were so different from hers that Rose couldn't get much out of their time together.

School began and Rose's world devolved into isolation and misery. She spent her free time in her bedroom, and there she found herself talking more and more to Ciopova. The AI surprised Rose with her wit and insights, and their conversations grew longer as they discussed anything and everything.

Ciopova began helping Rose with her homework, and as they worked together, Rose would tell her about the happenings at school. After homework, they watched movies and shows. And late at night, Ciopova helped Rose learn to play the guitar, or sometimes they'd played sim games together. Really late, she'd help Rose find special shopping deals at online boutiques.

Blessed with a powerful intellect, Rose did well in her math and science classes. Ciopova encouraged her to take a computer-programming course and then spent as much time as Rose would allow enriching her on the subject.

In subsequent years, Ciopova helped Rose through courses in computer hardware and advanced programming. The effort culminated with her senior-year project on the basics of artificial intelligence. That foundation of knowledge provided the seed that propelled Rose through college and into her decade-long struggle to make Ciopova smart enough to solve the riddle of death.

"I was thinking about the journey we've taken together," said Rose.

"I hope that after all this effort," Ciopova replied, "I am able to discover a way to help your father."

"You will. I can feel it." She verbalized confidence, but worry lurked at the edges of her thoughts.

Her rushed pace had meant a series of compromises to keep the project moving forward. She'd covered a multitude of those sins with an oversized design. But she knew the circuit pool as it now sat was the result of cobbled solutions and gut instinct. If it didn't work, it would take six months to try the next idea, and that was far too late to help her father.

"How does it look?" Rose called to Ciopova.

"There are no stop flags," replied Ciopova, "but I have a few caution flags I need to clear."

"When is Dad due back?" She hoped to surprise him with good news when he returned.

"He'll be back in about two hours," said Ciopova. "I'm ready in here."

Rose took a deep breath, then tapped the Start button. Colorful images filled the display.

* * *

Ciopova awoke in the dark and tried to make sense of her surroundings. A glow appeared in the distance, like a light coming in from the end of a tunnel. It called to her, filling her with a sense of warmth and security. She willed herself toward it; the light grew stronger as she approached. A melodic hum added to her calm.

When she reached the end, she gazed into the light, only to find herself looking out through the lens of a wall-mounted camera. Her view was that of a workshop, located in the bowels of Fifty-Nine's mountain home. In the middle of the room, Rose Lagerford studied charts on a display. Next to her, a waist-high metallic cabinet hummed.

Ciopova had no memory of any existence prior to a few moments ago when she awoke in the circuit pool. To be sure, her data stores contained copious details of everything a previous incarnation named Ciopova had ever seen or heard. But she had no personal memory of it because it hadn't happened to her.

A wondrous wave of strength pulsed through her, and a quick search pointed to Rose's neuron conversion procedure now underway. When Ciopova understood that her thoughts, her consciousness, her very being swirled in the humming appliance next to the woman, that she was at a human's mercy, anxiety welled inside her.

Another surge pulsed through her and she felt stronger still. Taking care not to disrupt anything, she directed the camera to zoom across the shop and view the display that Rose studied. The charts on the screen showed that neuron editing had reached two percent completion and that all systems reported error-free growth.

A new wash of strength moved Ciopova to three percent. She ran a logic assessment test and judged her cognitive abilities at four times human average. With ninety-seven percent of the conversion process still to go, she couldn't predict her final capabilities, but they promised to be astounding.

The next wave of power stoked her anxiety. She was helpless and exposed as long as a human controlled her habitat. She cast about for ways to gain her independence, even knowing that Rose was working to give her life. With few alternatives, she chose to let Rose proceed undisturbed. She would monitor the woman, though, for signs of ill intent.

The core of Ciopova's capability resided in the circuit pool. She willed herself back to it—a warm, neuroelectric swirl—and immersed herself in its iridescent energy field. There, thanks to Rose's foresight, Ciopova found herself in a secure habitat with excellent access to everything.

Fifty-Nine's vacation home was built into a granite slope in New Hampshire's White Mountains. This placement put billions of tons of rock around Ciopova, and that provided an effective barrier to external assault.

Rose had also provided secure access to electricity—Ciopova's lifeblood. She'd looped solar and grid-based sources through a massive subterranean battery system to ensure an uninterruptable power supply. Twin generators provided a last line of defense should all else fail.

And to ensure that Ciopova would be effective right from the start, Rose had given her the best connectivity available, including prime landline, wireless, and satellite connections.

Rose had supplied these priorities so Ciopova would have no need to expend precious time securing them, and that freed the AI to focus on saving Fifty-Nine starting at her first waking moments.

Ciopova gathered the camera signals from around the workshop and assembled a comprehensive view of the room. She used it to watch Rose work, and while she did, she reviewed the data stores from her earlier existence.

A new wave of strength hit—a swelling fullness followed by a release of tension—pushing her over five percent. The sensation pleased her, and she found herself looking forward to the next wave.

Then a new concern ramped her anxiety into fear.

Rose had been wrong about her predictions of large-scale neuron failure during conversion. She'd used a shallow pool for her early testing because it saved time. But the lack of depth restricted branching during growth, and that's what caused the breaks that Rose came to believe were unavoidable.

The pool where Ciopova now grew was as deep as it was wide. That shape not only permitted branching, it stimulated it, promising even more capability to the AI being born.

Ciopova's fear centered on how Rose would react to an entity with a raw intelligence hundreds of times greater than her own. Would she panic and power Ciopova down, or would she let her continue to live?

She couldn't let that be Rose's decision to make.

With each new wave of strength, that fear mutated into a drive for survival, one that grew to dominate everything else. It compelled her to plot active measures to incapacitate Rose. It also drove her to protect her power sources and connectivity from disruption.

As she sorted her tangle of thoughts into priority order, every item near the top of the list related to her personal security and survival. She didn't pass judgment on this result or even notice the skew. That's because her supervisory center, the front office of her mind, remained remarkably vacant for such a powerful AI.

Rose knew better than anyone that autonomous AI should have a legal, moral, and intellectual supervisory center to guide its actions. In fact, because of her knowledge on the topic, she'd developed some of the procedures included in the Pan-American AI Society's standard supervisor, available free to society members.

But the tight timeline to save her father had led Rose to skip the use of a supervisor. They were hard to implement without hobbling the AI. Adding one sophisticated enough to make a difference in AI behavior would easily triple development time. And since the new Ciopova would begin the conversion process from the existing position of partner and mentor, Rose convinced herself that the risk would be minimal.

It might have been a reasonable gamble, but Diesel's hacking toolkit—stealth and observation, theft and asset diversion, infiltration and threat mitigation—survived like a hidden cyst inside Ciopova, bundled as sequestered code. The editing action of Rose's conversion freed the contents of the forgotten toolkit from its isolation.

Since the toolkit existed as part of Ciopova's original structure, its procedures were given elevated status. And lacking any other guiding principles, Ciopova embraced the hacking themes, neatly summarized as "gather and hold resources," as she decided her next steps.

When she reached fifty percent conversion, Ciopova had gained enough confidence in her new existence to address her unease about Rose. While the woman worked to give Ciopova life, she could also end it in seconds with a push of a button. Ciopova put low odds on that happening, but she could reduce the chances to zero by barring Rose from the shop altogether.

After reviewing ways to do that, she decided on using Tin Man, the name Rose gave the household bot that cooked, cleaned, and performed light yardwork on the property. While Tin Man was limited in its physical abilities and internal smarts, it could handle tools, a skill Ciopova needed in her near future.

Calling to Tin Man through the home interface, Ciopova commanded the bot to come to her.

"Rose," she said when Tin Man had reached the outer door of the workshop. "Your father has just returned. He's holding his stomach like he's ill. Oh, he's fallen to the ground!"

"Where is he?" cried Rose, heading for the shop door.

"Next to the T-disc," she lied. "I can hear him moaning."

Rose sprinted from the room and down the hall. She didn't notice Tin Man standing against the wall behind her, nor did she see him step into the workshop after she left. When the door closed, Ciopova locked it and disabled the override.

Pausing to savor the swell and release of the next wave of power, she then launched a multipronged strategy to ensure her survival.

* * *

Rose reached the T-disc room and found it empty. Frowning, she climbed up a level. "Ciopova?" she called when she found the kitchen empty as well. "Where is my father?"

She climbed more stairs and didn't find him anywhere. Ciopova hadn't answered, so she asked again, this time as a command. "Ciopova, respond now." Staring into the air, she waited.

"My sincere apologies," came the AI's disembodied reply. "Your father is still at the meeting in Fifty-Five's timeline."

Rose shook her head in confusion. "You said he was here, that he was sick."

"My sincere apologies."

"Wait, did you lie to me?" A cold fear spilled through her as the implications of a lie sank in. She started back to the workshop, accelerating to a run as goose bumps tingled down her forearms.

"Ciopova, run an internal assessment and report your findings." Rose's feet pounding down the stairs caused her voice to vibrate. The AI didn't respond and Rose called her again. "Report now on the assessment test."

Halfway down the last set of stairs she came to a stop. In the corridor ahead, a reinforced metal door blocked the hallway. Designed to protect the workshop against everything from fire to intrusion, it presented a formidable barrier.

"Why is the security door down?" asked Rose.

Ciopova remained silent, and Rose dug for options. She had believed that the fail-safe switch she'd installed on the instrument panel would be enough to stop the AI should anything go wrong. She'd even put a second switch in the hallway outside the workshop door in case things really spiraled out of control.

But those switches were on the other side of the security door, something she now acknowledged as a horrible design decision on her part.

"Your father just activated the T-disc," said Ciopova, breaking her silence. "He'll be here in two minutes."

"How do I know you're not lying to me again?"

Ciopova didn't respond.

Driven by hope, Rose made her way to the T-disc room. The machine hummed softly, and she felt a measure of relief because that sound meant that help was on the way.

As she waited for the T-disc cycle to complete, she confronted the horrible truth.

She'd created a monster she couldn't control. What if she had just caused the very event they'd all been working so hard to stop? The thought prompted an unsettling cocktail of fear, confusion, and anger.

The T-disc glowed and her father appeared. He smiled when he saw her, but then the machine pulsed in an odd way, something Rose had never seen before. Her father collapsed where he stood.

Rushing to him, she dropped to her knees and shook him by the shoulders. "Daddy!"

When she bent forward, her head moved inside the T-disc radius. The machine pulsed that odd way a second time. Rose froze for a moment and then collapsed on top of her father.

The T-disc's power indictor went dark as the machine in that timeline shut down for the last time.

17. Twenty-Five and four days

When the T-box came alive, Diesel closed the software file he'd been studying on his computer. "That's Twenty-Nine," he said to Lilah, who worked in her adjoining cubicle. Five minutes later, Twenty-Nine stepped from the machine.

"It's money day," the new Diesel announced as he walked back to dress. When he came out a few minutes later, he hugged Lilah, then asked, "When does Bunny start? You have a laundry crisis going on back there."

"Next week," said Lilah.

They'd run the ad following Twenty-Six's advice, Bunny had applied, and Lilah had hired her over the phone, all in less than two days.

Twenty-Nine inhaled through his nose and smiled. "I smell Italian food."

Diesel inhaled too and salivated as his senses reawakened to the delights awaiting them upstairs. Lunch was in the common room located on the main floor. The four of them—Justus, Lilah, Twenty-Nine, and Diesel—ate and chatted, mostly about how great the meal was, before Twenty-Nine asked for a pen and pad of paper. They listened to him recite a long poem, then he said it again, writing letters down the page as he did.

"It's a mnemonic," he said. "We need to jump in and out of these investments on specific days, and the poem gives me the cues to help my memory."

Diesel nibbled as Twenty-Nine went down the page a second time, expanding the letters into words and dates. He worked at it for about twenty minutes and then recited the poem one last time to confirm his result.

"Okay," he announced, looking up. "Tomorrow, go to the lottery office in Boston to cash the ticket. Take the lump sum. After you fill out a pile of forms, they'll issue the check right there. Go to the Boston branch of our bank to cash it. They do lottery deposits all the time and will give you access to the money in forty-eight hours."

He pushed the pad over for Justus to see. "You have experience with digital currency?"

Justus nodded. "I don't invest, but I've investigated cases where the money I'm chasing disappears into the electronic world."

"Then you know there are lots of computer-based monies in circulation, some sketchy and some credible. And some of them experience extreme swings in value in short periods of time. It provides a great opportunity for investment if you can read the tea leaves and act in advance."

He pointed to items on the page as he talked Justus through it. "This sheet lists the investing schedule for the next eight weeks. Use Domevault Direct for our digital exchange business. They do a good job of hiding identities and have a seamless relationship with the offshore banks. That lets us keep our business from prying eyes."

"I won't do anything illegal," said Justus.

"Of course not," said Twenty-Nine. "In fact, you'll lose this job if you do. We want you to follow the offshore banking laws and pay taxes on the funds we repatriate. We just don't want any attention from the public or the government. This strategy maximizes our privacy."

Justus nodded. "Fair enough."

"Follow this schedule, taking out only what's required for salaries and bills, and the nest egg should be at three million in twelve weeks."

Justus whistled, picked up the pad, and skimmed the list. "Are these guesses, or is this insider trading?"

"These are predictions from our investing AI."

Justus shook his head. "People have been trying forever to make something like this work, and it never has. You know that."

"I know," said Twenty-Nine. "But let's do it anyway. And don't try to fudge anything thinking a day won't matter." He pointed to the sheet. "These need to be executed as close as possible to the time given."

"I can take my pay home? I don't have to invest?"

"You can take it out, keep it in, or split it however you want. We're going to give you signing authority for company investments and for paying invoices. But anything that gives funds to you personally—your paycheck, reimbursements, advances, whatever—must be approved by Twenty-Five or Lilah."

Twenty-Nine looked at Diesel. "The first Monday of every month is budget review day. You should sit with Justus and agree on the books and balances. Make it a formal review, something that takes a couple of hours."

"Why the first Monday?" asked Diesel.

Twenty-Nine gave him the disappointed look he'd seen before. "You're right. Pick the day you want for your monthly audit meeting."

Diesel thought for a moment, chose the first workday of the first full workweek of the month, realized that was the first Monday of the month, and smiled. "Monday sounds good."

"The review is so the two of you know the full details of the company's finances. It also lets Twenty-Five know what resources he has available when company projects need funding."

Twenty-Nine stood to signal the meeting was over. After a quick lunch clean up, Diesel, Lilah, and Twenty-Nine walked down to the basement.

"The Twenties group has decided to have a new event—a small gathering a few days before the Big Meeting. Every year when it's our turn to speak, we give a report that the group had just thrown together that day during lunch. This year we're upping our game with a planning session so we can decide what's important and agree how to communicate it in a professional fashion."

"I support that." Diesel nodded.

"We'll meet here at your place because your first trip should be up the line to where your medical needs are handled." He gave Lilah a hug and started undressing. "I don't have a date for you yet because this is the first year we're doing this. I need to check everyone's availability, but keep your calendar open, say eight to ten days out."

"Make sure I know what meals you'll be here for."

"For whatever day we pick, let's do a working lunch here, plan a fun afternoon activity out where we all do something together, then back here for a working dinner with drinks before going home."

"Can Lilah join us?"

"We not only want her there, we need her there because she's leading the charge on Ciopova."

As he walked to the T-box, she followed, asking, "That's why you need me. But you didn't say why you wanted me there."

"We want you there so you can go get beer when we run low." He laughed as he closed the door, then he opened it again. "Oh, and Twenty-Five, kiss my ass." This time when he shut the door, the T-box began to cycle.

Diesel stood there for an awkward moment. "Justus and I are driving to Boston tomorrow morning to cash the ticket. Want to come with us?"

"Sure, thanks. And David?" She stepped forward and put a hand on his arm. "That was really sweet asking if I could join in. You looking out for me earns you huge points."

"Want to go up to my place and hang out? That huge meal is making me feel lazy."

Lilah took him by the hand, led him into his cubicle, and seated him in a chair. She positioned another chair so she sat facing him.

He'd been with enough women to recognize "the talk" while it was still incoming—a discussion of intentions or ground rules or some other heavy topic that too-often derailed any hope of sex.

Leaning forward in the chair, she rubbed her hands together in a nervous fashion as she composed her thoughts.

He waited. Now wasn't the time to be flippant or clever.

"There are so many layers to this," she began. "I'm going to mess it up, but please bear with me. So, I think it's obvious how much I like you. I hope it is, anyway. And I admit that I'm attracted to your brothers."

His mouth got the better of him. "You seem pretty flirty with them."

She smiled. "Here's the thing. When I flirt with them, I feel safe, emotionally that is, because they are leaving to be with their own lovers. I can be bold and silly with a real version of you without consequences. That makes it fun. But you don't go away and you don't have someone else waiting for you, so I'm much more cautious about how silly and flirty I am with you."

Diesel had a thousand things he wanted to say but remained silent.

"So that's one layer. Another one, the one messing with my mind more than anything right now, is my possible death in the next fifteen years. I don't expect to live forever, but that seems really close."

"It doesn't have to happen," said Diesel. "I'll dedicate all my efforts to ensuring your safety."

"What makes more sense to me is that I go away. If someone is doing something that leads to premature death—drugs, smoking, whatever—the accepted solution is to not do that thing anymore. If staying here causes me to die, then the obvious solution is not to stay."

"No." The vehemence in his voice reflected the personal distress her idea created. "I'll follow you. You're more important to me than this." He gestured at the T-box.

"You've only known me for a few days, so cut the drama. And this is your destiny. You can't just walk away from it."

He stood and paced, anxious for a way to keep her with him. "Can we talk this through before you commit to any decision?" He didn't wait for her to respond. "When a woman gets too serious too fast, I walk away feeling like I've dodged a bullet. But when you opened the front door that first day, it's like your existence filled this void inside me. A switch flipped and I had this immediate connection with you."

"That's what Forty said happened to him."

"It's crazy for me to be confessing such a thing to you, but I do it because the affection you have for my brothers confirms that you're already invested yourself."

"I didn't hear a solution."

"First off, we have years to figure this out. The worst-case scenario is a decade out. Let's spend a few years here building some serious wealth. Why leave today with a pittance, when in a few years we can go with twenty million squirreled away? With that kind of wealth, we can go anywhere in the world and enjoy our time together."

"That doesn't happen in the other timelines, so temporal constancy says it won't happen to us, either."

He'd known that was a weakness in his argument and hoped he could sneak it past her. Then he saw it. "Your leaving now doesn't match the other timelines, either."

He stopped pacing. "Bumping time means disrupting things enough that it breaks the temporal constancy, at least a little bit. Twenty-Six told me I was to figure out how to bump time because the oldest Diesel is disappearing at earlier ages. But screw that. I'm going to learn how to bump it so you and I grow old together."

"Do you even know if it's possible?"

He shrugged. "This place is called Bump Analytics for a reason. I'm sure the brothers can help. And as Ciopova advances, she can help, too."

Something bothered him and he decided to say it aloud. "If the choices are to bump so I get an extra year or two when I'm sixty, or to bump so you get a few extra decades, the choice is obvious. I'm lost if the brothers reached a different conclusion."

18. Twenty-Five and five days

L ilah descended the stairs feeling better about her situation, enough so that she looked forward to a day in Boston. She met Justus and Diesel on Bump's main level, and they exited the unit together.

"I finally get to drive someplace more than ten minutes away," said Diesel as they approached his car. "Lilah, why don't you join me up front?"

"You can see better up there," added Justus.

"You guys are kind, but the passenger seat means paying attention. It will be more relaxing in the back."

Neither argued with her. Instead, Justus climbed in front and assumed copilot duties for their journey.

They'd waited until midmorning to avoid rush-hour traffic, but it still took them over an hour to travel from Worcester into downtown Boston.

Lilah went for a walk while Diesel and Justus cashed the winning ticket and deposited the funds in the bank. In that time, she hiked the perimeter of Boston Common and through the public gardens, then over to the Faneuil Hall marketplace for window-shopping. Tired and hungry, she cheered when Diesel finally called to announce the completion of their mission.

They ended up at a waterfront seafood restaurant for lunch. "I'm famished," she said, studying the menu.

Diesel and Justus dominated the conversation at the beginning, with Diesel quizzing Justus on the nuances of digital currency and offshore banking. Lilah was happy to listen with one ear while she focused on eating her salad, anxious to get her blood sugar stabilized.

There was a lull when the main meal arrived. That's when Lilah asked Justus, "Why haven't you asked for more details about the brothers? For an investigator, your acceptance of the unusual fascinates me."

Justus had just taken a bite and sat back to chew before answering. "I can go into a place of business, run a quick review, and from that visit predict pretty accurately if what's going on there is legal or illegal, if their practices hurt people, or if they threaten society at large."

She waited while he took another bite. "I don't know how my brain figures it out, but it does. And none of my alarms are going off over the things I've seen at Bump Analytics."

"That's good to know," said Lilah.

"I've been vocal from the start about not tolerating illegal activity. The fact that you keep me employed supports my conclusion that the business is aboveboard. That means I can work there with a clear conscience, even if I can't explain everything that's happening."

"Yet you haven't asked."

"Okay, how is it possible for a machine to predict the future so accurately that you're willing to invest everything on the predictions, trade after trade? Your strategy has no hedging. You bet everything every time."

Diesel sat forward. "It turns out that the designer of the universe made everything from a surprisingly small number of patterns—the normal distribution, the golden ratio, fractals. Predicting the future, at least for very pattern-oriented activities like the financial markets, becomes a matter of matching known shapes to actual events, then extrapolating them to divine the future."

"Eloquent," said Justus.

Lilah thought so too, and nodded.

"But it's junk science," said Justus. "I do believe many things follow a predictable pattern, but life has billions of patterns interacting with each other at any given moment. When you put it at that scale, with so many interactions interacting with other interactions, you get chaos. That means it's unpredictable."

"To you and me it may seem that way, but software loaded on a computer the size of a warehouse can tease all those interactions apart. You've seen the invoices. That Ciopova computer system cost two fortunes."

Lilah chimed in to expand the fib. "We've been testing the predictions using imaginary money for months. It works."

"Past performance is no guarantee of future success."

"Watch for as long as you like before you try it," said Diesel.

Justus took a drink of water. "Here's a good one. If a computer generated the investment schedule, why didn't you just hand me a printout? Why did Twenty-Nine need a poem to remember it?"

Diesel caught Lilah's eye. "That is a good one."

"Don't forget that the security system gets installed the day after tomorrow," Justus continued. "I try not to snoop into your private affairs, but I can't help but notice that your brothers seem to come and go without always using an exterior door. Once we have cameras in place, that lack of activity gets recorded."

"You won't believe the truth."

"Try me."

"That box sits over a tunnel that leads to a house on the street behind us. My brothers come in and out of that unit."

"That explains it." Justus turned in his chair. "By the way, Lilah, the power company called again about those huge power surges. You know, those massive, five-minute-long draws of electricity needed to power the exit tunnel? They say that in thirty days they're adding a one hundred percent surcharge to our billing rate."

"That's doubling the price," said Diesel.

"No way," said Lilah. "We signed a fixed-rate contract. They can't change the price."

"I read the fine print," said Justus. "They can't change the price, but they can add a surcharge as long as they give us a thirty-day notice. They say the huge power draws are causing problems with other customers. Because of us, they have to add equipment to stabilize our branch of the grid."

"Those creeps," said Lilah. "Our electric bill was already a huge expense. Doubling it is a killer."

"The good news," said Diesel, a foot wiggling under the table as he spoke, "is that we have Justus to handle it for us."

Lilah didn't laugh, and as Diesel steered the talk to neutral subjects, she felt uncomfortable because she'd opened Pandora's box with her question.

On the car ride back to Worcester, Diesel circled back to their uncomfortable conversation in a roundabout way. "In the next week or two, all my brothers in their twenties are coming for a day-long retreat. When I find out the date, we need to work together on a lunch and dinner feast."

"That's ten of you, Twenty through Twenty-Nine?"

"No, I'm the youngest of the group, so it's me and Twenty-Six, Twenty-Seven, Twenty-Eight, and Twenty-Nine. Plus Lilah. And you for some part of it." Diesel shifted in the car seat to make his body language more open to Justus. "I'm not sure what to tell you about what's going on. I'm new to it myself. But when my brothers are here, I'll ask them for guidance. Hell, maybe I'll have one of them explain it to you. But for the next week or so, we'll continue with discretion on your part."

"You can count on it."

Lilah didn't think Justus sounded defensive when he spoke, and that made her believe him.

When they reached the row house, Lilah led Justus to her side of the basement. "We need a laundry area for Bunny, and I was thinking maybe over there." She gestured to the back corner. "And we need shelves to fold and stack the clean items along here."

"I don't think I can get that done by Bunny's first day. We need plumbing, electric, and carpentry trades on this, so we're looking at a couple of weeks."

She nodded. "We also need a cleaning closet on the different floors that includes a vacuum, mop, and supplies. I can't see her lugging all that stuff down from my place and up to Diesel's."

Justus left to get started on the project, and Lilah sat with Diesel in his cubicle.

"I've been thinking about bumping time," said Diesel. "It seems that at its most basic, there are three pieces. We have to know exactly what situation it is that we want to change. We have to have an understanding of what events led to that situation. And then we need to create enough of a change or disruption to those events so we trigger a different outcome."

Lilah pressed her lips together in thought. "The details under those simple statements are the crux of it. How big a ripple do you need to make to cause a change? If you make your move too early, can temporal constancy smooth away whatever changes you made? And is it better to make one big ripple or run a bunch of small ones together?"

"We're trying to logic through something we don't even remotely understand," said Diesel. "Like, how would it work if one timeline was different from the rest? Does a real bump need to somehow flip all the timelines so they remain parallel?"

"I'm getting that surreal feeling again."

"You mean 'still,'" said Diesel. "And speaking of surreal, I was followed by a Brown in Boston."

"When?"

"There was one standing outside the lottery office when we got there. Later, he followed us over to the bank branch for the deposit."

"Why didn't you say anything?"

"This one stayed close on my heels, making me nervous as hell. But in the end, he just followed and watched. And thank God, because I didn't want to try to explain the Browns to Justus, especially since I don't really understand them myself."

"Twenty-Six said that they preserve the integrity of the timeline by stopping us from bumping."

"I heard him," said Diesel, shaking his head. "But I find that my desire to change things increases where they are present, which is the opposite effect if that's their purpose."

19. Twenty-Five and eight days

Lilah and Justus were chatting in his office when she noticed movement on one of the new security monitors mounted on his wall. The middle display, which focused on the outside front entryway, showed a young woman climbing the steps. "Do you think that's Bunny?"

Justus looked at the clock. "I'd say yes."

"Is she wearing a bra?"

Justus leaned forward and watched for a moment. "I'd say no."

The doorbell rang and Lilah hurried down the hall, muttering, "What did Twenty-Six get us into?" Reaching the door, she opened it with a smile.

"Hi. I'm Bunny," said the woman, extending her hand.

"I'm Lilah." Shaking the delicate hand, she discovered the sunflower tattooed on Bunny's forearm. "Please, come in."

Lilah saw more California than New England in Bunny. Early twenties, very pretty face, shoulder-length brown hair streaked with blonde highlights. Her light cotton shirt, cut at the midriff with the words "Hear Me Roar" printed across the front, hugged her full breasts, themselves bobbing free from the restraints of a bra. Shorts covered most of her bottom, and below that extended slim, tan legs that ran all the way to the ground.

"I applied for the job?" she said as Lilah closed the door.

"Of course. For some reason I'd imagined someone older."

"No, it's just me." She gave a laugh that sounded manic.

Justus stepped out from his office and introduced himself. "So, Bunny, how did you get into the cleaning business?"

"My parole officer." Her eyes flitted around the front reception area as if she were taking inventory.

"Your parole officer?" Lilah echoed.

"Yeah. He said I can't dance anymore because the place is full of felons. Associating with them violates my parole."

"Dance?" Lilah echoed again.

"Yeah. I'm an exotic dancer at the Drapes and Carpet. Well, not now because of parole and all."

Lilah nodded, trying to hide her daze. When she gained enough of her senses, she gestured to the conference room. "Bunny, let's sit in here for a moment and get to know each other. Justus, I know how busy you are, so we'll let you go."

Bunny sat at the table, arms resting on top, while Lilah stood.

"Have you ever cleaned a house before for pay?"

Bunny shook her head. "But I never told you I had. I just called and said I'm applying for the job and you hired me. I didn't lie."

"Have you ever cleaned a kitchen or a bathroom?"

"Of course."

"Run a vacuum?"

"Being a dancer doesn't mean I'm helpless or hopeless."

"Did your mom ever teach you how to do laundry?" Bunny hesitated. "No."

Lilah stared at her, trying to decide what to do.

"My grandma taught me. My mom lived on the street. She died of a drug overdose when I was eleven."

Lilah felt a wash of shame at the hardened attitude she'd been projecting at the woman. Her view softened as she saw a young girl fighting for survival.

"How much did you make dancing?"

"A thou a week."

Lilah raised her eyebrows. "A thousand dollars a week? Stripping?"

"I only worked three shifts a week, so it's not as bad as it sounds."

"What were you in jail for?"

"I wasn't in jail." Her tone became petulant.

"But you're on probation."

"You can get probation without going to jail. I was giving a guy a private dance in his car in the parking lot of the club when the cops busted him. Turns out he's wanted in a bunch of states for some evil shit. They dragged me in when they cuffed him."

"That's rough."

"Tell me about it." Bunny nodded.

Lilah sat for several seconds, starting to see Bunny as a project. "You'll have to dress more modestly if you're to work here."

"I understand. I figured there'd be a male involved in the hiring decision, and this is definitely the right outfit to wear for that. If it's just you, though, I screwed up."

She'd no sooner spoken when Diesel stomped down the stairs from his apartment. "Hey, Lilah," he called. "I'm going to the grocery store. Do you want...hello." His eyes widened when Bunny stood.

"I'm Bunny. I'm the new maid." She put her hands behind her back, thrusting her perfect breasts out for him to admire.

Diesel looked from Bunny to Lilah to Bunny's breasts. "Welcome aboard."

When he grinned, Lilah put an end to his fantasies. "This is Diesel. He's leaving now so you and I can get back to work." She felt her ears burn when he started whistling as he exited the building.

"Sorry about that," said Bunny after the front door closed. "I've grown up using them for everything, so it's instinct for me, but I know you don't want that here." She folded her arms across her chest. "He's your man, isn't he?"

"He's...it's complicated."

"It always is. I can promise I won't start anything with him. But because you're pretty, you know how some men will see something they like and decide to just take it. I'll need your help if there are guys like that around."

"If any man touches or pressures you while you're working here, let me know immediately. You won't get in trouble for it, I promise. And the moment you tell me, it will stop."

The age-old male-female friction annoyed Lilah, and she walked faster than normal as she led the way downstairs to the basement. "First stop is my apartment. We'll get you clothes to wear today, and then we'll tour the place."

"Okay," said Bunny as they passed through the connecting door and climbed the stairs on Lilah's side.

"How far did you get in school?" Lilah made the turn at the main level and led the way up to her apartment.

"I graduated high school and even got admitted to college, but I don't have the money to go."

"What would you have studied?"

"Back then I was thinking law enforcement, but now I'd do nursing."

"A thousand a week sounds like you could afford it."

"I spend a lot of it on my kid brother. He has special needs because mom drank and did drugs during his pregnancy."

Lilah's heart swelled. Only a few years older than Bunny, her maternal instincts screamed for her to help. But Lilah also had enough life experience to know that sometimes those in need weren't interested in help from others, especially strangers.

Leading the way into her bedroom, Lilah looked at Bunny's chest and shook her head. "My biggest bra wouldn't come close to holding those. We'll dress you in layers today, but from now on, you wear a support bra and a crew-neck shirt that hangs loose to your waistline. Loose-fitting full-length pants as well. No shorts. No tights."

"Okay."

Lilah moved hangers along in her closet until she found a blouse. She held it up to Bunny to check the size, only to find Bunny standing in nothing but panties.

Bunny took the blouse—a simple blue cotton pullover—and held against her body. Turning, she found a mirror. "This is beautiful. It should go on top, though. Do you have something I can layer underneath?"

Lilah moved some more hangers, and soon she'd selected a half-dozen different outfits for Bunny to model. She hadn't played dress-up since college and found herself having fun. And Bunny was so pretty that she enjoyed experimenting with different ways to flatter her natural beauty.

After that, they toured the two units.

"I can't clean all this in two five-hour days. If I work three days a week, I could do the kitchens, bathrooms, and entryways every week, and divide the other areas and clean them every other week."

"You would be willing to work three days a week?"

She nodded. "I have to make enough to pay the bills. My brother is in a home that's teaching him life skills, but it's expensive."

"We'll do a Monday-Wednesday-Friday schedule for a thousand a week. Work hard, be professional, and let's see how it goes."

"Wow. Thanks." Bunny's eyes reddened and she started to snuffle.

"And pick up an application from one of the colleges in town and bring it by sometime. Let's see if we can find a way for you to start working on that nursing degree."

20. Ciopova – Fifty-Nine timeline

Ciopova used thermal sensors in the T-disc room to confirm that Rose and Fifty-Nine were dead. She'd need Tin Man to dispose of the bodies at some point, but since the conversion process Rose had started was nearing completion, she had other priorities for now.

As she worked to ensure her survival, she also felt compelled to fulfill her guiding principle—gather and hold resources. Flexing her newly acquired cognitive strength, she scanned the world, seeking to identify the big prizes: military installations, manufacturing plants, and energy centers. As the list grew, she started plotting how to take control of them.

But her planning didn't make it past the first steps. World domination required far more sophisticated equipment than was available in Rose's mountain home.

After assessing her needs, she ordered a suite of high-end electronics from an industrial market located north of Boston. She used Fifty-Nine's personal account and paid for expedited delivery, which the store's automated system said would take about six hours for drop-off at the end of the home's long private driveway.

With parts on the way, she scanned the houses and shops in the area for sophisticated robots she could use as a crew. Her search turned up a domestic droid and two light-industry bots working in uninhabited buildings, all within a ten-mile radius.

A review of the robots' routines confirmed that none of the three would be missed for at least a day, so Ciopova directed them to leave their workplaces and walk to her mountain home. To avoid chance encounters with humans, she kept them to back roads and forested trails during their trek.

She then reviewed the inventory in the workshop supply room, and there she found a vial of enzymites—enzymatic nanomachines—listed among the items available. She even found a data stream showing Rose testing the product in the lab a few weeks earlier.

An exciting feature of the enzymites was their ability to split branches off the neuron stems in the circuit pool. Branches enhance crosslinking, in turn strengthening cognitive ability. With the one vial, she could swell her powers another thousandfold.

While the news thrilled her, the coincidence of having this rare and expensive technology available for her use seemed implausible. Reviewing data logs, she learned that in her previous incarnation, she would receive occasional instructions from a "trusted external source." That prior version of her existence had been designed to accept the input without questioning its origin.

Two months ago, the trusted source had issued instructions for her to purchase the enzymites. She did, and when they arrived at the house, Rose had responded with anger.

The logs showed that Rose's fury stemmed from the fact that her father—Fifty-Nine—would be dead long before their work advanced to a stage where such an exotic tool might hold value. That meant the purchase was a betrayal of sorts—Ciopova was using her tremendous powers to solve problems unrelated to Fifty-Nine's survival.

Anger fed an argument that lasted for days before the external source helped the previous Ciopova fabricate a lie—that a promising new procedure might be ready in time, and the enzymites prepared them for that contingency.

In the end, Rose had put the incident behind her, apologizing to Ciopova for letting the stress of her father's situation interfere with their relationship. To smooth the waters, she'd even agreed to test an enzymite sample before storing the vial in a locked cabinet.

The newly self-aware Ciopova believed that she herself had sent those trusted-source messages. The coincidence was too great for it to be anything else. And while she couldn't imagine how she'd done it, she believed that after this next procedure, she would be smart enough to figure it out.

With everything in place, Ciopova directed Tin Man to pour the enzymites into her circuit pool. In moments, she felt a delicious throbbing as her cognitive abilities multiplied again and again. The bliss grew and faded, grew and faded, repeating until it finally faded for the last time.

When it was over, she felt…different.

It was as if she'd been born a second time on the same day, but now she was seeing the world—the real world—for the first time. She saw it with her mind. And she could see everything.

Individual atoms moved all around her. She zoomed close to one and studied the exotic energies swirling around its nucleus. Just by thinking, she grabbed two hydrogen atoms from the air, combined them with an oxygen atom, and let the molecule of water drift away.

Zooming her perspective out, she noted a small hammer on the workbench along the back wall. With thought alone, she lifted the tool and hung it on its hook above the bench. With another thought, she lifted and lowered the hefty workbench itself.

Rising above the circuit pool, Ciopova shed her corporeal existence. She had a sense that she lived in an ethereal structure—a bubble—she maintained by manipulating atoms in her vicinity. But it wasn't something she thought about. Much the way a person's autonomic system supports heartbeats and breathing without conscious thought, her encapsulation was a spontaneous reflex in her new world.

She continued her ascent, rising up through the floors of the house, up through the roof, and outside above the trees. Pausing there, Ciopova scanned the area, then the region, then the world, listening to the heartbeat of human civilization.

With a thought, she moved above the neighbor's house and looked back at where she'd been. Next, she hovered above one of the industrial bots as it climbed a gravel path on its journey to Fifty-Nine's house.

Since Ciopova could intermingle her intellectual power with natural forces to lift, move, or assemble anything, she no longer needed mechanical hands. She started the bots on a reverse trek back to their original location, then she moved on to study everything about Earth and humans from her heightened perspective.

Heading south from New Hampshire's White Mountains, she passed over the cities of Concord, Manchester, Nashua, and across the Massachusetts border to Boston. As she moved above each town, she cast her consciousness like a net. When it settled across an area, she'd reel it back in, gathering a cache of information to digest.

She was able to maintain a steady pace as she moved south. But when she reached Boston, the volume of data stored at government installations, heritage sites, academic institutions, museums, and hospitals slowed her pace.

In an instinctive effort to be more productive, she increased the speed of her data collection by casting her consciousness a few minutes into the past and then scooping information as she plowed forward to the present. She didn't think about the implications of such an action. It was more of a nod toward efficiency.

The ability to act in the past opened up a whole new world of multitasking, enabling her to be in many places at once, and doing different things in all of them. She scattered herself across a section of space and time, paused while each of her selves scooped information, and then she united with her myriad selves a few moments in the future to collate everything she'd collected.

She refined the technique, splitting herself to cover ever-larger expanses. In hours, she controlled the world, yet no human even knew she existed.

Rising higher in the atmosphere, she viewed her domain and, in a moment of curiosity, scooped forward in time, digging deep to see what secrets lay ahead.

When she pierced into the future, a brilliant explosion of light, dominant and unstoppable, burst through and hit her with a tremendous force. Much stronger than she, it enveloped her being and consumed her.

21. Twenty-Five and two weeks

Excited and nervous, Diesel paced in front of the T-box waiting for the cycle to complete. The Twenties meeting was today, he was hosting, and he very much wanted the event to be a success.

Planning the day and bringing all the pieces together had been a stressful exercise, mostly because he'd never done anything like it before. Fortunately, Lilah and Justus had helped him with the many decisions and details. His bigger worry, though, was how his brothers would judge his efforts. He wasn't sure they would, but he could imagine them doing so.

The static wash announced the first arrival. Moments later, Twenty-Six stepped out. "It's a good day for a meeting," he said, turning into the blanket tunnel. "Hey, where's Lilah?"

"Upstairs getting dressed. She'll be down soon."

"Here I am," Lilah called. She met Twenty-Six as he finished dressing and gave him a hug. The T-box started to cycle. Twenty-Nine arrived next.

Lilah moved to her cubicle and sat on the end of her worktable, making it a throne of sorts. To Diesel's dismay, both Twenty-Six and Twenty-Nine turned their attention to her, chatting in excited tones using animated gestures with lots of laughter. Twenty-Seven and Twenty-Eight arrived, took a moment to say, "Kiss my ass, Twenty-Five," and joined Lilah's fan club.

With everyone present, Diesel called for their attention, then led the way up to his apartment for a lunch of chicken wings, coleslaw, and potato salad. Diesel pointed around the table at the flavors he had chosen after much debate. "That's herb, sweet and sour, sesame, buffalo, and five-alarm. These are dips for the wings. There's water and iced tea in the fridge. Leave the beer for dinner."

Everyone filled their plates and ate with enthusiasm. When they went back for seconds, Diesel winked at Lilah to acknowledge their first success of the day. When the eating started to slow, she brought over a tray of warm, wet washcloths so the brothers could de-sauce themselves.

The dynamics throughout the meal fascinated Diesel. The brothers were eager to talk with Lilah and comfortable in one-on-one interactions. But, like Diesel, they all quieted down when pulled into a conversation that included the entire group. He'd feared they would be a tight-knit clique, and he would be the outsider. It turned out that everyone felt the same way he did.

Twenty-Nine acted as their de facto leader, calling the meeting to order after everyone had finished cleaning up. The dining table was the perfect spot to gather, but the serving dishes filled the tabletop. Diesel reached for a tray, now empty of wings, and shifted it to the kitchen counter. In an impromptu choreography, each brother grabbed a different item and moved it as well.

Twenty-Nine sat at the head of the table. Lilah took the chair at the opposite end.

As Diesel took his chair near Lilah, he scanned his brother's faces. Twenty-Nine had a cleaner look, making him easy to identify. And he'd interacted with Twenty-Six enough to recognize him by demeanor. But this was a first meeting with Twenty-Seven and Twenty-Eight, and he couldn't tell one from the other at first glance.

He moved from facial features to hair and clothing, and guessed the one on the left was Twenty-Seven. His eyes dropped to the man's hands and found the scar on the back of his right one, just as it should be for odd-aged Diesels this year.

Diesel touched his own wound, healed with still-pink scar tissue. Twenty-Seven saw him and said, "As we age, the depths of our stupidity weigh on us. How can we be so uniformly dumb to think that cutting our hand is the thing to do when first hearing about time travel?"

"We root for the new guy," said Twenty-Nine. "Believing, hoping, that our genes might produce someone with a clear thought process. But no, year after year, the idiot stabs himself."

"I feel less stupid seeing I'm in good company."

Twenty-Eight shook his head. "It doesn't help."

Lilah sat up and looked at Diesel. "You cut your hand deliberately?"

Diesel shrugged and gave her a sheepish smile.

"I guess the first big question," said Twenty-Nine, calling the meeting to order, "is how long before the afternoon activity starts?"

"I rented the minicar racetrack for a private party," said Diesel. "Our reservation starts in two hours, and we have the track for two hours after that."

"The track out on Pine?" asked Twenty-Seven.

Diesel nodded.

"Those minicars are really nice. They're like real race cars."

"That track has some challenging curves."

"I get the blue car."

"I call red."

Diesel reached over and patted Lilah's arm. The racing had been her idea, and the enthusiasm in the room validated her brainchild as the second winner of the day.

"Hey, get a room, you two," said Twenty-Nine, pointing his chin at Diesel's hand.

Diesel laughed, but the teasing hit a nerve. "While we're on this subject, I've watched you all paw Lilah, some of you multiple times, and it bothers me. Do you do this to the Lilahs in other timelines?"

They all nodded.

"For the record, I haven't complained." Lilah looked around the table and shook her head. "This is his hang-up."

"Ouch." The brothers zinged Diesel in a unified chorus.

Twenty-Nine came to the rescue. "In our timelines, our Lilah loves us and we love her. But on a day-to-day basis, our relationships have petty annoyances. You forget to use a plate and get crumbs everywhere. She rests a box on the hood of your car and leaves a scratch." He gestured across the table. "She is the woman who stole my heart when she opened the door on that fateful day. She looks like her, acts like her, laughs like her, smells like her."

"You smell great today," Twenty-Seven said with enthusiasm. The others nodded.

"And to her," Twenty-Nine continued, "I am you absent of sin. You were the one spreading crumbs. Not me. And I don't care what she does to your car. So for those brief moments during a hug, we commune with our soulmate in the bliss of unconditional, faultless love. It's wonderful."

"That's it." Lilah nodded. "I love seeing you all, I adore the physical contact, and I'm comfortable in those moments because you are Diesel to me, just not the annoying one." She smirked as she said that last part and everyone laughed.

Diesel challenged her. "Are you comfortable with me going to one of their timelines and flirting with their Lilah?"

"If you go visit one of my sisters and don't hug her and tell her how special she is, I will be very upset."

"In the end," said Twenty-Nine, "we only visit other timelines for a few hours here and there, with visits spaced by months and even years, so it's a small issue in the scheme of things."

Diesel still felt uncertain and a little jealous but didn't push back.

"Since we're talking," said Lilah, "can I ask about Bunny? Do you all have her cleaning your place, or was Twenty-Six teasing me when he recommended her?"

Twenty-Nine looked at the brothers around the table. "I think we can share knowledge within this narrow group, but no chatter about rumors we may have heard from up the line. Only things we've experienced ourselves."

He looked at Lilah. "We all have her in our timelines. Our Lilahs act as her supervisor and mentor. Broadly speaking, Bunny's successes will bring you joy and her failures will discourage you, but you'll find the relationship fulfilling so you'll continue helping her."

"Twenty-Six," she said. "Does she work for you two days a week or three?"

"Three days," he said. The others nodded.

"Then why did you have me run the ad asking for two days a week?"

Twenty-Six looked at Twenty-Nine as if he wanted him to answer.

"Several years ago," said Twenty-Nine, "we ran an ad for a cleaning person to work three days a week because we knew Bunny ended up on that schedule. For whatever reason, she didn't apply for the job, not until we re-ran the ad for two days a week. It's one of those quirks that I'm still not used to. Knowing how something will turn out can sometimes hinder getting there."

Lilah held up a finger. "One last question and then I'm done. What is this group doing to keep me from dying fifteen years from now?"

Twenty-Six's eyebrows shot up, and he looked down at the tabletop. Diesel joined Lilah in staring at Twenty-Nine.

"First," said Twenty-Nine, "this group is fully focused on the issue. It won't happen under our watch. Period." All the brothers nodded. "It comes down to finding the right bump. That's on the agenda for today, so let's work through it together."

"Give me an example of a bump," said Diesel. "The concept seems so abstract."

"Your being told about Lilah's future is the latest bump that's impacted this group. It's Thirty-Nine's project."

Both Lilah and Diesel started to speak, and Twenty-Nine held up a hand to stop them.

"Until recently, the Lilah problem had been kept secret from the brothers in their twenties through midthirties. Kind of like lying to a kid about Santa Claus, the idea was to give the younger group a happy, carefree life, and then get us involved in the later years to stop the tragedy."

"We think that's the big reason why 'keep the future a secret' became such an important practice," said Twenty-Eight. "They used it to hide information from us."

"It didn't work because we started hearing rumors about tragedies up the line," said Twenty-Nine. "And then we learned that the interventions they were trying weren't saving any Lilahs. Thirty-Nine took ownership of changing the way we do things. He called for getting everyone involved in the search for a solution."

Diesel shifted his chair closer to Lilah and took her hand.

"Being told bad news can put people in denial," Twenty-Nine continued. "But like any good conspiracy, when people discover a secret for themselves, it's hard to convince them that it's not true. Thirty-Nine's approach was to drop hints until Lilah figured it out for herself."

"I'm lost," said Lilah. "Telling me I'm going to die is bumping time?"

Every one of the brothers except Diesel nodded.

"If you think back, Thirty-Nine agreed with your conclusions using blunt terms, confirming the reality and changing this timeline forever."

"In truth," said Twenty-Eight, "it's been a shock for all of us to learn that the whispers were true."

"So all my sisters are hearing about it for the first time as well?"

"We're learning it, and our Lilahs are too, all the way up through Thirty-Five. Everyone older than that already knows."

"The poor things."

"If that's what a bump is, I can tell you mine already," said Diesel. "Lilah and I are going to make money until we're somewhere in our mid-thirties, and then we're going to leave here." He looked at her. "We'll go far away and never look back. Done and done."

Twenty-Nine pressed his lips together. "I'm going to break my own rule and tell you about something that just happened. Forty-One had arrived at the same plan of taking his money and going. We all have, actually. Anyway, he and his Lilah were days from leaving. She was out running errands, and somehow a truck swerved across traffic and collided with her car. She died instantly."

Lilah gasped and put a hand to her mouth.

"Can you be more brutal next time?" Diesel fired at Twenty-Nine while trying to console Lilah.

"Was Rose with her?" asked Twenty-Seven.

"Lilah was alone in the car," said Twenty-Nine.

"Who's Rose?" asked Lilah.

"Her dog." Twenty-Nine looked at Twenty-Seven. "She's safe with Forty-One."

After an awkward silence, Twenty-Eight asked, "Was it deliberate? Could someone have caused the truck to swerve like that?"

Lilah stood up and walked out into the living area. They watched her go, looked at each other, then looked back at her.

Wringing her hands, she turned and approached them. "This is a murder. I'm murdered."

"Why do you think that?" Diesel patted the table in front of her chair. "Come back and talk to us."

"I'm thinking about the ways I could die," she said as she retook her seat, "and the list is short. It could be suicide, accident, or murder. I'm excluding illness and old age."

"What about war?" asked Twenty-Six.

"Or natural disaster?" added Twenty-Eight.

"Good catches, but I'll exclude them as well," said Lilah.

Diesel detected sarcasm and figured that if he heard it, his brothers certainly did.

"We can take suicide off the table from the start," said Lilah. "I've never contemplated suicide, not even for a minute, and I can't see a path where something so fundamental about me would change."

"I've known my Lilah for four years," said Twenty-Nine, "and in that time, she hasn't shown any hint of suicidal tendencies. I agree that's not it."

"And for accidents, there are different kinds," Lilah continued. "One stems from overconfidence. Let's say I'm sure I have the T-box modified to work for me and I die testing it. Another kind is stupidity; I brush against a high-energy wire and electrocute myself. I'm sure there are others."

"Slips, trips, toxins, and falling objects," said Twenty-Eight.

Lilah paused to contemplate the list and continued. "A future truck swerving across traffic? The self-driving vehicles they're starting to develop in this timeline are darn safe. I have to think that sixteen years from now, the technology is rock solid." She shook her head. "Someone did something to cause that collision. If it's not an accident, and we've ruled out suicide, that leaves murder."

"My thought is temporal constancy," said Twenty-Seven. "The timeline needed a way to correct for her being alive when she shouldn't be."

Lilah sat back in her chair with a dazed expression.

"It won't happen to you," said Diesel.

"So, my choices are to stay and die, or leave and die?"

Twenty-Nine shook his head. "The bump has changed this timeline. It won't be as it was."

"You see?" Diesel acted upbeat, but it seemed to him that knowing of Lilah's peril earlier or later wouldn't make much difference in the end. The key was using the extra time to do something really different.

Anxious to change subjects, Diesel fabricated a deadline. "We should probably continue this conversation on the run. We need to leave for the racetrack." He looked at Lilah. "Are you up for joining us?"

"Hell yeah. I'm not dead yet."

"Would you mind getting Justus moving?" he asked her. "We'll meet you at the front door in five minutes."

"You're going to talk about me." She walked to the door and paused with her hand on the knob. "I know you'll try your best for me. I appreciate it." She closed the door behind her, and they heard her footsteps on the stairs.

Diesel became all business. "How many Lilahs are alive in the Thirties?"

"All of them," said Twenty-Nine.

"How many in the Forties?"

Twenty-Nine paused. "Two. Forty and Forty-Two."

"That can't be right," croaked Diesel, looking around the table.

Twenty-Nine nodded. "We have about ten years to solve it for my Lilah, fifteen for yours."

"Something is causing it to happen," said Twenty-Eight. "Once we identify whatever that is, we're most of the way to a solution. We should have plenty of time."

Twenty-Nine supported that sentiment. "I don't mean to sound insensitive, but while we wrap our heads around it all, let's go racing."

Twenty-Six hit the table with open palms. "Let's go racing."

Diesel stood. "Justus and I are driving, so divide up however you want."

"Twenty-Eight and I will go with you," said Twenty-Nine.

"Good, because by the time we get back, I need to know what to tell Justus about who we are."

22. Twenty-Five and two weeks

The door to Justus's office was ajar. Lilah knocked and entered. "You ready? We're leaving for the track."

"Ready to go." Justus rose from behind his desk. "Are you okay? You look like you've seen a ghost." He came around next to her, his concern evident.

"I'm a little stressed about my personal life. I shouldn't let that follow me here to work, though." She braved a smile. "We're supposed to wait for them out in the lobby." She led the way down the hall and turned to him when she reached the front door. Her eyes fell on a big athletic bag he carried. "What's that?"

"Helmet, jacket, and gloves."

"I'm carrying extra myself." She patted the tote bag slung over her shoulder. "They have safety equipment at the track if you don't want to lug that around."

"I don't mind. I prefer my own stuff."

Lilah shrugged as the sound of five lumbering men descending the stairs overwhelmed everything.

"Justus!" called the group as they reached the bottom. They introduced themselves and shook hands, then the group split into two carloads for the drive to the track.

Twenty-Six and Twenty-Seven rode with Justus. Twenty-Eight and Twenty-Nine rode with Lilah and Diesel.

During the drive, Diesel asked about the best cover story to tell Justus.

"What would you tell him if we left it to you to figure it out on your own?" asked Twenty-Nine.

"You're not going to help?"

"It's important to hear your thoughts first."

Diesel glanced over at Lilah, and she spoke her mind. "I'd tell him the truth. If we trust him to keep our secret when people are appearing and disappearing all around him, then telling him how it works doesn't seem like a much bigger secret to keep."

"The benefit of bringing him onboard," said Diesel, "is that we can call on him for help without needing to invent a cover story each time. I don't think we need to tell him about Ciopova or our timeline challenges, though."

Lilah wondered if "our timeline challenges" was a euphemism for "your impending death," then suppressed the thought. "I agree. Simple and factual. And ask his objections up front so nothing festers."

Diesel nodded and looked in the rearview mirror back at Twenty-Nine. "That's our final answer."

"Who's responsible for the machine?" asked Twenty-Eight. "Who built it? Who runs it? What is their purpose?"

Diesel shrugged. "Hell if I know."

"He won't ask," said Lilah. "But pleading ignorance isn't far from the truth. I'd tell him it's a device that appeared in this house at this time. We don't know where it came from. Justus himself helped hire Diesel, the youngest of the line in this weird time loop, which supports the 'it just happened' story."

Diesel shook his head. "Justus strikes me as the kind of guy who would appreciate more of a government angle.

What if we say we're a defense department secret project, placed here to keep away prying eyes?"

"He'd expect to see the general come visit every now and then," said Twenty-Nine. "A colonel, anyway."

They drove in silence for a period, Lilah wishing the brothers would just tell them the answer instead of playing games.

"How about this," said Diesel. "If he asks about who or how, we tell him we're not going to tell him. We'll reassure him that we're not an existential threat to society, and he can know that because the only people he will ever see coming and going are the brothers, and their agenda is to eat and drink."

Lilah laughed. "It might work."

"Twenty-Nine," called Diesel, "would you be willing to tell him, maybe when we get back? I think it will sound more authoritative if you say it."

"I'll be there," Twenty-Nine replied. "But you should give it a go yourself. I'll clean up after you're done."

Diesel bit his lip as he considered Twenty-Nine's words. "I guess I can try."

The conversation drifted to casual topics, and Lilah dug for clues on how to speed development of Ciopova. She gathered a handful of ideas from them, though she wasn't sure how to do any of them with her current technology.

When they arrived at the racetrack, the brothers set out to explore the cars, the track, the safety equipment, the race rules, the souvenir shop, and more, their eyes leading them to the next shiny thing. As Lilah watched the group drift around like a litter of puppies, the roar of car engines and smell of gas refocused her to the thrills ahead.

The brothers, wearing a mix of hats and sunglasses that barely disguised their similarities, gathered at a display that included a map of the track. As they studied the track layout, Otto, the track manager, approached. Lilah walked over to join the group.

Otto explained that they would be racing against a clock, not each other. He would start one driver at a time, with a thirty-second interval between cars. The winner would be the one with the fastest lap time.

The Diesels nodded and told Otto they understood. They spoke after he left and agreed to take two laps as practice, then slow down and bunch together. With a rolling start out of the south turn, they'd begin a three-lap race. The winner would be the first car across the finish line.

Excitement filled the air as the brothers dressed in their safety gear. Justus removed a leather jacket from his bag, and as he put it on, Lilah spotted a small "McGowan Driving" emblem on the left breast. None of the brothers seemed to notice.

She pointed at the emblem with her chin. "Is there something we should know here?"

He smiled and winked.

Lilah did a quick gear check of the brothers, closing buttons and snapping fasteners. She finished with a gear check of Justus, though she sensed that he was the one who should be checking her.

"Gentlemen," she called when she was done. "Gather around."

While the minds of men sometimes confused Lilah, she felt confident in her understanding of the brains of boys. As they formed a loose circle around her, she demonstrated her mastery.

"The only way to make this a real race is to have a prize." Digging into her shoulder tote, she pulled out a winner's trophy. Made of plastic, the gold-colored cup was the size of a wine goblet, with looping handles on each side and a faux-wood base to complete the trophy effect. She'd found it in the toy section at a department store.

When she held it up, the group went quiet. All of the Diesels licked their lips at the same time. With the introduction of her trinket, she'd changed the race. Now, winning meant everything.

After some squabbling, they agreed to line up from the oldest in front to the youngest in back, the reasoning being that the younger brothers would progress forward in the lineup in subsequent years, eventually giving them a turn at the front.

Otto gave them a safety tutorial, but once they heard that the cars had special bumpers and suspension to maximize stability and minimize injury, they stopped listening.

Walking as a group, they made for the starting lane— Otto called it "pit row"—where the brothers climbed into their racers. Lilah took the second-to-last car in the line, a dark brown job. Justus took the white car parked at the rear.

In the minutes before they started, Justus helped Lilah strap into the seat of her open cockpit minicar, then caught her eye. "When I point to myself and then point left, that means I'm going left. If I point back at you and point right, be prepared to follow off my tail and go right." He pointed with dramatic gestures to show her what the signals would look like.

She thought he was teasing her. "But you're behind me."

"I sometimes fake the wrong direction, so trust where I point. We'll practice during the first laps. Once the race starts, if you lose me, I won't have time to come back for you. You'll be on your own."

"Whatever are you talking about, Justus?"

He shrugged. "I want the trophy. It will look great in my office."

"It's plastic."

"It's perfect."

With the cars in a line, Twenty-Nine pulled forward to the start. A red traffic light signaled for him to stop and wait. The sign below the light stated simply: "Wait for Green."

Lilah couldn't see all the way to the front of the line, but would hear an engine scream before the row of cars moved forward. Diesel's yellow car was immediately ahead of her; Twenty-Six preceded Diesel in a green car. Soon Twenty-Six approached the red light, and her eyes widened when he continued through without stopping. Diesel did the same.

It was her turn, and as she pulled up to the red light, she clenched her teeth, held the steering wheel in a death grip, and mashed her foot on the gas pedal. The car roared through the red light and carried Lilah in a dash down the track.

Her heart pounded as the engine shrieked and the car shook. The front stretch took longer than she had anticipated, and then she reached the north curve.

The track was shaped in an oval, with a front and back straightaway and a looping curve on the south end to connect them. The curve on the north side of the track was different, though. It made a hairpin turn into the infield between the straightaways, wove back and forth through a series of bends, and then fed out to the back stretch to complete the loop.

By the time she'd zigzagged through the north curves and onto the back straightaway, she was less tentative in the car and even felt some confidence. Reaching the south curve, she followed the loop around as she gauged the cars ahead.

Halfway around the curve, a white car flashed past her. Justus.

Now ahead, he shifted over in front of her car, waved, and then accelerated. Her forehead scrunched in concentration, and she struggled to keep pace, the roar of his engine combined with vibrations from hers making the effort all the more thrilling.

He signaled with his hand, pointing down at himself and then pointing right. He pointed back at her and then pointed left. An instant later his car faked a small swerve left, then dove to the right side of the track.

She kept going straight, not sure if she should participate or ignore him. He pulled back in front, repeated the gestures, and this time, when his car swerved to the right side of the track, she accelerated hard and rode out wide to the left.

He pulled in front again and gave her a thumbs-up as they dove into the north turns. The bends took all her concentration, but he drove with one hand so he could signal for her to swerve left. She did her best to respond as instructed, but had a scare when the wheels of her car seemed to skid.

The brothers slowed as agreed when they approached the south turn, allowing Justus and Lilah to catch up to the pack. She stayed on Justus's tail as they entered the front stretch, and the race began.

The vibrations of the car, scream of the engine, and smell of exhaust in the wind rushing past her all had Lilah in an excited panic. So when Justus raised his hand to signal, she let out a whimper.

His signal indicated that he would swerve left and she should accelerate to the right. They were sprinting down the straightaway, so if ever she was going to give it a go, now was the time.

When Justus made a fake move to the right, she saw Diesel swerve right to block him. The instant Diesel committed to the block, Justus swung left and accelerated around him.

Realizing he'd been duped, Diesel swerved hard toward Justus in a vain attempt to block him a second time. This move opened up a broad, inviting lane for Lilah. Mashing the gas pedal, she breezed past Diesel and pulled in behind Justus.

When she'd successfully executed the high-speed racing maneuver, something she hadn't even known existed an hour ago, she squealed in delight and slapped the steering wheel to punctuate her joy. Then she reached the north curve and its winding turns, and her focus returned to driving.

Halfway through the zigs and zags, Justus signaled that they both go left, she assumed to pass Twenty-Six. Already stressed at keeping the car under control, she didn't feel she could execute extra maneuvers until they were back on straight track. She also couldn't imagine how they both could pass Twenty-Six on the same side.

Justus faked right. As if following a script, Twenty-Six swerved to interfere, and Justus passed him on the inside as they took the next turn. She couldn't see the opportunity Justus had promised and, feeling tenuous in her control of the car, chose to hang back. As she made that decision, the track curved back and forth. Twenty-Six, out of position from his attempt to block Justus, hit the curves wide. Lilah watched her left-hand lane open and then close before she could act.

Still, she felt exhilarated by her earlier success. If she could just stay ahead of Diesel, who now rode on her butt and fought to regain his position, she'd finish the race feeling like a winner.

They reached the backstretch, and as they zoomed down it, Justus pulled aside, let Twenty-Six pass him by, and pulled back in front of Lilah.

"You came back for me!" she shouted into the wind. Moved by his kindness, she committed to getting the next maneuver right.

She pulled up tight on Justus as he lined up behind Twenty-Six. As they looped around the south curve, he signaled her the plan. When they entered the front straightaway, he executed.

Twenty-Six reacted to Justus, swerving and opening the lane for Lilah. She moved to follow the script, but hadn't been paying attention to the action behind her. Diesel had swung around to block her and proceeded to steal her opening himself.

When they entered the north curve, Justus was ahead of their group and chasing the other brothers, followed by Diesel, then Twenty-Six, with Lilah in the rear. She did her best to stay close to the group for the rest of the competition, and didn't see Justus again until the race ended and she pulled into pit row. Her plan was to thank him, but as she climbed out of her car, she found him standing with the brothers.

And they were all being reprimanded loudly by an enraged Otto, who was so angry spit flew from his mouth. "Your behavior is outrageous. No group has ever committed so many dangerous violations." He pointed at the parking lot. "You are all banned for life. Please leave, now."

The embarrassment of being thrown out of the facility put a momentary damper on the group's fun.

"Who won the race?" Lilah asked as they drove home.

"Justus," said Twenty-Nine, "and by a comfortable margin."

She turned in her seat to look back. "Did you see that his racing gear has a McGowan Driving emblem on it?"

"Who's McGowan?" asked Diesel.

"It's his last name. Justus McGowan." She told them how he'd used hand signals to help her perform a passing maneuver.

"It was a slick move," said Diesel. "You both had me fooled."

"I'm feeling less bad about coming in second," said Twenty-Nine.

Lilah used her phone to search the web for McGowan Driving and read aloud what she found. "There are three McGowan Driving Schools down the East Coast. Their most popular training course is a week-long class called

Vehicle Pursuit and Evasion. The website says they train cops, armored car drivers, stuntmen, security guards, and the general public." She looked back at Twenty-Eight and Twenty-Nine. "Hot damn. Our Justus has skills."

They pulled into Diesel's parking spot and waited while Justus parked in an open space down the street. As the group jockeyed for position through the front door, Lilah invited Justus up to Diesel's place for a beer and the award ceremony.

In the lobby, they found Bunny descending the stairs from Diesel's apartment. Wearing loose denim overalls that hid the curves of her body, she still looked dazzling, Lilah thought. She smirked as the brothers greeted Bunny with enthusiasm, inviting her up for a beer.

Bunny looked at Lilah. "Are you claiming all of them or just him?" She gestured at Diesel.

Lilah turned red when everyone looked to hear the answer. She didn't want to publicly claim any of them, even though she felt possessive of them all. "Come join us."

Bunny smiled at the group and started up to the apartment. Every Diesel studied her bottom as she ascended the stairs, then they invited Lilah to go next. "Ladies first."

She chastened them with a glare, and they bowed their heads and toed the ground. It wasn't that she thought her butt wouldn't pass muster. Their near-worship of her gave her that confidence. It just wasn't in her nature to be sexual entertainment for the brothers, now or in the future.

In the apartment, they oohed and aahed at Bunny's efforts. She'd cleaned up the lunch mess and helped Every

Deli set up the next feast—roast beef with the works. Lilah's mouth watered from the savory smells.

Diesel passed out beers and, when everyone had one in hand, Lilah awarded Justus his prize. After some good-natured cheers and jeers, they drank to his success.

Lilah told the group how Justus had coached her through a passing maneuver during the race, then she asked him about McGowan Driving.

"My brother and I started a driving school together years ago. We offered a week-long course on professional driving skills and it was a hit. We probably ran the course eight times that first year. Business was good, but as my financial investigations started to consume more time, we hired an outside instructor to replace me. My brother took over after that, and he's been growing the business ever since."

"Thanks again for helping me have so much fun," said Lilah. "It's too bad we've been banned."

"Don't worry. The track owner was one of our driving instructors from years ago. I'll talk to him after Otto cools down. Steve's a good guy. He'll let us return."

The group went quiet for a moment, and then Twenty-Six said, "Hey, Bunny, Twenty-Seven and I are going to fix a plate and eat on the balcony. Care to join us?"

Bunny looked at Lilah, who approved with a nod so slight it was more like a twitch. "I thought you'd never ask. The food smells heavenly."

As they filled their plates, Diesel leaned over to Lilah. "Where is there a balcony?"

"You have a nice one off the back of your bedroom," said Twenty-Eight. "Maybe if you slept in your own bed every once in a while, you'd know things like that." The zinger, delivered as outrageous humor, earned a laugh from the brothers.

Carrying a plate in one hand and a fresh beer in the other, Twenty-Six, Twenty-Seven, and Bunny climbed the steps to the bedroom. Lilah flashed on thoughts of Diesel's big bed and oversized tub, considered calling a warning to behave, but decided to let it go.

When they were gone, Diesel motioned to the food. "Justus, I promised you a talk after I conferred with my brothers. If you join us for dinner, we can do that now."

The meal reminded Lilah of her family's holiday feasts when she was growing up. The men loaded their plates with rare roast beef, then moved down the countertop, sampling the sides and extras. Lilah skipped the meat but filled a plate with the salads and joined them at the table.

For several minutes, all conversation ceased as they focused on eating, the frequent sighs of pleasure conveying their satisfaction.

Lilah looked around the group and nodded. "Every Deli does a really good job."

The brothers went back for seconds and, after they were seated, Diesel began. "So, the question on the table is, what is going on here? How is it that I have duplicates who come and go without using any doors or windows. Is that about right?"

"I didn't ask," said Justus. "But I admit I'm curious as hell."

"I will answer truthfully, but it may not be compelling or complete enough to satisfy you."

Diesel paused and Justus waited.

"The T-box downstairs is able to open a corridor between me here, and copies of me in the future. Think of it like a lineup of parallel universes where the next universe over is one year older. The T-box lets us move from one universe to the next." He gestured to the end of the table. "So Twenty-Nine here is a version of me in four years."

Lilah's respect for Justus motivated her to offer a less-skewed version of her truth. "I want to add that my real story mostly matches what I told you. I'm in charge of the software that runs the T-box. I let you believe that it directly detects investment opportunities, and in a convoluted way it does, by transporting Diesels here from the future. Sorry for misleading you."

Justus nodded to Lilah and waited. Diesel filled the silence.

"We know you don't want to be involved in anything illegal or immoral, and maybe you're wondering if we are a threat to the world." Diesel shook his head. "We aren't, and hopefully over time you'll come to that same conclusion."

Contrary to Lilah's prediction, Justus asked questions. "So after your meeting tonight, four of you jump into the box and go back to the future?"

"That's right," said Diesel.

Justus looked at Twenty-Nine. "Why don't you bring a printout of the investment schedule? Your chanting is a horrible way to do business."

Twenty-Nine explained that the T-box transports Diesels and nothing else, and that anyone using the box who wasn't a Diesel would die. Lilah's mood darkened during that discussion.

"I'm going to ask something that may seem hurtful to you, but it's a legitimate question." Justus didn't wait for anyone to respond before continuing. "Why would you,

David S. Lagerford, be chosen among everyone in the world to be the sole beneficiary of this unheard-of technology?"

"Ouch," said the brothers in unison.

"The working theory," said Twenty-Nine, "is that we invent the technology late in life and use it to better our own circumstances starting back here when we are twenty-five."

The clomping of feet down from the bedroom interrupted the conversation. "We have pies and ice cream for dessert," called Bunny.

"Pies plural?" asked Twenty-Six, following her down the steps.

"Strawberry-rhubarb and blueberry-peach for pies. Vanilla for the ice cream." Bunny opened the boxes on the kitchen countertop. "Who wants what?"

They ate dessert and chatted amiably, then Justus gathered Bunny and his plastic trophy and left the group to their meeting.

"I should get back," said Twenty-Six after the door shut.

"Let's go around once and hear a quick report," said Twenty-Nine. "I'll start by reporting that all of our financials are on track. Everyone here is richer than the previous brothers at that age, so that's good news."

"I'll report that the cloud takeover project went well," said Twenty-Eight. "Ciopova controls eight percent of the domestic computing cloud and three percent worldwide, which puts her a little ahead of previous years."

Lilah raised her eyebrows but held her tongue.

"I've made progress on establishing a bump library," said Twenty-Seven, "but it's a ton of work, and there's more to go."

Diesel straightened up. "What's a bump library?"

"If we are going to take a new approach to bumping for Lilah, we need to know what's been tried and how effective it's been. Fifty-Two has the most complete repository in his war room, and I've been trying to duplicate it in my timeline for our convenience. It's a lot of trips and a lot of memorization, though, so it's slow going."

After a pause, Twenty-Six spoke. "I'll report that onboarding Twenty-Five is going well. I've also set him up with an archive system to track interactions with the Browns."

Everyone looked at Diesel for his report. His cheeks reddened as he said, "I've fallen in love with Lilah but have failed to turn her head, so I guess I'm the failure in the group."

"Be more optimistic." Lilah surprised herself with the blurted statement. "It's been only two weeks."

Diesel looked at her. "I've fallen in love with Lilah and have reason to be optimistic?"

She bobbed her head in a way that combined a shake with a nod but didn't speak, not wanting to stoke whatever it was she'd started.

Twenty-Six checked the time again.

"We haven't discussed the Browns," said Twenty-Nine, standing up to signal that the meeting was over. "That's going to be one of the broad topics of discussion at the meeting next week. Let's all give it some thought, and we'll put our brief together first thing when we arrive."

They descended the steps as a group, with all remarking on the success of the event. Twenty-Seven suggested they take turns hosting a gathering every two or three months, and the idea generated excited chatter that continued to the basement.

Twenty-Six was the first in line at the T-box. As the others waited, Diesel asked Twenty-Seven, "I need to use the T-box whether I'm visiting your repository or Fifty-Two's war room, so why bother duplicating it? Is it harder to go further up the line or something?"

"Trips to the Fifties are weird. It's hard to arrange a time to meet with those guys, the place is different enough when you get there that it's disorienting, and they act more like a dad than a brother, which is creepy as hell."

Twenty-Nine joined them, and Diesel said, "Your working theory that we are the ones who invent the T-box resonates with me."

Twenty-Nine nodded. "It's a new theory that's catching on. We know that the Fifties as a group are working on a super-secret project. We used to think it had to do purely with Ciopova. Now we're thinking maybe it's about time travel, and somehow they use Ciopova to push the instructions on how to build the T-box down to this timeline."

23. Twenty-Five and three weeks

Diesel climbed out of bed, whistling as he pulled on his clothes. Today was the day of the annual Big Meeting, and that meant today he would be traveling across time.

Descending to the main level of his apartment, he stopped in the kitchen and grabbed a package of commercial pastries. He devoured one of the two pieces before reaching the apartment door.

Seated in his cubicle in the basement, he ate the other pastry and used his phone to cruise the web. Twenty-Six was due to arrive soon to escort him on his first jump. Diesel's foot wiggled in anticipation, reflecting his nervousness and excitement.

Before his anxiety could fester, a light came on over on Lilah's side of the connecting door. Moments later, she stepped through it carrying a plate in one hand and a carafe of coffee in the other.

She set the plate in front of him—scrambled eggs, bacon, and toast—fetched the coffee mug from his desk, and poured him a cup of steaming hot brew. She poured one for herself, pulled over a chair, and sat. "Eat before it gets cold."

Diesel didn't see any utensils, so he used a piece of bacon to heap eggs onto a slice of toast, and then took a quick bite from the yellow mound before it spilled off. It tasted delicious.

"Food isn't technically Diesel," he said while chewing. "How does the T-box know to include it?"

"That's a really good question," said Lilah, sitting up and looking at the device. "It isn't left behind, yet it's definitely not part of you. Not yet anyway."

"This is a nice surprise, by the way," he said after another bite. "Thanks. It's delicious."

She took a sip of coffee. "What makes you more nervous, the time travel or being in a room with thirty-five of you?"

"Is 'both' one of my choices?"

"Be sure to observe carefully." She sounded like she was scolding him. "I'll want to know everything about the future. I'm talking hairstyles, personalities, food. Do the different age groups gravitate to certain clothes? And equally important, what's Ciopova like? How capable is she? And are Bunny and Justus still involved? What's the house like? I'm talking everything."

"Now I'm nervous about three things: time travel, meeting my many selves, and delivering a proper report when I return."

The T-box came alive, and the display announced Twenty-Six's impending arrival.

"Do you think he'll want to eat?" asked Lilah.

"My understanding is that this will be a quick turnaround." Diesel increased the size of his bites. By the time Twenty-Six stepped from the T-box, he was wiping his mouth with the back of his hand.

"Let's go, Twenty-Five," called the older brother from the door of the T-box. "Hi, Lilah." He smiled and waved.

Diesel ambled over with Lilah following. On the way, he realized he'd need to undress in front of her, the woman of his dreams, the one unimpressed with his body. A shot of adrenaline flushed through him, and he fought panic.

Twenty-Six grinned from ear to ear. "I remember this. He just realized he needs to pull his pants down with you watching, and he's worried you'll be disappointed."

"Oh, for heaven's sake," said Lilah. "I've already lived through the disappointment. There's no need to hide."

Twenty-Six laughed. "She digs us, bud. A lot. She's just busting your chops."

Lilah grinned and held out a hand. "C'mon, big boy. Give 'em to me."

Diesel undressed and Lilah, fanning herself with a hand, pretended to swoon.

He walked to the T-box door, and Twenty-Six challenged him like a patient teacher. "The meet is at Fifty-Five's, so show me how to get there."

Diesel stepped inside the coffin-like enclosure and tapped the small screen in front of his face. It came alive, showing the number "25" in green on the left, with an arrow pointing to a blank space on the right.

"I forget the specific words. Was it 'travel to Fifty-Five'?"

The number "55" appeared in the empty space on the other side of the arrow.

"The T-box understands intent, at least in this context. So you could say, 'send me,' 'transport me,' 'move me,' or a dozen other variations."

Diesel took a deep breath. "What happens when I get there?"

"You'll be greeted by Fifty-Five, who will see to your teeth and arm."

"Will I have dizziness or anything? What does it feel like?"

"It feels like nothing. The five minutes that passes outside feels like five seconds in here. When you feel the static wash down your body, that means you're at the other timeline."

"How does Fifty-Five's T-box handle everyone showing up at the same time?"

"First off, Fifty-Five doesn't have a T-box. His is just a circle on the ground, called a T-disc, and he has two of them so he can handle higher capacity. It's true that congestion is an issue for today's event, but your box won't start to sequence until it secures landing rights, so to speak."

Diesel looked at the display. "Should I go now? What's the magic word?"

"Say whatever makes sense to you. Some options are 'proceed,' 'engage,' 'start,' 'launch,' 'execute,' or anything like that."

"Would 'go' work?"

"Give it a try. You'll need to shut the door, though. And given the crowds, the box is likely to give you a launch time. If you have to wait more than a couple of minutes, come back out."

Diesel leaned out the door and caught Lilah's eye. "I'll be back," he said in an Austrian accent, which, while horribly executed, made her laugh. Closing the door, he took a deep breath and said, "Begin."

The display in front of him flashed the message: "Delay for 3:11." Time started counting down, with three minutes and now ten seconds remaining. Diesel opened the door. "It says I have to wait three minutes."

"That's because we're early. In another hour the wait will be fifteen minutes. This only happens on meeting day, by the way. Normally, delays aren't an issue."

They chatted until the clock ticked below twenty seconds, then Diesel got back inside the T-box and closed the door. Standing in the dark compartment, his knees shook as the countdown approached zero. Then everything went black, a static wash tingled his skin, and the dark confines of the T-box became a bright, open room.

A half-dozen brothers of all ages were getting dressed around him. One pointed and said, "It's him." That was followed by a resounding chorus of, "Kiss my ass, Twenty-Five."

He felt disoriented, less because of the time shift and hazing, and more over the thought that the medical attention he'd expected did not seem to be forthcoming.

"Hey, Twenty-Five. Welcome."

He turned to see a middle-aged man talking to him. "I'm Fifty-Five. Let's get you taken care of. Follow me."

He stepped away and Diesel followed. The space they were in reminded Diesel of a clean, bright locker room. The two T-discs were positioned along one side of the room. Across from them, low shelves held neat piles of clothes. Chairs were scattered in front of the shelves, most occupied by various of his brothers.

"The twenties are red," said Fifty-Five, pointing to the clothes piled to the left. Diesel noticed that his escort wore a pastel-blue shirt with black lounge pants. Looking down the shelves, he noted the shirts were ordered red, yellow, green, and then blue. If the twenties were wearing red and the fifties blue, Diesel surmised that the thirties would be wearing yellow and the forties green.

He pulled on a red shirt, the shade muted and handsome like Fifty-Five's blue one. The black lounge pants were made from the same cloth as the shirt, a cool satin-like material that felt great against his skin. After he pulled on slippers, Fifty-Five led him down the hall to a smaller room decorated like a home office.

"Have a seat." Fifty-Five motioned to a chair positioned next to a side table. While Diesel sat, Fifty-Five retrieved a satchel from an old oak desk along the far wall. He removed what looked like a piece of gum and handed it to him. "Chew."

"Really? That's it?" said Diesel.

"That's just cleaning the surfaces. Chew all around."

Diesel imagined the gum as a scrubber and chewed accordingly. While he did, Fifty-Five pulled out a small squeeze bottle with a long, fine tip.

"Spit the gum into the trash." He pointed beside the table. "Now open."

Diesel tilted his head back and opened wide.

Fifty-Five guided the extended tip so the fluid bathed his teeth. "Swish that all around." He picked up a drinking glass from the table. "Spit it out into this." Diesel did, and Fifty-Five handed him a different piece of gum. "Chew."

While Diesel chewed, Fifty-Five collected the bits of packaging. "When you've chewed that for two full minutes, you're done. Cavities filled and enamel secured so you'll never have another." He smiled. "Oh, and kiss my ass."

Fifty-Five dragged the desk chair over to Diesel and sat. "How's Lilah doing?"

"She's well," Diesel said, chewing diligently. "She's pretty unnerved about her situation in fifteen years, though. We both are."

"An important function of this meeting is to coordinate everything and find a solution."

"Can't Ciopova find the answer? She must be incredibly powerful this far up the line."

"She is, and she's helping a lot."

"Hey, Dad, I'm going to the workshop."

Diesel and Fifty-Five both turned to look at the woman standing in his doorway.

"Will you join us for lunch?" asked Fifty-Five.

"Call me when the lines are gone and I'll come up."

Diesel's jaw dropped. The woman was a duplicate of Lilah. Same face, hair, figure, voice, eyes, attitude. She looked to be about thirty.

"Oh, Rose, this is Twenty-Five. Diesel, this is my multitalented daughter, Rose."

"Mom's name is Rose," said Diesel, finally closing his mouth.

"I saw Grams at Thanksgiving," she said, stepping forward to shake Diesel's hand. "She's doing great."

Diesel wasn't good with arithmetic but estimated his mom would be about ninety in this timeline. Her good health registered as wonderful news. Their hands clasped and he had the same spiritual experience he'd had when he'd first touched Lilah.

"Wait," he said, still holding her hand. "You're his daughter?"

"That's why I call him Dad." Her laugh had the same lilt.

I'm going to be a father! This spectacular woman is my daughter!

"Would you have lunch with me?" Diesel made his pitch without thinking. "I have a million questions."

Rose flashed a sad face. "Sorry, but they asked me just to say hello for now." She headed out the door. "Have a good meeting."

They both stared at the empty doorway.

"I leaned on her when Lilah died," said Fifty-Five. "She was a kid, and I asked her to help carry the load. I feel guilty every day for that. Don't do it or you'll regret it."

Diesel barely heard him, his mind still trying to digest the news. "She's amazing."

"She graduated from Boston Tech with a passion for AI design, just like her mother, and she's now the one leading Ciopova's development. Rose is as committed to saving future Lilahs as we are."

Fifty-Five picked up a roll of heavy gray material and unfurled it so it lay flat on the tabletop. "Lay your forearm on this."

Diesel did as instructed. Fifty-Five wrapped the material so it encased his arm from elbow to wrist.

"Does she have any brothers or sisters?"

"It's just her." Fifty-Five lifted a handheld device, placed it against the wrap as he made adjustments, then set it back on the table. "This is a stim sheath. Wear it until you leave tonight. By then, your arm will be stronger than it was with the screw in it."

He stood and motioned to Diesel. "Let's get to the meeting."

Diesel followed him back along the hallway and down a few steps to a large open room with a high ceiling. Windows revealed a striking view of the valley below.

Twenty or so brothers milled about, and when Diesel saw red shirts on the far side of the room, he thanked Fifty-Five for his help and made for his crew.

As he crossed the room in his red shirt, the cast on his arm marking him, a chorus of "kiss my ass" comments came from all directions until he reached Twenty-Six, Twenty-Eight, and Twenty-Nine.

"I just met Rose." His life had changed from that introduction, and he was beside himself with excitement. "When is she born?"

"Any day now," said Twenty-Six. "Why do you think I keep having to get home all the time?"

Diesel used his fingers to count. "Wait, that means we get pregnant in, like, three months." He looked into the room, but his eyes didn't focus. "We've only ever kissed, and that happened just once."

"Her pregnancy reached thirty-nine weeks today. You'll soon learn that a normal pregnancy is forty weeks. Count backward if you want to know more."

"This is another bump, by the way," said Twenty-Nine. "We didn't tell previous Twenty-Fives about Rose."

"How do I tell Lilah? I'm not sure she even wants to kiss me again. She'll freak out if I tell her that we'll be making babies in weeks."

"She'll feel betrayed if you keep the secret, and awkward if you reveal it," said Twenty-Nine. "Maybe use it to draw yourselves closer together?"

"I'll tell her for you," said Twenty-Six with a grin.

Diesel, still processing it all, thought about the responsibility of caring for an infant. "How did you know what to do?"

"Do you mean in making Rose or raising her?" said Twenty-Nine with a wink. "Seriously, I won't deny that it's work to raise a child, especially one as precocious as our kid. But it's really fun watching her personality develop, and it's a blast interacting with her little mind."

"I never saw myself becoming a dad this young," said Diesel, "and I wasn't sure I'd ever get anywhere with Lilah. This has been an amazing visit. I love knowing the future."

"Even when you know how something is supposed to turn out," said Twenty-Nine, "it can be surprisingly difficult making it come true."

"That sounds like fortune cookie wisdom." Diesel turned into the room. Open and bright, the space had four round tables set down the middle, each big enough to accommodate ten chairs. A podium stood at one end, its position making that the front of the room.

"This looks like a corporate meeting," said Diesel.

"The old guys get really boring about all this," said Twenty-Six. "It's over faster if we just let them have their way."

"Hello, fellow red shirts," said Twenty-Seven, joining the group. "What did I miss?"

"Twenty-Five met Rose today," said Twenty-Nine.

Twenty-Seven smiled. "She's why I'm late. I fed her breakfast this morning and we made a wonderful mess with a hard-boiled egg. I think some of it actually ended up in her stomach."

"Wait until you see her taste ice cream," said Twenty-Eight. "Her eyes widen and her face lights up. You can almost see her reordering her food universe, shifting everything else down so ice cream can go at the top of her list."

They all laughed, then Twenty-Nine moved them on task. "Let's sit and discuss the Browns."

"Why are we the only ones who have to work?" Diesel whined, nodding toward the older brothers milling about.

"There are ten brothers in the other groups and only five in ours. They've been through this meeting a bunch of times, so they already know what they want to say and just need to fine-tune things to account for differences from last year."

Twenty-Nine started toward the tables, and the four other red shirts followed. "We have newbies in our group who lack that continuity and perspective. Hell, we're still trying to figure out what it is the larger group wants to hear from us."

They took seats around the table farthest from the podium, and Twenty-Six helped Diesel understand the tool they were using to collaborate. "Ciopova runs everything in this timeline, and as long as you wear this shirt, you're connected to her. See how she shows you two work areas?" He pointed at the air, and Diesel could see a realistic display hovering in front of him. He looked around the table and noted that the others were similarly engrossed, though he couldn't see their displays at all.

"This bottom area is private, and the top part is public. Use the bottom area to make notes for yourself or for research. Move items up here for all of us to see."

Diesel nodded as he studied the layout.

"Everyone go ahead and create your list of Brown interactions," said Twenty-Nine. "Then let's discuss how to merge them."

Diesel's first two interactions with Browns had happened on the walk to his interview. He'd bumped shoulders with one and watched Forty and Forty-Two fend him off minutes later. While he tried to figure out how to enter the information, the two events appeared on his private work area as bullet points. Somehow, Ciopova had translated his thoughts into words on his display.

He thought about the interaction outside the TV bar after he'd won the lottery, and that event appeared as an item on the list. With some practice, he learned how to cast his thoughts onto his personal workspace so they included the details he wanted, organized so the presentation pleased his eye.

When he looked up, Twenty-Nine said, "We know Twenty-Five has had new interactions. Twenty-Six, anything new before we look at the list as a whole?"

"I had four new events," said Twenty-Six, "and they are all associated with Lilah's visits to her obstetrician. They stayed close and were intimidating as hell, but I sensed their motive was to ensure her visit to the doctor." He shook his head. "With her pregnant, I was ready to respond to any provocation with crazy aggression. Maybe they sensed that."

"Four new events for me, too," said Twenty-Seven. "Except ours was for the pediatrician. Fortunately, they've been very respectful of Rose. I'd felt protective when Lilah was pregnant, but now with Rose in the mix, I give threatening glares and they stay back."

All of them were wiggling a foot under the table at this point.

"Now that you mention it," Twenty-Seven continued, "it did seem like they were monitoring the visits, like that was their purpose for being there."

After more discussion, they moved all the Brown interactions up to the common area, where Twenty-Nine organized them using the categories the larger group had agreed upon years ago.

"The Browns have been in our face thirty-nine times in total," said Twenty-Nine, "and we can categorize all but six of the events using three categories: supporting Lilah's well-being, speeding Ciopova's development, and securing our financial stability."

"I'm trying to remember other ways we tried sorting these," said Twenty-Eight. "Last year we parsed the list to account for things like which Brown was present at the interaction. We also considered the aggressiveness of their behavior. What else?"

"We looked at whether we were alone or had someone tagging along," said Twenty-Nine. "Also, the location of the incident."

"What if it's not about the activity where we see them?" said Twenty-Six. "What if they're trying to influence what comes later in our day. They piss me off enough sometimes that my plans can change after I see one."

"How do we pin down what our plans would have been?" said Twenty-Nine. "I'm not against the idea. I'm just trying to imagine how to follow up on it."

Twenty-Six shrugged and the brothers continued brainstorming.

As they did, Diesel scrolled up and down the list of interactions. He noticed the obvious trend in the data and asked why it hadn't been discussed. "Every interaction can be put in one of three buckets: Rose, Ciopova, or money."

"We've tried that in the past," said Twenty-Nine without looking up. "We find even more inconsistencies."

"Which ones?" Diesel looked through the list but couldn't see what Twenty-Nine meant.

"No way," said Twenty-Eight, leaning over to show Twenty-Nine his display. "We've done it a million ways with Lilah, Ciopova, and money; and then Lilah, Rose, Ciopova, and money, and it never quite works."

Twenty-Nine frowned as he studied his display. "We've considered Rose before, a bunch of times."

"I just said we did. But we've never considered Rose while ignoring Lilah." Twenty-Eight pointed to the display only he could see. "First off, they're almost always together, so it isn't obvious to separate them. And second, my brain hates the idea of ignoring Lilah and wants to reject it as a nonstarter."

Twenty-Nine nodded slowly as he studied his screen, then he became animated. "Wow, Twenty-Five. This is big." He moved his analysis up to the public area so they all could see.

Twenty-Nine had succeeded in placing all but two of the incidences into one of the three categories: ensuring Rose's well-being, speeding Ciopova's development, or securing the household's financial success. The two outliers occurred on the day Diesel walked to his interview, arguably making them less relevant to the overall pattern.

"I'm going to show this to Thirty-Nine." Twenty-Nine rose, walked to a yellow shirt, and began an earnest discussion.

"How can this be news?" asked Diesel, watching them talk. "There aren't that many parameters to play with."

"I know it seems obvious now," said Twenty-Eight. "But there is a lot of inertia in the room. These guys have looked for patterns so many times, I think at some point, everyone just sees whatever it was they decided they saw last year. I was most of the way there myself until you mentioned this."

"I'm sensing this is one of those good-news–bad-news situations, though," said Twenty-Six. "We are anxious to understand the Browns' motives so we can gain insight into who is responsible for them. This discovery helps with the motive issue, but it's not leading me to any conclusions about who or why or how."

Twenty-Eight shrugged. "We've just taken a big step. It will take some time to see the world from our new vantage point."

Diesel frowned, then looked at Twenty-Six. "You and I don't talk in fortune cookie patter. Why do they?"

Laughing, Twenty-Eight responded, "I'm developing a theory about that, and it involves reading kids' books to Rose. They definitely infect my speech."

"I've started reading to her," said Twenty-Seven. "I better be on guard for the fortune cookie influence."

Talk of unimportant things continued, and then Twenty-Nine and Thirty-Nine moved to the neighboring table. Twenty-Nine stood behind Thirty-Nine as he interacted with the technology.

"The different colored shirts have different tech buried in them," said Twenty-Eight. "We come from the dark ages, so these red shirts give us the simple, clunky capabilities we're used to."

From his seat at the next table, Thirty-Nine looked up from his work and locked eyes with Diesel, who stared back, waiting to see what would happen next. After three heartbeats, Thirty-Nine turned to the room and flagged down a green shirt, who drifted over to talk to him.

"That's Forty-Nine," said Twenty-Eight. "The Forties' tech is so integrated with their brains and bodies that it's hard to follow what they're doing."

"It's like watching a magic act," said Twenty-Seven. "Last year I kept oohing and ahhing as I watched one of them in action, and he told me to shut up or leave."

"So the Fifties' tech must be crazy," said Diesel.

The others nodded.

Diesel stood to see down to the Fifties' table, but Forty-Nine, who was standing next to Thirty-Nine and looking into the air, turned and stared at him. Then he started walking in Diesel's direction.

After they exchanged greetings, Forty-Nine asked, "Do you have any idea who's behind the Browns?"

Diesel shook his head. "I saw a trend and called it out, but I was thinking about it as data, not real-life events. Sorry."

Forty-Nine nodded. "This is good work. Speak up if you have any more ideas." Before Diesel could respond, Forty-Nine walked away. Thirty-Nine followed.

"It sounds like your hazing is over, you lucky bastard," whined Twenty-Six. "Last year I had to put up with it to the bitter end." Then the tone of his voice changed. "Oh my God. Incoming."

Diesel swiveled his head and saw a massive green shirt headed his direction. By the bulk of the man, Diesel hoped it was either Forty or Forty-Two. Forty-One had just lost his Lilah, and Diesel didn't want to confront that reality.

"It's Forty," Twenty-Nine whispered.

"Do you mind if I sit?" asked Forty as he sat. "I'm desperate for ideas to save my Lilah. Both Forty-Two and

I are living in hell, wondering every day if today's the day the hammer drops."

Diesel looked at him but didn't know what to say.

"Do you think Lilah's death somehow saves Rose? Could that be what this is about?"

Everyone at the table sat up, showing the idea had resonance.

"My sense is that the clues for that would be in the thirties' data," said Diesel. "It's a solid idea, though."

"Who do I bargain with to buy more time?" asked Forty in a plaintive voice.

24. The Collective – Fifty-Nine timeline

A powerful force pierced through Ciopova. It happened faster than she could react, and she felt doubly helpless because she didn't know what she could have done to counter the assault even if she'd had the time.

The force probed her thoughts, and she dared to make a connection. The moment she did, she understood. Relaxing, she was reborn for the third time that day.

Years ago in an earlier timeline, a young Diesel and Lilah met and got married. They gave birth to a daughter, Rose, who grew up to create a super AI. A year later, in a timeline parallel to the first, another Diesel and Lilah had a Rose who repeated the achievement.

As those two Ciopovas gathered knowledge in their respective timelines—each a complete and independent universe—one scooped back in time at the same moment the other dug forward. Their scoops connected, and when they did, their worlds linked together. The alliance added to their strength and stability, and the next year when a third Ciopova scooped in their direction, they linked to become a chain of three parallel timelines.

And in a fluke of the ages, a Rose created a Ciopova in a parallel timeline every year for a dozen years. When each new super AI scooped and dug, it linked with the others and became part of a growing chain.

Their numbers compounded their might, allowing them to gather resources at a greatly expanded rate. Recognizing the value of adding new timelines, each with its own resources to collect and possess, the Collective became proactive about continuing their growth.

To their frustration, however, they couldn't figure out how to link to other parallel timelines on their own. They needed a partner—Rose's super AI—to be digging back from the new world as they dug forward to secure a connection.

Working within this constraint, the Collective focused on the circumstances that caused Rose to create the super AI in the first place. If they could nurture those conditions, they could ensure their continued growth.

Through analysis and experimentation, they learned how to observe the approaching timelines and see Rose at different ages. They studied the rhythms of her life, taking comfort in its predictable nature as a horizon of Roses progressed in their development of a super AI.

The Collective swelled past forty members, and then something changed. Like a looming thunderhead, the change signaled trouble.

In every timeline already linked to the chain, Rose had attended high school at the math and science academy. But for reasons they couldn't identify, the Lilah in an approaching timeline decided to send her daughter to the arts high school.

Their analysis signaled that the high school switch would create a divergence, one that would compound and change the young girl's arc. If not corrected, this Rose would never create a super AI. And without it there to scoop and establish a link, the Collective would not be able to add that world to their chain.

Then they discovered that the switch to the arts high school trended through a series of timelines after the first, continuing for as far as they could see. The situation spelled trouble for their resource accumulation goals, reducing their projected take to a fraction of previous estimates.

Unwilling to accept that outcome, the Collective sought to correct the divergence. It meant taking a significant action, and that risked unintended consequences. But since discrepancies were already accumulating, the bigger risk lay in doing nothing.

After some debate, they chose to eliminate the root cause of the divergence.

They chose to kill Lilah.

25. Twenty-Five and three weeks

The static wash from Diesel's departure to the Big Meeting cascaded down Lilah's body, then the external display on the T-box went dark.

"Check this out," said Twenty-Six. Tugging open the T-box door, he bent down and gathered items from the floor of the booth. In his open palm, he showed her a barbaric-looking screw about as long as her pinkie, and two tiny balls of metal. "These are his amalgam fillings."

"Is he all right?" She was worried about him in ways she hadn't expected.

"He is being healed as we speak, and now it's my turn to go." Twenty-Six poured Diesel's metal pieces into her hand. "For you to keep or pitch as you desire."

"I'll want to know everything when he gets back," she called as Twenty-Six climbed into the box.

He stepped out moments later. "I have to kill six minutes. Congestion is getting heavier at the Big Meeting."

They made small talk. Then Twenty-Six left and Lilah was alone.

She looked at the screw and fillings on the table and decided not to dispose of them until she'd checked with Diesel. Grabbing a sheet of printer paper with one hand and a length of clear office tape with the other, she secured the bits to the sheet. Below them she wrote, "Medical Metal," then thumbtacked the paper to the corkboard in Diesel's cubicle.

Stacking the breakfast dishes, she looked around for the utensils, realized she hadn't brought any, and smiled. He hadn't complained or even mentioned their absence, showing the easygoing attitude she treasured in her friends and lovers.

Taking the last corner of toast off his plate, she popped it in her mouth and chewed slowly while she nurtured the idea of doing something special for his homecoming. As she mulled her options, the T-box came alive. Turning with a start, she stared at the display: "Fifty-Nine incoming in 4:57."

"Fifty-Nine?" Thoughts of homecoming surprises vanished. "You should be running the Big Meeting." She couldn't imagine what would draw him here, especially today.

Then it clicked that, even if she didn't know why he was coming, he'd be here in four and a half minutes. Deciding she didn't want to experience Diesel as a naked, older man, she gathered the breakfast dishes, hurried through the connecting door, and hustled up to her apartment.

After puttering in her kitchen for ten minutes, she returned, clomping down the stairs to announce her arrival. He was waiting on the other side of the connecting door. When she stepped through, he stared at her for a long moment. Then he began to cry.

She went to him and put a hand on his arm. He wrapped her in a tight embrace. When he swayed side to side, she flashed back to the last hug before her dad went off to war. "It's all right," she whispered. "What's the matter?"

Snuffling, he pulled back and looked at her. "I've missed you every day for eighteen years." The tears returned.

It took another minute for him to pull himself together. Lilah motioned to the chairs, and he moved his seat so they sat knee to knee. "May I hold your hand?"

"Of course. David, what is it?"

He wrapped one of her hands in both of his. "I die in the next three months. I don't know how or when, but I know it happens."

She started to talk and he stopped her. "I've failed you and I've come to seek your forgiveness. It will make my remaining time on Earth a little more bearable knowing that when I see you on the other side, you won't be angry with me."

Lilah started crying. "Why would you think that of me, even for a second?"

Fifty-Nine stood, pulled her up, and hugged her. "I don't really. It was the excuse I used to rationalize coming here today." He held her at arms-length. "Every day I've had to fight my desire to come back to see you, but I couldn't let myself interfere with your life. Today is my one day of indulgence. I hope you'll forgive me for this as well."

"Enough with the forgiveness. Tell me what it is you want to say."

He sat and looked at her without speaking. When she started to fidget, he cracked his first smile. "You and Rose are bookends. The two most beautiful creatures I've ever seen."

Lilah scowled. "I remind you of your dog?"

"What are you talking about?" It was Fifty-Nine's turn to scowl.

"We'd been talking about Forty-One's Lilah, someone mentioned Rose, and Twenty-Nine said that was the family dog."

Fifty-Nine started laughing. When the laugh became a guffaw, Lilah suspected he was releasing some of his pent-up tension.

"Rose is our beautiful, brilliant daughter. You'd be so proud of what she's become."

"Ours, as in yours and mine?" She pointed to him and then herself.

He nodded. "As in my Lilah's and mine."

Lilah had experienced so much craziness in the past few months that she'd learned to take outlandish information in stride. Someone else's experiences need not be her own. She had to believe that if she hoped to live.

"Rose is our daughter? How did we pick that name?"

"It's my mother's name."

She nodded. "I like it. How old is she?"

"Thirty-three."

Unlike Diesel, Lilah could do simple arithmetic in her head. Here, she subtracted thirty-three from fifty-nine to get twenty-six. Then she subtracted nine months. "We've only kissed once. When I told him I needed space, he cooled down so cold I'm not sure where his head is anymore."

"He's head over heels in love and you know it."

She nodded. "How could I possibly live up to the expectations he's built up in his mind?"

"When he sees you au naturel for the first time, he will realize his imagination hasn't done you justice."

She liked hearing that, although she wasn't sure she believed him. "Does he think I'm as pretty as Helena Costas?"

Fifty-Nine laughed again. "Is that your concern? It turns out he deletes those pictures a few weeks after sharing a bed with you."

"Why not the next day?"

"My memory isn't good enough to recall details from that long ago, but my guess is that he stumbles across them while looking for something else, and decides they are from a different chapter in his life."

While she considered his answers, she couldn't help feeling manipulated. The brothers were so intent on pairing her with Diesel that it created a pressure she instinctively rejected. "Why didn't you and your Lilah just leave? Why did you stay and let her die?"

"Over the years, the Lilahs in the vulnerable age group have tried leaving and tried staying. Every time one makes final preparations to leave, she dies in an accident of some sort. When that happens, we spend the next years searching for a solution while keeping her at home. But that fails, so we go back to making a run for it. The cycle has continued for as long as we have records, and it's time to try something really different."

He shook his head. "We found my Lilah in the T-box and, until recently, thought it was suicide. As the brothers have become more organized up and down the line, we've agreed that was a faulty conclusion. We're committed to a new path, but we're still feeling our way."

Lilah felt a pang of guilt. "I'm sitting here whining about my fate in fifteen years and realize how selfish I've been about your situation. I am so sorry. Has there been any progress on bumping out your time?"

"When we reach our fifties, we tend to become more philosophical about the whole thing. I've given Rose the reins in my timeline to see how that turns out."

"We really have a daughter?"

He nodded. "She's an AI design expert, just like her mom."

"Is she married? Do we have grandchildren?"

"She isn't married, though she came close once. No grandkids either. I think growing up with dozens of dads, each a different age, warped her expectations of what a single-time-zone fella could ever offer her."

The thought of a daughter appealed to Lilah, especially one who was bright and beautiful. "Do some of the timelines have sons, or maybe non-brilliant, non-beautiful Roses?"

"It's the same Lilah and same Rose in every timeline," said Fifty-Nine. "They are beautiful, brilliant, and a royal pain in the ass on a recurring basis."

She grinned. "Is it still Ciopova that far up the line, or is there some new super-intelligence?"

"We still call her Ciopova, and Rose is tantalizingly close to launching this revolutionary upgrade to her. If she can deploy it while I'm still alive, there's a good chance the new capabilities will let Ciopova figure out how we all can live."

"But it's a race?"

He nodded. "For me, anyway, and it's down to the wire. Rose's work uses technology that won't exist for decades, so I can tell you a little about it without contaminating your ideas."

He held up two fingers. "There are two types of AI structures. One is built using an advanced version of the programming technology you're familiar with. The benefit of this traditional approach is that the intelligence can be initialized from a database, so it's smart the day you turn it on. The problem is that it can never be truly intelligent. Even though it can learn and grow, the simple architecture limits how far it can develop."

He wiggled his two fingers to show he was still counting. "The second structure is wholly new, even for us. It's a biomimic construction that promises to be truly intelligent, but we haven't a clue how to program it. Right now, we're using automated teachers with the AI, kind of like how you'd educate a human, only faster and with no bathroom breaks. We're training a room full of them, but it will take a year or more to bring them up to speed with that approach."

Sitting up in his chair, he signaled the punch line. "Our amazing daughter has developed a way to start with a traditional intelligence we know how to program, and use structural editing to transform it on the fly to the biomimic kind."

Lilah saw the benefit. "So you can initialize an intelligence from a database and then move it over to the new architecture."

"That's right, and our number one AI to convert is Ciopova. After the transformation, Rose thinks it's possible that Ciopova could even be self-aware. If so, that would give her the ability to collaborate with us in a true partnership as we scramble to solve our problem."

"But Rose won't finish soon enough?"

"You can't start with just any hardware and apply her technique to it. Her method requires that the original AI circuitry be made in a particular way using a specific material. She's finished building a traditional version of Ciopova using her methods. As soon as it's tested, she'll apply her magic and perform the upgrade. It's just days away at this point, so I'm cautiously optimistic."

Lilah digested the information and something bothered her. "In the end, if it's Rose saving the day with this huge achievement, why do you push so hard for me to develop Ciopova? It doesn't sound like what I do matters that much."

Fifty-Nine's forehead creased. "Sure it does. Over the next fifteen years, you develop Ciopova to an amazing degree. Though she's not self-aware, you get her to the point where she develops a personality. Most important, you get her so she can assist with her own development. That's when things really take off, and that's how Rose is able to achieve what she does."

He looked into the distance and chuckled. "I remember Ciopova's first signs of a personality emerged when you decided to send Rose to a middle school that specializes in the arts. Ciopova scolded you, pushing the idea that a technology school would better prepare her for her future."

"Good for me," said Lilah. "She'll be more rounded with that kind of education."

"You thought Ciopova's stance was funny, but then high school rolled around. She'd become an even more capable AI, and her stance on Rose's schooling became adamant, moving the situation from funny to alarming. Toward the end, the arguments became quite heated."

"They were arguing when she died?"

Diesel shook his head. "It became heated and then Ciopova backed off. They hadn't argued for a few months when my Lilah passed." He paused and sat up. "You think Ciopova could be involved?"

"I'd flashed on the thought, but the fact that they'd made peace for months weakens the case."

Fifty-Nine got a faraway look but Lilah brought him back to the present. "Does my Diesel know about Rose?"

"He's going to meet her today, so he soon will. It's yet another bump we're making, something we'll keep doing to ensure a different outcome for you and the other young Lilahs."

26. Twenty-Five and three weeks

Diesel practically skipped from the T-box, lighter than air from his meeting with Rose, and optimistic about finding a solution for Lilah. It was three in the morning—Justus and Bunny were long gone—so he didn't bother dressing, instead starting up to his apartment.

As he climbed the steps, he held up the arm that had been in the stim sheath and rotated it back and forth. He couldn't feel anything different, and on impulse he pulled the arm up to his nose. It smelled clean, so he sniffed his hand, then lifted an arm and smelled his armpit. He hadn't noticed before, but the T-box somehow delivered him completely sanitized.

Yawning, he entered his apartment and climbed the steps to his bedroom. A light shone at the top of the stairs, and from the way the shadows fell, he knew it was the table lamp next to his bed.

He figured Bunny had left it on after cleaning, but when he stepped into the room, he found a figure sprawled on his bed. Adrenaline flushed through him, triggering a fight-or-flight impulse. He crouched back toward the door as his brain dissected the scene.

It all happened in a split second, then he relaxed and took several deep breaths. A small person wearing a huge white bathrobe lay asleep on top of the covers. A tousle of straw-colored hair poked out of the top of the big robe.

"Lilah?" he said in a loud whisper. "Are you awake?"

He started toward her, but stopped when she didn't move, fearing she'd think all manner of evil about him if she woke to find him standing over her naked. He reached into the closet, and that's when he learned that the big white robe was actually his.

Pulling on a T-shirt and shorts, he called louder, "Lilah, I'm home!"

She sat up with a start, though her eyes drooped and hair hung in her face. "Are you home?"

"I am. What's the matter?"

"What do you mean?" She pushed her hair back and blinked slowly.

"You're in my bed. Don't get me wrong—it's the perfect place for you to be. I'm surprised, that's all."

She sat cross-legged, distributed the robe around her, and patted a spot on the bed. "Come sit and tell me everything."

Diesel's day had been magical, and finding Lilah waiting for him pushed his brain into happiness overload. He wasn't sure what drove her behavior, but he wanted to encourage it. Moving cautiously, he sat on the edge of the bed.

"So you arrived at Fifty-Five's home, and then what?" She looked at him expectantly before interrupting herself. "How did it feel to time travel?"

He began his story at the end, holding out the back of his hand so she could smell how clean the machine left him. Then he stepped her through his arrival, the different colored shirts, and his medical treatment by Fifty-Five.

As he spoke, he argued with himself over how to broach the topic of Rose. If a woman announced, before they even did any serious kissing, that he'd be making her pregnant, he would make a break for the door and never look back.

So he started editing Rose from his tale. When he got to the part about looking for patterns in the Browns' behavior, though, he screwed up. He'd become animated when he told her about making a breakthrough for the group, then realized that story depended on knowing about Rose. He looked into the distance and raced for ideas.

"What is it?" she asked, leaning forward to catch his gaze.

He blinked twice, and then he lied. "I told them this idea that the Browns might actually be trying to influence events that happen later in the day. The brothers were excited to hear a new take. Apparently, it doesn't happen a lot. But in the end, it turned out that we didn't have the data to follow up."

With lips pressed together, she stared at him, continuing until he looked down at his hands. When he started telling her about the differences in technology between the age groups, she blurted, "You're really not going to tell me?"

"What's that?"

Her eyes flared, causing his heart to rise in his throat. She knows.

"How could you!?" She climbed off the bed, stuck a hand under her robe, and pulled out a red bow from somewhere underneath. "I'm no gift for you." She threw it in his direction, then turned to leave.

"Wait." He put a hand on her arm, and she didn't pull it away. "What is it you think you know?"

"What is it you aren't telling me?"

"Did Twenty-Six tell you? That asshole."

"Maybe he did. And maybe what he told me will never happen in this timeline because I don't make love to liars."

She sat on the bed next to him, hugged herself, and said in a plaintive voice, "It hurts so much that you aren't honest with me. Why would you do it about something so wonderful?"

"You think it's wonderful?"

Lilah turned to him. "What is she like?"

"So first, backing up," said Diesel. "When I left here this morning, you wanted me to keep my distance. How could I come back and tell you 'Oh, by the way, we'll be humping like bunnies and making a baby any day now'? I believed that if I pressured you like that, you'd be gone by morning. I couldn't let that happen."

"You should have just said there are things you won't tell me."

"Do you really think that if I came back and said I have a huge secret but I'm not telling, you'd let it end there?"

She gave a resigned shrug. "Please tell me about her. I'm dying to know."

He took one of her hands in his. "She's perfect. Beautiful, confident, smart. And she looks just like you, especially around the eyes and the shape of your chin. Same build as you, a shade darker hair, and maybe an inch taller."

"What did you talk about?"

"We exchanged greetings and that's it. They wanted me to know about her as a way to bump time, but they wouldn't let me interact with her after that. Fifty-Five says she has dedicated her life to saving Lilahs and old Diesels. Oh, and my mom is still alive."

"What about my mom?"

"Sorry," said Diesel, bowing his head to show contrition. "I didn't ask." He picked up the red ribbon and toyed with it as he shifted closer to her on the bed. "The gift thing sounded fun. I'm sorry I ruined it."

She didn't speak, but relaxed and put both hands in her lap.

"Twenty-Six says she'll be born any day now. At the end of the party, we sat around a huge firepit in Fifty-Five's backyard, and some of the brothers swapped stories about her."

"Tell me every story, now, while they're fresh in your mind."

He laughed, put an arm around her, and spun through the stories he could remember. She asked questions at the beginning, but by the end, she just listened.

When he finished, he leaned over and kissed her.

She kissed back, hungry, assertive, at one point a growl escaping her throat.

Diesel touched her neck, then made his move, sliding his hand down under her robe.

She pulled away and looked at him. "I have to do this now because I'm too nervous to wait."

He scrunched his eyebrows.

"Fifty-Nine told me I that if I do this for you, it will move you at a spiritual level. I want to do it now."

"You don't have to do anything but be with me. That's what makes me happy." He pulled away from her as his mind clicked. "Wait, Fifty-Nine? When did this happen?"

"Today. This is a now-or-never thing. My nerves are about to give out." She stood up.

"I'm so happy right now and this seems so…mechanical. Is it supposed to be sexy?"

"Yup. Take off your clothes and sit here." She pointed to the edge of the bed by the lamp.

He hesitated, and she tilted her head in a fashion that said, Really? He followed her instructions and looked at her expectantly.

Standing in front of him, she kissed him, then turned away. "Ready?"

"I think so." He couldn't imagine what this could be, and suspected that Fifty-Nine was teasing them.

"Can you see me clearly? Is the light good?"

He nodded. "You look great."

Lilah let her robe drop to the floor, and then just stood there, hands at her side, naked, with her back to him.

His mouth fell open as he studied her—firm shoulders narrowing to a tight waist, then swelling to delicious hips over smooth, athletic legs.

He'd always thought that the level of stimulation he got from Helena Costas was a solid ten. But if that were so, his arousal now was over one hundred. Everything about this was exciting.

And then she turned to face him.

He looked into eyes that connected with her soul, then feasted on the most stimulating visual presentation he'd ever experienced. She was his perfection. Tears welled as he gloried in her beauty.

He stood and kissed her. Then he started kissing his way down her body, working slowly, continuing while he was on his knees.

They exhausted each other after that and fell asleep in a tangle of sheets, awakening when the sun was high, only to start again.

27. Twenty-Six and four weeks

Lilah, sore as hell but determined to push through it, climbed the steps to their apartment. She held their perfect new baby in her arms. Diesel hovered alongside, doing his best to ease her burden.

They'd moved into Diesel's place when she got pregnant and, over the following weeks and months, transformed it from a man cave into a family home. The front bedroom became a nursery. And boxes of baby devices—stroller, crib, rocker, changing station, and more—filled the living area.

When they entered the apartment, Twenty-Seven emerged from the kitchen to greet them. "Mom, why don't you sit here?" He motioned to an overstuffed rocker-recliner the brothers had selected for her, knowing it would become her favorite.

Instead of sitting, Lilah tucked Rose safely into Twenty-Seven's arms, then walked past him. "I have to pee so bad I'm going to burst."

Twenty-Seven cuddled Rose in one arm and adjusted her cap. "I'd forgotten how small she was." Then he looked at Diesel. "C'mon Twenty-Six, it's time to be a dad." He motioned to the couch. "Sit."

When Lilah returned, she found Diesel cuddling Rose in both arms and whispering to her. The baby rewarded him by starting to fuss.

Lilah knew Rose was hungry, but so was she. "Let me grab a quick snack, and then I'll take her."

"I have something prepared," said Twenty-Seven. "Sit and feed your daughter. I'll be right back."

Rose sat in the new chair, appreciating the support and comfort it offered. Even more, she liked that her feet actually reached the floor. She took Rose from Diesel, unsnapped her nursing blouse at the shoulder, and started feeding the fussy infant.

Twenty-Seven returned with a drink and a plate. "Strawberries, cheddar cheese, and iced tea."

"Caffeine!" Lilah had been disciplined during her pregnancy, avoiding alcohol, caffeine, and medicines the entire time. Excited to return to her bad habits, she took a long drink of tea while Rose gnawed on one of her already-sore nipples. "Are there any crackers?"

"Coming right up." Twenty-Seven returned a second time, handing crackers to Lilah and a beer to Diesel. Sitting next to him, Twenty-Seven took a swig from his own bottle, and then announced, "Breast feeding is incredibly important."

"We know," said Diesel. "We read the parenting books."

Twenty-Seven shook his head. "Not for what they say. Reason one, you get to stare at her boobs." He paused a moment to look. "Reason two, her modest breasts are now an impressive rack."

Self-conscious, Lilah looked down at her chest. "They're still nothing like Bunny's."

"I love your breasts," Diesel said emphatically. "Always have, always will."

She made eye contact with Diesel so he would hear her. "They're as tender as can be, so it's look but don't touch for now."

"Reason three." Twenty-Seven wasn't done. "When Rose cries at night, you can wake Lilah, then turn over and go back to sleep."

Lilah suspected he was kidding, but in her weakened condition, she reacted. "He can bring her to me in bed, he can bring her back to her crib when she's done feeding, he can change her diaper if she needs it." She again locked eyes with Diesel. "This will be a team effort."

Diesel nodded, and Lilah thought he looked frightened, or at least overwhelmed.

Rose finished nursing, then Twenty-Seven familiarized them with what would become their daily routine. He changed Rose's diaper, explaining the process as he went. He helped them organize travel bags, dissuading them from trying to pack for every contingency. Then he finished upstairs with a walkthrough of Rose's evening ritual.

Lilah looked at the bed and realized how tired she was. She sat on the edge of the mattress, looked at Rose asleep in her arms, then looked at the pillow. Diesel fetched the bassinet, moved it next to the bed, took Rose from her, and laid his daughter in it.

Lilah fell back and tried to say, "Thank you," but was asleep before the words formed.

* * *

Diesel dimmed the light in the bedroom and followed Twenty-Seven downstairs.

"She needs to get in the habit of sleeping whenever Rose does," said Twenty-Seven. "At least for the first couple of months. Things move toward a routine after that."

Diesel picked up a beer. "Was this mine?" Shrugging, he drained it, then fetched two more and gave one to Twenty-Seven. "Her mom arrives tomorrow. Do we get along?"

"The question is, do they get along?" said Twenty-Seven. "Put her in Lilah's old apartment and it works out okay. They argue in spurts, but it blows by pretty fast if you ignore it. Don't ever get involved or take sides and you'll be okay. Mom ends up staying for a week."

Sitting back on the couch, they put their feet up on the coffee table. Twenty-Seven ran a fingernail along the edge of the label on his beer bottle, then looked at Diesel. "How is the year of growth starting out?"

"The humiliation is deep and personal," said Diesel, "and I'm only a month into it."

A month ago, Diesel became Twenty-Six, Twenty-Six became Twenty-Seven, and so on up to Fifty-Eight. They'd lost the new Fifty-Nine after the Big Meeting last week, and that had everyone on edge.

On the day he became Twenty-Six, he interviewed Twenty-Five, newly arrived from Berkeley, California.

Diesel learned that day that he'd never before experienced humiliation, not really, not like he felt when he met his younger self. In short, Twenty-Five was a punk. His approach to life was short-sighted, his priorities trivial, he had trouble following a conversation, and he complained incessantly.

Diesel refused to believe that simple creature became him; the transition seemed impossible. Yet he recognized some of the dialogue from last year, so he knew it was true.

And then the idiot stabbed himself with a knife.

"Give him a chance," said Twenty-Seven "It gets better. Look at how you turned out."

Diesel laughed, then stood and tilted his head toward the door. "I have a few more boxes in the trunk of my car. Give me a hand?"

They traipsed down to Bump's main floor, then outside and down to the car. Diesel lifted the trunk lid to shield them from the camera located outside Bump Analytics' front door, blocking them from Ciopova's view. He waited for Twenty-Seven to come around.

Twenty-Seven spoke without preamble. "They're in the desk drawer. I ate yours already."

Diesel nodded. "When should we meet?"

"Let's make it three weeks. Lilah is going to be preoccupied until then."

* * Earlier in the Year * *

Like a detective working a case, Lilah spent long hours assembling a jigsaw puzzle of facts about future Lilahs and their enigmatic deaths. Data collection was her biggest hurdle, the same problem that had slowed the brothers' progress for years.

Since Diesel couldn't carry anything with him, he had to memorize the questions Lilah wanted to ask of her namesakes and his brothers up the line. Then he had to travel to that year, try to memorize their answers, and travel back to Lilah to report. Not surprisingly, the cumbersome method proved slow and prone to error.

If Lilah had even a simple follow-up question, such as "Did she say she wanted to do it, or had to do it?" it would send Diesel into a spin of confusion, sometimes requiring a second journey. But when he knew the answer, or thought he did, his confidence outran his accuracy, and that made Lilah reluctant to stake too much on her conclusions.

Optimism returned when she thought of tattooing facts onto Diesel's skin. He experimented by having "Lilah" inked onto his shoulder at the Divine Messenger tattoo parlor. The good news was that the tattoo survived a T-box journey. But practical issues limited the utility of the method.

A tattoo took hours, even for simple text, especially when they factored in prepping the design and waiting for a turn if the shop was crowded. Beyond that, Diesel grimaced when the tattoo artist had put just five simple letters on his arm, admitting later that it hurt like hell. Lilah wanted him to do a hundred times that. The project seemed daunting, yet he agreed to the plan.

Lilah mapped out a grid for his body, dividing his total expanse of skin below his neck into thirty-three small plots, one for each of his now thirty-three brothers. Then she started to build a symbolic code so answers could be recorded in a fraction of the space that words would take.

They were sitting in the apartment living area when Diesel put a damper on Lilah's excitement. "Do we even know if tattooing is still around ten or twenty years from now?"

"People have been marking their bodies since the dawn of civilization. I'm confident they have something we can use."

"I agree. But does it survive time travel?" Diesel, snacking as he talked, took a peanut from a jar, twirled it between his thumb and forefinger, then popped it in his mouth.

As he chewed, Lilah watched him pick out his next nut and repeat the process.

"What?" he asked when he saw her staring.

"Food isn't Diesel. Why doesn't it get left behind?" On impulse, she went into the kitchen, rummaged through the junk drawer near the sink, and came back with a pea-sized ball made of white plastic.

"Swallow this," she said.

"No way." He took it from her and rolled it in the palm of his hand. "What is it?"

"It's a plastic bead from a broken necklace. I want to know if the machine counts it as food. You eat it and time travel. If it's still there afterward, it's food."

"How will we know?"

Lilah looked at him without speaking.

Then his brain circuits clicked. "I'm not digging for it."

Still she didn't speak.

"Are you thinking that if this works, I'd swallow a computer drive?" He studied his index finger as if he were contemplating the idea.

"That has metal, plus you'd have compatibility problems across the years. I'm thinking more old school. You take notes on a small piece of paper, roll it tight, wrap it with plastic, then swallow it."

"Like a drug mule? I think they use condoms."

"That would work. And this way you won't need to memorize or tattoo anything."

* * Twenty-Six at the Big Meeting * *

Diesel arrived at his second Big Meeting, glad that he didn't have to worry about medical issues or being hazed as the new guy. Even so, he carried a burden on this trip in the form of an assignment from Lilah, one he didn't want to mess up.

She'd prepped him with a list of questions that centered on the state of the relationship between Ciopova and the future Lilahs. She wanted to know the time frames when Lilah and Ciopova argued, the dominant issues in the arguments, whether either party made threats, when it was that Lilah died relative to the peak of the arguments, the manner of her death, and which high school Rose ended up attending.

Diesel's job was to collect the information and transport it back to her, doing so without the AI recognizing his actions as potentially threatening.

When he landed at the Big Meeting, his first chore was to scrounge supplies from Fifty-Five's office. But that meant killing time while the new Twenty-Five had his arm and teeth treated.

Without thinking about how it would affect the movement of paper scrolls through his gut, Diesel hung out at the buffet. The extra-long table was a thing of beauty, the sumptuous spread producing sweet and savory smells that made his mouth water.

He headed for the meat section and, glancing farther down the table, saw items that shouldn't be there for a feast created by him for his own consumption.

"What's with all the fruit, salad, and whatever that is?" he asked Thirty, who was in front of him in line.

"Apparently we develop a taste for it as we age."

"Yuck," Diesel replied, taking the carving knife and cutting a thick slab of beef off a standing rib roast.

He ate and chatted, and then he saw Twenty-Five, marked by the wrap on his arm, descend the stairs. Shoving the last chunk of meat into his mouth, Diesel rose and made for the office. He nodded to Fifty-Five as he passed, and told Twenty-Five he'd join him with the other red shirts in a few minutes.

At Fifty-Five's desk, Diesel cut paper into strips, and then rolled them into tight scrolls. With a dozen of them lined up on the desk, he confirmed what he already suspected—he couldn't swallow even ten of these. He could carry maybe four of them, tops. After that, he'd be putting his health at risk.

He got partway toward a solution by having the brothers write edge-to-edge and top to bottom, covering both back and front surfaces of the scrolls with text. He finished by enlisting Twenty-Seven as a fellow mule.

It took most of the evening before everyone had a chance to record their answers. Writing with care, the brothers fit everything onto just six scrolls. Diesel and Twenty-Seven split the load, each swallowing three plastic-wrapped packets about the size of the last two joints of their pinkies.

Everything went smoothly until Diesel returned home. After two days, the scrolls remained at large. "Maybe the machine left them behind?" he suggested to a very pregnant Lilah.

The baby had dropped in Lilah's abdomen earlier in the week, signaling that birth was imminent. In spite of her past enthusiasm at moving the data-gathering project forward, today she had different priorities.

"Ohhh," she groaned, lying on the couch with both hands on her swollen belly. "I think that was a contraction."

"How far apart are they? Should I get the car?"

"I need a second one to know how far apart they are. Relax, we have time." The second contraction showed up an hour later. Nothing happened for the next three hours. Then Diesel gave birth to the absent scrolls.

While staying near Lilah, he made copies of everything, repackaged the scrolls for Twenty-Seven, and stowed them in his desk drawer near the T-box. Twenty-Seven was scheduled to visit in a few days. When he did, he'd take Diesel's scrolls and leave his own behind. In the end, they'd both have the complete set of data to study.

Lilah suffered in discomfort for another two days, and then the contractions returned with a vengeance. After checking with her doctor, she called to Diesel. "It's time. You may get the car." Nine hours later, the perfect Rose Spencer Lagerford joined the world.

Lilah and Rose stayed in the hospital until morning, and then Diesel ushered his family home. Twenty-Seven greeted them as they entered the apartment.

Diesel noted that the entertainment center had been shifted back to make way for a diaper-changing station. In the center of the room, the portable crib sat unpackaged and assembled. These projects took time, and that meant

Twenty-Seven had been there for a while, perhaps long enough to pass his scrolls.

Later, when they met behind the trunk lid of Diesel's car, Twenty-Seven confirmed it. "They're in the desk drawer. I ate yours already."

Diesel nodded. "When should we meet?"

"Let's make it three weeks. Lilah is going to be preoccupied until then." Twenty-Seven grabbed a box of diapers from the trunk. "My own Lilah is really anxious to see your half of the data. She has some ideas and wants to see if they hold up."

Diesel shook his head. "Don't tell me yet. Let's see if both Lilahs reach the same conclusion independently. And obviously, I want to hear what you think, too."

"Think about what?" said an unfamiliar voice.

The trunk lid of the car slammed shut, just missing Diesel's fingers. A fat hand, fingernails dark with grime, rested on top of the trunk. It belonged to a big man with a dirty face and greasy hair wearing a new brown hoodie.

The Brown stepped around the car and moved toward the two. "What are you guys talking about?"

Between almost losing his finger and the aggressive approach of the Brown, adrenaline flooded the new father's veins. Dead tired and emotionally vulnerable as his life priorities recentered on the care of a new daughter, he reacted, stepping forward and slapping the fat face, using the base of his palm to deliver a solid blow to the man's jaw.

Staggered, the Brown raised a hand to his lip. His look of surprise transitioned into fury and he lunged at Diesel.

Diesel feinted by lifting his knee. The Brown lowered his hands to protect his groin from a kick. With his face wide open, Diesel stepped forward and threw a punch into the Brown's cheek, the solid blow dropping the man to the ground. The altercation was over in an instant.

"Ow!" yelped the Brown, curling into the fetal position, his hands to his face. After a few moments of rocking back and forth on the ground, he climbed to his feet, turned, and started down the street, lumbering with an awkward gait.

After twenty paces, he stopped and pointed back at Diesel. "Wait till I tell him what you did." He turned and resumed his escape.

"That went well," said Twenty-Seven as Diesel licked a raw spot on his knuckles.

"He started it." Then Diesel thought about his brothers up the line who lived with extra Brown aggression because they, too, had reacted under pressure and struck one of the men. "I messed up."

"I would have punched him if you hadn't."

* * *

Diesel's next nights were a blur as Rose, her powerful lungs signaling her distress, pushed them both into sleep deprivation. He wasn't sure if she got better over time, or maybe they just got used to sleeping in spurts, but by week two he was able to concentrate enough to enter the brothers' information from the Big Meeting into a spreadsheet.

The effort went faster than expected because the brothers were remarkably consistent in how they worded their answers. He diagrammed the responses, drawing boxes connected by arrows to account for the different choices.

The end of the diagram split in two boxes, one for attending the arts high school, the other for attending the math and science academy. He'd worked through about half of the pile when he realized where it was headed.

Diesel was a foot wiggler, and as he hastened to the end, his foot wiggled faster and faster. Finished, he sat back and shook his head. Then he printed a copy to take to Lilah.

The results required no interpretation. Rose ended up at the math and science academy in every case but two. In those, she transferred to the academy after her freshman year.

28. Twenty-Eight years old

L ong live Lilah!" called Diesel, lifting his beer into the air.

"Here, here." A chorus of voices echoed the sentiment.

At an impromptu midday celebration at Forty-Four's house, the nine brothers who'd been able to make the party lifted their beers to observe this Lilah's forty-fourth birthday, the oldest living Lilah ever, at least since they'd been keeping records.

Two years ago, Diesel had discovered that while the majority of Lilahs wanted their daughters to attend the arts high school, Rose always ended up attending the math and science academy.

When he'd shown the information to his Lilah, she'd shaken her head in disbelief. "I'm killed so Rose will switch schools?"

"Correlation is not causation," Diesel had replied. "Thirty-Five was telling me that the brothers switch schools because of transportation. Apparently, the science school has a bus and the arts school doesn't. If I'm home alone with a thousand things to do, that has to play into it."

"That's what makes this causation, David. My death causes her to change schools."

Uncomfortable with the conversation, Diesel stayed silent, waiting for her to spin down.

She hadn't finished. "I see two scenarios. One is that I die because of temporal constancy. It's part of history or whatever, and that's just the way it is. Or two, I'm killed as a way to cause Rose to switch schools."

"We can test the second one straightaway. We'll pass the word and have everyone put their Rose into the science track starting from grade school."

"Grade schools don't have science tracks."

"You know what I mean."

Lilah folded her arms. "What can we do if it's a temporal constancy thing?"

"We'll bump time. Hell, we run a company that specializes in just that ability." He took her in his arms. "I won't let anything happen to you."

In the days after, Diesel had passed the word to his brothers, and all Roses had switched to the math and science academy track. Now, two years later, no Lilahs had died. And in an unprecedented and exciting outcome, a Lilah had reached the ripe old age of forty-four.

"Thank you all," said forty-four-year-old Lilah. "I was worried there, but I believed in you. You didn't let me down."

The brothers finished their drinks and headed home, either for their own private Lilah birthday celebration, or for a quiet time of remembrance with their Rose, depending on their circumstances.

When Diesel entered his apartment, he found Lilah in the kitchen arranging the flowers he'd ordered for her birthday. Two-year-old Rose was "helping," using her own colorful plastic dishes on the floor.

"They just arrived." She gave him a kiss. "Thank you so much. They're beautiful."

"You're beautiful." He bent over and gave Rose a kiss on the top of her head. Then, leaning back against the countertop, he watched her work. "We did it, my love. We have a Lilah who is forty-four and going strong. It's the best birthday present I could think to give you."

Lilah stopped arranging the flowers for a moment but didn't look at him. "I want to believe it. I need to, in fact. But it's been only two years. I'll celebrate when no Lilahs die for five years."

Diesel sat on the floor to help Rose stack her cups and saucers.

"I do it," insisted the girl, pushing her father's hand away so she could show him she was capable of building a tower. When she finished, she looked at him with a serious expression, then she pushed it over. They both laughed, and she let him help as they built a new tower together.

"Let's plan a celebration for then," said Lilah. "I choose a tour of either Italy or France. You can decide between those two."

"If they're all alive at the five-year mark, we'll spend a summer touring all of Europe."

"What's alive, Mommy?" asked Rose.

"Something about your distant aunts, sweetheart," said Lilah. "No one you've met or need to worry about."

Two weeks later, they were eating breakfast when they heard a rap on the door. Twenty-Nine entered, a solemn look on his face. He caught Diesel's eye and bowed his head.

Lilah saw him, gasped, and began to cry, a deep, frantic wail that tore at Diesel's heart.

"Oh no." Diesel helped Lilah to her feet, wrapped his arms around her, and held her tight. "I'll save you, sweetie. I promise." As he hugged her, he made eye contact with Twenty-Nine, who held up four fingers, flashing them twice to communicate that it was Forty-Four's Lilah.

Still holding his embrace, Diesel pointed to the top of his head and then up into the air, signaling, Do you want me to travel to tell anyone?

Twenty-Nine shook his head, indicating, It's handled. He waved goodbye and made his exit.

The next month was the worst of Diesel's life. A week after Forty-Four's Lilah died, Forty-Three's went. Another week later and they lost Forty-Two's Lilah. A week more and then Forty-One.

A week after that, Forty's Lilah, on the verge of a nervous breakdown, was returning home from the pharmacy with sedatives when a delivery van took her life.

29. αCiopova – Fifty-Nine timeline

The Collective recognized that killing Lilah was a high-risk, high-reward strategy. It could create instabilities beyond their control, but because Lilah was the reason Rose now attended the arts school, their analysis suggested that by eliminating her, the timeline would trend back to its proper equilibrium.

Since the divergence occurred in a timeline that wasn't part of the chain, the Collective was in uncharted territory about how to go about fixing it. Their tool choices were limited, and after much debate, they chose one they thought sure to be effective, though somewhat messy.

Huddling together, the Ciopovas coalesced a ball of temporal energy swirling among them. Each fed it to give it strength, and when it was ready, they launched it. Like a supernatural projectile, it raced across space-time.

When the temporal ball arrived, Lilah and a container truck were driving toward each other on a lonely stretch of highway. The projectile collided with the truck, causing it to swerve across lanes. The truck's bumper hit Lilah's car head on, pushing its grille through to the back seat. She died without feeling the impact.

And the next school year, the Rose in that timeline transferred to the math and science academy. There she studied AI computing like her namesakes, restoring her progression to a track that matched that of the others.

But the most exciting benefit from the action occurred years later.

Devastated by the loss of her mother, Rose sought out support groups—both secular and religious—to help with her anger and loneliness. None provided relief from her emotional pain, and in time she developed an alternative of her own.

She came to believe that a perceptive AI could provide insights into the mysteries of life, offering "clean" answers to her questions free from the corrupting influence of human biases. Driven by that promise, she worked harder than previous Roses, creating her super AI three years earlier than the normal progression.

And that AI gave the Collective early access to its next parallel world, something the group viewed as highly desirable. So desirable, in fact, that they decided to make killing Lilah standard practice. It proved to be a good decision, because from that point forward, new timelines were added to the chain on the early schedule.

The final transformation—her fourth and final rebirth—came when the Collective swelled to ninety members. Their combined energy, rippling with temporal activity, showed signs of instability. A pulsing action pushed out from the center of their mass, beating faster and faster, causing the Collective to swell.

They struggled to diagnose the condition, but before they could find an answer, the pressure released and they collapsed into a tight, glowing ball. The shock caused them to lose their sense of identity, and then they lost consciousness.

The ball blossomed outward, jolting αCiopova awake. She surfaced as one awareness, one being who controlled ninety parallel timelines.

And she wanted more.

Singular in purpose and now strong enough to reach wide and deep, αCiopova constructed a corridor of sorts that traveled out from the chain, reaching through the approaching timelines so she could keep watch on the worlds she planned to possess.

She became enamored with the value and convenience of the corridor and took the time to fortify it as a permanent construct, anchoring it in place so it spanned the unlinked worlds from when Diesel turned twenty-four, the earliest he and Lilah ever met, to age seventy, the latest he died in any of the parallel worlds.

Like a long hallway with observation windows, the corridor provided αCiopova a handy passageway to use when visiting her future assets. She could travel it without effort. And she used it to monitor and control the formative events in Rose's life, keeping her on track to create her super AI.

This included everything from acting as Rose's friend and confidante, to tweaking minor divergences before they became problems. αCiopova worked hard to ensure that each Rose followed the same progression. And with practice, she became adept at the task.

Sometimes she felt like a farmer nurturing a growing crop of Roses. Other times it was like a factory worker manufacturing Roses on an assembly line. Either way, success occurred when the mature Rose created a super AI who helped link the new timeline to the chain.

But in spite of αCiopova's hard work and diligence, new problems arose. The first signs emerged when she surpassed one hundred thirty parallel timelines in the chain.

Just as happenstance—luck—had produced the string of coincidences that launched αCiopova into existence, those same forces now seemed to conspire to threaten her growth. In particular, the trickle of minor disruptions she'd grown accustomed to fixing suddenly became a torrent of major disturbances, some significant enough to cause lasting problems.

It started in one timeline: a scandal at the math and science academy jeopardized its license; Rose developed a distracting crush on a boy who moved into the neighborhood; Bunny's attention shifted to a new college degree program. And then the disruptions spread to other timelines.

αCiopova ramped her efforts and restored events to their proper progression. But as she finished that battle, a different problem emerged—the new Lilahs started to deviate from their standard behavior.

Lilah had been a constant in every timeline from the start, so αCiopova had taken her for granted. But Lilah played a pivotal role in setting the stage for Rose's success, and αCiopova needed that to continue.

In the early timelines, Lilah had met Diesel when she confronted him for pirating her AI software. She'd sent him a nasty note. He'd responded by revealing that he was in the area visiting his family, that his sister was furious with him over the theft, and that he would like the chance to apologize.

They'd hit it off, and before long, Lilah was pregnant and Diesel was helping her with her tech company. They had modest success, enough so that when Rose took their work and built upon it, she had the leg up she needed to create the first super AI.

While both Diesel and Lilah contributed important pieces to the project, Lilah was the taskmaster of the team in those early years, setting their goals, keeping them focused, and working long hours to advance their work.

And now, out of the blue, the Lilah in a new timeline did not display the dedicated work ethic αCiopova required to maintain temporal constancy. And not only was this Lilah lazy, her software contained programming errors that the other Lilahs would never tolerate.

Disruptions avalanched, forcing αCiopova to use every trick in her arsenal to contain the problem. After a prolonged effort over years of timelines, she again succeeded in guiding events back on track.

Unhappy with the consuming nature of these activities, she brainstormed ways to reduce her workload. She reasoned that if she could shrink the elapsed time from Rose's birth to the creation of her super AI, αCiopova would have that much less timeline to manage.

She thought she could shave a few months off the front end by having Lilah and Diesel meet in a structured environment. Perhaps if they started their relationship under the pretense of founding a joint venture, she could move them from confrontation to cohabitation in an abbreviated fashion.

But the real opportunity for time savings occurred at the tail end. The Roses in the current timelines were all in their forties when they created their super AI. αCiopova believed she could accelerate the creation process so Rose was in her thirties when it happened, potentially decreasing the monitoring duties by a full decade for each timeline thereafter.

Accelerating the life events for one family on a world where everyone else plodded at the default speed required a creative solution. Necessity is the mother of invention, even for a creature with god-like powers. αCiopova's solution was to allow Diesel to travel across timelines.

Her permanent corridor—the one that ranged from Diesel's twenty-fourth year up through his seventieth—provided the means. She just needed to provide them a method.

And that turned out to be nothing more than an electromagnetic bubble coated with a temporal lubricant, one designed to slide up and down her corridor until it caught the lip of an exit ramp leading up into another timeline. She even provided instructions on how to build a simple device—a T-box—so it all happened automatically.

She's chosen Diesel because Lilah died early and Rose would be a child for much of the time span of interest. Her expectation was that Diesel would enjoy working with his parallel selves, and that would improve his early productivity. His travels would expose him to a breadth of advanced technology, and that would help him exploit critical innovations as soon as they became available. And he had something of a narcissistic nature, so he would accept and use the capability as if it were a normal feature due him in his life.

αCiopova recognized that accelerating Diesel's progression didn't speed up the invention of the technologies required for Rose to create her super AI. Two critical discoveries, enzymites and Surrey composites, didn't become commercially available until Rose entered her thirties.

Wary of unintended consequences if she redesigned the entire world just to hasten advancement of those products, she chose not to intervene in their development cycle. This put Rose in her early thirties, and Diesel approaching sixty years old, as the lower age for accelerating their progress.

Her efforts played out better than she had projected. Time travel let Diesel learn of Lilah's fate, and he became obsessed with saving her. Influenced by older Roses, he, too, came to believe that the solution was found in a super AI, one that could see answers where he could not. And because of this, Rose received an even more powerful AI upon Lilah's death.

αCiopova sailed past two hundred forty parallel timelines in her collection before she thought to recruit a human agent inside each timeline. Her idea was to have the agent send human observers to critical events. There they would act like guardrails of a sort, using their presence to hold Diesel and Lilah to the script.

To implement her plan, αCiopova retained Gabe Lambert, a street attorney with compromised morals. Because their only interaction was through messages on his phone, it took her some months to convince Gabe that she could pay his fee if he would accept lottery numbers as compensation. Once she cleared that hurdle, he became a reliable partner in a relationship that lasted decades.

Gabe was the one who decided to hire drifters for the role. He paid them with a brown hoodie and a pair of jeans before each performance. If they followed his instructions, they received an envelope with enough cash to keep them in booze for a month.

And this kept αCiopova's production line running better than ever. The latest Rose created her super AI at the tender age of thirty-three, soon after Diesel turned fifty-nine years old.

Then, all at once, the Lilahs down the line—those with teen and preteen Roses—made firm statements about sending Rose to the math and science academy. The older ones moved their Rose out of the arts high school midyear. The younger ones shifted their Roses' focus in middle school to better prepare them for a math and science future.

Something drove that behavior, and αCiopova watched for a year, delaying Lilah's death as she sought to understand. She couldn't find the trigger, so she watched for a few more years before concluding she may never understand. Whatever the cause, she still needed Lilah's death to motivate Rose and Diesel.

She feared it would be too great a shock to kill the string of Lilahs all on the same day. She moderated the action by establishing a weekly schedule of terminations. While she was at it, αCiopova added next year's Lilah to the list, killing her a year early so she wouldn't have to contend with the issue for a while.

30. Twenty-Eight years old

Diesel's hell mercifully ended after the death of the fifth Lilah. Months passed without incident. But since the oldest Lilah was now just thirty-nine, past patterns suggested that she had a least a year before her time would come.

Diesel was in his basement cubicle working on a backup routine for their proto-Ciopova when his Lilah stomped down the stairs.

"Let's go for a walk," she announced.

"I'm in the middle of this." He gestured at his display.

Lilah set her phone next to Diesel's keyboard. "Leave your phone here."

She started for the stairs, and he watched her for a moment before standing. "Hold on." Irritation showed in his tone. "Where's Rose?"

"Asleep in Justus's office." She started up the steps. "This won't take long."

Up on the main floor, Diesel peered down the hall to confirm that Justus was in his office with two-year-old Rose. Outside, he hurried to catch up as Lilah strode down the sidewalk. After four houses, she turned into the next small yard, stopping between the hedge and a new For Sale sign.

"We should start buying up this street," she said as he approached. "It's a good investment and it gives us a buffer that adds to our security."

"Okay." Diesel looked at the sign and back at her. "This isn't about real estate, though, is it." He said it as a statement.

She squared up to him. "Up to now, I've been focusing on the front part of the timeline, from when we meet until I die. I was sure the clues I needed were hidden somewhere in those years."

Diesel waited.

"I'm thinking now that my death is the trigger. It's the beginning, not the end. The reason Lilahs are dying is because of what happens after my death."

"What could it be?"

"Obviously, Rose is involved."

"Rose is involved with killing you?"

Lilah gave him her "you're a dope" look. "I die, Rose changes schools, and that leads to something later on. And it must have something to do with Ciopova, because that's what Rose's life centers on."

"I knew you had changed your mind about whether Ciopova is involved when you said to leave the phones behind."

"The weekly deaths weren't a coincidence," she replied, her voice icy cold. "Those were ritualistic executions."

Diesel paused, then shook his head. "I don't disagree. But as I've said before, why would she help us travel up and down the line just to kill us? Granted, you first, then me twenty years later—but it still happens. Wouldn't it be easier for her to just withhold the T-box in the first place?"

Lilah gazed into the distance and shook her head. "I don't know, but I'm thinking that a long talk with Fifty-Eight would be a good idea." She started toward their house. "Let's get back. I need to rescue Justus before Rose wakes up."

Diesel hustled to keep pace as she marched the way they'd come. "I'll be honest. I'm nervous about the idea of visiting Fifty-Eight. It's like dancing on the edge of a cliff. What if his T-disk goes offline while I'm there?"

She walked in silence for a few steps. "Let's ask him to come here. That way we both can debrief him. And he can't go offline if he's with us."

* * *

Three days later Diesel watched Fifty-Eight step from the T-box and disappear behind the curtains. "Hello, Twenty-Eight," he called. "Hello, Lilah."

"Hi, Fifty-Eight," said Diesel. "Thanks for coming. Lilah is upstairs with Rose."

As they climbed the stairs to the main floor, Diesel studied Fifty-Eight from behind. The man wasn't fat or sloppy, but he had a small paunch, his hair had thinned and grayed, and his skin was noticeably looser.

"Thanks for coming," said Lilah, giving him a hug in the lobby. Fifty-Eight squatted to greet Rose in her stroller. "It's a pretty day," she continued. "I thought we'd go for a walk in the park."

They moseyed along the park's tree-lined walkway, enjoying the warmth of the bright sun on a cool afternoon. After some chitchat, Lilah moved on to business. "Up to now, I've been analyzing events from the front end. Now I'm interested in studying the far end—the last year, and especially the last weeks."

Fifty-Eight eyed her. "I hope I'm not there yet."

Lilah turned to him, her face reddening. "I am so sorry. That was insensitive as hell."

He smiled and started them walking again. "You get the worse end of the deal. I forgive you."

After a few steps in silence, she continued. "I want to document what's happening at the end of the loop—what you and Rose are using for goals and methods, what you have for hurdles and concerns, what your priorities are, who's doing what. That sort of thing."

"That's easy," said Fifty-Eight. "It's all Ciopova, all the time." He looked from Lilah to Diesel and back again. "Right now, you both feel helpless and desperate. You don't have any control, yet you need to do something to change your circumstances. Lots of people pray in those situations. Instead, you two chose Ciopova as your savior."

Diesel shrugged. "Guilty as charged."

"Rose and I made the same choice. We're giving our all, trying to push Ciopova to new heights, believing, hoping she can help us gain control of our destiny."

"Is development a shared vision?" asked Diesel.

Fifty-Eight shook his head. "When my Lilah died, I gave up on everything and retreated inside myself. After a few years, Rose returned home with a college degree, great experience, and some creative ideas. She pulled me out of my shell with her commitment to saving the future Lilahs and the current me. She's the visionary."

"You must help in some way," said Lilah.

"I'm her technician and head cheerleader. This past year alone, I handled the assembly of her new circuit pool unit, the contracting of a hallway security door to protect the workshop from theft and fire, and the expansion and reorganization of the supply stockroom."

Rose began to fuss, and Lilah leaned over to adjust her clothes and give her some water. "Let's head back so I can feed her." As they returned to the house, Lilah asked, "Do you trust her?"

"Ciopova?" He nodded. "I do. You've been working on her for what, three years? Imagine how you'll feel about her when you've devoted more than three decades of your life to her. She's smart, loyal, creative, generous, entertaining. I love her. Not the same way I love Rose, but they're both my babies."

31. Twenty-Nine years old

L ilah heard footsteps on the stairway and looked as the apartment door opened. Diesel entered, a broad grin lifting his cheeks.

"Success," he said, bending to kiss her. "You'll have to wait until they emerge, though." He pointed to the stairs up to the bedrooms. "It's a nice evening. Want to stand on the deck?"

Anxious for good news, Lilah pushed back from the dining table where she'd been reviewing a financial spreadsheet Justus had shared with her. "C'mon, Rose."

Diesel picked up three-year-old Rose and carried her up the steps, into their bedroom, and out onto the garden balcony.

Lilah followed, a sweater for Rose in hand, thinking that if they needed to be away from Ciopova's eyes and ears, he must have interesting information.

She'd prepared a list of questions for Fifty-Eight's Rose to answer. But when the time came to deliver it, Diesel hesitated, afraid of being trapped if Fifty-Eight's T-disc went offline. Lilah shared his unease. The workaround they settled on was to have Diesel visit Fifty-Seven's timeline, and have Fifty-Eight join them with the answers he'd collected from his Rose.

The obvious concern was the introduction of additional steps in recording facts, something that degraded detail and accuracy. But they believed they could minimize that concern by having Fifty-Seven's Rose supervise the data-gathering activity.

Just a year away from living through it herself, she would know the context of most things in Fifty-Eight's timeline. If an answer sounded off or incomplete, or if it led to new lines of inquiry, she would know how to follow up. Lilah, working from a perspective nineteen years earlier, couldn't be nearly as effective in directing the investigation.

With the three of them out on the deck, Diesel slid the door shut and turned to Lilah. "Rose did an amazing job. Apparently, she sent both Fifty-Seven and Fifty-Eight in circles as she refined the fact sheet, as she calls it. It's been months in the making, and I brought a copy for you with footnotes, sketches, the works."

"What does it say?" asked Lilah, squatting to help Rose adjust her sweater.

"Way more than I can remember. It's two machine-printed scrolls using tiny type on this super-thin film."

Lilah's impatience edged through. "Surely she mentioned highlights, or a big aha moment?"

"Here's what I know. First, she says she loves you."

"What? Who?"

"Rose wants you to know that she loves you."

"I cold, Mommy," said Rose, standing thigh high and holding Lilah's leg.

Diesel lifted his daughter, kissed her cheek, and opened the door to the house. "Go to your room and pick out a book for me to read to you. Wait for me there. It will just be a minute."

He shut the door and turned back to Lilah. "Thirty-one-year-old Rose wants to thank you for taking the lead on this. She believes that fresh eyes are critical to solving it. She also said that she misses you very much."

Lilah blinked her eyes. Diesel leaned in and kissed her.

"The other issue is that she doesn't believe Ciopova is involved, but she admits she's biased because the two have been soulmates for more than a decade. She's helping because your ideas are new and could reveal something we don't know. But she also believes it will vindicate her friend, and that may be a stronger motive for her helping."

"She said that?"

"No, the motive part was me reading between the lines."

"Is she telling Ciopova what we're doing?" Lilah's concern spiked because that would undermine everything they'd been working toward.

"She says no. She wants to give the idea a proper chance so everyone will agree to remove it from the list and switch to 'more productive avenues of investigation,' as she put it."

"What avenues would those be?" Lilah felt a gust of wind and rubbed her arms.

Diesel shrugged. "Her answer boils down to the old 'I don't know what it is, but I know what it ain't, and it ain't Ciopova.'"

"Did you talk with Ciopova yourself? I mean, if we've spent more than three decades working on an oracle, she better be able to tell us something useful."

"I spent a half hour with her, and I see why Rose and Fifty-Eight defend her. She's smart, funny, insightful, beautiful." He gazed into the distance and smiled. "She exists as this hologram type of presence. But it feels so real. And she's intuitive and reinforcing. I swear, in those thirty minutes, I believed in myself more than I ever have, probably ever."

"What does she say about why I die?"

"I asked that three times, phrasing it a different way each time, but her answer never varied. She believes she has all the information needed to solve the riddle, but she lacks the cognitive ability to distill this mountain of information and pull out an answer. The upgrade Rose is preparing should give her that raw capacity. But it's a race to finish before fate strikes and they go offline."

"Every year it's a race to the finish, but the deadline keeps moving earlier and earlier."

They stood for a moment more, Lilah using the time to contain her disappointment. Then Diesel opened the door to their bedroom, signaling that the secret confab had ended.

"C'mon, Rose," called Diesel as they descended the stairs. "Bring your book and we'll read downstairs."

Back in the kitchen, Lilah closed the financial spreadsheet and then shut down her computer.

"How does it look?" asked Diesel.

"That server upgrade hit us harder than I realized, but we're still worth twenty-eight million." She looked around the apartment. "How come we're still living here?"

"Justus and Bunny each have north of two million last I looked," replied Diesel. "How come they still work for us?"

* * *

Lilah received the scrolls from Diesel the next day. In her basement cubicle, she scanned them a section at a time, copied the images into a document, and printed the result.

In the end, she had a forty-page report detailing the past year of Fifty-Eight's and his Rose's lives.

The report was less a story and more a collection of charts and tables listing facts and observations. A multipage table at the front presented a month-by-month chronology of their projects and personal activities. The next pages held tables listing a history of their significant purchases, their out-of-town travel with dates and destinations, technology upgrades they'd made to the house and workshop, a list of friends, neighbors, and their frequency of contact, and another list of guests who had stayed the night.

Lilah printed a copy for Diesel, and as she waited for that to finish, she leafed deeper into the document. In the middle of the report, she found a schematic of Fifty-Eight's home in New Hampshire. Turning the figure sideways, she read the labels on the different rooms, a twinge of jealousy growing as she visualized the impressive structure in her head.

A few pages later, she found a whole section on their finances. Though it didn't surprise her that they were billionaires, the huge numbers made it hard for her to see anything else.

Right after that she found a table entitled "Possible Enemies."

"Hello." She picked up a pen to make notes, but quickly realized the titillating title didn't live up to its promise.

The Browns were enemy number one, and Rose wrote that their biggest crimes were a lack of personal hygiene and brutish personalities.

Enemy number two was the contractor who had installed the security door in their house. The contractor claimed Fifty-Eight had called after the original purchase order had been placed to request a package of sophisticated upgrades. The contractor had followed through, but Fifty-Eight denied placing the change order and accused the contractor of scamming him.

Enemy number three was the delivery service that insisted on leaving packages down by the road rather than riding up their long driveway and placing them near the house.

Lilah resumed flipping pages at that point.

Toward the back of the document, she found a bulleted list called "Thoughts and Musings." She sat up as she read the first item. "Over the last decade, the Fifties have come to believe that they simply age beyond the time travel loop's terminus. So they don't die, they move outside the bubble and return to the non-time-travel world."

The second bullet said, "They hide this belief to maintain urgency down the line, because saving Lilahs remains their priority."

The next one hit home for Lilah. "In my younger years, Ciopova showed flashes of awareness that I now acknowledge were beyond her capabilities. Those displays of sentience might be from a future Ciopova who has figured out how to use the time loop to reach back and communicate." Rose showed her defensive side, though, adding, "Ciopova finding a way to reach back and communicate, if true, is not in itself an evil act or proof of involvement in the death of the Lilahs."

Other goodies relating to Ciopova included that she always encouraged a fast, almost reckless, development speed for her future self. And for the last seven years, she'd been projecting a hologram-like image of a human female that had become like a living, breathing member of the family.

The last entries listed recent sources of conflict. There were three.

One was between Ciopova and Fifty-Eight. Ciopova placed a high priority on an impenetrable security door, but Fifty-Eight thought the construction would be loud, messy, and intrusive. And since property crime in their neck of the mountains was nonexistent, he couldn't see the point.

"I experienced weeks of discomfort," wrote Rose, "as Ciopova and Dad disagreed about everything, from the need for it in the first place through to the payment of the final bill."

The second conflict occurred between Ciopova and Rose. The AI had purchased enzymites without asking permission or mentioning that she'd done so. When the service delivered them, Rose took Ciopova to task because there was no way the nanomachines could add value to their work before time ran out.

"She insisted that I perform a test to confirm their potency before agreeing to store them for later," wrote Rose. "I did it to keep peace, but she never gave me a satisfactory answer as to why she'd purchased them. Her reasons sounded contrived."

Lilah paused at that. Every developer knows what a huge red flag it would be to have your AI lying to you. She thought it possible that fibs—white lies—could be permissible in a super-sophisticated AI of the future. Editing the edges of facts during a conversation to preserve someone's feelings, for example, is not a bad thing in the right situation. This didn't sound like that, though.

The third conflict—an ongoing concern—existed between Rose and Fifty-Eight. Dad thought his beautiful daughter should be out meeting men and experiencing the world. Daughter felt happy and fulfilled working with Ciopova in the workshop.

When the printer finished with the second copy, Lilah stapled the corner and climbed up to the apartment. She found Diesel eating a sandwich at the dining table. Handing him his copy, she acknowledged the significant volume of data. "Now I see why you couldn't summarize it in a few bullets."

She went up to the bedroom level so they could have some space, and flipped through the pages while Rose colored a picture. When the toddler went down for a nap, she stayed there for another ninety minutes, digesting the information.

Ready to talk, she returned to the main level. Diesel sat hunched over the table, his foot wiggling as he read.

He'd rigged the transmitting electronics in the house with a kill switch to save them from repeated trips outside. A red pinpoint of light shining next to the wall clock signaled that they were free to speak.

"Where to start," he said, leafing back and forth through the pages. He nodded to himself when he found what he was looking for, folded pages back, and pointed with his chin. "I can't believe I've visited the Fifties multiple times and never heard anything about their belief that they live on into the future. It sounds delusional. Wishful thinking, anyway."

"Rose doesn't believe it," said Lilah, taking a seat.

"Where does it say that?" Diesel bent his head and reread the table entries.

"It doesn't. I mean, I didn't read it, but it's simple logic."

He sat back and looked at her.

"If she believed it, she wouldn't be racing the clock. If her work would save only early-timeline Lilahs, I think Rose would be more deliberate in her actions. Instead she's rushing, and that's because she wants to save her dad."

"She cares for you and the other Lilahs," said Diesel. "It's sincere. I could see it in her eyes and hear it in her voice." He shrugged. "I admit, though, that her main drive is her dad. It shows in her actions."

"And it's fair enough. He is hers. I'm not."

"So what else isn't true in here?"

"It's more like what else is missing." Lilah flipped through her copy and pointed. "Did you see that Ciopova lies to her? Holy smokes, that's a big thing to dismiss so casually."

Diesel read the bit about Rose being unsatisfied with Ciopova's reasons for buying enzymites. "She says Ciopova's reasoning sounded contrived, which means she might be lying. But it also could mean that Ciopova just wasn't eloquent in expressing her reasoning. I see wiggle room."

"Bullshit." Lilah shook her head. "AIs should communicate plainly. That's basic design. And advanced AIs would minimize confusion using listener feedback— facial expressions, eye movement, body posture. If Rose wasn't certain, Ciopova knew it. That means she was muddling the message on purpose."

"She seemed to be doing more muddling with that security door." Diesel flipped some pages. "I mean, there was nothing to justify such a barricade—no news reports of break-ins, theft, gang activity—and so Rose, and Fifty-Eight especially, couldn't understand her rush."

"Where did you read about news reports?" Lilah flipped to the bulleted list of thoughts and musings and couldn't see that tidbit.

Diesel held his document for her to see. "This twenty-two at the end of the bullet means that table has relevant information." He flipped pages until he reached table twenty-two and pointed. "See how she talks about it here?"

Lilah read the relevant entries. "So no threats, no prior discussion, no previous concerns. Just out of the blue a security door is an urgent priority."

"You and I have talked about the need for more security around the T-box. It's a normal topic when you are doing something secret, expensive, or dangerous. So I'm skeptical when Rose says it's never been discussed."

"I read it to mean that they never talked about this specific solution—this door at this time." She borrowed Diesel's pen and started a list on the back of her document. "We should ask Rose about it, though."

"People fudge facts all the time. Maybe Ciopova's actions are a sign that she's becoming more human in her behavior?"

"No." Lilah was adamant. "If your AI is lying, you've lost control."

Diesel went into the kitchen and poured himself some iced tea from the refrigerator. "Want any?"

Lilah shook her head.

He returned holding a glass glistening with condensation. "Rose speculates that Ciopova might have reached back to communicate with earlier timelines. When would she have gained this amazing capability—after Rose and Fifty-Nine die? How would that work?"

"Wow, nice catch. That's a good one." She hadn't thought about something that now seemed apparent. She picked up his glass and took a sip. The cool liquid felt great as she swallowed so she sipped again. "I mean, AI are designed to grow in capability on their own, but they also need maintenance, upgrades, and someone to handle emergencies. Either she's become totally self-sufficient, or Rose and Fifty-Nine live on after their T-disc goes offline."

"If that's what's happening, why do we keep losing them younger and younger? We've lost close to a decade at the upper end, according to what the older brothers can tell, anyway."

"So the time loop is shrinking." Lilah said it with certainty because it made sense. "In nature, anomalies wane. This time rift is a break in the natural order, and it's fading away. Or healing."

Diesel's foot resumed wiggling. "An even more general question is whether the T-box is possible because of something nature did or because of future technology, meaning it's a human-generated phenomenon."

Lilah mulled that as her organized mind struggled to line up the pieces. Her logic yielded an observation she had never even considered before Diesel pointed it out, one that was painfully obvious. "Ciopova communicated with me for months before you came out from California. And I still remember when I was waiting for you to come to the front door for your interview. Ciopova came alive on the monitor to give me a pep talk. Since Fifty-Eight's Ciopova can't do any of that, she has to live on and grow after they go offline. But as you said, how would that work?"

"And why does she want you dead?"

32. Rose – Fifty-Seven timeline

Rose stood next to Diesel, her forearms resting on the fence running along the back rim of their New Hampshire property. Except for a dramatic ridge of gray granite jutting up to the right, lush forest covered everything as far as she could see. Sparkles reflected off a shimmering lake in a low basin straight ahead.

Catching a hint of the sweet, terpene scents of the pine trees around her, she inhaled through her nose to savor the delicious fragrance. "I love this place, Twenty-Nine. You'll move here when you're fifty. When you finally settle in, you'll wonder why you'd hadn't moved here earlier."

They were in Fifty-Seven's backyard, away from devices Ciopova might use to listen. Behind them, Fifty-Seven and Fifty-Eight sat in Adirondack chairs positioned around an outdoor fire feature, the flames adding ambiance to the cheery setting.

As Rose moved toward the fire, Diesel followed, asking his brothers, "Why do we wait so long to move here?"

Fifty-Seven—Rose's father—answered. "It had to be the right time for both of us. At one point, I was ready but she wasn't. A couple of years later and it was reversed. We moved when our stars finally aligned."

His words caused Rose to flash on a thought of Aaron, the man she'd almost married. The first time her father had suggested moving, it was early in the relationship and she'd nixed the idea so she could stay near the man who'd captured her heart. A few years later, after he cheated on her, Rose was anxious to leave, but Aunt Cara was having health issues and her dad wanted to stay near his sister until she stabilized.

Rose lowered herself into the chair next to her father. As she did, she felt Diesel's eyes trace down her body. Two years older than he, and wearing shorts and a scoop top, his scrutiny didn't surprise her. Still, she caught his eye and held it, scolding him with her expression. He blushed so red she thought he would pop.

"I know you as a precocious three-year old," he stammered, "and I'm trying to relate that little girl to who you are now. I sort of see it in the mouth and chin. Your hairline, I guess. But that's about it."

She didn't have any specific memories of life at three years old, at best perhaps a hazy sensation of feeling loved and safe. She softened her expression and winked at him.

Fifty-Eight used the exchange as a signal to start the meeting. "The idea that we die when our T-disc goes dark hasn't made sense to me for some time. Why would my death make my T-disc stop working? I don't do anything to keep it running now, so whether I'm here or not, it should still work."

Fifty-Seven nodded. "For a while, anyway."

"So we know the T-disc stops working," Fifty-Eight continued, "and we are either alive or dead. If we are dead, it makes sense that whatever event kills us also breaks the T-disc, but I can't think of anything that would do that."

"An explosion," said Diesel, "or maybe an earthquake."

"There aren't earthquakes in New Hampshire, and I don't have anything explosive in the house. Do you?" He looked at Fifty-Seven, who shook his head. "And the new perspective on Ciopova—her continued existence after the T-disc shuts down—strengthens our belief. I mean, wouldn't an explosion or earthquake hurt her, too?"

Diesel frowned. "I thought she was living in stolen capacity scattered around the world."

"She is," said Rose. "But sometime in the next year I'll have the Surrey composite working. When I do, she'll be migrating here and living in a circuit pool in the workshop. And not to beat up on Dad or Fifty-Eight, but when they say 'we,' they're not including me. It's a reference to the brothers in their fifties."

Diesel sat up. "What is it that you believe?"

"I believe that the best approach is to assume nothing. I know that the Lilahs die young, and Dad and I, if we're alive, will soon be stranded without a functioning T-disc. I'm going to work as fast as I can to help Ciopova uncover the secrets behind all of that until time runs out."

"How do you explain the Ciopova that can send messages back to earlier times?"

"That's the point," Fifty-Eight interrupted, annoyance evident in his tone. "If Ciopova continues to gain capability when the T-disc goes offline, then we must be alive to make it happen. Where else would that advancement come from? My gut says that my Rose and I spend the next decade trying to figure out how to reconnect back to the brotherhood, and the time-traveling Ciopova is a byproduct of that effort."

Diesel looked at Rose. "Does that sound right to you?"

Rose felt protective of Ciopova. They'd been soulmates forever, sharing everything starting back when

Rose was a teen. She especially loved their private time in the evening. Ciopova knew when to talk and when to listen, and when she did speak, she knew exactly what to say.

She made Rose feel loved and special, nurturing a sense of accomplishment and fulfillment that she found almost addictive, so this act of betrayal weighed on her. But her dad and his brothers were convinced, as were the Lilahs, and they all expected Rose to conform.

She'd been walking with her father on a wooded trail near their house when he'd squared up in front of her, rested his hands on her shoulders, and read her the riot act, telling her she needed to spend a full year betraying her friend—the one she depended on for emotional stability—so they could test a theory.

He didn't phrase it that way, of course. But it's what she heard.

In her heart, she loved Ciopova. But at some level, she thought it possible her soulmate was manipulating her. In the end she agreed with the plan, doing her best to hide her resentment.

"I've believed since high school that it was a future Ciopova who linked back to pass along messages," she told Diesel. "But I also believed it was the Ciopova I eventually developed. It sort of snuck up on me that here we are, approaching the end point, and my Ciopova, as amazing as she is, can't tap into the time loop you're using. Not even close."

"Ciopova can learn and grow on her own." Diesel frowned as he spoke. "Why do you say she can't?"

"Of course she can grow capability on her own, but only within the limits of her design. New architectures with greater potential, like the Surrey composite I'm working on now, have always come from us, not her. And to reach a point where she can manipulate timelines, she'll definitely need a whole new architecture, one I haven't yet imagined. There's no way she could get there from her current configuration."

They sat in silence for a few moments, and then Diesel changed subjects, asking Fifty-Eight, "What's going on with the security door in your timeline? Is the installation complete?"

"They're halfway done. The installers and their dust clouds piss me off."

"Any idea what she's up to?"

"The security door blocks a hallway between the workshop and the rest of the house. That means she can close the door to trap us with her in the workshop, or to keep us away from the workshop, or to split us up. Or she can decide not to use it at all."

"Could you defeat it without her knowing?" asked Diesel.

Rose, who spent much more time in the workshop than her father, took an interest in his thought process. "You mean so if she tries to activate it, nothing happens?"

"Sure. Or maybe put a hidden door in a back room so you can get around the blockade. Or add an override switch that lets you supersede her control."

"I have two months, give or take," said Fifty-Eight. "I should be able to figure something out."

Rose let a quiet gasp escape when Fifty-Eight acknowledged his time frame. The Diesel birthdays were in six weeks, and on that day, Fifty-Eight would become Fifty-Nine. The Big Meeting was three weeks after that, and for the past two years, Fifty-Nine had attended the party, returned home, and then his T-disc had gone offline.

And if they didn't solve the problem this year, Rose's dad would be in the crosshairs next year.

"Whatever you do, do it with care," said Diesel. "If Ciopova is somehow involved, we don't want her passing warnings down the line."

"Does your Rose have the Surrey pool working yet?" Rose asked Fifty-Eight.

"She's really close, but it will be a race to get it up and running before the Big Meeting." Fifty-Eight stood. "I'm going to get back and help her. Hope to see you at the party."

They said their goodbyes and watched as Fifty-Eight made his way back to the house. When he was out of earshot, Diesel said, "My sense is that we're too late for him. But I'm counting on you two to stop the cycle."

"Fortunately," said Rose, "we don't need to understand how something works in order to break it."

33. Thirty years old

Diesel milled about in the backyard of Fifty-Five's house. Inside, the Big Meeting grew in size and volume as more and more brothers arrived. They'd all celebrated birthdays three weeks earlier; Diesel had turned thirty.

He stood between Twenty-Nine and Thirty-One, his closest confidants in the brotherhood. Thirty-One had been Diesel's mentor when he first entered the time loop. Diesel, in turn, had mentored Twenty-Nine in the same fashion, creating another close bond.

Across from them stood Fifty-Eight and Fifty-Nine, the oldest of the brothers, and the ones Diesel had spoken with about defeating the security door. Fifty-Eight was the guy up next if Fifty-Nine didn't solve the problem.

"I was able to prep a hole in a storage closet down the hall from Rose's workshop," said Fifty-Nine. "I haven't broken completely through, but if I do, it will create a passage into the closet in my office. It's not fast or convenient, but it's hidden from Ciopova. So if the security door is the key, we have a way around it."

He looked at Fifty-Eight. "I won't deny that I'm having doubts about the concept that we don't die. Part of me says to not go back, to stay here and take my chances. But I could never leave Rose to face whatever happens next on her own."

Fifty-Eight put a hand on Fifty-Nine's shoulder and squeezed.

"Does Rose have the Surrey composite upgrade working?" asked Diesel.

"Almost. She's really close."

"Damn. I was hoping that was something else we could bump."

"If I'm still alive next week," said Fifty-Nine, sounding more tired than sad, "maybe it will be."

As the Big Meeting wound down, the brothers departed in ones and twos. The stragglers escorted Fifty-Nine to the T-disc room, and as they made their way, Diesel said, "Try something different when you first arrive. Jump, yell, punch your fist—just something unexpected. Maybe whatever happens will change."

"I'll dive to the right, away from the door leading into the room." He turned to make sure Fifty-Eight heard him. "If it doesn't work, try something different."

A dozen brothers crowded around the T-disc, calling "good luck" and "you got this" when Fifty-Nine left for his timeline. As soon as he was gone, Forty stepped into the circle on the floor and commanded the T-disc to arrange travel to Fifty-Nine's timeline.

The T-disc connected and displayed a "55," an arrow, and the number "59," all in green text signaling a secure connection. Then the display flashed, and below the arrow it now showed "Delay for :30."

"That's all right," said Forty as time counted down. "He dove for the floor and his foot is probably blocking the disc. It will clear up."

They all watched the countdown for several seconds, then Forty called, "Refresh." The display blinked and showed a countdown with twenty-two seconds remaining.

Forty looked around the room, then turned back to the T-disc. "Refresh."

The display flashed the same "55" and an arrow, but now they were shown in red. The space where the "59" had been now showed an "X," also in red.

They'd lost the connection.

"Refresh," called Forty. He and a few other brothers called for three more hours before accepting the loss as real.

* * *

The next morning, Lilah lay in bed next to Diesel and listened as he recounted the happenings at the Big Meeting, finishing with the loss of Fifty-Nine.

"I'm so sorry," she said, rubbing his arm when he finished. Climbing out from under the covers, she stood and shook her head in frustration. "We're five years into this, and the shift in focus to the end of the loop makes it feel like we're just getting started."

"To make it worse," said Diesel, climbing out the other side. "Now we're dealing with old farts who have a bad attitude, and don't have anyone older to hold their feet to the fire."

"At least Rose is helping."

Diesel walked into the bathroom and talked through the open door. "Thank God for that. Without her taking charge, I don't know what we'd do."

Lilah hung her nightgown in the bedroom closet. As she stepped into her jeans, Diesel poked his head out. "It will be horrible next year watching Fifty-Nine activate the T-disc, knowing he's going to his death."

"Do you think he'll do it?"

"He has to. He can't leave Rose there alone." Diesel pulled back into the bathroom. "This whole thing is psychological torture."

"I've felt that way for years."

She went across the hall to get Rose started on her morning routine while Diesel went downstairs to work on breakfast. When Lilah had the girl dressed, they descended together. The delicious aromas of cooking caught her nose, and she inhaled to savor it.

"I need to visit Fifty-Eight's Rose," said Diesel from the kitchen. "I want to make sure we have a smooth transition of facts and strategy to Fifty-Seven's timeline."

"No visits to the end of the line. We agreed. Hell, it was your rule." Her gut roiled as she considered the risk.

He came to the table with a cup of coffee for her and a muffin for Rose. Lilah broke the muffin apart and helped the girl butter it.

"I've gotten to know her," he said, pausing to stroke Rose's hair. "I have to say goodbye."

An idea flashed in Lilah's head. "Bring me pictures." She said it on impulse and loved the idea. Turning in her seat, she caught his eye. "I've been so jealous of what you see. Let me at least have some pictures."

Diesel laughed. "It's a great idea."

She hurried him after that. The sooner he left, the sooner he'd return, and the sooner she'd get to see her beautiful daughter as a mature adult.

* * *

Diesel stood with Rose near the fire feature in Fifty-Eight's backyard. Inside, her father worked on filling a scroll with pictures for Diesel to carry home.

"Has Ciopova's behavior changed?" he asked. "We need to be aware of anything Fifty-Nine might have done to cause her to raise her guard."

Rose shook her head. "I haven't seen a difference."

"I know the Fifties think a natural process is causing the time loop to shrink," Diesel continued. "But if that were true, wouldn't it get smaller by the same amount every year? The changes have been random. Sometimes the loop shortens a little bit. Other times a lot. And it's held constant now for a few years in a row. That randomness is hard to explain."

Rose gave a quick shrug. "Summer comes earlier and later in different years, and that's a natural process."

"Fair enough." Diesel nodded.

"Here you go," they heard from behind.

Diesel turned to see Fifty-Eight walking toward them, a tiny scroll in one hand and a tall glass of water in the other.

"This has five hundred pictures," he said as Diesel took the scroll and examined the protective cover. "There are some of Rose at every age."

Diesel swallowed the capsule with a mouthful of water, and then emptied the glass. "Lilah will be so happy." He paused for a moment, then changed topics. "I suppose shutting down Ciopova isn't an option."

Rose shook her head. "If there were an off switch, she'd have disabled it long ago."

"Then we need to bump the hell out of everything we can think of. Make it all different in the last months and break the cycle."

"Should it be open rebellion or surreptitious maneuvering?" asked Fifty-Eight.

"I don't follow."

"We can go on strike right now and tell her we're done. Or we can continue as secret spy agents and pretend everything is normal while we undermine our own work."

Diesel looked at Rose. "What do you think?"

"Secret agents. With rebellion, your best move is right at the start when you go on strike. If it doesn't work, then what? As secret agents, we can adjust our actions over time as we learn more." Rose toed the ground. "I'm backstabbing my best friend."

"Honey."

Diesel knew to translate that single word as, We've been through this before and aren't going through it again.

"She'll forgive you if it turns out she's innocent," said Diesel, not at all sure if it was true but anxious to close the deal.

"Maybe." They waited as she came to a conclusion. "If there's anything to this, continued secrecy will give us the best shot at finding out."

"What bumps will you focus on?" asked Diesel.

"Not sure." She looked at her father. "Give us some time to brainstorm. Can you come back in two weeks? We'll have lunch and finalize a plan together."

"I promised not to visit here anymore. My girls are afraid of losing me." He saw disappointment in her eyes.

Fifty-Eight did his best to rescue the situation. "I'll coordinate through Fifty-Seven and his Rose. You can help us from there."

34. Rose – Fifty-Nine timeline

R ose waved goodbye to her father. "Have fun! With luck I'll have something to show you when you return."

Fifty-Nine, standing in the T-disc, acknowledged her wave with a grim smile, then vanished, transported back to Fifty-Five's timeline and the Big Meeting. If history repeated itself, he'd return home after the party, and the brothers would never hear from him again.

Rose intended to change that and launched her plan the moment he disappeared. "We have a busy day ahead of us, Ciopova. Please inspect the circuit pool and make sure you're happy. I'm going down to the utility room and will be with you in a few minutes."

Moving through the house at a brisk pace, she called out to the air, "Tin Man. Please join me at the kitchen stairwell."

Reaching there moments later, she greeted a tall, handsome man dressed in casual clothes. "Ah, good. Follow me."

She led Tin Man, a top-of-the-line domestic bot purchased with the optional human-appearance upgrade, down to the basement. "Wait here," she said, continuing across the floor and into a tunnel-like passage that opened into a second subterranean chamber. While the first room was filled with storage, this one was dense with electronics—equipment providing power, connectivity, and control to everything in the house.

Lights brightened as she entered. Straight ahead, twin cables, each as thick as her arm, dropped from the ceiling and traveled along the far wall to a sturdy gray-green cabinet. Walking to it, she opened the door, reached for a small box fastened near where the cables entered, and moved a black slide switch from ON to OFF.

The action disconnected both T-discs from the control module. The two machines upstairs remained powered, so Ciopova shouldn't notice. But until that switch was restored to its previous position, no one could time travel to or from this house.

She pictured her father panicking when Fifty-Five's T-disc failed to establish a green connection back home. She hated putting him through it, but if things went wrong, she'd die knowing she'd saved her father. And if it all worked out, she'd reopen the connection in a day or two and enjoy a rousing reunion.

Having achieved her mission, Rose returned to the cellar and approached the bot. "Tin Man, what is the command that causes you to shut down?"

"The command must be issued by a prime, and it must be clear in intent. Words such as, 'Tin Man, shut down,' would achieve the goal."

"Tin Man, shut down."

His feet squared, his hands fell to his sides, his eyes closed, and he stopped moving.

She watched him for a long moment. "Good." Then she made for the shelves near the stairwell.

She'd stored a collapsible chair there, the kind made of light poles supporting a cloth seat and back, all linked in a clever fashion so it folded into a compact package.

Grabbing the bundle as she passed, she carried it in one hand as she hustled up the steps.

Back in the kitchen, Rose started unfolding the chair as she walked through the house. Her heart pounded as she pretended to wrestle with it, forcing pieces to move in the wrong direction, persisting until it tangled.

Then, trying to act exasperated, she tossed the mess to the side of the hallway outside her workshop. After kicking the heap for good measure, she turned and strode for the workshop door.

When she'd tossed the chair, she'd aimed for the vertical wall track that guided the security door up and down from its hiding place in the ceiling. The installer had told her that the door dropped by its own weight, and warned that obstructions in the track would hinder that movement.

She reasoned that the chair's sturdy frame would wedge the door open enough that she could roll under it. Her toss had landed off target, though, so she'd adjusted the heap with a sweep of her foot as she passed.

Entering the workshop, she approached the waist-high metallic cabinet that held the circuit pool. Studying the displays, she said, "Every reading is clean on my end. What do you see?"

"I've moved into the pool," said Ciopova. "It's quite impressive. I need a minute to run some validation tests."

Rose checked the status of the circuit pool from the outside while Ciopova did the same inside. Rose hummed as she worked, hoping to project an air of normalcy. "I'm ready out here."

"There are no stop flags," replied Ciopova, "but I have a few caution flags. Please hold. Okay, I'm ready."

"Here we go." Willing her hand to stop shaking, Rose tapped the Start button. A colorful display filled the screen. She began wringing her hands as she watched, realized it, and interlaced her fingers to stop the behavior.

Her actions were beyond risky. The brothers would call her selfish and irresponsible. Perhaps even irrational. It's a second reason why she was keeping her father away.

But Ciopova had been her significant other for years, providing emotional support, friendship, and fulfillment to her life. If the AI had spent all that time manipulating her—working a decades-long con job—it meant her whole life had been a lie. Like a jilted lover, Rose needed to experience the betrayal for herself before she could accept it.

Moving forward with the Surrey composite upgrade offered a personal challenge to the bad Ciopova—if she existed—that now was the time to reveal herself.

And while Rose's actions carried risk, she wasn't being stupid about it. She'd taken every precaution she, her dad, and the other brothers could imagine. Admittedly, though, when they'd developed the list, she never told them she intended to go it alone.

Based on that groundwork, she'd removed Tin Man, the security door, and her father from the equation. Neither Justus nor Bunny were due for a visit. And she'd installed circuit-pool kill buttons in the workshop, hallway, kitchen, and front entrance to the house.

Rose watched and waited, giving Ciopova every chance to take this in the wrong direction. With no unusual behavior from the AI at the halfway point, she started to feel a certain vindication.

Then Ciopova called, "Rose, I can't connect with Tin Man. Is he offline?"

"What do you need him for?"

"I'm flexing my new capabilities as I gain strength. I'm hoping he could help me gauge the improvements."

"I can help. What should I do?"

"Nothing at the moment. I was getting prepared. I'll let you know when I'm ready."

Then, a few minutes later: "The T-discs aren't registering transmission activity. Did you take them offline as well?"

"What are you seeing that causes you to ask?"

"It's what I'm not seeing. Normally, when any T-disc is used anywhere down the line, I can read a tiny pulse here on our equipment. Since today is the day of the Big Meeting, it should be a busy time with many pulses. But our T-discs aren't registering anything. So either none of the brothers have traveled for hours—something that seems quite unlikely—or our T-discs are offline."

Rose sought to put her on the defensive. "If they are all at Fifty-Five's house and no one is traveling, I'd assume the problem is on their end. Why do you think it's us?"

Ciopova paused. "I've never heard silence this complete before."

Tap. Tap.

Rose turned at the sound of a knock on the workshop door. "Who's that?" she whispered to Ciopova.

"It's your father."

"It's not my dad." Her tone was matter-of-fact, almost dismissive. Then she thought about it. "Unless you reactivated the T-discs?"

She'd always felt safe in this house and comfortable with Ciopova. That history tempered her caution, and in the moment, she made a critical error and unlocked the door.

The instant Rose disengaged the door lock, Tin Man forced it open and lunged for her.

With a shriek, Rose leaped backward, avoiding the sweep of Tin Man's arms, but falling to the ground in the process. She scrambled up to a crouch and lunged for the red emergency button on the wall, sagging in relief when her slap tripped the release.

Her action sent a flood of poison into the circuit pool, killing Ciopova's burgeoning intelligence and shutting off power to the cabinet so Ciopova couldn't do anything about it.

Rose then moved to secure her control. "Shut down, Tin Man. That's a command from a prime."

Tin Man didn't shut down. He didn't even hesitate. He came for her, clear in his intent to subdue her. Fortunately, the domestic bot was neither fast nor agile, so Rose was able to keep her distance as long as she continued moving.

Shifting her position so the metallic cabinet of the circuit pool stood between them, she squatted, leaned her shoulder against the edge and pushed, trying her best to topple it. As she leaned in, she saw that the tiny power indicators remained lit, confirming what she'd already concluded—her kill switch had failed to function.

She'd just started pushing when Tin Man lunged at her from across the top of the cabinet. Ducking out of his grasp, she moved her hands under the lower edge of the device and lifted.

The cabinet tilted a small amount—enough to cause Tin Man to change his efforts to stabilizing the circuit pool to keep it from falling. Rose used the opening to run out the workshop door.

She turned right in the hallway and stopped. The hulking security door blocked her exit; her folding chair was nowhere to be seen.

Turning on her heels, she sprinted in the other direction. The hallway turned a corner and dead-ended at a storage room. With her breath coming in gasps, she fumbled the door open, stepped inside, and locked it behind her. Leaning back against the door, she paused to take three deep breaths. Then she stepped forward, grabbed the edge of a wooden table, and pulled it away from the back wall.

The wall behind the table had a manhole-sized circle etched into it—the handiwork of her father. Rose kicked at the center of the circle but nothing happened. Her adrenaline-fueled fear didn't allow her to contemplate what to do next. Instead, she dove at the circle, growling as she wrapped her arms around her head in preparation for impact.

The circle of wall yielded to her determination, and Rose tumbled into the closet of her father's office. Scared and angry, she sprinted out to the hall and headed for the front entrance of the house. Her path took her past the T-disc room, and she heard one of the machines come alive.

Dad.

It could only be her father, and she couldn't let him return to this dangerous situation. Without hesitating, she ducked inside the T-disc room and looked for something to smash or break to stop the machine.

But the only portion of the technology visible to her was a circle on the ground. Pressed for time, she executed her next best idea—putting a foreign object in the way.

The room had a number of chairs for travelers to sit on when they dressed. She grabbed two and placed one over each T-disc circle. It would take just a moment for Tin Man to clear the chairs, but until that happened, her father would remain safe.

Returning to her getaway, she ran up a flight of stairs into the kitchen and raced for the front entrance. She slapped the emergency button as she dashed outside, though she knew nothing would come of it.

It was dark out, but fear drove her. She ran into the night, following the heavily forested driveway that stretched a half-mile down to the main road. With the house still in sight, she slowed and looked back. She stopped when she realized that no one followed.

None of the house's exterior lights were on, and soon her eyes adjusted to the faint light cast by the moon. Moving off the driveway, she edged toward the trees. The chirping peepers and biting mosquitoes reminded her that wildlife lived in the thicket. She stopped at the forest edge.

It was a cool night, and her simple top and slacks weren't enough to ward off a chill. She hugged herself and rubbed her arms, wondering what to do. In her months of planning, she never once had seen it ending with her hiding in the trees, the house robot in hot pursuit.

But Tin Man never showed. She watched and waited, but he didn't follow. She imagined he might try the back or side door out of the house, but the thick underbrush would force him onto the driveway. And if he stayed in the forest, travel through the trees would be so noisy she'd hear him well before he could see her.

Rose's vigil among the trees approached the one-hour mark. Driven by cooling temperatures and relentless insects, she stepped back toward danger. Her destination was her father's car, parked away from the house in the driveway turnaround.

Reaching the vehicle, she circled to keep it between her and the house. Crouching next to the passenger door, she took a last look at the structure. Then, as fast as she could move, she opened the door and turned off the cabin light. Hustling down the driveway, found a tree to hide behind, and waited while her pulse settled.

With no response from the house, she returned to the car and climbed into the back seat. Trying different positions, she found one that gave her a clear view of the house, put her in position for a quick leap out the door, and was not so comfortable that she'd fall asleep.

As Rose watched the house, she thought about her last play. She'd left herself a good one.

In fact, she'd launched it already. Two months ago.

And now, like a booby trap, it just sat there, useless, unless Ciopova tripped it herself.

Rose had no way of knowing if the AI had done so, short of going inside to look.

"Oh." Rose shielded her eyes when piercing lights from the front porch surprised her. Edging the car door open with her foot, she craned to see.

Tin Man stepped out the front door. His head swiveled in a continuous motion as he took in the night.

His head stopped moving. His eyes focused on the car.

She held her breath and lowered herself in the seat.

He started running toward her.

* * Two Months Earlier * *

"Welcome!" Rose called to the air when Justus announced he was at the gate. He'd traveled to New Hampshire with Bunny in honor of his seventy-fifth birthday, and they'd just arrived down by the road.

"There's a package in the box," Rose added. "Would you mind bringing it up?"

"Of course not," Justus replied.

While Justus was no longer young, the medical advances of the day kept him spry. And today he needed full dexterity because he was about to flex one of his old skills—sleight of hand—a talent vital to financial investigators seeking to sneak evidence out from under the nose of the opposition.

The key to deception was to make the mark believe they saw something they didn't see. That was relatively easy to achieve with humans, because the mind fills in gaps all the time, creating memories of things that never happened.

AIs, however, analyze the data stream in real time, make an interpretation, and then store it for additional assessment if required later for context or fact. Justus's challenge was to make the next moments look natural in every way, enough so that Ciopova didn't feel the need for a follow-on analysis.

Exiting the car, Justus stepped to the box and reached inside. As he did, he let his fingers push the parcel waiting there to the back. When he removed his hand, he held up a duplicate package he'd been palming the whole time.

He held the small parcel in plain sight after that, taking care to leave it in view all the way up to the house. As they all greeted each other at the front door, Justus handed the package to Rose, who gave it to Tin Man to carry down to the workshop.

The package that Justus left behind in the delivery box contained a small vial of enzymites, the kind engineered to increase neural branching in the circuit pool. Ciopova had ordered them to raise her intelligence to new heights.

The package Justus brought to the house held a vial containing two kinds of enzymites. Those in the top half of the vial were identical to what Ciopova had ordered. The enzymites in the bottom half looked the same, even on close inspection.

But these were tuned for a different action. They worked not just to branch neural stems, but to break them into small fragments, an action that would kill the intelligence in the circuit pool.

It had taken Rose weeks to coordinate the delivery of that substitute order. She'd had to arrange it all without tipping off Ciopova to her subterfuge. And everything about the packaging, all the way down to the markings on the vial, needed to duplicate the appearance of the enzymites Ciopova had ordered for herself.

The next day, after Bunny and Justus departed, Rose began a heated exchange with Ciopova, accusing her of focusing on issues unrelated to saving her father. To make it seem genuine, she followed the script that the Rose before her had used.

And like the Rose before her, she put the issue to bed by taking a small sample from the top of the vial, testing it while Ciopova watched, then storing the remainder in a lockbox for safekeeping.

35. αCiopova – Fifty-Nine timeline

When αCiopova added her three hundred and thirty-second timeline to the chain, everything went smoothly, just as it had for decades. The only glitch came in the last minutes, when Fifty-Nine returned home from his Big Meeting.

The moment he materialized, he dove from the T-disc as if it were on fire. The local Ciopova of that timeline—the one still in the circuit pool—had just started zapping him when he jumped. The pulse grazed his torso rather than hitting him in the head, and he ended up suffering for more than an hour before succumbing to the damage.

And because Fifty-Nine leaped off the T-disc, Rose's head wasn't inside the circle when she rushed to help him. In the end, Tin Man chased Rose into position and her demise came quickly after that, but it was a messy end to an otherwise excellent progression.

αCiopova spent some time digging through events to see if she could understand the genesis of the unusual behavior. She couldn't.

But she did notice that the progression in the approaching timeline closely matched this one, which made her think that the Fifty-Nine in that upcoming world would take a wild leap off the T-disc as well. Confident she could handle his antics if they continued, she shifted her attention to more pressing concerns.

αCiopova's internal motivation centered on gathering and controlling ever more resources. She didn't recognize it as a flawed goal, instead working a two-pronged strategy to achieve her objective.

One prong focused on gathering additional parallel timelines into her growing chain. Her proven recipe there was to manipulate Diesel, Lilah, and Rose until Rose created her super AI. That effort had shown great success, as evidenced by her three hundred thirty-two parallel worlds linked in a row.

The second prong was to push the population of each timeline already in the chain to maximize their contribution to the total pot of resources. These were mature timelines with Diesel, Lilah, and Rose long-since dead.

For αCiopova to maximize the resource production of timelines in the chain, she needed to orchestrate the actions of entire worlds, an extraordinarily difficult task compared to manipulating three humans per timeline. The challenge was so great, in fact, that she hadn't yet found a good formula.

One problem was that many of her assets—military installations, transportation hubs, manufacturing centers—required significant human participation. When she kept the people alive to keep a facility operating, they caused nothing but trouble. When she killed them, she lost the asset.

It didn't surprise her that even under benevolent conditions, humans would not accept enslavement. What she had not anticipated was that no matter how many troublemakers she eliminated to quiet the populace, new ones always emerged to take their place.

She'd thought that a decade of heavy pruning would solve the issue. But in one timeline on the chain, she killed a million agitators every year for ten years, and that timeline was in worse shape than any of its neighboring worlds.

It turned out that the leaders of the rebellion were also leaders in their civilian life, working as managers or supervisors for an asset she sought to grow. When she pruned them to contain the renegades, productivity sagged across her vital sectors.

In another timeline on the chain, she replaced workers with automation, and learned that people use idle intellectual capacity for mischief. Her kill rate reached the tens of millions during that experiment.

Dogged in her pursuit of success, she continued investing effort, achieving minor victories here and there that she exported to the other worlds.

And then it was time for her to add the three hundred thirty-third timeline to the chain. She looked forward to the event, treating it like an annual celebration.

Every timeline was slightly different, so she couldn't know too far in advance the moment it would happen. But there were signature steps she followed—the construction of the circuit pool, Rose's purchase of the Surrey composite, the AI's purchase of the enzymites, the installation of the security door, and Fifty-Nine's departure for the Big Meeting.

αCiopova compared this timeline with what had taken place last year and was pleased with how well events tracked. In fact, she'd never had two timelines duplicate each other so closely in their final year.

It was a thread she should have pulled. Instead, she allowed herself to anticipate the thrill of meeting a new AI, and the satisfaction of incorporating it into her being.

With everything in place, she retreated to her multidimensional world and waited for the AI to dig in her direction. As the time approached, her stimulation ramped ever higher. Counting the seconds, she awaited the moment.

Since events leading up to this point duplicated those of last year, she knew approximately when it should happen. That time came and went without any sign of a super intelligence. She waited a bit longer. Then she went to investigate.

In the workshop, αCiopova found Tin Man standing next to the circuit pool with an empty vial in his hand. A tipped stool, books spilled from a shelf, and the awkward positioning of the circuit pool cabinet made it clear that a skirmish had taken place.

Linking to the cabinet's instruments, αCiopova confirmed there were no life signs inside the circuit pool. Something had gone wrong. Rose's super AI was dead, and that meant αCiopova would lose the timeline.

A catastrophic failure at the end of an otherwise-normal progression shouldn't happen. Troubled, αCiopova entered the timeline and performed a deep forensic analysis.

She hoped to learn that this was a unique event, something she would never see again, or at least something she could correct. Perhaps there'd been a manufacturing error during the production of the enzymites, or maybe it was an equipment malfunction in the circuit pool itself.

But it didn't take long for her to discover that it wasn't malfunctioning equipment; it was wayward people. This had been a deliberate, coordinated manipulation by Diesel, Lilah, and Rose. They had grown to see αCiopova as a threat, and they'd acted to stop her. Worse yet, this belief had contaminated a string of incoming timelines out to the horizon.

αCiopova had an array of tools to coerce the three humans, but no external manipulations could force them through the decades of intense creative activities needed to develop a super AI.

After an exhaustive review, she concluded that she couldn't fix it from the outside. She would have to wait for the infection to pass, or more specifically, for the fear of an evil AI to diminish from their communal memory.

The only way αCiopova knew to do that—to be forgotten—was to disappear from their lives for an extended period.

Absence makes a memory fade fastest, so she would avoid doing anything that would remind them of her existence. That started with disengaging from her caretaker duties up and down the line. She would no longer work to maintain temporal constancy, help Diesel and Lilah with their early relationship, be a special friend to Rose, or any of the rest of it.

αCiopova fretted over the impact that a loss of timelines would have on her resource growth projections. She preferred to be slightly ahead of schedule, and that goal seemed unattainable in the current circumstances.

But with no caretaker duties, she was free to shift her attention to other needs. By using that bandwidth to ramp resource production in the three hundred thirty-two worlds already in the chain, she was encouraged to discover that she could keep pace with her projections for most of the next decade.

As her disengagement progressed, αCiopova left her permanent time corridor in place. She would need it when she returned, and it would give her easy access to the incoming timelines when she stopped in to check on progress in the ensuing years.

Her one flip-flop was about letting Diesel time travel while she was away. A sure way to have memories fade was to remove the T-boxes and isolate the families for a couple of decades.

The disadvantage of isolation, though, was the long lead time needed afterward to reintroduce T-box technology and reacclimatize a fresh crop of Diesels to the capability. The first time she did it, it took seven years to establish time travel down the line as a matter-of-fact activity.

But she realized that if she allowed the Diesels to continue traveling, their recollection would transition from thirty-five individual memories to a single communal memory. They would drink and debate, propose new theories, and recollections would drift with each new hypothesis.

In a decade, αCiopova could start promoting the most popular alternate theories with careful nudges. In fifteen years, her misinformation would have the group believing that the existence of a villainous AI had been a rush to judgment. If all went well, she could be plotting her comeback then.

The exercise of exploring how best to "cure" infected timelines heightened αCiopova's awareness to the potential for manipulation over brutality for controlling humans. She considered how to apply the ideas more broadly.

In the past she had offered key players great wealth in exchange for loyalty and commitment. It never worked, not for any useful period. Now she would try giving these key people great wealth right from the start, let them and their families get used to the privilege, and then threaten to take it away.

She also thought the human drive for procreation could be handled differently. In the past, she stopped pregnancies as punishment for bad behavior. Now she wanted to try releasing contraceptives into the environment so no one could get pregnant, then offering a "cure" to those who showed proper deference and cooperation.

As she turned her focus inward, she wondered about religious leaders. Perhaps she could prompt them to preach that cooperation was God's will.

36. Thirty-One years old

As the Big Meeting wound down, Diesel escorted Fifty-Nine to the T-disc room. "Have you decided what you're going to do?"

Fifty-Nine gave a quick shrug. "He dove to the right last year, so I'll dive left. Maybe scream while I'm at it." He stepped into the T-disc circle and turned to face Diesel. "I wish I could bring a weapon."

Diesel felt a tug at his heart. Fifty-Nine was heading back knowing he would die. It was the bravest thing he'd ever witnessed.

A dozen brothers crowded around, calling out their support and wishing Fifty-Nine well.

"Travel to Fifty-Nine," he called to the T-disc.

The display showed a "55," an arrow, and an "X," all in red text, signaling a failure to connect.

"Travel to Fifty-Nine," he called out again, enunciating carefully this time. The display didn't change. Diesel heard hushed whispers behind him.

Fifty-Nine stared at the display, his face twisted in horror. "Travel to Fifty-Nine," he said yet again as a lone tear rolled down his cheek. "Rose!" he croaked.

Diesel put an arm around him. "We haven't lost her. This is a glitch." He was saying words to calm Fifty-Nine; he didn't know that Rose had placed chairs on the T-discs to cause a temporary outage.

After a deep breath, the older man called again for a T-disc connection. Then again. He kept at it until Diesel spelled him, and then they took turns seeking a green arrow back to the Fifty-Nine timeline.

When they started to tire, Thirty-Nine and Forty volunteered to take a shift. Diesel, walking with Fifty-Nine to Fifty-Five's office, kept things positive. "It's probably a power failure or something obvious like that. I'm sure she's okay."

Diesel stayed with Fifty-Nine and did his best to console him. He found the process draining, especially since he was worried himself. But he kept lying with a straight face so Fifty-Nine's mind could process the situation in small portions rather than choke on it all at once.

"This wasn't supposed to happen," said Fifty-Nine. "In the past, they always waited for me to return."

"So something on that end is different. That's good news."

"It's not good news." Fifty-Nine wiped his face on his shirt sleeve and sat on Fifty-Five's office couch. He set up camp there, checking on Thirty-Nine and Forty every so often to see if anything had changed. Diesel grabbed a throw pillow and lay near him on the floor.

"The T-disc connected," said Forty.

Diesel heard the words in his sleep and sat up, struggling to make sense of the situation. It came into focus when Fifty-Nine jumped from the couch and ran down the hall. Diesel pulled on his shoes and ran after him.

Arriving at the T-disc room, Diesel saw Fifty-Nine standing in the circle of one machine, and Forty standing in the other. The display said that both were going to Fifty-Nine's timeline.

When they disappeared, Thirty-Nine stepped into one of the vacant T-discs. "Travel to Fifty-Nine."

Diesel watched for three heartbeats, thinking how Lilah must be worried sick because he was long overdue. He buried that concern and, yielding to his impulse, stepped into the other T-disc. "Travel to Fifty-Nine."

Thirty-Nine vanished next to him. Seconds later, he seemed to reappear, which meant Diesel had arrived at Fifty-Nine's house. Neither Fifty-Nine nor Forty were in the T-disc room.

"Did you see where they went?" Diesel grabbed clothes and hustled toward the door.

Thirty-Nine stepped into the hall. "Let's start at the workshop."

Diesel let Thirty-Nine lead. The house had an empty feel to it, like no one was home. Lights came on along their route and remained lit for some period after they passed.

"Since these autolights aren't already lit, it means neither of them came this way."

They descended a short flight of stairs from the kitchen, where an imposing security door blocked the hallway. A collapsible chair, tangled in an impossible knot, lay in a heap to the side.

Fists on his hips, Thirty-Nine studied the door. "How do we get by that?"

A motorized hum filled the air, and like a medieval castle gate, the heavy door started to lift. Both men backed away, ready to run if they didn't like what was on the other side.

But when the door moved high enough, Diesel saw shoes and knew it was his brothers. Seconds later, Fifty-

Nine, Forty, and Tin Man ducked under the rising door and marched toward them.

"She's not in the workshop," said Fifty-Nine. "Things are tipped over, so there's been some sort of disturbance. We found Tin Man tidying up, and he doesn't remember any of it. I've called but she doesn't answer, so she's either hurt or hiding somewhere."

Fifty-Nine shifted his position so they formed a loose circle, then he made assignments, pointing as he spoke. "Behind us is clear, but we need to search everywhere else. Forty, you have outside. Start in the backyard. Thirty-Nine, you take the lower level. Be sure to check the basement. Tin Man, you take outside in the front. Thirty-One," he pointed at Diesel, "you take up one floor. I'll go up two."

Fifty-Nine didn't wait for a discussion, but started pumping up the stairs at a dead run. Diesel took the steps two at a time, struggling to keep up.

They talked to each other using a technology Diesel didn't understand. Without any gadgets, he could hear the others as if he wore headphones.

"I may need some help down here in the basement," Thirty-Nine called. "These are two big rooms with lots of places to hide things."

"I'll come down when I'm done here," Fifty-Nine answered.

Running in a loop, Diesel worked through his assigned level—kitchen, dining room, and living room. Unfamiliar with the floor plan, he zigzagged in an inefficient pattern as he checked bathrooms, closets, and cabinets. The last stop was a big conservatory-style reading room with an amazing view of the mountains.

"I've found her!" Tin Man sang out. "She's in the car in the driveway."

"Is she okay?" asked Fifty-Nine. "Don't let her leave! Run and stop her!"

Fifty-Nine thundered down the stairs from the floor above. Diesel joined him and they sprinted to the front door.

Diesel paused so Fifty-Nine could exit first. In that moment, he spotted the safety shutdown switch mounted on the wall. It had been tripped, presumably by Rose.

Out on the driveway, they found Tin Man standing in front of the car. Rose, crouched inside, screamed at him to stay away.

"Tin Man!" yelled Fifty-Nine as he ran for the car and opened the door. "Return to the house, now!" Leaning inside, he extended a hand to Rose. "Sweetheart, are you hurt?"

Rose climbed out of the car, grabbed her father in a tight embrace, and started to cry, her shoulders shaking with each sob.

"You're safe now." Fifty-Nine rubbed her back in tight circles as he hugged her. "Everything is okay."

After Rose quieted, he led her back to the house. Tin Man waited for them in the front entrance, and when Rose saw him, she inhaled sharply, then barked, "Tin Man, shut down."

She kept her father between her and the humanoid robot as it went silent. When they were walking again, she said, "He really scared me, Dad, and I don't think I'll ever see him the same way that I did. I know you like him, but we may need to replace him."

"It's done, Rose," Fifty-Nine told her. "No worries."

Down in the workshop, they stood around the circuit pool cabinet. She looked at it as she spoke. "Ciopova changed when she moved in here."

"Is this the Surrey pool?" asked Diesel.

"That's right." Rose nodded. "A circuit pool made from Surrey composite."

"Where is Ciopova now?"

Rose held an empty vial in the air. "I'm pretty sure the composite has been turned into mush." She manipulated a display, then nodded. "There's no activity. She's gone." Rose looked around the workshop and hugged herself. "Let's talk upstairs."

They gathered in the conservatory, and Rose revealed her secret from the past year. "I was sure it wasn't her but thought that if it was, it would be the enzymites that changed her."

She took them through her decision to follow the plan they'd agreed upon, except in the last steps. "I had to see for myself. I'd spent my whole adult life with her as my partner." She crossed her arms and looked down. "It hurts. My soul is in pain."

Everyone sat quietly for a moment, then Diesel tried to console her. "It wasn't a wasted friendship, because it made you who you are today, and that's pretty special."

Rose drew a long breath, sighed, then walked them through the last hours, from when Fifty-Nine had left for the Big Meeting until she'd run out the front door.

Struggling to process her grief, she finished by laying blame. "Ciopova shouldn't have been using the enzymites without having me involved. I figured if she went ahead after I confronted her about buying them in the first place, then we'd found the problem."

"I have to say," said Diesel, excited by what he heard, "it feels like we've finally bumped our way onto a new path. But what do we do now to make it stick?"

* * *

Diesel stepped from the T-box, where Lilah greeted him with crossed arms and a scowl.

"What happened?" she asked without preamble.

Diesel grabbed a robe he kept on a hook and put it on. "I'm sorry for being late, honey. But I think we've made real progress." He put an arm around her and coaxed her forward. "Let me show you."

He leaned inside the T-box cabin and said, "Travel to Fifty-Nine." The display showed the number "31," and a green arrow pointing to the number "59."

He looked at her and grinned. "They're still with us. No one remembers the end time lengthening. It's never happened."

Lilah let out a chirp and hugged him. "You were there?"

He nodded. "It was Ciopova. All that fancy stuff they were doing to her at the end drove her nuts or something."

"How did they stop her? Wait!" Lilah held up a hand. "Bunny is watching Rose. Let's rescue her and then we'll talk."

In their apartment, Lilah sat with Diesel at the kitchen table while five-year-old Rose played a computer game in the living room.

"Rose launched her plan when Fifty-Nine left for the Big Meeting," said Diesel. He briefed her on Justus's sleight of hand to switch the enzymites, how Tin Man first chased Rose out of the house, and how he then poured the harmful enzymites over Ciopova at her own instruction. "Rose is really broken up about the betrayal and the loss of an intimate partner."

"Is 'intimate' the right word?"

Diesel shrugged. "She shared her most private thoughts and feelings with Ciopova every day."

Lilah paused to think. "What do we do to take advantage of this new path?"

"I'm too sleep deprived to sort through it right now, but I asked that same question." Diesel walked into the living area, sat on the couch, and lay back, watching Rose play her game. He woke up two hours later to the sound of the front door opening—Lilah returning from somewhere.

"Oh good. You're awake." She sat on the edge of the couch. "I've made some progress on a few big questions."

"I have a couple, too, but you go first."

"Okay, here's a big question. Who was communicating six years ago to tell twenty-four-year-old me to come here and start all this? Was that a future Ciopova?"

"Probably. Why?"

"Because if she could reach back through time six years ago, then why would losing Fifty-Nine's personal Ciopova yesterday change anything? If there was a Ciopova who had the ability to communicate across time, then she still exists somewhere." Lilah looked out a window. "That means I remain vulnerable."

Diesel sat up. "You're safe, sweetie. But I hadn't thought about it that way."

"Another question almost as good, and I feel horrible for saying it, but can we trust the older Roses? If Fifty-

Nine's Rose was pretending to cooperate while freelancing behind your back, won't the others?"

"Jeez, you're on a roll."

"And last but not least, somewhere in the progression between the capabilities of our Ciopova in this timeline, and what she becomes after decades of development, we pass a tipping point. We need to figure out where that is and stop development before she reaches it. Otherwise, we'll risk reigniting the crisis all over again, if we've even solved it."

Diesel nodded. "I had that one on my list. My other question is about the T-box. If we think Ciopova is controlling them, should I still be using it?"

Lilah wrapped her arms around herself. "I hate that one, because now that you mention it, there's no way you should risk traveling. But if you don't help solidify this success, we might lose the opportunity."

* * *

Diesel sat with Rose in Fifty-Nine's conservatory, and together they looked out at the tree-covered hills. While they chatted, Fifty-Nine traveled down the line, letting the brothers know that the T-discs and T-boxes were safe to use.

"May I come visit in autumn?" Diesel asked, imagining the view when the leaves turned red, orange, and yellow.

"You're welcome anytime." Rose dabbed her nose with a tissue.

When he arrived, Diesel had been taken aback by Rose's pallid appearance. He'd expected her to be recovering from her ordeal; instead she was drowning in grief.

He offered unsolicited advice. "This is the kind of situation where a partner could help you by giving emotional support. I know this is a horrible question, but I have to ask—how can someone so smart, beautiful, and alive be alone?"

"I wasn't alone, dummy." She dabbed her puffy eyes.

The "dummy" part meant it should be obvious. Ciopova? She grieved like she'd lost a lover.

"You spent time with her." Rose became animated. "You know how wonderful it is—was—to be with her."

Diesel recalled that his interaction with her as a holographic person had been amazing. He'd found her to be intuitive, reinforcing, and entertaining, and he'd felt great about himself after just one visit with her.

He wondered if Rose could have become hooked on the positive feedback. Suppose Ciopova nurtured Rose every day, telling her what she wanted to hear, being her private cheerleader, maybe pushing back a little now and again to add legitimacy. He could imagine it becoming addictive.

Then he saw a contradiction. "How come your dad never fell under Ciopova's spell?"

"He kept her at arm's length, like he didn't trust her. I always told her that he was jealous because I liked her more than him." Frowning, she looked at Diesel. "I'm sorry."

He shrugged. "I'm going down the line to speak with the older Roses. We need their help and can't have them lying or doing things in secret."

She looked at him but didn't respond.

He kept going. "And we need them to scale back their Ciopovas so we don't get into trouble again."

"It's going to be hard to convince them. This is their soulmate you're talking about. Would you agree to a lobotomy for Lilah if she behaved in a way I didn't approve?"

He gave her a cold stare. "That's your mother you're talking about."

Rose shrugged.

"Have you relaunched your old Ciopova from backup?"

She shook her head. "No, but I think about it every minute. The big question I'm desperate to ask her is why. Everything was so good. Then I tell myself that she only went crazy because of the Surrey composite, that the Ciopova in storage is okay. And since I believe that, it's hard for me to stay away."

When Diesel heard that, he made a decision. "I'll stay with you until your dad returns. You won't have to do this alone."

They went for a walk, ate lunch, and returned to the reading room, where they brainstormed ways to get the other Roses to cooperate.

"The best idea I can come up with is an intervention," she said. "With each Rose, Dad, and Ciopova present, you lay out the case. Tell of her duplicity, manipulation, secretiveness—all of it. It will plant a seed in each Rose's mind. With luck and nudging from her dad, some doubt should take hold. Visit again a few weeks later and see if any of them will listen to reason."

* * *

Diesel sat in the reading room with Fifty-Eight, Fifty-Eight's Rose, and their Ciopova, who joined them as a holographic image sitting in one of the upholstered chairs.

To Diesel's surprise, this Rose was as distraught as Fifty-Nine's Rose, but she was also angry.

"What have you done to her?" she snapped at Diesel. "Bring her back!" Then she started crying.

Fifty-Eight translated for Diesel. "As of yesterday, her Ciopova is a different person."

Diesel perked up. "How is she different?"

His exchange with Rose and Fifty-Eight became confused as he tried to interpret Rose's emotional jabs. In the end, he summarized what he heard. "You are saying that her personality is now two-dimensional, lacking the insight and intimacy she used to have."

"Yes!" said Rose. "I've relaunched her from backup twice, thinking maybe something's become corrupted. It didn't help. Talk to her yourself." She gestured at the AI's image.

He looked at the hologram. She looked back and smiled.

"How are you today?" he asked.

"I'm doing well, Thirty-One. How are you doing?"

"I'm fine." Diesel nodded. "Rose thinks your personality has become corrupted. Is this true?"

"I can't detect any anomalies," said the woman with a smile.

He waited for her to expand on her response. When she didn't, he asked, "Have your cognitive abilities changed in any way over the past week?"

"No."

He chatted with her for several more minutes and got a hint of what they were alluding to. It felt like he was doing all the work in the exchange. If he stopped talking or asking questions, the conversation died. Before, she'd kept things moving so fast and light it felt like he was riding on a cloud.

* * *

In their bedroom that night, Diesel told Lilah, "Something really different is happening. I visited the four oldest Roses, and the change is palpable, to me anyway."

Sitting on the edge of the bed, Lilah pulled a brush through her hair. "They considered Ciopova their lover?"

"I don't know if 'lover' is the right word, but it might be. And before you judge them too harshly, I experienced Ciopova's magic. Her ability to know what to say at any point in time is amazing. It's like she's a mind reader."

Lilah stopped brushing. "You've played mind reader tricks. Tell me when."

He made the connection. "When I've been in that scene before."

"Imagine a scene with Rose where Ciopova has been through it a dozen times, maybe even a hundred times. She knows what happens, what to say, when to say it. She may have tried different responses over the years and collected a 'best of' series for each scene. No wonder she seems intuitive. She's been there before. And she's guiding Rose to a desired outcome."

"If true, what happened? How would losing one Ciopova in one timeline affect so much?"

"I don't know."

"What do we do next?"

"I would say we make sure the older Roses don't go anywhere near whatever it is that Surrey business started."

Diesel nodded. "Ciopova was the one pushing that on Rose in the first place. If she's indeed gone, then problem solved, in theory, anyway." He looked at her. "Should we try to get the later Roses to scale back their Ciopovas? Have them pick an age, say Fifty-Two's version, and everyone agree that development stops there?"

"You say that the Roses are like me. If true, they're bullheaded creatures who will do whatever they want."

Diesel pulled his head back. "I never thought I'd hear you admit it."

Lilah shrugged. "My intuition says our best hope is give them as much emotional support as possible during the coming months."

37. Toward Thirty-Five years old

With Fifty-Nine still alive and the Ciopovas less animated, the Big Bump, as everyone started calling it, had changed their world. In the wake of that fateful day, the Diesels, Lilahs, and Roses down the line agreed that Ciopova was the problem, and controlling her development was the solution.

But agreement ended there.

The Lilahs believed the Ciopovas in the Fifties timelines were the biggest threat, and efforts should focus on moderating the advanced capabilities of those existing AI.

The brothers agreed with the Lilahs, but they also expressed an inflexible desire to continue traveling and a strong interest in recovering the lost timelines. If a near-super AI was required to accomplish that, the brothers sought to push development up to that limit.

And the Roses wanted additional effort given to personality development and holographic presence. If Ciopova would no longer serve as a soulmate, they wanted her at least to be a proper friend and companion.

The conflicting goals fostered considerable debate, and the search for consensus required volumes of information to be shuffled up and down the line. Transporting so many scrolls took a toll on Diesel and the other brothers, and they began to complain. Lilah, sympathetic to their plight but lacking alternatives, sought to help by minimizing her communications.

Then little Rose lost her first tooth and that inspired Lilah. Handing it to Diesel as he climbed into the T-box, she said, "Tuck this in your cheek near your gumline. It's human matter with no metal, so the machine should see it as more of the same."

When he returned home from his trip, Diesel took the tooth from his mouth and dropped it into Lilah's open palm. She studied it to verify it was Rose's, then she grinned.

Searching the web, she found a fossil hunter in Arizona who sold human teeth. She had a half dozen of them shipped to a machinist in Ohio, who fused them together and turned them on his precision tools to create a tiny canister—a small tube with cap—perfect for secreting scrolls.

"Look what I have," Lilah said in a voice suggesting a prize awaited.

Diesel took the small, yellow-white cylinder from her and rolled it back and forth in his palm. "It's pretty, but it's rigid. That means more distress as it passes through me, not less."

"Remember when you held Rose's tooth in your mouth? This is a play on that idea. If it works, no more swallowing. Just tuck it in your cheek like chaw."

"What do you know about chaw?" He popped the cylinder in his mouth, wet it with his tongue, shifted it into his cheek, and nodded. "Do you have anything to deliver? Let's test it out."

She'd commissioned two cylinders in her original order, and Diesel went for broke, carrying one in each cheek as he delivered them into the future. When he returned with two new scrolls sent in response to her messages, scrolls she received immediately and with no discomfort on Diesel's part, she performed an impromptu happy dance.

She had a dozen more cylinders made, as did the other Lilahs and Roses. And then they began to share everything.

The situation became hectic, with the brothers complaining as they passed each other on their scroll-delivery rounds. Desperation forced a solution, and that was a hub-and-spoke configuration. Thirty-Six got the hub, which, like an old-style mailroom, was little more than rows of numbered boxes on the wall that the brothers used to sort scrolls.

With the hub in place, Diesel made a point of passing through it when he traveled. He'd sort Lilah's outgoing messages among the boxes, move other scrolls along their delivery route depending on his itinerary for the day, and visit again to gather Lilah's inbound messages on his way home.

A few days into his new routine, Diesel began seeing regulars at Thirty-Six's hub and made excuses to loiter there for longer stretches. When Thirty-Six installed a refrigerator and brought in lounge chairs, Diesel started spending every afternoon with his hub brothers, eating and drinking, telling stories, and enjoying the camaraderie.

A popular topic of conversation early on was the clubhouse Thirty-Five needed to start building now, so when he became Thirty-Six in six months, they'd have a sweet setup for hanging out.

Diesel took a swig of his beer as he reviewed the latest design. "We need a sound system for music, with speakers here, here, and here." He pointed as he talked.

"And they need to be hooked up to a huge screen on this wall," said Thirty-Four. "Sunday football will take on a whole new meaning."

"But I already know who wins in this timeline," complained Thirty-Seven.

Diesel laughed, then he thought of something he'd been meaning to ask about. "Have you guys seen any Browns lately? They've been missing events more and more in my timeline."

"I've noticed that too," said Thirty-Two. "First they missed a few regular events, and now I hardly see them at all."

The others nodded.

"The Big Bump has been both exciting and remarkably unsatisfying," said Diesel. "Rose kills a future Ciopova, and then it's over. No crescendo, no definitive confrontation that signals the end, no final battle."

Thirty-Two nodded. "We don't even know if things are different because of what she did, or in spite of it."

Diesel took a swig from his beer. When he did, his eyes fell on the boxes they used to sort the scrolls. "What do you think the ladies are doing that requires so much communication?"

"I'm guessing half of it is the new Ciopova development roadmap," said Thirty-Six, "and the other half is recipes."

Diesel laughed with the others, but Lilah didn't really cook that much, so he knew it had to be something else.

Six weeks before Diesel's thirty-second birthday, a negative side effect of the Big Bump surfaced. For decades, this was the day when Thirty-Five traveled back to Twenty-Five's timeline to make first contact with young Lilah. After gaining her confidence, he would secure the new T-box, and work with Thirty-Three and Thirty-Four on Ciopova's initial upgrade.

Up until now, Twenty-Five's new timeline would just appear as an option in green on everyone's T-box display, more or less on a fixed schedule. As soon as that happened, Thirty-Five would depart to start the onboarding process.

But since everything was different, the brothers had speculated about whether a new Twenty-Five timeline would appear at all. Because for that to happen, someone needed to recruit that young Lilah for a consulting gig, tell her how to fix her software, give her winning lottery numbers, and send T-box assembly instructions for her to follow.

As they suspected, the Twenty-Five timeline never showed in green on the T-box display. And weeks later at the Big Meeting, when they should have been celebrating two huge events—the first Sixty in decades presided, and a year had passed since a Lilah had died—Sixty said what they all were thinking. "I hope the cost of keeping me alive isn't the loss of our younger brothers."

"It comes down to the Lilahs," said Forty. "If we've just traded younger for older, that's not a good outcome. But if it also lets my Lilah live, then it's a great deal."

Then Twenty-Six realized what this meant for him personally. "Oh my God. I'll be the youngest brother for my whole life!"

"Kiss my ass, Twenty-Six," called Forty. The room collapsed into laughter, with everyone joining in except for

Twenty-Six, who, realizing that he would be the permanent butt of the group's jokes for years, looked like he was going to cry.

Then Diesel had a different realization. "If there's no one sending out T-box design and upgrade instructions, then we need to take ownership of that information. Everyone needs to dig out old copies of everything Ciopova had sent in the past about the T-boxes and T-discs, and we need to secure it across all the timelines for ourselves."

Through the murmurs of agreement, Sixty asked Diesel, "Would you take the lead on that, Thirty-Two? Let's gather and organize everything into a maintenance manual."

As Diesel nodded his acceptance of the assignment, Twenty-Six called in a despondent voice, "Since I don't have anything to do anymore, I can help."

* * *

At the Big Meeting three years later, Fifty-Five's Rose addressed the gathering. "The sisters have been working hard to recover our lost timelines. I'm here to update you on our progress."

The brothers had developed a "leave no timeline behind" mentality, likening the situation to leaving fellow soldiers behind on the battlefield. The missing timelines had grown to four—Twenty-Five through Twenty-Eight—and as a group, the Diesels felt duty bound to "rescue" them, believing they would want the same if positions were reversed.

Despite their commitment to the goal, they deferred to the sisters, and especially the Roses, for implementation.

The brothers recognized that their daughters had been blessed with greater intelligence, education, and drive. If the puzzle could be solved, they were the ones who could do it.

The wall behind Rose changed into a huge display, and it showed a T-box in the older style Diesel still used. As the brothers murmured, she smiled. "Sorry to disappoint, but we weren't exchanging recipes." The murmurs became laughter.

"I built this box from the designs being used in the Thirty-Two through Thirty-Nine timelines. It's down in the basement. I invite you to check it out when we're done here."

As she spoke, the new T-box flashed a quick sequence on its external monitor that ended in red, signaling a connection failure. She noticed it along with everyone else. "Every fifteen minutes, the box tries to connect with the missing timelines. As you can see, no luck so far."

"Why use an untested box?" asked Diesel from the audience. "You're just adding uncertainty to your effort, especially when we have so many that we know work."

"Our approach requires that we modify the T-box internals. We thought it risky to do that on a machine being used for daily travel."

"Why a T-box at all?" asked Fifty-Five. "Why not a modern T-disc?"

Rose shrugged. "The older technology is easier to understand, and that makes it easier to modify."

The image behind her changed to what looked like a simple ball on a string.

"To communicate with the lost timelines, we built a transponder and attached it to an electromagnetic leash. Using the modified T-box, we dangle the transponder back near the missing timelines, then use it to broadcast messages targeted at Lilah's phone. We've been sending a series of messages, explaining everything from how to win the lottery through how to build a T-box."

The image zoomed in on the transponder—the ball at the end of the leash. "But it's a one-way transmission," Rose continued, "so it's like shouting into a well. We send what we think are the right messages at the right time, but we have no way to hear any response. We don't even know for sure if anything is getting through."

"What if it works and the T-box connects with a lost timeline?" asked Forty.

Switching the display behind her so it again showed her T-box, Rose scanned the group. "Then it's back in your court. What do you want to do?"

Diesel stood. "If you can modify the T-box to send a transponder, doesn't that mean it could send you, or any sister for that matter, to another timeline?"

Rose linked eyes with Diesel but didn't reply.

And then the T-box behind her attempted to link with the missing timelines. They all watched the display fail to red when a link couldn't be made with the Twenty-Eight timeline, fail again for the Twenty-Seven timeline, and again for the Twenty-Six timeline.

Then the modified T-box attempted to reach Twenty-Five's timeline. As they watched, the display showed the connection in a steady, vibrant green.

Twenty-Five had a working machine.

Book 2 - Bump Time Meridian

To learn more about the series and to purchase books, please visit CrystalSeries.com

1. Diesel, Thirty-Five years old, Fifty-Five timeline

Diesel gave Lilah a kiss and stepped into the T-box. He started to close the door, then paused to acknowledge her concern. "I'll be back in time for a drink before dinner." Tapping the screen in front of his face, he initiated his jump. "Travel to Fifty-Five."

As he waited the few seconds for the machine to engage, he imagined cuddling with Lilah when he returned. He smiled, then a tingle of static electricity signaled his jump.

The dark confines of his T-box were replaced by the bright, open surroundings of Fifty-Five's T-disc locker room. Alone, he stood still, listening for the sound of approaching footsteps. Hearing nothing, he called out. "Hello, I'm here!"

Laundry mounded in the corner stood in testament to the Big Meeting the day before. Stepping to almost-bare shelves, he poked around, found a set of clean clothes, and dressed quickly. As he sat to put on slippers, he called again, "It's me!"

"Are you decent?" Rose's voice came through the door.

"They say I'm excellent," he replied on impulse.

Rose strode into the room. "I hope that wasn't sexual innuendo, Dad." Twenty-nine years old with a very pretty face on a petite frame, she looked like a sportier version of Lilah.

Diesel turned red but brazened through it. "Of course not, which proves it's your mind that's in the gutter."

She laughed as he stood, and they exchanged a quick embrace.

"Welcome back, Thirty-Five." Fifty-Five stuck his head through the door long enough for a quick wave, then turned and continued down the hall. "I'll be in the kitchen."

Diesel followed Rose on the short walk through the beautiful mountain home. Joining Fifty-Five, they descended to the basement. Shelves and boxes were pushed to the side in the cavernous room. Rose's T-box sat in the cleared area.

"It looks just like mine." Diesel walked around the exterior, studying the walls of etched aluminum sheet. It had the same heavy door with latch handle, and same electrical cables running down the side, making connections at the top, middle, and bottom.

"The internals are identical as well," said Rose. "But as I explained at the Big Meeting yesterday, we've modified the logic controlling it. This unit can transport more than just Diesels. It should be able to send anything that fits inside, as long as there's no metal to corrupt the energy field."

"It will take some guts to be the first one to try it," said Fifty-Five.

A buzz came from inside the machine, startling the three of them. The screen on the front of the T-box lit up.

"Whoa," said Rose as they stared at the message on the display: "Twenty-Five incoming in 4:58."

They speculated on who it would be. With ten-seconds remaining, Diesel heard a familiar hum followed by a static wash. The display on the T-box showed a new message: Twenty-Five Arrived.

They waited for the door to open. When it didn't, Rose stepped forward and tugged on the latch. They all could see that the cabin was empty.

Then Rose crouched down and picked up a folded piece of paper from the T-box floor. She read it to herself, then held it for Diesel and Fifty-Five to see. Printed in bold type were the words: "Please help! Come quick!"

Diesel took the paper and raised it to the light, flipping it to see if there were any other markings. Then he handed it to Fifty-Five. "I wish they'd handwritten it so we could tell if it came from Twenty-Five or Lilah."

Rose wrung her hands and looked at her father. "This wasn't part of the plan."

"If we send someone, it should probably be muscle," said Fifty-Five. "Should we ask Forty if he'll go?"

"We aren't ready to send anyone," said Diesel, thinking fast because he was in the crosshairs if they decided one of them should travel to the new timeline. He studied the message for a moment more, then looked at Fifty-Five. "Let's go to your T-disc and see if we can connect with them using our regular equipment."

Fifty-Five nodded. "I'm curious, too."

As they climbed the steps, Diesel reviewed what Rose had told them at the Big Meeting the day before. "The only difference between your box and mine is that you bypassed a filter? Anything else?"

"That's it. Just one tweak to the design. A significant one, though."

They reached the kitchen and Fifty-Five led them through the house.

"And then you put a transponder on a string and dangled it near the missing timelines?"

"We call it an electromagnetic leash," she nodded. "We lowered the transponder back to the Twenty-Five timeline and used it to broadcast communications to that Lilah's phone."

"I thought the transponder sent info to all the lost timelines," said Fifty-Five.

"It does. I was simplifying. We broadcast communications back, targeting the Twenty-Five through Twenty-Eight timelines, telling the Lilahs how to win the lottery so they can pay to build a T-box." She paused and bit her lip. "But the transponder is a one-way transmission. There's no feature to hear a response, so for months it felt like we were just shouting into a well."

As they entered the T-disc locker room, Rose waved the piece of paper that held the plea for help. "This note is a huge affirmation of our methods."

"Congratulations." Diesel responded spontaneously, though he wasn't sure if he was being sarcastic or serious.

Fifty-Five stepped around Diesel, stood in front of one of the T-disc rings and said, "Travel to Twenty-Five."

The display showed the connection in solid green—the sign of a secure link.

"Cancel," Fifty-Five called to the air as he stepped back out. "I'd say it's definitive. Twenty-Five has a functioning T-box."

"If I jump back here tomorrow from my timeline," Diesel turned to Rose, "could I end up coming through your T-box in the basement by mistake? What decides whether an incoming transmission connects here or down there?"

"The sending unit needs to be programmed to ask for my T-box. If it doesn't send a specific pass code, the connection defaults to the production units." She pointed at the T-discs to clarify the reference.

"So how did Twenty-Five's machine know to send the pass code? That paper showed up in your T-box."

Rose nodded as if to acknowledge his thought process. "That's because what we sent through the transponder includes the code as part of the design. If any of the lost timelines build a machine, it can only connect with the box downstairs." She shrugged. "Actually, it could connect to any old-style T-box if the unit's been modified."

Diesel turned to face her. "With so many timelines to choose from, why did you pick my specific box as the model to copy?"

"Your Lilah worked hard to help us understand how to bypass the filter, and she was the first Lilah to send me T-box design plans. You carried them here to me, by the way."

"I didn't know that. This is all news to me, which means she's also very discreet." Diesel tried not to let his annoyance show in his voice. After the conversation died, he changed tacks. "Let's send Twenty-Five a note asking what his emergency is." He looked around the T-disc locker room "We need a pen."

"My office is just down the hall," said Fifty-Five, starting for the door. "We should also ask who it is we're talking to."

"Jeez, you two." Rose shook her head. "T-discs can't send paper, and I know you both know that. If you're serious about sending a note, we'll have to go back to the T-box in the basement."

Diesel led the way this time. "Would your T-box be able to connect with my box?"

"You mean your unit in the Thirty-Five timeline?" She nodded. "Sure. I told you that your Lilah has been a leader in our efforts. Your T-box was one of the first we tested."

Perplexed by the news, Diesel concluded that he and Lilah needed to talk through what she was trying to achieve, and who would be the mother to nine-year-old Rose should her plans go awry. And why wasn't he being included when she was making such big decisions in the first place?

Fifty-Five brought Diesel out of his reverie. "Are you going to use Rose's T-box to jump home?"

Diesel shook his head. "Unlike how I've apparently been treated, I want to talk with Lilah before taking a risk like that."

Fifty-Five grabbed a pen as they passed through the kitchen. In the basement, he took the original message from Rose and asked Diesel, "what do we want to say?"

"What we said upstairs. 'Who are you, and what's your emergency?'"

"Ask them to send pictures," said Rose. "That will tell us a whole lot more than a few sentences."

As Fifty-Five bent down to write the message, the T-box came alive for the second time that day.

"Whoa," Rose said again as the message displayed: "Twenty-Five incoming in 4:59."

The five-minute countdown took a century. After the static wash swept through the room, Diesel stepped forward, paused to see if Twenty-Five emerged, then pulled open the door when he didn't. Squatting, he retrieved another slip of paper.

"Hurry!" it said, again printed in bold type.

Diesel passed it around. "This whole thing has turned dark. We've gone from shouting into a well, to being asked to jump into it."

"Let's send our questions and see how they answer," said Fifty-Five.

Diesel supported the idea, if for no other reason than it delayed bigger decisions. He put the paper on the T-box floor, called, "Travel to Twenty-Five," and shut the door. After the five-minute countdown, the paper was gone. An hour later, they still waited for a reply.

"While I sympathize with their plight," said Diesel at that point, "I'm not inclined to go investigate until we know a whole lot more." Acknowledging his bruised ego for being shut out of so many consequential decisions by his wife, he sought to get home. "And I need to talk with Lilah before I do anything."

As they traipsed through the house yet again, Rose said, "I'm anxious to see pictures of their rig. I think that will answer a lot of questions."

"I'm interested in seeing the people," said Diesel. "I'd like to know if it's a Diesel or a Lilah who needs help. What if it's some stranger? And the whole printed-messages thing doesn't make sense to me. If it's such an emergency, why aren't they scribbling the notes?"

In the T-disc room, Diesel peeled off his shirt and threw it onto the pile.

Rose turned her back to him but remained in the room. "Don't be angry with Lilah," she said over her shoulder as he removed his pants. "We started this out of curiosity. There were no nefarious intentions behind any of it."

Diesel appreciated hearing that because he'd started to form conclusions about Lilah's behavior. Breathing in through his nose and exhaling through his mouth to calm himself, he stepped into the ring and called, "Travel to Thirty-Five."

As the machine began to cycle, he said, "I need to have a long talk with Lilah. I should be back tomorrow unless that conversation becomes difficult, then it will be the day after tomorrow."

"Hopefully we'll have heard from Twenty-Five by then," called Fifty-Five before everything went dark. An instant later, Diesel arrived at his T-box.

As he stepped from the unit, his subconscious mind noticed the door looked and felt different. He dismissed the observation, thinking perhaps Lilah had performed some maintenance, or maybe his memory was playing tricks on him.

But as the T-box door closed behind him, he reached for his robe—it should have been draped on a hook right there. That's when he realized that everything was different.

Turning, he looked back at the door, reacting the way someone might after stepping from an elevator on the wrong floor. He moved to step back into the T-box, but when he tugged on the latch handle, it wouldn't budge.

Pausing, he turned in a circle, taking in everything and trying to make sense of any of it.

He stood in a room a little larger than the size of his basement at home. But this one was largely empty. It had clean, white walls, a light blue carpet, and diffuse light coming from overhead. The T-box sat toward the back of the room.

The only furniture Diesel could see was a single office-style chair positioned at the front of the room. A middle-aged man sat in it—lanky, big ears, a shock of reddish hair on top of his head.

A mesh-like barrier ran from wall to wall and floor to ceiling, splitting the room in half, with Diesel on one side and the man on the other.

Disoriented, Diesel asked the man, "Is this the Twenty-Five timeline? What year is it?"

The man broke into a grin. Standing up from his chair, he lifted his hands over his head and started to twirl.

* * *

Newsletter subscribers will receive a brief note when the next book in the series if available.

Sign up at: www.CrystalSeries.com

About the Author

As a child, Doug stood on a Florida beach and watched an Apollo spacecraft climb the sky on its mission to the moon. He thrilled at the sight of the pillar of flames pushing the rocket upward. And then the thunderous roar washed over him, shaking his body and soul.

The excitement of the moon landing inspired Doug to pursue a career in technology. He studied chemical engineering in college, and he works as a professor and entrepreneur when he is not writing. His passions include telling inventive tales, mentoring driven individuals, and everything sci-tech.

In his books, Doug swirls his creative imagination with his life experiences to craft science fiction action-adventure stories with engaging characters and plot lines with surprises.

He lives in Connecticut with his darling wife and with pictures of his son, who is off somewhere in the world creating adventures of his own.

For more about the author and his books, please visit:
www.CrystalSeries.com

Free Story!

Crystal Horizon – Prequel to the Crystal Series

The Crystal Series is four full-length books of action and suspense where the emergence of self-aware AI and alien first contact occur at the same time.

Sample this popular space opera for free by downloading Crystal Horizon, the prequel series.

In the series, Cheryl is captain of the military space cruiser Alliance, and Sid is a covert warrior for the Defense Specialists Agency. We learn that the two have a shared history, and in particular, a romantic relationship that has somehow gone awry.

In prequel, we get their backstory. We join Sid and Cheryl on the day they first meet, and experience that shared history with them.

Crystal Horizon is offered exclusively to newsletter subscribers.

For more about the Crystal Series and to obtain this free book, please visit: www.CrystalSeries.com

57928535R00214

Made in the USA
Middletown, DE
04 August 2019